Scorch

A.D. Nauman

Soft Skull

2001

Scorch

ISBN: 1-887128-64-6

copright ©2001 by A.D. Nauman

Printed in Canada

Editorial: Nick Mamatas
Design: David Janik
Cover Illustraion: Paige Imatani, Bad Monkey Studio

Author Acknowledgements:
I wish to acknowledge the encouragement and contributions of Alan Friedman, my writing professor at the UIC Writers' Program, and of my brilliant friends and fellow writers from the old "Nauman Circle": Marina Lewis, Sarah Smith, Gina Frangello, Cecelia Downs, Chris Daniels, Tim Imse, and Charles Cannon. Also, for their lifelong support of my writing, I wish to thank my mother, June Anderson, and my sister, Connie Busch. Lastly, I wish to acknowledge three special people whose celebration of my work has made my efforts feel truly worthwhile: Mark Spann, Becca Manery, and Dion Ewald.

Soft Skull Press

107 Norfolk Street
New York, NY 10002

buy this book and other great
softskull titles at a big discount at
www.softskull.com

For
Charles and the Circle

"When he had first come to Packingtown, he had stood and watched the hog-killing, and thought how cruel and savage it was, and come away congratulating himself that he was not a hog..."

Upton Sinclair, *The Jungle*

one

Arel Ashe had a good life: she'd never been raped or beaten, had been robbed only nineteen times, had avoided marriage, and best of all had an evening job at the Sunco Public Library, where she could watch TV after the twelve hours at her day job. She watched the old favorites on the ten-foot screen: "Real Life Spouse Murders in Action," "Lady Killers," "Man Eaters," the local news.

Still, she was unhappy. She sat on her stool like a jar of old pennies, feeling her insides scrape when she shifted. The library was airless, a tight place trying to look limitless, its ceiling-to-floor mirrors reflecting tall plastic videoracks and the images of tall plastic videoracks—an infinity of wobbly orange towers packed with tiny square videobooks bordered in lime, grape, mango, or cherry, each square crammed with the big face of the videobook author who could tell you how to get a million bucks in two weeks or a great tan, butt, bust, car, job, house, man.

The videobooks eyed her. She tried to sit naturally. She turned to watch the snow fall against its black backdrop through the one window. Was thirsty again.

She turned the TV on and off, because she could, and tensed at the adscreens, which were on a circuit that couldn't be controlled. All evening the adscreens had been off—a blank beige stripe around the top of the walls—and at any moment might spring on, with trumpets and snare drums and millisecond images flashing from right to left: a hand, an eye, a lower lip, the left half of a woman's surprised face, then a soup can or a bag of potato chips. Then silence. Sometimes her dreams were like them.

She tried to relax, rolled her head, was instantly sleepy. She checked the clock: three more hours till closing.

Then the front door alarm wailed and actual customers came in. Actual people. She watched them on the security screens under the counter: two guys. The first was a perfect man—his hair, the color of his head, sculpted into short blunt swirls around his skull, his eyes emerald. He wore a thick padded gold lamé jacket with a miniature American flag on one sleeve, gold bluejeans and cowboy boots. Behind him was a guy with dark hair. They moved from the third screen to the second, to the first, then to the counter.

"Happy New Year!" said the blond, though it was already mid-January. "Mind if we. . . *look*?" his tone deep and low. He leaned toward her, startling her. She was not classically attractive—she was light-haired and lean, but short and past thirty.

"Why didn't you call up our list?"

The dark-haired friend replied in a strange locked-up voice, "He likes to touch things."

The blond drum-rolled the countertop and yanked one of the Dr. Aslow videos off the purple counter display. "Hey! You need to see this again," he commanded the friend, who shrugged.

"We recommend it highly," Arel said mechanically, then added cheerily, "It really helped me!" though it hadn't, really, and she wondered why she'd said it had. Or maybe it had.

The blond and his friend vanished into the forest of racks, and she was alone again. Sitting. Dr. Aslow's neckless head smiled wisely at her from atop the trilogy. She'd watched all three in one night—"Getting Happy," "Staying Happy," and "Getting Happy Again"—and the next day had taken his advice, had gone out and bought a car that was a little too expensive—and she did feel happier. But then time went by and she grew heavy again.

Happiness was such hard work: you had to exercise to control your hormones, concentrate to control negative thoughts, gulp down herbal pills. Then at the end of each day you sank into bed with heavy limbs, muscle settling onto bone, air descending like layers of old foul wool.

She heard the guys knocking around in the depths of the videoracks, clicking videos in and out of their slots, and grew self-conscious. Pictured herself sitting at the counter looking self-conscious. Turned on the TV. She flipped through the channels, past "Real People Videos" and the Sunco newsmags, past a Paterco Public Education Channel show on killer animals and their unsuspecting prey, and stopped at the Holoco Film Classics network. An old Dolla Dare movie was starting.

"What's on?" said, not the blond, but the friend.

"This," Arel replied, glancing over, gazing back at the screen. "An old Holoco adstory." Dolla Dare was running in five-inch glitter heels down a wide street of mansions, her arms outstretched and breasts bouncing in a transparent blouse. She was happy, rich, and uninhibited. Handsome shirtless men peered out their windows lustfully, as their ordinary wives towel-dried their hair in the background.

Arel said, "The one where Dolla Dare fucks married men in their cars but only if they're Holoco cars. You've seen it. In the end she meets a really rich guy with a bunch of Holoco cars and they do it all around his circular driveway."

"Huh."

"Much too obvious," she continued in a put-on voice of authority. Her day job was in Sunco's Adstory Department, and she had a theory that the best adstories were the ones that made you think things you didn't know you were thinking. She had theories about many things, which made people frown—not the theories themselves but the fact that she had them. *If you're so smart why ain't you rich?* they'd say and she never knew how to answer.

The dark-haired guy disappeared and she turned off the screen, turned it on again, off and on again, watched Dolla have sex in a couple of cars, switched to "Real People Videos," which was about another marketing director—who else could afford to be on it? His personal theme song was playing and the cameras were following him down the street, catching every moment of his important day. She started to squirm. Started to flip through the channels again. Pulled at her collar. Glanced up at the adscreens, then down at the Dr. Aslow display. Then asked herself, as she did every evening at about this time: Why am I unhappy? Why am I so unhappy?

The answer was always the same: She didn't have enough money. She needed more money. If only she had more money. Why didn't she have more money? Damn.

She slouched, wanting to disappear behind the counter displays. Her and her big job in Adstories—*ha*. She was still a crummy junior assistant, still earned the same salary as when she started eight years ago, still sat in the same damn cube, lived in the same damn minuscule one-room apartment, where every night before she could open the sofabed she had to fold up her dinette set and roll it into the closet and wedge it between her luggage set and the twenty-gallon stock pot, and her furniture—God. More than two years old and embarrassingly out of style. She had the new car but only one—she had to drive it on the weekends too. She was not who she thought she'd be at age thirty-two. You weren't supposed to blame your parents for your crummy life but she did anyway. Blamed the only parent she'd had— her mother—who was so *weird,* boasting about being a philosophy professor, until the university downsized and she found out just how useless she was, barely able to waitress at the airport coffee shop. Then walking in front of a stray bullet and getting herself killed four days before Arel's tenth birthday. *God damn.* Arel tried to sit straighter, tried to catch her breath. Lately, for some reason, she'd been thinking about her mother.

The blond reappeared with a stack of videobooks and cried out, "Don't watch this!"—in a friendly, helpful way—and snatched her mini-remote, "Let's watch Grab Bag!" He clicked to SuncoSites and the huge screen broke into hundreds of tiny twirling squares. From the other end of the library the dark-haired guy said, to apparently nobody, "Everything in this world is too big or too small," which made Arel look at him. What an odd thing to say. She kept looking: He seemed familiar. But he wasn't handsome. He was trying to spin a videorack, which only creaked around in a lopsided, resisting tilt. He got mad and smacked it.

"Hey! Careful with that!"

"Here we go!" said the blond to the screen. So upbeat, with such an amazing face—the perfect width, the least line of bone along the jaw, the forehead sloping at just the right angle. She looked at the screen with him, at the rotating pictures of people to date and stuff for sale—refrigerators, snowmobiles, cancer treatments. The blond stood entranced, his videobooks stacked on the counter, his thumb pressing into the sharp hard corner of one of the boxes.

"You have to bring these back tomorrow," she said.

He was suddenly boisterous: "No problem! I'm between evening jobs temporarily and guess what—no don't! My friend here hasn't had an evening job for over a *year.*"

The friend lurked behind him, looked embarrassed.

"God," Arel blurted.

The blond went on: "The free time's nice though. Know what I'm doing?" He tapped a fingertip on his temple. "Strategizing. How to make a million bucks in the next two months. Know what I'm doing? Writing songs. Entertainment. That's where the bucks are."

"Wow. Really?" Stupid. She hadn't had sex in three months and wasn't flirting well.

"Hello, I'm Kyler Judd."

"Arel Ashe." Her smile grew until her jaw hurt. He seized her hand to shake it, rocked from foot to foot.

"That's Ben."

"Ben?"

"My parents were weird," Ben replied in his suffocated voice.

"Ben's out on a ledge!" Kyler said and actually put an arm around him, squeezed his shoulder. "Ben the Brain—that's him! Knows all kinds of techie stuff—but he *thinks* too much—that's his problem. Not me, not me—I'm a *doer.*" He squeezed Ben's shoulder again, tried to bounce him up and down.

"Are you guys gay?"

"What? No no!" He let go of Ben's shoulder. "We work together. Guess what we do—no don't! We're teachers! Can you believe that? Holoco High. But not forever. I'm marketing, he's technical." He bounded back from the counter, then forward again, ground his palm into the rough surface. "See, we're like a team. I'm the big picture man and Ben does things like mix up chemicals. New products! That's where the bucks are. We're gonna make a killing—no lousy five-buck-an-hour job for us—no offense. It came to me one day in a flash—this idea for a new product. Guess what it is! No don't—"

The faster he talked, the slower she thought, until all activity in her brain stopped. His new product was a cleanser for scrubbing up the billboards on your house. She tried to admire his enthusiasm, but she had a theory that only stupid people were enthusiastic. Life called for skepticism and fatigue—for going to work, going to work, and going home in an endless cycle of riding, parking, walking.

"Ooh! Ooh ooh!" Kyler began to bounce again and pulled out his sellfone, which must have gone off. She tried to read the tiny screen upsidedown: a newzip from Celebrity Line. Kyler read aloud, "Dolla Dare's got a new show! God! Don't you just love Dolla? Hey Ben!"

Ben did not reply, stood bored on the other side of the room. Arel began swiping out the videobooks, which were all about making a million bucks by inventing new products or writing songs. Kyler remained enthralled, glancing back and forth from the huge library screen to his tiny sellfone screen, not knowing which to watch.

Then Ben, trying to spin another rack and not looking at her, said to her: "You're not long for this world."

"What?"

"They'll start closing these old libraries. Who has time to come in? They'll merge their lists and you'll be on the street. By the end of this year,

I predict."

"Oh please!" she replied too loudly. "Back to delivering burgers."

"Nah," said Kyler, tucking away his sellfone. "We'll get you on at the school. Night supervisor's a cushy job, though some kids stay past midnight studying. Did you know that the government used to run the schools?"

"Yes, I did know that."

He explained it anyway: "They taught stuff like history and then people didn't have any job skills and corporations had to retrain everyone! God!"

She was preoccupied, swiping and reswiping a videobook that wouldn't beep, and though she usually didn't say things that popped into her head, said: "Of course what do we know about it? Big Brother Government and taxes—our grandparents barely remember them."

Kyler looked disturbed, but Ben looked up and stared at her.

"Whoa!" Kyler bellowed. "That's pretty retro! You don't look like a Commie organizer to me! Ha ha!" He winked, to show he was kidding, then tweaked her chin, to show he thought her stupidity was cute.

Ben was still staring, and she started to feel it. She tried to catch glimpses of him, started to think he wasn't really bad-looking: tall, kind of pale, nose and lips long and thin but right for his face. He'd taken off his dull gray jacket and was letting it drag on the floor. He had on an old thin knit shirt, tight across his chest and the small round muscles of his arms and shoulders. Her glance stuck on the shoulders. It was like her to like the peculiar one.

Kyler noticed, rolled forward on the ball of one foot, "This guy is out on a ledge. Wild horses! Too smart for a school teacher—used to be in biomed engineering—major bucks there—then bam! Something happened," then, in a whisper, "but he never talks about it. Ben the Mystery Man—that's what I call him." Then boomed out: "Hey Ben, tell her about the time you got yourself fired! That's a riot!"

"You got *fired?*"

Ben tightened, took back his gaze.

Kyler laughed. "Tell her that story! Cracks me up!" Silence. "He'd be in his cube and forget what he was supposed to be doing, right?"

Ben replied flatly: "I got interested in other things. That weren't applicable."

Kyler held his sides laughing and Arel giggled, liking the feeling of laughing with Kyler at Ben, until Kyler abruptly stopped laughing and picked up his videos.

She didn't want them to go. She leaned across the counter, poked Kyler's elbow, "My day job's in Adstories."

"Really?" Kyler replied and stopped leaving. "Well, you're launched!"

"No not really, I'm just a peon."

"What? What is this I hear? *Negative* talk? 'Talk positive—be positive—succeed!'"

"I know, I know, but, I don't know—it seems harder than I thought it would be—succeeding. Do you ever think that? You have to be so energetic and enthusiastic, and personable and stylish."

"Uh-huh, uh-huh," Kyler examined her, looked doubtful.

"And for me to get promoted I'd have to write original adstories on my own time and submit them to this Committee, which has a big meeting to critique people's work!"

He kept nodding, then: "Hey! I bet you could do that. You seem like a real smartie. You know what your problem is? You think too much! You gotta be a doer! That's how you win the game. Right Ben?"

Ben had become hypnotized by Dr. Aslow's bright purple display.

"So get to work!" Kyler commanded and barked at Ben, "Hey Brain!" And they left.

She watched them on the row of security screens—front door to sidewalk, through the parking lot, to Kyler's chartreuse sports car, a brand new Holoco Mazda Machete, and she was alone again. She looked back down the row of screens—lot, walk, door, right racks, left racks, then—on screen one—herself, pale behind the red-orange counter, looking down. She seemed like a stranger. What was it her mother used to say?

Then the adscreens sprang on and she screamed. Bright images raced around the walls like frantic rats: a dancing tuna, a bottle cap, a tire swing, a leaf, a cartoon aardvark, then legless Air Morgans running running running from screen to screen, the noise of a cheering crowd rising until she had to cover her ears. Then it was over, and she felt herself breathe again.

What had she been thinking? Yes—Kyler. Kyler was right. Kyler was happy. You gotta be a doer! She sat straighter on her stool, turned off the TV, whipped out her miniwriter. "Just do it!" she told herself. "Be a doer!"

She positioned her hands above her miniwriter, ready to go. Then stared at the little black screen. First she needed an idea. She looked around the room. How did people have ideas? She looked around, looked around. Waited for something to occur to her. Looked up and down the videoracks, at the tiny wise faces encased in colorful boxes. Her eyes drifted to the work-out section, where the videobooks didn't have faces, just body parts, and something occurred to her—an idea. "Yes!"

Sunco had just acquired a new company—the Illindiahio Plastic Surgery Corporation—and needed an adstory to get viewers to have even more plastic surgery. She accessed the character menu and marked a few types: handsome celebrity doctor, sexy blonde, assertive-yet-cooperative wife, and the tense career woman, who could be the scorch. Scorches, she'd noticed, were people like intellectuals, feminists, do-gooders, old government officials—silly unattractive people with no real skills, who disagreed with the main message of the story and looked foolish in the end. Arel had figured out this definition by herself, though it must have been written down somewhere once.

She typed:

> Lunching at posh restaurant, three long-time friends, just past thirty, unhappy women, sensing that something is wrong with their lives but not knowing what, not even knowing how to find out.

Wife:	I'm going to make a change! I'm getting a breast- booster!
Blonde:	Wow, really? I've been thinking about making a change too. I've always wanted a nasal tip tilt, but I'm not sure I have the courage to do it!
Wife:	We can go together! There's strength in numbers!
Career Woman:	Well, I know I could use some thigh molding, but I won't do it. I resent societal pressure to be thin!
Blonde:	If you can improve yourself, why not?
Wife:	I'm doing it to feel good about myself. I don't care what society thinks!

Arel's mind raced. She couldn't think of a middle for the story, so she wrote the end:

> The wife throws a party at her posh suburban home, after the surgery, and all the men buzz around her and the blonde, saying things like, 'You look great—new hairdo?' and the career woman comes in wearing a dress that makes her hips look really huge and no one pays attention to her. As she's leaving, walking down the trellised walkway to her car, the camera zooms in on her butt, and the wife and the blonde glance at each other and can't help but laugh.

Arel held the miniwriter at arm's length, read the screen, read it again. Was this good? It was like everything else on TV. She reread it, and another thought popped into her head: This isn't good. This is stupid. She laid the miniwriter on the counter and stared at the screen, stared so long that a Paterco ad began to scroll across it: *"Stuck? Never give up! Call Dr. Script! Expert advice that WORKS! $5.99 a minute!"* Not a bad idea, but she couldn't afford it. She couldn't afford anything. You had to be rich to get rich.

She picked up the miniwriter and threw it across the room, heard it bust open on the carpet.

"Shit." Now she would have to buy a new miniwriter. She sighed, sat, thought, then rummaged around in the trash for an old adflyer, found an old pen in the drawer behind the counter, and wrote on the actual paper: SCORCH.

That was the problem: the scorch wasn't funny enough. You had to get people laughing at the scorch so they couldn't stop to think about what he was really saying. Jonquil Adams and Austin Carl, Sunco's star writers, had just done a great scorch in one of the Home Products sitcoms: a dark skinny rat-nosed nerdy intellectual guy was making a long speech about the evils of owning too much stuff, about how possessions entrap you and debt imprisons you, and when he finished, the camera panned back and all the main characters were asleep and snoring. It was hysterical.

Arel kept trying, wrote out:

```
Career woman says: "Well, you two look very nice, but I'm
glad I didn't have plastic surgery, I'm glad I'm who I am.
I'm different, and I for one like me this way." Wife says:
"Well, that makes one of us!" and everyone at the party
laughs.
```

Better. That was better. Not bad. Good, even, maybe. And Arel imagined the laugh track roaring and started to laugh too, her voice alone in the room. She closed her eyes tight, imagined herself in a brightly colored crowd, imagined everyone laughing together, all together, and felt almost happy, almost seen, not so alone.

*   *   *

She spent the next morning at Sunco thinking of the various brilliant lines in her screenplay, smiling secretly, strutting by other people's cubes, taking little breaks because she deserved them. Then she discovered that

Jonquil Adams and Austin Carl had already submitted a story idea for the plastic surgery account. She sat in the Sunco Faste Sandwiche Shoppe in a two-person booth with three other people—Kadence and Koo, also assistant juniors, and their team leader, associate junior Ormer Bell. Koo had the news:

"It's an incredible story, phenomenal—Jonquil and Austin are incredible, phenomenal. It's about this 14-year-old girl who gets raped by seventeen guys who pour battery acid all over her and stab her with plastic forks and cut off her nose and leave her to die. That's the first scene. Then this man comes by who happens to be a plastic surgeon—Doctor Hampton Drane—and he rushes her to the hospital. So, it takes months and months of reconstructive surgery, and you see her at different stages—you know, at first she's really gross, then she gets a little better in each scene—and in the end she's so beautiful that she becomes an international supermodel who makes millions of dollars every day. And of course she lives in New York, and really gorgeous men throw themselves at her, but all along she's in love with Hampton Drane and keeps going back to him for little changes—like to her hairline, elbows—whatever. Then it turns out that all his other female patients are in love with him too because he's made them all so beautiful, and it's really suspenseful because you don't know if he's going to marry this girl or not. But in the end he does, because she's the only one who's not jealous of all his other beautiful patients, and in the last scene they get married and move into this gorgeous mansion full of gold antiquey-looking things."

There was a long pause. Kadence finally said, "God. That's so graphic."

"Audacious." Ormer shook his amazed head, and there was another long pause, until Arel blurted, "Why do they stab her with plastic forks?"

"Huh?"

"The seventeen guys who rape her. What are they doing with plastic forks? I mean, what—they just happen to be carrying plastic forks in their pockets? They're on the way back from a family picnic, and one of them has the fork bag?"

"What does that matter?" said Ormer, always annoyed with Arel. "It's a terrific image."

"Why?"

"Huh?"

"What makes it a terrific image? I think it's, well, kind of stupid. Isn't it just like that movie Holoco did last year, where a bunch of guys raped a girl and stabbed her with plastic knives?"

"What's your point Arel?" Kadence spat. Kadence and Ormer were versions of each other—big and beige, long-faced, tilting over the table like dangerously tall skyscrapers. Arel preferred Koo, who was not so tall and too simple-minded to be sardonic.

"Well, my point is, it's...it's stupid. Doesn't anyone agree? Is it just me?"

"Oh, we all agree—it's just you," Ormer said and they all laughed. Even Koo, who might have secretly seen her point. Ormer went on, "I think it's brilliant. What else could it be—it's Adams and Carl." Kadence and Koo nodded, mouths serious, eyes flicking from side to side. Always agreeing with the slightly senior male. Arel began to twitch.

Then Kadence said slyly, "You didn't by chance have your own story idea to pitch, did you?"

"Well—"

"Ahhh," they all understood.

Arel got angry. "I admit my idea isn't as good as theirs but I still think theirs is a little stupid. Who's the scorch?"

Everyone frowned and chewed, chewed, waiting for someone else to know the answer. Long moments passed. Kadence said, eyebrows thoughtful, "I don't think you particularly need a scorch in a biofiction—see, it's based on this real guy, Doctor Hampton Drane. He's the president of Illindiahio—a real good-looking older guy. I saw a picture of him in Jonquil's cube. He really did treat a rape victim once, although she didn't become a supermodel or anything like that. She looks okay though—Jonquil's got a picture of her too."

"I thought you needed a scorch in everything. Everything seems to have one," Arel said.

"Does it?" Koo replied. "What would it be in a serious piece like The Hampton Drane Story?"

Arel tried to think, but her head was as empty as everyone else's seemed to be. She began to feel hollow, from her feet to her head. What was it her mother used to say?

Ormer crunched up his sandwich wrapper. Lunch was over.

They rode up together in a silent elevator. In the mirrored walls, imprinted with the thousands of various Sunco company logos in colored glitter, Arel saw her face—a streak of pale beige crayon encircled by the logo for Dazzle World, a discount chain selling over ten thousand shades of finger nail polish. She looked at Kadence and Koo, tall and short, their silvery hair in poofs with big head bows, Kadence's fuchsia and Koo's mango.

Their short tight suits were fuchsia and mango too, of course, Kadence's with the wide rhinestone lapel on the left, Koo's on the right. Ormer was dressed in his silky Caribbean mauve, his shoulders padded out to twice the size of his hips. His hair stylishly short on the sides and tapered into a long oily V at the neck. Arel's hair was still in the old zag style, hanging and banged, because she could no longer get up early enough every day to poof, poof, tie, and spray. Her suit was last season's shade of cucumber and her shoes, which she'd gotten a year ago from a resale site, were flat with round toes. The elevator doors opened and she was relieved not to look at herself anymore, marching at the end of the line through the cubicle maze to her stall, which was piled with the latest urgent work to be done. She stepped into her cube, sat down, and once again time stopped.

Two more episodes of "Movers and Shakers" had come over her fax to audit. Scripts were piling up in paper skyscrapers and soon Ormer would come looking for her with his long sarcastic "Well?" Ormer leered at Kadence and Koo but never at Arel.

She pulled out her checklist and slogged through the first episode of "Movers and Shakers," checked off the various cleansers and polishes appearing in the background in the various scenes, then went through the episode again with the values checklist, marking down the number of references to the various desirable values—the importance of clean tiles, the importance of clean dishes, the importance of clean clothes, on and on. "Movers and Shakers" was a sitcom produced by Home Products, which also owned the Grasshopper Earth-Mover Company, so the series was about three beautiful earth-mover factory workers ("Movers") who worked nights making milkshakes ("Shakers") at a malt shop, which they kept very clean with various brand-name cleansers. In this particular episode, the ugly union organizer gal was trying to make the beautiful blonde Lulu read a pamphlet. Beautiful brunette Lalla points out that the union gal wouldn't have time for pamphlets if she had a boyfriend. Lil, a beautiful redhead, decides to fix up the union gal with a male friend who's not very attractive, who ends up falling in love with Lalla instead, who leans bustily across the sparkly clean malt shop counter.

It was just like an episode from the year before, in which Lulu's homely male friend fell in love with Lil, who recommended a Home Products shampoo to make his hair fluffier, instead of the ugly union gal, whose hair was lusterless.

Arel banded her checklists onto the top of the script and her head, full of lead, rocked forward onto the stack of pages. Three o'clock. Four and a half hours to go. The mini-digits blinked on the miniclock scotchtaped to the side of her cube: 3:01, 3:01, 3:01, 3:02. Her eyes closed, opened: 3:02, 3:02. . . Closed again. The office was quiet. The room was large but padded, and footsteps on the carpet swooshed like a distant wind. She thought about Kyler Judd, his glossy hair like gold in the fluorescent lights, his face beautifully even and smooth. She thought of fucking him in the library on the floor behind the counter. Facing him. Seeing his face. Her legs bare and wrapped around his thighs, his pants open, a huge perfect penis tilting out. Then it wasn't Kyler's face but Ben's, his brown eyes melting, his lips spreading into a wild smile. Then it wasn't Ben but Ormer Bell, on the table in the sandwich shop, her face pushed down into wrappers and paper plates, him pounding her from behind, finishing his sandwich, making remarks to Kadence or Koo. Then it was none of them. But someone's arms were around her, someone's chest against hers, hands stroked the sides of her hair, tenderly traced the line of her collarbone. She hugged her stack of papers, imagined a massive dick pushing inside her, ground her crotch into the seat of her chair, got off, and fell asleep.

When she opened her eyes it was 4:30. She bolted up, hair flying on waves of static electricity. Anyone could have walked by. She padded fast to the bathroom, rinsed out her mouth, combed her hair, then trudged into a stall and sat on the toilet. She kept reading and rereading the ads on the stall walls: "Tired? Exhausted? Fatigued? You may have ATS—Always Tired Syndrome. Mention this ad for a discount at Dr. Dreem's Fatigue Clinic," then the Sunco logo. She pulled off square after square of toilet paper: "Pinkie's Diet Center," said the first square. "NatureMade Tampons," "Jock's Pleasure Parade," "Advertise Here!"

Back in her cube, she unbundled the next episode of "Movers and Shakers," in which the homely union organizer scampers around the factory trying to make people give up their lunch half-hours to go to a union meeting. She makes an impassioned speech about the pay raises they'll get if they formed a union, and Lalla asks, "Just how much of our pay would go to *union* dues?" which makes ominous music play and the union gal's eyes shift uneasily behind their Coke-bottle lenses.

At 7:30 Arel got up and went for her coat. In the bathroom, Kadence and Koo were repoofing their hair.

"Hi Arel," said Koo in her ever-friendly high pitch. "You okay?"

"You know maybe I'm getting sick. I actually fell asleep in my cube. Was anyone talking about it?"

"No." Kadence peered down at her. "I wouldn't worry. You were very odd at lunch."

"I was. I was so odd. What if I'm getting sick? I'd hate to lose a day's pay. God."

"Don't worry!" Koo's small face drifted in the mirror like a smilie balloon. Then all three of them rolled up their sleeves, pulled their Flame-Offs out of their purses, and strapped the slender tanks onto their forearms. They folded their sleeves down over the plastic tubes, and, palming the squeeze triggers, put on their coats. No one spoke in the elevator, but going out the door they called out suddenly friendly bye-byes.

*   *   *

Shivering, she rushed through the old underground walkway to the old lot, spotted her little red mock sports car—the thing she most loved. A Sunco Toyota Zinger, with only seven more years of payments. She trotted toward it, reached out for it, ran her hand along its fender, stooped over the hood to sweep the day's adflyers off the windshield. Then climbed down into it, turned the key in the ignition. The dashboard was silent: she'd paid an extra fee to disconnect the voices, tired of inanimate objects talking to her.

On the highway, as usual, traffic crept. She got stuck behind minitrucks and megavans and a bus painted to look like a giant stick of cinnamon gum. She crept, crept, then stopped in the tunnel. She sorted her junk mail. Took her last Bit-o-Burger out of the mini-fridge, popped it into the mini-wave, ate it in one bite, was still hungry. Taillights and headlights and the adscreens flashing on the tunnel walls hurt her eyes. She rested her head on the steering wheel and closed her eyes but still saw the images: Coke ads, car ads, clothes ads—bright, dark, bright—a woman's thigh, a nose, dogs running down an alley, a sailboat, a finger in red hair, a topless woman bending over a topless man with a basketball. She opened her eyes and saw them again. Thirsty again.

At the other end of the tunnel the Chicago skyline glared in winter darkness—a carved pumpkin's mouth in neon—the green glass highrises separated by the shorter older rotting buildings. The old bleak brick flashed its block-letter messages: Fly FunAir, Call CopCo, See MansionWorld. The ads on the highrises were more sophisticated, in sync with the neo-post-modern style of the jeweled chrome outlining the huge windows and the spikes of gold and silver on the roofs. Poetic messages wrote themselves across the buildings in elegant script: "Almatti, my darling"..."Zulu Beach— toast the sun"..."Devven Lee designs me." Traffic crawled. Ahead, past the tunnel, rich people were flying onto the express lanes, their embossed fender emblems winking in the flood lights at the entrance between the express lane police cars.

She rolled ahead an inch, another inch, another. Then the honking began. An armless corpse dropped from the overpass onto a car roof and slid off onto the pavement between lanes, which made people honk more—now they'd have to steer around it until the Sunco body sweepers came. Buying the city streets had been Sunco's biggest mistake: there was no room to expand and people began to associate Sunco with inconvenience. Arel remembered it clearly. A tearful vice president had taken all the blame and resigned on prime time television. Committees were formed and a PR campaign was launched pointing out the advantages of sitting in traffic for several hours a day. She remembered the jingle—"Oh it's fun to sit on the Kennedy, on the Kennedy in your car..." Commuters were shown working on minicomputers, chatting happily on their sellfones, eating, sorting junk mail. But of course Americans were too smart for such a ploy and another tearful VP resigned: Americans deserved the best, he burst out—Convenience. Then everyone felt sorry for Sunco, which seemed to be trying so hard, and was satisfied when the current CEO came up with Express-Choice— everyone knew it was only a matter of time until everyone was wealthy enough to buy their way into the express lanes.

In the meantime, traffic in the regular lanes crept, crept, stopped again. And now she had that annoying jingle in her head. The honking intensified. Three lanes over, a man jumped out of his Pontiac Predator and started shooting at the guy honking behind him. Arel didn't have the bullet-proof glass option but was too tired to duck. She could see the honker smiling, smug behind his bullet-proof windshield, the bullets bouncing off. Finally the guy with the gun stopped shooting, ran over and kicked the other guy's hubcap, huffed back to his car. Arel was hungry.

She'd be late opening the library, but she pulled off the highway anyway, rolled past the abandoned cars smashed and burning on the roadside, and into the McDonald's drive-through. Steadily, efficiently, ten lanes of cars rolled through the long bank of orange and yellow archways. She punched in her McCharge number and her order: a McHealthy-Steak, the diet Mini-Fries, McPeas, a double-jumbo diet Coke. A happy, real human voice came over the speaker: "Would you like to try a Chocolate McClare tonight?"

"No thanks."

"Would you like to buy a limited-quantity nylon McJacket for spring— cobalt, daffodil, or ruby?"

"No thanks."

"How about a subscription to McKids-R-Us magazine, which comes with valuable coupons that will save you money at all McKids-R-Us toy stores, clothing stores, gift shops, daycare centers, play centers, movie theaters, and children's hospitals?"

"No!" How irritating: they'd gotten her demographics wrong.

Her food sped through the pneumatic tube and she rolled back onto the highway, eating, slurping. But still thirsty, and late opening the library again.

✳   ✳   ✳

At the library door Ben was waiting with the videobooks. His hair and clothes were neater and straighter than the night before: He'd looked better disheveled. She was embarrassed, thinking of her afternoon fantasy, taking the bag from the hueless, unfamiliar hand.

"Where's Kyler?"

"Oh, he really wanted to come." Ben seemed out of place in the foreground, stiff in an old collared shirt. "Really. He likes you. He says you're going to write adstories for our new products and we're going to be The Three Musketeers. And they'll make a movie about our lives." He plunked a mini-taper onto the counter. "That's his new song. He really wants your opinion."

"God, what energy he has! Writing songs, inventing products."

"All the girls go nuts for him."

She stared at Ben, his eyes cast down, eyebrows permanently frowning. There was a kind of silence with the TV off and no one moving, but the heater whirred in the background, horns honked and car alarms wailed in the distance. At any moment the adscreens would pop on. She watched his eyes until he caught her, then she looked away. She'd been in love once, at fifteen, with a beautiful short blond boy with aqua eyes, who'd climbed through her window in the house where she lived after her mother died, with her Great Aunts Ashley and Tiffany.

"So you want to hear this?" Ben asked.

There was nothing to do but nod. He turned on the mini-taper and Kyler's voice announced: "Hello Arel! This is my latest—'I Used to Be Manic, But Now I'm Just Depressed.'" A guitarathizer bleated and Kyler sang:

I used to be manic,

Ran around in a panic.

Had to be sure that the boss was impressed...

But since you left me honey,

I know this sounds real funny

But I don't feel like money,

I just feel depressed...

The singing stopped, the tape purred, silent.

"That's it?"

"That's the first verse. He writes first verses."

"It sounds familiar. Is it familiar?"

"It's like an old Burba Rae John song. That's his angle. He accessed the copyright laws and found out exactly how many words and notes he had to change to avoid getting sued. It's bound to be a hit. Not a bad scheme. He'll make his million. He'll have everything."

"A million bucks, great looks," and again she said something that popped into her head, "a brain full of nickels."

Ben laughed—a surprisingly normal laugh. "I thought you had a thing for him."

She found herself shrugging, wanting Ben to like her. His face was calm and intelligent, black and white with shadows. She tried to find something else to look at. She'd forgotten about the boy climbing through her window. She looked at the mini-taper, grinned, "So why do you hang with him?"

"Oh, he's a good guy. He's like a friend. He calls me Ben the Brain."

"He gets you women."

"Mostly he gets himself women." Again, the normal laugh.

"You get the ones he doesn't want." Her face hardened and they had to avoid each other's eyes for a moment. He began to spin the mini-taper on the countertop, trying to keep it at an exactly even speed.

"He really does like you. He says you're out on a ledge. He likes people like us." The mini-taper stopped spinning and he stared at her, too long, with his uncomfortable eyes, not casual. She didn't reply. The silence grew too long and he picked up the mini-taper. "So," started to go.

She called after him, "Boring!"

He stopped, turned, not posing. "What?"

"Boring—copying an old song. I see it all the time in Adstories."

"It sells." He looked at her, looked right at her—he liked her—she could tell. But still he was about to go. So she said, "Do you ever try to think thoughts that wouldn't occur to you?"

His eyebrows raised, for once not frowning, and a grin spread crooked across his thin face. He walked toward her. She looked down and watched the back of his head on security screen two, at his dark hair—short, thick, tender. His back grew smaller on screen two as he appeared on screen one. She saw herself on security screen one, looking down.

"You want me to stay awhile?" he asked.

"Up to you."

"I can stay awhile." He leaned close, too close, too intense, and she leaned away. The boy who climbed through her window had dumped her and she'd wailed, thrown herself against the walls, begged him to come back. Then he did and she dumped him to show him how it felt. She let her face drop and there she was on the security screen: dim as the trim on the videoracks, head like a small brown nut.

"You're not smooth," she criticized.

"No. Plus I wear this old gray jacket. But you don't mind."

"Don't tell me about myself. People telling me about myself are always wrong."

"Always?"

Silence. She felt his nearness, looked at his hand—not big, not rough or soft—not like a man's or a woman's. She kept a distance, made him wait for her. He waited, waited. Then she climbed up on the bottom rung of her stool and reached for him. He wasn't surprised. His lips were thin, like hers, cool and too wet. He tasted like mint toothpaste, school rooms, car exhaust. She thought of letting him in behind the counter but imagined some Sunco boss happening to look at the security tapes and firing her. And there was no room on the floor between the videoracks.

"I know what you'd like," she said.

"Yeah?" His voice was anxious, all his mystery gone. Men were so predictable. She smiled, campy, and walked around the counter, hooked a finger into his shirt collar, and led him through the racks to a door at the back of the library.

"What's in there?"

"The old storage room."

"Yeah?"

She pushed the door open and turned on the light.

"Wow," he said. "Books."

Boxes were stacked to the ceiling, tossed into the middle of the room, flaps up and full of dust.

"Why don't you clear all this out?"

She shrugged. "No one ever told me to. No one cares they're here."

He began to look at the books, opening and closing their strange covers. She hopped onto a box to be taller than he was, turned his face upward, raked her fingers through his hair, kissed him. Then he forgot about the books and tried to get as much of his tongue into her mouth as possible. He pushed up her skirt, slowly at first, then yanked down her underpants. She knelt, unzipped his pants and pulled out, of course, an ordinary penis. She wanted to wrap her legs around him—to face him. But he whacked her sideways off the box and before she could turn toward him he kicked her forward onto her face, grabbed the back of her hair, shoved her face-down into a low pile of boxes. "Ow." He pinched her wrists in one of his hands over her head and forced his dick in from behind. Paused to catch his breath. She inhaled a mouth full of dust. For awhile he banged the front of her pelvis into the edge of the box, then he grabbed her hair and banged her forehead against a stack of hard books.

"Ow. Quit," she said and his fingers loosened and rested on the sides of her skull.

"I'm sorry," he panted. "Don't you like that? What do you like?" He sank his teeth into her shoulder, too near the bone, then hit her on the head with a book.

"Could you—" she hesitated.

"What?"

It was too weird to say.

"What?"

"Be gentle?"

There was an embarrassed silence. But he whispered, "Okay," and ran his hands slowly down her neck and back, reached inside her shirt with fingers like feathers, petted her like a kitten. His chest brushed her back. He groaned quietly, then loudly, and his thrusting got harder and faster.

Not much time left: She pictured a woman's nude torso, a giant dick plunging in. Or a topless waitress tied down to a table top in a posh restaurant while the diners lined up. No, she was tired of that one. A line of men in Devven Lee's, waiting to try on jeans, a salesgirl on her knees unzipping them one after another, in front of the security camera—Ben was distracting. Then it was over.

"Sorry," he sighed.

"No, it was good." She wasn't as sore as usual. She felt him trying to straighten her skirt for her. Kind of nice. When she turned, he was looking for her panties.

"You're nice," she said. But facing each other, they were awkward. He looked weird stuffing his too-short shirt tails into his pants, which had pleats. His hair was lumped up on one side. Would she want to be seen with this guy in a restaurant?

She tucked in her blouse and pushed back her hair and there was no next step. She felt herself dropping again, a tiny stone into a wide dark well. She was tired. She wanted to be alone.

"Well," she said. "Time to close the library," though it wasn't. She seemed to do this often: lie. She looked at his long bone of a nose, his eyes fixed to a history book. She could probably find a guy with a better dick. Maybe Kyler.

He followed her back through the racks. "Call me sometime, or I'll call you."

"Sure, fine."

"Good."

"Mm."

He left, and the hum of silence squeezed her brain. Two more hours till closing.

She sat, sat, mind wandering. Who was the last guy she'd had sex with? Some guy she'd met in a dateroom. She turned on the screen, clicked to SuncoSites, went into a room, a chat in progress:

Axman:	Pix? Who got pix
SexE:	oh ok
Fukmee:	sup to all the sexy ladees
Goddes:	Fuk U
Axman:	send th pix
Sexee17:	the modling agency?
Axman:	this room sux so bad
Atemine:	sumone pisst
Goddes:	Where are you?
McFreak:	Fuk u fuk u

God. She clicked off: you couldn't talk to anyone anymore. She clicked on Op-2-Shop, rode around the merchandise for awhile, then turned into the Hare-Care room, then into the cover of a magazine on the coffee table, into the Horoscopes:

> Scorpio: Longer hours on the job will add up to big bucks in your future! Passionate Scorpio can be stubborn—being more cooperative at work is the key! Tomorrow is a good day to spend money! Big surprises in your love life—Click on Dr. Starr to learn more! ($5.99/minute)

She gazed, then clicked back to the TV: lately she hated the feeling of being pulled into the Net. She flipped past "Real-Life Incest in Action" and "High School Massacres," past the Paterco Public Arts Station with its teasers for *Moll Flanders, Car Crashes of the Royals,* and yet another remake of *1984.* Flipped to the Holoco Premiere channel, which was airing the new Dolla Dare news show, "Here's Looking at You, Kid." She thought of Kyler. Kyler was so perfect. Dolla came on screen. Dolla was so perfect. You have to be a Dolla to get a Kyler, Arel thought, sighed, sat, watched.

Dolla and her camera crew were riding a scaffold up and down a ritzy Gold Coast highrise, peering into people's windows with cameras and bright lights. At first the show was pretty dull—people sitting in their living rooms watching TV. "God, people," Dolla complained, "What a bunch of bulimics you are"—then, knocking on a window—"Hey you! What are you, some kind of compulsive? Get a life, schizoid!" Dolla was dressed like Catwoman in tight black leather, her bright blonde head disembodied, floating in the night. The scaffold moved along and finally found something interesting: a middle-aged man and a girl having sex on someone's white fur coat. He was holding her legs up on either side of him, like he was driving a wheel barrow, and she was trying to keep herself propped up on her elbows—not an easy position to keep. With each hard bang she and the coat slid forward on the marble floor, and he was irritated, dragging her back each time and banging even harder the next time.

Then he turned and saw Dolla Dare out his window with TV cameras on a scaffold. "Now *here's* a *show!*" Dolla raved into her microphone and gave the man a thumbs up. She waved the cameras in closer and the man dropped the girl, jerked the coat out from under her and put it on himself. Arel had to laugh—the sleeves were much too short. Then the man ran to a desk, pulled out a gun, and started shooting through the window. For a moment there was chaos as the cameras whirled. A guy on Dolla's crew fell off the scaffold. When the cameras settled again, Dolla was kneeling and shooting back through the window at the man, who, along with the girl, had taken up a position behind his sofa. Dolla and the man both had bad aim. Still it was exciting—vases exploding behind the man's head, the camera crew huddling terrified at the edge of the scaffold. Finally Dolla and her crew began to sink out of range, down in front of another window. The man inside was sitting alone, apparently tuned to the Dolla Dare show, because he bounced and pointed at himself on the screen, bouncing and pointing at himself.

*　　*　　*

The next morning the people from Adstories Promotions rounded up all the young women in the building, made them put on their coats, crowded them into the elevators, and herded them into the front lobby. Hampton Drane was coming in a limousine. The young women were to rush at him adoringly as he got out of the car, while Promotions snapped stills and ran their video cameras.

But Hampton Drane was late, stuck in traffic on the bridge, and the young women stood sweating in their coats in the elevator lobby, crowded against pots of extravagant waving ferns. Arel was pinned between two chrome planters, the big woman from Human Resource Improvement pressing closer and closer with each ripple of the crowd. "Oh, excuse me," she repeated, "oh"—her head and body fat and pale, her eyes small and lashless, her hair too short. Sweat snaked down her cheekbones like slow tears and dropped onto Arel's shoulder.

At noon he arrived. The outpouring to greet him, however, was not a success. They had to go through the revolving door one at a time, and Doctor Drane had to stand at the open limo door, waiting for a crowd to accumulate. The tall thin head of Promotions, who looked like Ormer Bell, clucked and moaned and finally put Doctor Drane back into the limo and sent him around the block to arrive again in the proper crowd.

Going around the block, the limo got stuck in traffic. The women waited for another forty-five minutes, this time in the cold. In the photographs, they would look raw, red-eared and mean, clutching their coat sleeves with mittenless hands.

Arel was on the periphery when Hampton Drane re-arrived and stepped into the mob. She saw the silvery-white side of his head, his neck wrapped in a ruby lambswool diamond-studded scarf. The side of his coat was smooth, ostrich-colored, glistening in frigid sunshine. He went fast into the revolving door, and the women lined up on the sidewalk to re-enter the building one by one.

Back in the lobby, Arel kept drifting to the end of the elevator line. It was already 1:30: she could kill another hour just trying to get back upstairs, and then would only have to spend five more hours in her cube. The crowd thinned and she peeled off her coat, scarf, woolly hat. The sides of her hair rode up on waves of static—good for another 15 minutes in the bathroom with the hairspray. The crowd moved faster and she found herself in the last small group in front of the elevator doors. When they opened, she ran in the other direction.

The only place to go was the sandwich shop, which was closing. She looked in. Young black men in hairnets mopped off surfaces, swung chairs onto tables upside-down, fast and efficient, reminding her how she'd intended to be more enthusiastic on the job. Bobbing round among them was the sandwich shop manager, a young small white guy in a boy's-sized suit, his short hair sprayed to his skull, his lips chomping in a tireless critique of the mopping and chair-raising performances of the black men. She walked back to the elevators and waited. The tall chrome corridor hummed, eyed her. An elevator arrived, she got on, the doors closed, and in the mirror she watched herself push every button between the first and fifteenth floors.

The elevator jerked up, stopped, swooshed open, closed. Five times, ten times. When it reached the fifteenth floor—her floor—she let the doors close again and ran her finger up from fifteen to twenty-five. Jerk, stop, open, close—it felt exactly right.

On the seventeenth floor, Hampton Drane got on, alone.

"Hello," He was twinkling, cheerful, grinning at her untamed hair. He turned to push a floor button.

"Can you believe it?" she blurted. "Some obsessive-compulsive must've pushed all the buttons."

His smile broadened. The elevator stopped, opened, jerked to a start—Hampton Drane now part of the rhythm of her life.

"My name's Hampton Drane," he said and shook her hand. He was older than she'd expected and wasn't behaving like a rich person.

"I know," she said. "I'm in Adstories."

"Oh, a writer. Will I be working with you?"

"No, no. I'm a peon. I don't even like working in Adstories." She stopped, shocked. She'd never said it out loud before. Possibly she'd never realized this before. Hampton Drane continued to smile, leaning against the mirrored rail, short and tall at the same time.

"I would have guessed that. I'd say you don't like anything about Sunco. You feel like you don't belong. You're unhappy but you don't know why and you don't know how to find out."

She looked at him with his too-nice smile, replied sarcastically, "I suppose I'd feel like I belonged if I had some plastic surgery."

Suddenly the smile was gone and his face became a mask—slim, overtanned, full of tiny symmetrical lines. The lips unsmiling were acceptably thick. The eyes were round, retreating.

"Did I say you should change something?"

"Isn't that what you're selling in the Hampton Drane Story?"

He was silent, then began slowly, "Most of my patients are the victims of accidents and violence. I make them bearable, not beautiful. That story—"

"Oh my God! You don't like it either!"

Then the doors opened again and four guys from Promotions piled on.

"Doctor Drane! Where have you been?" Each took a turn exclaiming: "Where did you go?" "We had three more senior executives to meet!" "We just looked up and you were gone!" They formed a membrane around him— the head of Promotions, two other guys who also looked like Ormer Bell, and Brick the black guy, head of the Multicultural Diversity Division, which made sure the ads would sell to ethnic groups. At the next floor they piled off, sucking Doctor Drane along with them.

Arel rode up one more useless time, then rushed back to fifteen, ran through the maze of cubicles to tell Ormer about the elevator ride. By quitting time, everyone had heard.

Kadence and Koo derided her in the bathroom.

"Arel had a vision of Hampton Drane in the elevator," Kadence pretended to explain to Koo. "This apparition told her he liked her script better than Jonquil and Austin's."

"I never said that." Arel sagged.

"Why was Hampton Drane roaming around the building by himself?" Koo asked Kadence.

"Why, looking for Arel, naturally. His soul mate. He just took one look at her in the crowd on the sidewalk, and out of all those women—well. He couldn't resist those shoes."

Koo giggled.

"And that blouse," Kadence continued, and Koo giggled again. "I remember when those were in style."

Arel was silent.

Kadence looked down the sinks with her long creamy face, her lipstick seamless, her eyebrows perfect teal semicircles. "You've got an attitude problem, Arel. You're going to lose your job."

"Let's go," Koo said, suddenly upset, fumbling with her Flame-Off. Kadence looped her arm through Koo's and marched her out the bathroom door and down the corridor.

Arel waited. Long enough for them to be down in the lobby, through the front door, into the parking lot, into their cars. Long past the time she thought she would go, long after the hardest-working junior assistant had packed up and left. She'd be late to the library again. But she couldn't picture herself walking out, riding down: she couldn't picture herself at all. The camera always followed the attractive girls strutting away arm in arm, not the scorch. Once again she was unseen, internal, a mole traveling beneath other people's lives of pinky-cream skin tones, well-placed gestures, photogenic glances.

*   *   *

She crept down the dark street stairs into the old tunnel that led to the old parking lot. Most of the lights were out. She walked while her eyes adjusted to the lightlessness and imagined she could see. Forms slumped on either side of the tunnel—people or bags of trash. She heard a moan and slowed down, palmed the squeeze-trigger of her Flame-Off, aimed at nothing. The lot through the old tunnel was dangerous but saved her $4.30 a month, and she had a theory that rich people get rich by saving three bucks here, two bucks there, never picking up the lunch tab. You had to be cheap with little things to be extravagant with big things. That's what she'd figured out and that was right, she knew, growing angry. She was smart and she *would* be rich someday.

She went up the tunnel stairs and into the lot—dark and darker patches of asphalt, speckled with frozen cars, their alarms wailing and screeching. She started across the lot. As she walked, the car alarms began to click off, and for a moment she heard almost silence, heard the sound of her soft crunching footsteps and traffic above like a slow tide always coming in. Then she heard a sound like footsteps behind her, starting and stopping, starting and speeding up. Then nothing. She was imagining footsteps behind her. The moon was only a half and cast a numb useless light. She palmed the trigger of her Flame-Off: there were footsteps behind her. Then nothing. Silence. The air stiffened.

At her car she hesitated, didn't put the key in the lock. She wasn't going to let someone steal her car. She stood. Nothing. She'd force him out. She waited, waited, until an airless voice said: "Give me the purse and I won't kill you."

He appeared between two cars in the row behind her: hatless, his face wide and chapped, his ears and hair curling out surprised, his jacket massive, olive, ripped, buttonless at the throat—something someone had found in a dumpster and passed from one homeless person to another.

"Come *on*." He came toward her. She'd never done this before. She stepped away from her car to avoid damaging the paint. His shoulders moved through moonlight into shadow, then tilted forward, ready to reach. One hand appeared briefly in the light—large, its flesh thin but its bones thick, their contours showing white through the skin—a hand painfully pale.

She fired and the tendril of flame hit his sleeve, traveled up in a ragged wall. It was fast. He backed away and tried to shake it off, but it jumped onto his chest, devoured the old jacket cloth and the shirt underneath. He began to scream, whipped from side to side trying to think what to do. She thought of yelling, "Roll on the ground!"—easy for her to think of, leaning comfortably on her car. The flame ran up his neck and she smelled hair burning, then what must have been flesh. His hands tried to tear the fire off his face. Round and round he went in a bright dance. She felt his warmth. He whirled away from her, into another line of cars, and finally sank between two of them. His screaming stopped but she could still hear him burning. She'd never used the Flame-Off before. The beauty of it was you didn't need good aim—hitting any body part would do. The instructions recommended aiming for the groin, but hitting the arm seemed very efficient.

She got into her car. Felt herself slam the door. Key in hand. Ignition. Key in hand. She couldn't move, saw her hand, in grainy light, statue hand, tiny creases and ledges of bone, shallow indentations. Chiseled by a long-gone artist. Blue veins like frozen rivers, connecting, reconnecting. Skin between veins not white. Mottled, shadowed. Skin sinking into valleys between veins and bones. Her hand an entire landscape—a whole world.

"No," she said out loud. She felt nothing for that scum. Nothing. Her hand moved across nothing and the key went into the ignition and turned and the car backed out and she breathed in ice, clicked on the heater. Drove out of the parking lot, up the ramp. Did not look at the lit parts of her hands clutching the steering wheel.

She tried to move thoughts in her head. Turned on MTV. Shook her head hard. Familiar images danced brightly off her dashboard: teenaged girls in pink short shorts and pasties wiggled across the screen, singing "You're so exciting" in the same voice. They were the same girl—one picture repeated and repeated to make a row of paper dolls. She turned up the volume and began to feel normal again. Thought of relaxing on her stool in the library, imagined discovering something good to watch on TV.

Then started thinking. An entire row of cars could have gone up in flames. Really, the Flame-Off was kind of dangerous. She could get in trouble. If some rich guy lost his car, he could hire the police to find her and sue her. She drove fast, resisted looking back, then turned to the Helicopter News: another shoot-out at the Fried Chicken Express, a sniper on the roof of a Toys-N-Stuff, but no parking lot fires. At stoplights she tried Hotnews on her sellfone: *Dolla's New Show An Instant Hit! Dr. Aslow Tour to Include Chicago!*

At the library she watched two full hours of Flashnews—millisecond images of more snipers, shoot-outs, a mutilated blind woman, hockey stars and basketball stars and soap opera stars at the airport—still no parking lot fires. She called Ben.

"Did you hear anything recently about cars burning up in a parking lot downtown?" He hadn't, but thought she sounded odd. "I'm just concerned about this possible parking lot fire."

"Is your car there?"

"No, no—" Did the Flame-Off instructions say to put out the body before leaving the scene? She wished she hadn't called Ben. She didn't want to tell anyone. Then, suddenly, "I had to torch some guy tonight—a young guy."

"Good for you! Did you know that more than half the people who carry Flame-Offs are too timid to actually use them?"

"Oh?"

"You think you started a parking lot fire."

"Could you come over please? Would you mind? It's pretty weird here all alone."

He hesitated but agreed.

✳   ✳   ✳

Waiting, she worsened. Her breathing felt like gulping. She pictured a line of cars vanishing in a wall of flame that leapt onto the highway and roared down its concrete sleeve, dropping off in ribbons of fire bombs through the city. The whole world standing still, burning up. People beating at flames with bony bloodless hands. She grabbed Dr. Aslow's "Getting Happy" and popped it in the video player.

His slow, melodic voice calmed her: "Getting happy..." Soothing, encouraging. Dr. Aslow's face appeared big and bald and lime on the screen. "What does this mean?" His face shrank into a little gold-rimmed oval and floated over scenes of Mexico, China, India.

"We live in the greatest nation in the world," said the reassuring voice. She relaxed, watched the pictures of Bombay: people starving, ugly, shabbily dressed, pushing each other in the streets. Someone was running with a dead chicken.

"This is how the rest of the world lives. No one is happy in other countries. Everyone wants to come and live here, where we have the highest standard of living in the world." His face floated over neighborhoods of mansions, several Rolls Royces sparkling in every circular driveway. Good-looking people in good-looking clothes emerged from the mansions and climbed importantly into their cars.

"But what does this *mean?*" Dr. Aslow's face looked puzzled in its oval. "What does this mean to you personally? You may be thinking to yourself, 'I don't live in a mansion. I only have two cars. I only own two or three tuxedos. My girlfriend isn't as beautiful as these women. She needs to lose a few pounds. She doesn't dress that well.'

"What does this *mean?* Getting *happy*. *Feeling* happy. *Happiness*. What *is* happiness?"

He made her wait until he floated to the end of the mansion street, circled around, and started back again.

"Here in the greatest nation in the world, we live better than anyone else in the whole world. We *are* better than everyone else. But we're impatient. We don't all live in mansions. But we're great *because* we're impatient. Our impatience drives us on to reach our dreams—our mansions, our cars, our women. Now, what does this *mean?*"

At the end of the mansion street, Dr. Aslow's pleasant, paternal face grew to full size. The camera panned back and he reclined slightly in a leather chair in a room with gilded wallpaper.

"We're all on a journey—to our dreams. We *dream*. We *ache*. We *deserve* the good things. But we're still on our journey—we're not *there* yet. You say, 'I'm tired of this journey. I want to be happy *now*.'

"Of *course* you do. We *all* do. That's human nature. The difference is that we live in the greatest nation in the world and *we are free*. We *can* buy now—be happy *now*. Be *happy!* It's as easy as following my easy three-step Aslow plan." Snapshots of happy people appeared on the screen in a valentine around Aslow's face. "Step One—identify your objectives. What do you need to buy *right now* to make you happy? Make a list! Step Two—read over your list. Check off the items you might be able to afford *right now*. But don't be stingy with yourself—be generous! Aren't you worth it? Does it cost a little too much? Buy it anyway! *Feeling* like a million bucks is the first step to *getting* a million bucks. Go on—*dare* to *feel* like a million bucks."

His voice grew excited, signaling an extremely important point. "Remember, no one *makes* you happy or unhappy. *You* are responsible for *owning* your happiness. *You* are the key to your happiness. Take control.

Don't be a victim. Don't *blame* others for your unhappiness. *Choose* to follow my plan, *choose* empowerment!"

His voice relaxed again into contentment.

"Step Three is the easiest step of all. Just go out and buy things! Make
a day of it! Put on your best clothes! Walk around like a million bucks! Make
the salespeople think you're loaded. Show them you're better than they are.
Don't haggle over the price like a poor person. Throw the cash around! At
the end of the day, you'll feel like a million bucks—"

At last Ben walked in. "You're watching Dr. Aslow."

She paused the tape. Aslow's face froze in a pleasant half smile.

"Have you ever watched it twice?" she said. "It seems different the second time."

"Huh?" He peered at the screen, took off his jacket, dragged it on the
floor. Men were so different in person. She turned off the screen and wished
he hadn't come. He'd expect sex after coming all this way without wanting
to and she didn't feel like it. She was angry.

"Yeah. You watch it twice and you see things. He keeps saying, 'What
does it mean?' and he never tells you. He doesn't even tell you what 'it' is.
And what's with that voice? It's like he's trying to hypnotize you."

"Huh?" His eye was caught by a woman in a lavender lace bra on an
eggplant videobook cover.

"This has been the worst day of my life! People at work hate me and
I'm going to lose my job!"

He looked alarmed, then uncomfortable, standing awkwardly, not
knowing what to do with his jacket. Then, kindly, mechanically: "I can see
that you're very upset."

"Oh bullshit! What is that, some line out of Aslow's 'Getting Along with
Venutians.'"

His eyes squinted into two hurt slits. "I'm sorry. I don't know what to
say."

"Well obviously! I'm going to lose my job—"

He barked: "Don't be so melodramatic! I'm sure everything's fine."

Long silence. Then Arel said, "You shouldn't have come."

"Well, I didn't want to."

"Then why did you?"

"You begged me to."

"I did not."

Suddenly the adscreens sprang on and screamed around the room:
strippers and boxers and the latest cure for ulcers. She pressed her elbows

over her ears, bent forward, screamed along with them.

"For your information," Ben said calmly, "I was working on something important. You're like everyone else. No consideration for me."

She looked up. "Consideration for you? I was the one who got mugged."

"Oh I see—poor you. Poor little victim. What were you doing wandering around after dark anyway?"

"Leaving work!"

He tilted his head, looked tired, looked as though his next response might not be the usual one, "Arel," he said.

She blurted: "I feel bad about that guy."

Angry again: "What, that guy who attacked you? Christ." He put his coat back on. "Everyone I know is addled."

He started to leave and she panicked, thinking of sitting alone till midnight with thousands of dead videobook eyes watching her. She even called out, "Ben!" but couldn't think what to say next, having used up all her true feelings down to one level and not knowing what lay underneath. He hesitated, not wanting to go either, she could tell, but the dramatic exit was in progress and there was nothing to do but throw himself out the door, which floated shut behind him on a puff of air, latched slowly, air-tight.

She wanted to hide behind the counter, to never be seen again. She wanted everything around her to look different. She wanted to fall asleep and wake up as someone else.

She crept through the racks, leaving the counter unmanned, and shut herself into the little dim storage room. She curled up on a dusty box top and tried to sleep, but the insides of her eyelids were as bright as the adscreens, the videobook fronts, the bald fluorescent bulbs. Her eyes couldn't help but slide open. She wanted to cry, but her eyes were too dry.

She climbed off the box and sat on the floor against the wall, hugged her knees. Like when she was a child and sad about something. Her mother would sit next to her on the floor, wrap an arm all the way around her. She was thinking about her mother, for the first time in years. It was the old boxes and dust and books in stacks, reminding her. Years. She raised a foot and kicked a book off the top of one stack, then kicked off the next one, then the next, thought of her mother. Another book dropped to the floor and Arel thought she recognized it, the front cover a shadowy photograph of men and women with cardboard signs on handles. She picked it up. It was the kind of book her mother would have had, or maybe she did have it, in some pile, on some dusty shelf: *The History of Labor*. Arel opened it, and, intending to look at the pictures, started to read.

two

For three months she read. Words bunched up in her brain like cars at the toll booth: false consciousness, class consciousness, mode of production, secondary labor force, alienation, hegemony. Her Mini-Meanings definitions didn't fit the old sentences. "Alienation: Being left out of the group"; "hegemony: authority." "Consciousness-raising," she said out loud, then recognized it. This was her mother's word. She remembered something her mother had said, in her almost-laughing voice: The fish will be the last animal to discover the water. The clarity of this memory was startling, and in the humming silence of the storage room Arel looked around at the blue-carpeted walls, ceiling and floor and tried to see.

Gradually the odd words became familiar, seemed to mean things, joined together to form rickety towers in her brain. She had to make an effort to keep them in place. Stuck in traffic on the Kennedy, falling asleep in her cube, she felt these new slender structures slip too easily into the swamp of fatigue and frustration at the base of her skull. She held on. She began to recall the features of her mother's face: narrow, pale. When she finished *The History of Labor* she found another old book with a lot of the same words in it—*The Rise and Reproduction of American Corporacracy*. The swamp in her brain grew firmer and she grew confident, formed a plan: to liberate the suffering masses from their capitalist oppressors.

It was a simple, three-step plan. Step One was to surreptitiously raise consciousness by slyly dropping forgotten historical facts.

She sat in the usual booth with Ormer, Kadence, and Koo in the Sunco

Faste Sandwiche Shoppe awaiting the perfect moment to plant another seed of discontent. She sat across from Ormer, seeing only the left side of her face in the mirror, fused to the back of his head.

"You're quiet today," Kadence commented to her and Ormer's black eyes shifted, fixed on Kadence's face, and they both seemed to smirk.

"Yeah!" Koo buoyantly agreed. "No tidbits?" Koo liked hearing Arel's forgotten historical facts. Koo said to Kadence: "Yesterday she told me that you used to be able to call the police and not get charged. Isn't that nice?"

"Koo," Ormer pronounced, "your brain is a cotton ball. It wasn't *free*. The police were paid through taxes, and everyone had to pay whether they got robbed or not. And then the police were such incompetents they never solved any crimes. You'd call to report your car was stolen and you'd fill out a long form and you never saw your car again."

Arel should have had a reply to this, but for a long moment she thought of nothing but her car being stolen, and she got choked up. Koo crunched a Curly-Peel, and Kadence began compressing wrappers into small tight wads. Arel recovered and said: "Did you know that people used to only work eight hours a day and they got paid for taking vacations?"

"What?" Koo exclaimed. "That's so nice!"

Arel had spent days trying to understand this concept. "And they only had to work one job."

Kadence replied, "Oh sure if you have no ambition and never want to improve yourself. Like my grandparents. Gag. They had this ghastly old refrigerator that was five years old and completely the wrong color, and no carpet on the living room walls and no TV in the shower. And a ghastly old computer with wires all over the place! So unattractive! I'm surprised at you Arel."

Koo said, "My father told me that when he was a kid he had to ride ten miles to school everyday on a bus."

"And his father paid taxes," Ormer reminded, "which was un-Constitutional," going on instructively, "Our country was founded on the principle of no taxation."

Kadence nodded, pulled a roll of sugar-free breath-mint life-savers from her purse, popped one in her mouth, and they all sat cracking hard bits of food between their molars.

Arel blurted, "Did you guys know that *1984* was, like, written *before* 1984?"

"Where do you get this stuff anyway?" Kadence frowned.

A long silence as three pairs of eyes drifted indifferently from one side of the room to the other. She straightened up, rocked, cocky, and prepared to throw a monkey wrench into their brains.

"I've been reading books!" she said, loud and defiant.

Kadence and Koo sucked on their straws with little bird mouths and Ormer yawned. No one was shocked. No one wanted to know what books, where? No one cared. Arel looked into the black mouth of her second double-jumbo diet Coke, still thirsty, seized it, knocked the ice chunks around it, faster, faster, loud and wild. Coke splashed out and she exploded: "Don't you think we're all alienated by the hegemony of adstories? Don't you think we experience our lives as meaningless and worthless because we can only sustain a sense of self-worth through these illusions we have about ourselves and our conditions?"

Their eyebrows jumped up into their foreheads, and for a moment they all forgot to blink.

Koo said, "What's hedge money?"

Ormer intervened, "What are you babbling about Arel?"

At last she had their attention, and now she was terrified. She began, "I mean, well, isn't it kind of a problem that all our TV shows are produced in Adstory departments?"

"That isn't even true," Ormer grimaced. "Newsmagazines have their own departments. Journalistic integrity and freedom of the press and all that bull."

Koo chirped, "Like that new show—'Thirty-two Seconds'! Last night they did an in-depth story on the Paterco megastore layoffs and how customers now have to wait 2.4 minutes longer for service."

"But everything else is adstories!" Arel yelled. "All fiction is advertising! We're all being brainwashed by the capitalist bosses who want to oppress us by selling us stuff to make us happy but we end up not happy because, because, they don't really want us to be happy, or something like that, and who can figure out any of this anyway when every time you try to have a thought the goddam adscreens come on and you forget what you were even trying to think about in the first place!" She took a breath. "And then if anyone did manage to have a thought that challenges the dominant culture they get turned into a scorch, see? Everyone else thinks they're just stupid or weird or too stuffy or something and they're not taken seriously because they're like that in adstories—see?—I'm a perfect example! The more I say the weirder you think I am and the less you listen so I may as well not say anything at all!"

Silence, rolling on relentlessly—the perfect underlining of her stupidity.

"My my," said Ormer.

"Can we have a policy please?" Kadence intoned. "No lecturing your co-workers at lunch? All morning my head hurts, and all afternoon it hurts worse. Lunch is the only break it gets."

"You must think we're pretty stupid," Koo put in, sounding hurt. "You think we're all just brainwashed or something. We know the difference between what's real and what's just on TV."

"Well put, Koo," Ormer approved and Koo beamed. Then he stared at Arel with half-closed lids. "I thought you were beginning to shape up around here. You seemed almost, energetic. More, invested. As you know it's review time, and I've recommended a 1-point raise for all three of you, and one of you will be promoted to associate junior—that's a 2-point raise."

"Two percent?" Arel gasped. A *raise?* It was like, extra money for nothing! And, had Ormer said something almost nice about her? She'd never been praised at a job before. It was what she'd always expected, had never gotten, and now it felt like a miracle—like the Coke machine accepting your dollar bill at last.

"Are you in the running or not?" Ormer eyed her. She looked at the side of his face, pinkly well-shaved, the crease from his nose to the side of his mouth just beginning to deepen. She imagined his hands on her butt, wedging it between two stacks of paper on her desk in her cube, spreading her legs with his thighs. She'd fuck him for two percent. Even one percent.

"Yes!" she chirped, trying to sound invested.

After a long silent moment, Kadence said, "Arel. Your hair is at an all-time low."

Then Ormer's long hands mashed his lunch wrappers into a giant loose ball of green and orange —their cue. They piled out of the booth and headed for the elevators, the women in their little clicky shoes in an eager line after Ormer, who strolled. Kadence shouldered little Koo out of the way and ran alongside Ormer, wanting a date more than a promotion. Arel jockeyed into position on the other side of him, only as tall as his shoulder pad. He'd be looking down at the top of her hair. Were blonde streaks glimmering in fluorescent light?

Then a pair of elevator doors opened on a pale silent crowd riding up from the vending machine mall in the basement. She got onto the elevator, turned, and saw the faces again in the mirror—corpse-white, unblinking tiers of them—her own face in front, lined, the color of earth. Ormer's voice dropped down from above, "So many opinions for such a short woman," and the doors snapped shut.

*   *   *

When she felt uneasy, she thought of Ben. She hadn't spoken to him for three months, since the night she'd torched the guy in the parking lot, but she'd seen him once, through her car window as she drove by Holoco Pre-Exec High—a short detour off the main route to the library. She'd seen him rounding up a class of freshmen on the sidewalk, his arms raised and wide open, not confined to his usual narrow cylinder of space, and he was smiling, gathering up the shuffling mob of boys and girls. Kyler was there too, at the edge of the crowd on the curb, jabbering to an attractive red-haired teacher.

She wanted to call Ben. Reading was lonely. It was silence and slow time passing. She imagined telling him all the things she'd found out: "Did you know you used to be able to drive all over the city without ever paying a toll?" Imagined him being interested, imagined talking that was not struggling. She'd tell him about her mother, her hair the color of pecans, her smile reckless, saying to someone going out the door, "Our legacy to the next generation will be the inability to imagine." What did it mean? She'd ask him and they'd figure it out together, lying naked in bed, propped up by a mound of purple pillows. Then they'd fuck slow and easy in the center of a double-jumbo king-sized bed draped with mauve and gold silk.

At last she called him. He was actually there, in person, on the phone.

"Hi, hi. Ben?" Dry-mouthed. "Would you like to get together some time maybe when you're not too busy next week maybe or whatever, whenever's convenient?"

He wanted to come over that night. He said he'd meet her at her place.

She ran to the bathroom and tried to poof her hair with a comb and a mini tube of Natural Beauty styling gel and half a can of hairspray. It was more of a lump than a poof, but she could leave the lights off. She peered down her shirt: the bra was plain gold satin—no bows or lace, rhinestones or feathers—but acceptable.

She closed the library early and drove fast along the seamless neighborhood streets, passed the bright clumps of all-night megastores packed with tired people buying groceries, lottery tickets, booze and drugs, sweaters, shoes, dinette sets. Above the flashing rooftops of the megastore malls hung the moon and the first two moonboards, just launched—one a red and white striped circle blinking Coca-Cola, the other radiating the chunky square Bud logo. The real moon between them looked small—surprised and sad.

She sped into the wide bright entrance of her mall park—Brook Stream Woody Meadows—and around the outer residents' lanes toward the south end, where her apartment building was fitted onto the corner of the mall like a soup can, short and stumpy above the Holoco Discount Emporium of Salad Dressings. She pulled up to her entrance and saw him, dark and tall in the center of a gritty cone of light. His coat was black, glossy like his hair, his face still winter white. She walked toward him.

"Hi." She thought she'd put her arms around him but instead put her key in the door lock.

"You look great!" he said, nearly bouncing. She watched him examine the full length of her bare legs. "Your hair's a little different."

"You got a new coat."

"No—just another old coat."

They went through the outer glass door, through the cube-sized carpeted foyer to the oak-veneered inner door. She shook out her key ring, couldn't find the right key. "How's Kyler?"

"Fine. The same. Still doing that Sign Shine thing—he's really persisted with that one. Doesn't need me to mix up any new chemicals, though. He figured out it's more cost-effective to change the label on Stove Shine. Turns out Stove Shine is really Fridge Shine with a different label. He asks about you."

"Ahh—" she replied knowingly. "He stills needs the adstory writer."

Ben smiled and they went through the next cube-sized foyer to the bullet-proof door. She punched in her security codes.

"So," he said, waiting forever, and she smiled, finally got the door open. The elevator lobbies in the south end complex—the cheapest apartments at Brook Stream Woody Meadows—were long and narrow, with thick, graceless elevator doors and only one plastic swan fountain. "What subversive activities have you been up to?"

She smiled. He read her mind, she thought, and she giggled. "I've been reading old books."

"Yeah? Those books in the library?" Enthusiasm, just as she had imagined. She went on: "Some of it's hard to understand because there are words we just don't have anymore. Did you know that kids used to get alphabet letters written on their papers—grades—instead of money for doing their school work?"

"Oh yeah. I knew that—" he stopped. Looked odd. No elevator was coming and he tensed up, mashed the button again and again with an angry thumb. "Yeah," he started again, "You'll like this," completely calm. "Holoco quit giving out real money in their elementary schools. They've got this fake stuff now—school dollars—schollars—get it? Ha ha. Turns out the little kids didn't want to spend the real money in the school store. They wanted to save it instead."

"These elevators never come." She took his hand and led him into the beige-carpeted stairwell. They ran up one flight, then another. She stopped abruptly on one landing, said breathily, "I can't wait to tell you everything I've been reading about!" Then grabbed his hand and ran him up two more flights, their footsteps far-away heartbeats. Each landing had a security camera mounted on the wall and when they got to her door Ben stood and stared into its tiny round lens. She fumbled for the right key, dropped it, tried to put it in upside-down. "God."

His voice behind her said, "I guess we can't get in," low and sexy, and she felt his hands on her shoulders, sliding down the tops of her arms, his nose in her hair, his teeth on her neck. He kept biting as he peeled off her coat, jacket, blouse, skirt, underwear—he took off all her clothes. All of it. He turned her toward him and crouched to peer into her face. By the time she got his coat off and his shirt unbuttoned he'd pulled off his pants, underwear, socks and shoes. All of it. His chest was narrow, black hair on white skin, his stomach concave. She kneeled but he kneeled with her, lowered her onto the floor on her back. Then he actually climbed on top of her. Intended to face her. The camera must have been enough of a turn-on for him. He kissed her, pressed down on her, one thigh hard and warm between her legs. It had been years since a man had lain on top of her. He licked her ear, bit her cheek. She watched as he finally moved his other knee across her thigh, then slowly pushed in. Her mouth went dry. He said her name, twice, then said it again twice—he never got it wrong. Her eyes closed and there was nothing in her mind, no movies playing, only the feel of him pushing in.

"Jesus *Christ,*" she said, managed to open one eye and found him looking at her. His face so close. He looked right into her, not at outside parts of her. She started to pant and couldn't stop. This was not going to be the usual orgasm—the thigh-tensing, mind-roaming type. No monologue running in her head, only the sound of herself catching her breath and the feel of him inside her, until some restless inside self squeezed out and her body went limp. Her mouth so dry. She took his face in her hands and licked out his spit until she wasn't thirsty anymore and his weight sank into her, his arms pressed her sides. She dragged the ends of her hair out of her mouth.

Her arms and legs wrapped around him and they held each other on the hard gray indoor-outdoor carpet under the camera and felt something like privacy.

But time passed. Soon he'd have to go home and get enough sleep to function at work the next day. She had to be up at 5 AM. She would have to work seventeen hours after three hours of sleep.

"I'm glad you called," he whispered. "I gotta go."

"I know."

She watched him crawl from his pants to his shirt to his socks, collecting everything before putting anything on. She almost said "I love you." But said out loud, it wouldn't seem true. Held inside, it stayed warm and intense.

"Do you have your keys?" he asked.

They were still in the door, hanging by the one pushed half-way in upside-down.

He slipped his arms into his coat sleeves. "I'll call you tomorrow."

"Yeah?" She wondered, really?

He mouthed bye and left her lying naked on her back on the floor. She listened to him thud down four flights of stairs and out the door, then she balled up her clothes, rose, and realized she could have invited him inside, to spend the night. She remembered the camera lens aimed at her back and imagined its cold metal casing imprinting a circle in her skin, a hole the size of a silver dollar, big enough for her to spill out of.

*   *   *

In her cube the next day she gazed across the piles of scripts on her desk and prepared for Step Two of the Arel Plan: Sabotage adstories.

She wasn't sure exactly how to do it. Just *do* it, she told herself. Quit thinking so much. Just—be a doer! But she kept sensing her thoughts—bright debris shooting randomly from endless soundless explosions. She tried to line up words in long rows, tried to have thoughts like sentences in books. She pulled out her sellfone and called Ben.

"Hey! You caught me!" he said.

"What?"

"Between classes."

"Oh." Pause.

"So how are you?"

"Nervous," she replied and felt better admitting it, though she seemed to be more nervous talking to Ben than enacting her plan to unravel capitalist America. She cleared her throat. "I'm about to sabotage an adstory."

"Yeah?" He was interested. "You're out on a ledge. How are you doing it?"

"That's the problem. I don't know."

"Which adstory?"

"'Movers and Shakers.'"

"God I hate that show. Make Lalla and Lil have a lesbian love affair—you know, by themselves, without any guys watching. That'll really piss people off."

"I don't want to just piss people off."

"Oh."

"Anyway Lalla's getting married in the season finale."

"Make Lulu and Lil go along on the honeymoon."

"I can't change it that much." Pause. "Anyway, people would like that, wouldn't they?"

"I would."

"You would"—an opportunity to talk dirty. "You like the strangest stuff." She giggled, remembered holding him so completely naked, feeling his stomach against her ribs.

"Make Lalla fuck the hotel staff while her husband's sleeping on the beach."

"Ben," she laughed, then wasn't happy. He was thinking of Lalla, not her. She swiveled toward her mini-screen and called up the latest episode. "I can't make that big a change." Then whispered to herself, "Start small."

She scrolled up the screen to a stage direction. "Listen to this," she said, reading, "'Lulu sits gracefully on table and crosses legs.' I'm adding '. . . and delicately picks her nose,'" she laughed out loud. Then scrolled down to the union organizer's speech about how women were treated in the workforce and deleted the knowing glance between Lulu and Lil. "God!" she said. "What power!"

"Arel—aren't you going to get caught doing this?"

"Nah. These scripts pass through so many hands—Austin Carl will think Jonquil Adams made the changes, Jonquil Adams will think the Vice President's assistant did it—on and on. They'll never trace it to me."

"I'm glad you have that worked out."

"I'm gonna make Lalla's boyfriend a real asshole. Here he is at the end of the episode doing the candle-light dinner thing with strolling violinists at the malt shop to pop the big question."

"Make him take a call in the middle of his proposal."

"Hey that's good." She found the spot. "He pops the question while he's on hold."

"He forgets he's proposing and starts talking about the business deal instead."

"No—it's a call from some old girlfriend."

"I hear you typing. You're sure you won't get caught?"

"Never." But she jumped when Ormer cleared his throat behind her. "Hi Ormer!" she said weirdly and whispered "Ben, bye" and clicked off her sellfone.

"May I have a moment of your valuable time?"

"I didn't see you."

"Obviously not. I'm assuming you want to try for the promotion."

"Oh yes."

"Associate junior means turning over another four scripts a week. Here's today's. It airs the first of April, so it has to be done immediately. However if you have time to chatter on the phone you probably have time to do this. Are you still working on 'Movers and Shakers'? What's it doing on your screen?"

"I—uh. Punctuation error."

"What?" He squinted at the screen. "I expect this on my desk before lunch." He strode away and Arel picked at the rubberband on the new bundle, compressing several other bundles on her desk. Ormer hadn't needed to deliver it in person. The company didn't need to use paper at all—probably some executive somewhere had discovered that piles of paper were more intimidating to employees than peaceful green humming screens.

She tugged at the fat rubberband and looked at the title page: "Life-Threatening Lust"—a Special Arts Theatre Presentation for Sunco's home nursing company. The profits for this subsidiary must have been down—the movie was scheduled to follow the 'Movers and Shakers' wedding extravaganza episode. She lined up her checklists next to the script and began to read: It was about a handsome young lawyer and his wife, who had become fat and didn't understand him anymore. The movie opened with a lustful afternoon in the lawyer's office, with him doing several of his female clients, a secretary and her daughter, and a lady with a poodle who'd inadvertently gotten off the elevator on his floor.

Then one of his unmarried female colleagues, whom he'd done previously, bursts into his office and demands that he leave his wife to marry her. When he refuses, she turns into a psycho-killer bitch. Various body parts from his previous lovers begin arriving on his desk by express mail. Still he refuses to marry her. So she moves into his attic, darting out at night with a butcher knife to stab his upholstered furniture. Eventually the wife becomes suspicious, and the lawyer nails boards over the attic door to hold back the psycho bitch.

But one night the psycho bitch busts out and strangles the fat wife's pet hamster with a shoelace. The fat wife finds it the next morning, hanged on the pull cord of her favorite Tiffany table lamp. Choking back sobs, the fat wife creeps suspensefully around the house, peering into closets and behind doors, while all along the psycho bitch is right behind her—which the audience knows by the way the camera angle turns and jerks and reels around, depicting how a psycho bitch would see a wife.

In the climax scene, the two women fight face to face in a chaos of table legs and Tiffany lamp shards. The hamster is seen arcing through the air, trailing the shoelace behind it. The psycho bitch crushes the fat wife's legs with a portable marble fountain and in the same instant the grandfather clock falls symbolically onto the bitch, cracking her spine. The lawyer begins to feel grief-stricken and fixes up two rooms in the attic—one for his wife and one for his former lover, now both confined to wheelchairs. Grieving, he calls a home healthcare agency to send a nurse to look after the tragic women. The nurse turns out to be a tall wet-lipped redhead in a tight white uniform, and as the credits roll, the nurse slips out of her expensive silver coat and wiggles next to the lawyer on the couch to comfort him.

Arel sat for a long time, her eyes stuck on the last word, her thoughts not moving. Then she cried out, "Sabotage!" loud enough for people to hear, though no one did. She pulled up the script on her screen, sat, squinted at it. She tried making the wife thin and the lover fat, but that didn't seem logical. She inserted a phrase directing the nurse to look with concern at the two attic doors, just before she peeled off the silver coat and ran her open palms down her thighs.

Arel scrolled back to the fight scene. What if the camera panned back and revealed that the lawyer had been standing on the indoor balcony through the whole fight, looking on?

Her phone chinked. "Hello?"

"Hey," Ben said. "Are you okay?"

"Oh, yeah."

"Let's get together." Pause. "Soon."

"Yeah. Okay." She said, trying to sound warm and emotional, but sounding remote instead. Why did that happen? Inside her was a door on a stiff hinge that kept slamming shut before any real feeling could get out.

The only time to see each other was between midnight and five in the morning, but they made a date anyway.

"Great," she said, sounding insincere again, anticipating the lost sleep and the next day's fatigue. "Bye!" Clicked off her phone.

She turned back to the script, felt its mass. Felt overwhelmed. It seemed unchangeable, sprawling across her desk like one of the ancient pyramids, structures pressed onto the horizon so long they seemed more a thing of nature than something constructed by men.

∗   ∗   ∗

Four days later Ormer appeared in her cube. "What have you been doing to the adstories?"

"Huh?" She couldn't believe it. What an idiot. Had she really imagined she wouldn't get caught?

"Jonquil Adams wants to see us both immediately in her office. Something about changes to the adstories."

"Huh?"

"Will you get your butt out of that chair?"

Her bare feet felt around under her desk for her shoes. God. She'd be fired. She'd never get another job. She'd be evicted and lose her car and end up dying on the street. She stood, tucked in her blouse. Couldn't swallow. She tried to shake the wrinkles out of her jacket, which had been balled up on the file cabinet.

"Want to drop by the beauty salon for a few hours before we go up?"

"I'm coming," she said, pawed her hair.

In the elevator, Ormer said nothing. She tried to rest her hands at her sides but they trembled, twisted the fabric of her jacket. She looked at the cool shimmer of Ormer's ecru sleeve, at a pinstripe with emerald threads lazing through it. She tried to hold still. Watched the number above the door: 20, 20, 20, 21. . . Jonquil Adams was fifteen floors above them.

When the elevator doors opened Ormer moved fast. She jogged to keep up. The halls were wide, the ceiling high—there was even a window. Around the corner were Jonquil's four secretaries—in real mahogany cubes—on the periphery of a wide open space adorned with real plants and strings of tiny glitter balls. Arel and Ormer went right in.

Jonquil's office was so huge they had to look around to find her: she was posed, tall and creamy and dressed in grape, between wall-sized posters of her greatest successes—Lalla, Lulu, and Lil, wild-haired and big-smiled with heads tossed back and photographed nude from the chest up, and the giant frank star-lit face of Hampton Drane. The opposite wall was a mirror, duplicating the tableau in silver, grape, and flesh.

"Ormer Bell." Jonquil propelled forward in steady heels to shake hands. Jonquil had a body made for striding. Her hand was as perfect as a photograph, coming at Arel for a shake. Arel looked up, saw the chin and the solid sweep of hair like onyx.

"Arel Ashe," Jonquil enunciated and led the way into a small cushy living room-like area. Arel and Ormer sat in amethyst chairs and Jonquil stretched out on the ruby sofa, beyond the glass coffee table and panda-skin rug. She pulled the script out from under a pillow, flung it on the table.

"How long has this woman been with us?" Jonquil asked Ormer.

"Four, five years," he guessed.

"In one of those god-awful cubes." She lit a cigarette—she'd be able to afford the cancer treatments. She lunged forward and rifled through the pages of the script. "Have you seen this?" she asked Ormer. "Listen to this. In this scene, the union organizer is going on and on about how women are discriminated against in the workplace. At the end of her speech Arel added, quote, In a capitalist system women are culturally devalued so they can be used as a cheap secondary labor force."

Silence. Dust particles drifted through a streak of sunlight toward Ormer's crossed knee. Arel couldn't look at Jonquil, so she looked at Ormer, looking at Jonquil. A slow confused frown crept down from his eyebrows to his lower lip. His eyes began to widen, widen, then his lips slightly parted, in amazement, in horror: Jonquil was smiling.

"I mean, Arel, where did you find this stuff?"

"Pardon?" Arel croaked.

"It's so *authentic*. Where did you *get* these *words?*" Jonquil laughed out loud.

"In some old books."

"You've been reading old books? God, what a great idea! It seems so obvious though, doesn't it? Listen to this: 'Alienation is not the name of an old sci-fi flick,' says the union organizer. 'It is when we are able to sustain a sense of meaning only with the help of illusions about ourselves and our condition.'" She laughed more—huge gut laughs, a snort through the nose. "Condition!" she shrieked. Ormer smiled palely. She flipped excitedly to the end of the script. "And listen to what else Arel did. During the proposal scene, the fiance gets a phone call—are you listening Ormer?—from a sexy young client and he leaves Lalla sitting there while he closes the deal! Just one little detail and pow—the character is so *focused*. It shows you what a go-getter he is!" Jonquil threw her shoulders forward, dropped her voice. "And immediately the audience wonders, Will Lalla get mad?" Then, booming: "And she doesn't! Lalla knows what's in her best interest. What savvy! This guy is obviously going places, she's not going to screw it up just because her feelings get hurt. We really get a glimpse into Lalla here, into the complexity of her inner thoughts. Lalla really comes alive!" Jonquil glowed at Arel. "Wonderful! I must admit," now almost whispering, "sometimes it's kinda hard to tell the girls apart, isn't it?"

"Huh? Oh I don't know. They all have different color hair."

"Modesty! How fresh!" Jonquil's hand flew to Arel's knee, gave it a squeeze. "I'm not too big to admit it. We've just plain gotten stale with this show. A smart new creative eye is just what we need on this. Ormer why has this woman been working here for five years with no promotion?"

"Promotion?"

"Why have you been walling her up in one of those god-awful cubes all this time? Surely even you could spot her potential."

"Potential?"

"What are you a parrot? Caw caw, Ormer wanna cracker?" She laughed the mean wild laugh of a successful person. Arel looked into Jonquil's eyes: grape, like her suit. Jonquil moved a shoulder toward Arel to shut out Ormer. "Are you working on any original screenplays?"

Arel smiled. Step Three of the Arel plan was her screenplay. "Actually, I am. The Hampton Drane Story Part Two."

"Wonderful! Wonderful! Needs a better title. Ormer, you brainstorm with Arel on the title. Do you think you can handle that?"

Ormer looked plastic, in a hard immobile slouch. "Sure."

"Then I'll schedule the Committee for a critique." She pulled out her Mini-Manager, flipped it open. "Three weeks from today. That means submitting in two."

"Two weeks?" Arel choked. "That's kinda soon. It's really only half finished. I uh, I've been having trouble figuring out the last few scenes. . . "

"Arel!" She threw up her hands in a big, teasing gesture. "You can do it! The trick is, don't think about it too much. That's the way you win the game. Just do it!" She winked at Arel, stiffened at Ormer, "I expect you to be supportive of her efforts."

"Of course," he said, then rose, remarkably loose, and waited for Arel to stand up.

"Is that all?" Arel asked Jonquil, who was now punching up various things on her Mini-Manager screen, looking alternately surprised and pissed. Arel continued, "It was so great to—" Ormer grabbed her elbow and led her fast out the door.

"Lesson one," he said when they were out the door. "Leave when it's time to leave. Nothing is forever."

He was jealous. She was thrilled. She watched the back of his glittering jacket billow in and out with his agitated steps, the back of his neck red behind the pointy black rat tail of his hair. *She* had caused this. She *had caused*.

In the elevator he remained wordless and red. Years and years of ridicule at lunch. Of him never desiring her. She smiled even though he could see her gloat reflected to infinity. Then she laughed, her body finally free of its weights, rushing up. She burst into wild laughter, threw out her arms and yelled, "Yes!" Success! Revenge! His eyes avoided her. He squinted at the numbers blinking above the elevator door, the squint tightening, his pupils almost gone. He was falling, she knew, as she soared. Even the sinking of the elevator had no effect on her. At last she would have an existence outside of crowds and tunnels, cubicles and dropping boxes.

✻ ✻ ✻

That night she closed the library early, got a bottle of champagne at the Booze and Snooze drive-through, and drove to Ben's place to surprise him. She'd never been there. He lived at Park Forest River Oak, a Holoco mall park, above a bulbous Mega-Gourmet Coffee and the country's largest space-savers store. She rang his bell.

He was awake but confused and different in his own place, leaning out the door in a red plaid flannel robe.

"What are you wearing?"

"Arel?"

"I'm sorry, were you sleeping?"

"I was working. Did we have a date?"

"It's a surprise!" She held up the bottle. "I got a raise and a promotion!"

"Yeah?" He smiled, but not as enthusiastically as she'd expected. He held the door open for her, and she walked in.

His place was even smaller than hers. And he had no stuff. What he did have was old or weird or both. In the corner by an old computer under the only lamp in the room was a real-looking skeleton, on a coat hanger, wearing some kind of kilt. On the other side of the skeleton was another computer, or pieces of one, in a kind of pile. His sofa-sleeper was black-and-white checked. She drifted across the room, stood between the skeleton and a row of old yellowing pages stuck onto the wall. There was a picture of Mars that wasn't generated—that seemed to be drawn by hand, childish, with childish hand-writing in the corner: "Sarah." She wanted to touch it but was afraid it would disintegrate, it looked so old. Beneath the hand-drawn Mars were several generated pictures of thick wormish structures that seemed distantly familiar. She frowned, tilting toward them. "What are these pictures?"

"Huh? Oh they've been up there for ages," he said. Then yanked them off the wall. She tried looking at some other part of the room, but everything was old and worn, everywhere, as though Ben was a person with a past but no present.

"Where did you get that sofabed?" she couldn't help saying. "My god—is that ancient thing a TV? Don't you have any stuff?"

"Are you finished critiquing my lifestyle?"

Neither of them was smiling.

"I'll go," she said, then didn't.

He stood watching her, until it was clear she didn't want to go. "You can stay. I'd like that. I was just, just—very preoccupied with a new project."

"Oh." She squinted at his computer screen. Then she tried smiling, gave him the bottle of champagne and he stood, holding it in both hands, staring at the cork. She said, "Jonquil Adams liked my changes and made Ormer promote me!"

At first he didn't respond. Then: "She liked it?" Silence. "Weren't you trying to piss her off? I don't get it. You sound like a regular company gal."

"No I don't." She frowned at him. "Anyway, see, now I can operate from a position of strength." This sounded familiar, like something from Aslow's first trilogy, "Getting Along at Work," "Getting Ahead at Work," "Getting Your Boss's Job."

"How could she like your changes?"

"Well. She completely missed the point."

"And that's not a problem?"

"Well. I see what you mean. I was too subtle, that's all. Next time I'll be clearer. I'm currently writing an original screenplay for Jonquil that will really pack a punch."

"Listen to you." He studied her face and she shifted, guilty. About what? For eight years she'd dreamed of getting promoted and now her dreams had come true. She was actually happy. She was. Striding from her car to Ben's door she'd felt real—could picture herself striding, passing in and out of squares of light cast by streetlamps in the parking lot. Looking confident.

"My screenplay—" she said, hearing her voice sound haughty, "is really gonna shake things up. It's a sequel to the original Hampton Drane Story. I assume you saw that."

"I don't watch a lot of TV."

She didn't know how to reply. He kept staring at her. So he thought she was "selling out." Fine. He was weird. She didn't need him—people in power can fuck anyone anytime. She'd had plenty of lovers in the past. She'd just get another one.

"Arel?" His voice tentative.

"What?" Hers defensive.

"Suddenly you're different."

"Bullshit." She lifted her chin and thought of making a dramatic exit. But her chin began to sink and she sat down instead, on his black and white checks, not wanting to leave at all. He was weird but she kind of liked that. He stayed on her mind. She was tired of the search for replacement lovers, tired of moving on, having to forget the men she'd begun to love: their voices, their smiles, their bodies. She had a system. She would forget them from the bottom up—feet first, face last.

She looked at Ben's face, frowning at her. A rough black beard was appearing below the softness and whiteness of the skin beneath his eyes. The contrast drew her in. But love was a thing from adolescence; she didn't know how to love as an adult. She could either run to him and beg him to love her or hide behind a windowless wall. She might have cried, but her eyes were too dry. She was becoming a desert, thirsty and tearless, a layer of sand that could be carried off by any brief wind.

"Arel?"

"Yeah?"

"I'm a wet blanket," he said.

"What?"

"I'm sorry I spoiled your surprise. I'm happy for you. The promotion and the raise—if that's what you wanted."

She rose. "Thanks. I'd better go now."

"No, stay. You can stay."

"I'd better go," she replied, needing the relief of leaving.

"Okay," he said stiffly.

The night was too cold for late March, but walking back through the scattered squares of light she began to feel all right again, kind of happy, even, hearing her heels click on the pavement, more confident, feeling her body loose inside its clothes, seeing her short but shapely legs stretch as she twisted herself into the low bucket seat of her almost-sports car, almost like Dolla Dare's legs in pantyhose commercials.

*　　*　　*

The next day Ormer appeared in her cube in a new cobalt suit, with glossy shoes and eyes to match and hair slicked back into a perfect black solid, no deviant strand coming loose. Her eyes couldn't settle. His face and neck looked airbrushed; he was a fashion centerfold. If only he'd been blond. He handed her an orchid.

"Free for lunch today?" His voice was not sarcastic. "Noon?"

She couldn't speak. Nodded. He clicked his tongue and left. He'd never clicked at her before. Her blood rushed up and she was back in the old fantasy: his hands sliding up the sides of her torso, his eyelids heavy with lust.

She ran into the bathroom and shrieked at herself in the mirror. She was all wrong. Her suit was so old it was almost pastel, with deep creases like a screaming mouth across the back of the jacket. She whipped it off and shook it, put it under the hand dryer. Then wiggled out of the skirt, which had smaller creases to match. Eventually Kadence and Koo arrived.

"Congratulations on your promotion!" Koo burbled. Her face was excited, close to Arel's in the mirror, her hand almost touching Arel's shoulder. "I like that you got promoted even though you're different."

"What is that supposed to mean?" Kadence stood teasing her hair with rough jerks.

"Well, you know, Arel's not so. . . I mean, she's kind of. . . I don't know. Earthy."

"You mean ugly and plain. And why exactly are you standing in the bathroom in your underwear, Arel?"

"I'm trying to get the wrinkles out." She was dousing the jacket with water and putting it back under the dryer. "I have a lunch date with Ormer."

A long buzzing silence, and Kadence left the bathroom. Koo said, "Wow."

"This is hopeless!" Arel shrieked. The wrinkled suit, the flat hair, what to say to Ormer Bell for an entire half hour—these things were big enough to occupy her entire brain.

"You'll be fine! I can help." Koo always helped. She hung the jacket and skirt over a stall door and pressed on the wrinkles with the heels of her hands. Then she poofed Arel's hair and made up her face as Arel gazed in the mirror, recalling past transformations at beauty parlors: skin and hair completely different, bone and muscle just the same, the nose asserting itself through the new filmy outer layer, the eyes with the same sad down-turn, same slow blink. Koo slapped her back as they walked out of the bathroom. Ormer was waiting at Arel's cube.

He took her in the elevator up to Chez Tres Chic at the top of the Tower and even paid her entrance fee. The walls and ceiling were covered with jagged bits of mirror, bordered with ivory and strips of diamond chips. The floor was ebony. Diamond necklaces hung from the ceiling, and mirror balls rotated to make everyone's skin shimmer.

They sat, and Ormer ordered $10 cocktails, smoothed a silk napkin onto his lap. Past his shoulder Arel saw her face in a mirror fragment: she could see how someone might think she was pretty, from a distance, though the extra-poofed hair seemed silly, like colorless cotton candy atop her skull.

"Hampton Drane," announced Ormer, as though he had just come in. Then—"Part Two"—snapped on like an exclamation point.

"Oh."

Their cocktails arrived, pink and foaming in tiny glasses.

"Tell me about it."

"Hm, okay, well—" She paused, drank. Tried to remember it. She recalled it in bits, then chunks, then whole scenes. Suddenly it seemed like the stupidest thing she'd ever thought up in her entire life.

She finished her drink and wanted another one. Ormer ordered one and stared. She had to start talking; he was buying her drinks and lunch. "Needs a better title," she said.

He waved it away as nothing and his hands struck her as elegant now, not effeminate, suspended above the glass-topped table, reflected everywhere she looked.

He said, "Soooo?"

"We-ell. . . " Dread solidified in her throat. "We-ell. . . "

"A-rel."

"Okay. What happens is, Hampton Drane closes his lucrative practice in Cincinnati and moves back to Chicago. . . to treat torch victims." No response. "He prowls around the streets at night looking for them and takes them to his special clinic and treats them—free of charge." Still no response. "Then he gets to be friends with this one young homeless guy who got torched in a parking lot, and he invites him to live in his mansion permanently, and the young guy goes around with Hampton Drane to rescue dying torch victims, and they start a community in his mansion, and all of Hampton Drane's wealthy friends are sure that these homeless people are gonna rob him and murder him in his sleep, and then in the end. . . they don't." Silence. "Of course there's a love interest—a smart brunette—and there's a really hot sex scene of course." Though she'd had them making love gently, facing each other, but that would be boring on screen, she now realized. "Then at one point the young homeless guy's family is looking for him because they love him, but maybe that's kind of corny."

Their lunch plates arrived. Ormer remained perched over his, his head cocked, and Arel began the slow process of winding a noodle around her fork. She listened to the chinking of plates, the low sexy laughter of women at the bar.

Then Ormer began to nod. "Interesting."

"Do you really think so? You really do? Really?" His eyes shifted, squinted, dropped. She went on, "It needs work. I'd really value your input. I can make changes, no problem." Thoughts flew in her head. He liked it. Did he really like it? Her drink was gone. But he thought it was good. No, he was lying. She was too gullible. She had to stop believing everything everyone told her. No—no—she was too suspicious. That was her problem. She had no savvy—that was her problem. She extended an arm across the table, as Jonquil might have done, but it was ridiculously short. Maybe he really did like the story. More likely, he thought it was passable and was sucking up because Arel was Jonquil's new pet. He bought her another drink and she downed it. There must have been salt in it—she was still thirsty, she only wanted more. *More, more* hummed in her head and Ormer was everywhere, everyone, in a thousand shards of glass around her. His voice coming from no where said: "You made Hampton Drane a do-gooder."

She frowned and nodded to express nothing and examined the noodles on her fork.

After another long pause he said: "You've made a hero of the scorch." He understood. He'd gotten it exactly. Their eyes met and the understanding welded them together, was unbearable.

"Well, yeah," she replied.

"Different. Very. How would you ever sell it to the committee?"

"I have a theory—the Theory of the Different."

"You have a theory. With a name."

"I think people are tired of the same old stuff. Don't you? Anyway, Hampton Drane will like it. I'm going to send him a copy."

"Ah."

"I still have time to make changes, though. Jonquil said you were supposed to give me a hand. Remember?"

"Mm." He took a bite of noodles, chewed, swallowed, gazed past her shoulder. He must have been looking at himself in some bit of mirror. Then, instead of speaking, he took another bite, chewed, gazed some more. "Needs a better title."

"I agree, a hundred percent."

"How about, Hampton Drane: Man With a Mission."

"That's so great! Thanks Ormer. But you know, I think, I think there's something else—something's missing, I think. Something's been nagging at me—"

"No," he said abruptly. "No no! Don't change a thing." Then he leaned forward and paid her the greatest compliment, "It *works*."

His foot under the table brushed against hers and she looked down through the glass top, saw all their knees. When she looked up he was wiping his lips, running the tip of his tongue along the edge of his teeth, gazing past her. Then he looked at her, didn't speak, closed his eyes. Rubbed them with a tired thumb and forefinger, opened them again. Full of tears? He began to say something, stopped. Then reached right across and took her hand, squeezed it, leaned toward her. "I'm with you," he whispered.

She felt the upward surge again, watched her face turn red in a crescent of mirror. She wasn't smooth. He rose and held her chair as she stood up, teetered, held his arm to the elevator. She remained posed on his arm down twenty floors and made heads turn when she strode off the elevator with him into the maze of cubicles.

✳   ✳   ✳

The afternoon of drinking made her especially thirsty. So on her way to the library she went to the Booze 'n Snooze drive-through, bought a double-jumbo bottle of rum, and dumped a fourth of it into her diet Coke. She sucked it up through the super-straw, missed a turn, and ended up in a MegaSnax drive-through getting munchies. Flame hot 3-D Doritoes, the extra large bag. She stuffed them in her mouth as fast as she could, washed them down with rum and diet Coke, then had to get more diet Coke, which then needed more rum. She was late opening the library.

She sprinted in and turned on the Party Channel. Spewing Cannibals' remake of "Teen Angel" was playing and she hopped up onto her stool and danced. She didn't particularly like the tune, but the beat was strong. The adscreens popped on, and frozen dinner boxes danced round with her. She kicked out her legs, sending her shoes into the racks, and looked up to see one flying over the head of an amazed Kyler Judd.

"Hi!" he screamed over the music. "Guess ya didn't hear me come in!"

She turned off the TV. "Hey Kyler!" She hopped onto the counter, threw out her arms, jumped down, as though she thought she could fly.

"Whoaaaa!" Kyler said, attempting to catch her. "Ya okay there, Arel?"

"God, Kyler," she said, throwing her arms around his broad hard shoulders. "I forgot what a beautiful, beautiful man you are!"

"Oh!" he replied, grinning, giggling, sniffing her breath. "Thanks!"

"Did Ben tell you? I got promoted, I got a raise, everyone loves my screenplay, I'm totally launched!"

"Yeah, Ben said. What are you doing to that boy anyway? He moons around like a love-sick teenager."

"Oh?" She didn't want to think about that. She started to dance again, to no music. "Come on, dance with me."

He slightly reddened. "Well, actually Arel I came in to chat about Sign Shine. I figured, now that you're so big-time, you could really launch me!"

"Hey, baby," she said, close to his face, "I'll launch you." She ran a finger down his bicep.

He just stood there. But not uninterested—she could tell. "I figured you could write me up some campaign to pitch to someone—Holoco, Sunco, whoever."

"Paterco," she said.

"Yeah," he said, let out a little nervous laugh.

"So I scratch your back, and you. . . will. . . do what for me?"

Another nervous laugh.

"Okay," she stopped dancing, panted, took a sip of the double-jumbo rum and diet Coke. Pretended to be serious. "Now, the best adstories are the ones with lots of sex in them. So we need to think sex. Sex sex sex. Let's do that now." She pitched forward and smelled his neck, which smelled of Sex—the cologne. She frowned into his face. "Are you thinking of sex, Kyler?"

"Oh, always!"

"Good. Now, tell me what exactly you're thinking."

Slowly he smiled, then grabbed her face and kissed her, thick-lipped and full of tongue. He put his arms around her waist so she wouldn't stagger backwards. She wasn't used to a man with so much confidence. He pushed her against the counter and pressed his body against hers, kissed her more, then leaned back so that he could see her face, or so that she could see his. Even so close, he was perfect. He was a fantasy. He chewed on her neck, shoved his hands up under her shirt, unhooked her bra in one skillful pinch.

"Hey," she whispered, gently pushing him back. "Wanna see my secret room?" She walked him backwards through the video racks to the storage room.

"What's in there?" He was so excited, she laughed. He'd be expecting medieval torture devices or cages of large zoo animals and he'd be even more surprised by their absence, by just a room, private, with some boxes of books. She threw open the door. "What is it?" he asked.

"It's an old storage room!" she said.

He peered hopefully into boxes. "What's in here?"

She replied in a suggestive voice, "Books. You know what I do with them?"

"What?"

"Read them."

He stood a few feet from her, his face still delighted but puzzled. She looked down, saw the smoky cover of the one she'd just read: *The First American Dream*. She couldn't help saying, "Did you know that almost half the people in this country used to vote?"

"No kidding?"

"And there only used to be two political parties?"

Then, wanting to keep up, he said, "I'm very interested in politics. Did you know this is an election year?"

"Oh, oh yeah."

"That Paterco guy's been President a long time, hasn't he?"

"Yeah," she said, trying to remember. Then Kyler rested his hands on her shoulders and she let their weight press her down, till she was sitting on a box, eye level with his fly. The stale taste of rum and diet Coke and Doritoes was still in her mouth, which opened and pressed into the material of his pants. She licked the zipper, cool, pushed her chin against his huge hard bulge. Felt his hands brush against her forehead, heard the clank of his belt buckle, the unzipping. She leaned back and watched him pull out a perfect penis—not just thick but long, the head perfectly proportioned. "God, Kyler," she said and stared at it. Then lunged forward and stuffed as much as she could into her mouth and down her throat. Inhaled deeply to avoid gagging. The room was soundless. She heard an unnatural buzzing in her brain. Then felt a surge up her windpipe and had to pull away. Suddenly wanting to cry.

She looked up, at the perfect angle of Kyler's chin. The slope of his shoulders and biceps and forearms made her run her hands up as far as they would go, then down again. He was electric. He could star in a Dolla Dare movie. He ran his open hands down her neck and sternum and pushed her backwards on the box. Rolled her stockings down to her toes and worked his way back up with his tongue. "Oh—" and some other sound spilled out of her mouth. This was skill. Kyler was a man who learned well, who'd wasted no time questioning his teachers.

He stood suddenly and shoved his dick in, started slow, then sped up fast, rolled her onto her side, then onto her knees on the floor, lifted her onto another box, banged her against the wall. Dust went up her nose and she concentrated on suppressing a sneeze. *This guy could do an aerobics video,* her thoughts chattered, *one, two, three, and—Jump to the left, now to the right. . .* He went on forever, and her mind wandered: a cheerleader and the football team, all the cheerleaders and the football team, Kyler and Dolla Dare.

Her thigh muscles began to ache. She tried counting positions but lost track. She ended up spread face-down on the floor, bruised, exhausted, and thinking of zoo animals. Through the whole event, she'd forgotten to look at his face.

"Good?" he panted on the floor beside her. He was about to spring up and, what—do deep knee bends? She held him down, gazed at his sweating, unfamiliar face. Sex made strangers of people. She closed her eyes, made him stay on the floor beside her, and as usual the sex began to seem better in retrospect. Not just better—incredible. She kept her arm across his chest until he quit panting, was rested and ready to do it again.

*   *   *

The morning of the Committee meeting, she waited in her cube and thought about Ben. For two weeks she hadn't returned his calls. What was there to say? Promotion, raise, upward mobility, Kyler, possibly even Ormer. Ben didn't seem to belong on that list. She'd only needed him when she'd had nothing else. Now she was about to have everything—every distant promise was about to be kept.

"Arel," came the voice and she jumped. Ormer seemed less polished than usual, not so certain. "It's time."

She followed the back of his billowing jacket to conference room A and was not calm. People accumulated around the long brown table but didn't look at her. People began to sit: various identical guys from Promotions, Demographics, Assessment, all in Ormer suits with the latest oiled-solid hair. Arel and Ormer sat across from them. At the head of the table was the VP's personal representative, Ayla Horn, a twitchy shapeless woman in a mannish suit who fluttered around with folders and agendas for future meetings, her feet puffing out the tops of her shoes, the bulges of her calves strangely low on her legs.

Jonquil Adams and Austin Carl entered last, busy and bored, tall in sweeping clothes that matched their hair today: black for Jonquil and gold for Austin.

"Are we all here?" Ayla Horn asked, as though someone might reply, "I'm not."

Arel's leg began to swing.

"Okay I guess we're all here," Ayla said doubtfully and continued to pull things out of her briefcase: a coffee mug, a mini-manager, a mini-recorder. She announced the date into the microphone, then laboriously recited the name of each attendee. Arel's leg swung higher. Ayla finished, paused, then blurted, "Does anyone else think it's hot in here? Is that thermostat working?" She got up to look at it. Levas, the Demographics trainee, was helpful and got up with her. They poked at it, mumbled. Ten minutes gone by.

"Levas," Ayla said, "run down the hall and see if conference room B is open."

He actually left. Arel stopped swinging her leg, but her foot started to jiggle. Ayla asked Austin Carl, "Don't you think it's stuffy in here?"

He pursed his lips.

"Are you hot?" she asked Jonquil, apparently intending to proceed around the table. Levas returned: Someone was using B. "We'll just have to suffer," she chirped, sat, waited for Levas to drag his chair up to the table. Then, "Okay!" Thank God.

Then, silence.

"Well," Ayla said, "I assume everyone here has read this." More silence. "Have we all read this?" God. Another pause. Pages flipped. Ayla continued, slowly: "I found the end. . . mmm. . . confusing." A sudden grunting of agreement.

Cantor, head of Promotions, said, "I found the ending implausible."

"Yes," agreed Ayla, "Implausible."

Suddenly Jonquil Adams was in the conversation, speaking in a fast low voice directly to Arel: "The problem is your character, Arel. You've got a real motivation problem here." Her fingers opened and closed to emphasize her point. "You have to ask yourself, Arel, *why* is my character doing this? *Why* is he doing that? You have to ask yourself, what would *I* do in that situation? Why would I do that? See how that works? As he is, Arel, your character is not convincing. He lacks motivation for his actions."

"Yes, yes," nodded Ayla.

"Very one-dimensional," said Cantor.

"I just didn't like him," Dorvan from Assessment blurted. "What's this guy doing anyway? What is he, some kind of do-gooder? How would someone like that get to be a successful surgeon? It's implausible."

"Mm," Ayla moaned, and a silence descended. Was it over? Arel tensed to run for the door. But no one got up. Pages turned, turned. By accident, Arel caught Jonquil's eye, blurted out: "You're very helpful."

"Mr. Carl," Ayla said. "We haven't heard from you."

Austin Carl stroked the top of his eyebrow with the tip of his index finger. "Yes, well, I did start to glance through this. Nothing particularly stood out for me. Implausible, I thought. Overwritten."

"Mm, mm."

Pages turned.

"And how about you Mr. Beal?"

"Bell," Ormer replied.

"Bell—yes—did I say Beal? I meant Bell. Isn't that funny. I know your name of course. I know a Nella Beal. What was I thinking? Bell, Bell—" she enunciated into the tape recorder.

"It doesn't matter," Jonquil barked.

"No, no, where were we?" Ayla went on, "The style—yes, overwritten. We prefer simple language, of course. We're not trying to be artistes here. Page 25." Pages flapped, everyone happy for something to do. Ayla continued: "Hampton Drane says, 'The Communists are no longer around to sell us the rope by which to hang ourselves. We'll have to manufacture it ourselves.' What is that?"

The others searched through the preceding pages for the answer.

Arel croaked, "That's a reference."

"I see. Very overwritten—words like 'manufacture.' Why not just say 'make'? Is that what you meant, Mr. Carl?"

He winced.

"It doesn't sound natural," said Cantor.

"That's why he doesn't come across like a real person," realized Levas, who smiled kindly at Arel.

"That's just editing," Jonquil barked again. "She could clean that up in an hour. The main problem, Arel, is that your character lacks consistency." Heads nodded.

Arel straightened up, began in a careful, loud-enough voice, "I was trying to do something different. I have a theory that people would like something different—"

"Oh I agree, a hundred percent," Jonquil said. "Too much sameness on TV. Absolutely. Drives you nuts, doesn't it? Now the first Hampton Drane story was quite different—a love story between a prominent physician and a grotesquely scarred rape victim. A wonderful story. But see, Arel, it was still plausible because he made her beautiful again."

Arel caught herself nodding, made herself stop. "But our idea of what's plausible is a function of our culture."

Everyone looked at her.

"God," Jonquil realized aloud. "You really talk that way, don't you?"

"You're all completely missing the point!" cried Dorvan. "How is this supposed to sell plastic surgery?"

"I wondered that too," Ayla remembered.

Cantor added, "It doesn't. Or it's so incompetent it isn't clear."

"It certainly is incompetent," said Levas.

"Frankly I couldn't get through the first page," said Austin.

"It's the worst thing I've ever read!" Dorvan said.

"It makes me think you don't understand the concept of adstories at all," Ayla accused.

"I wondered that too," Levas put in.

"Five years is a long time to be here without catching on," Jonquil commented.

"Is that how long she's been here?" Austin groaned. "I thought she was just hired."

Ormer finally spoke: "There've been other complaints about her work. Reports of sleeping in her cube, making personal phone calls, loitering on elevators."

Arel turned toward him and looked right into his face. Betrayed. He'd known all along how the Committee would react. She thought she might really cry: for eight years they'd seen each other every day, eaten lunch together, ridden elevators together, followed each other through revolving doors, stood side by side on the pavement turning up their coat collars before leaving for the night. Brothers and sisters didn't see each other that often, or know each other that well.

"Not much of an employee at all, huh?" Ayla frowned.

"I think we should fire her," Ormer said.

Silence. Across the table the row of young associates were shocked, then nodded in wild agreement. Suddenly awake, Austin Carl said, "Why not?"

Jonquil leaned in, "It's probably best for you, Arel. This line of work is apparently not for you."

"Then we all agree!" Ayla called Security. Everyone began to file out of the room.

"Wait—" Arel blurted. Two security guards appeared to take her away. She yelled, "Ormer!" but Ormer was hovering over Ayla, unaffected, eyebrows raised, eyes roaming sideways. A guard took her elbow. "Wait! Ormer!"

The guards escorted her to her cube and watched her pack her pencils, her miniclock, the photograph of her car.

"Can I make one phone call?" she asked. It wasn't allowed. "Can I pee?" They gave her three minutes.

In the bathroom, Kadence was leaning against the sinks, and Koo was examining her red eyes in the mirror.

"Arel!" Koo said. "Ormer just told us! I can't believe it! You were doing so well. You were so cheerful and cooperative! I don't understand."

Kadence turned her superior face to show that she did, but her movements were tense, her superiority self-conscious. She realized, perhaps, that if one of them was not safe, then none of them was. That the man she'd been chasing for years was an easy betrayer. Arel watched her range around and nearly hit her hand on the sink, too tall for the space, her desires and expectations too large for the cell she'd been stuffed into. She felt sorry for her, knowing how it felt to feel your desire like a panic, to realize at last that the constant urgent whispering, *I need. . . I need. . .* is always a sentence unfinished.

"I'm running out of time," Arel said and assembled her Flame-Off on her arm. Koo pulled a paper towel out of the dispenser and made Kadence give her a pen. "Here's my phone number." She scribbled. "Call me. Don't disappear, okay?"

"Okay." They smiled at each other. Kadence yanked back her pen, jerked the zipper shut on her purse, and the guards began to knock.

*   *   *

Outside, she expected to feel awful, but didn't. Outside, in the middle of the day, it wasn't cold for May after all. She'd never felt the sun so strong on the street, and a feeling spread through her, smooth—an assurance that she would be all right.

But she turned the corner and the wall of skyscrapers threw its cold shadow on the concrete and Ormer's stony face invaded her brain. She shivered, pushed through a crowd, stepped over bums asleep or dead on the ground. The sound of gunfire carried on the wind off the lake. From rickety stalls vendors yelled, "*hot*dogs. . . *cond*os. . . *time-share yachts*. . . " A dark-skinned man began walking with her. "Spare a ten, baby?" "Get away." A dark-skinned woman darted out from a doorway: "Buy some silver, lady? Genuine jade? Handcuffs?" Arel turned south, then east. "Ma'am. . . ma'am. . . ." Two black boys appeared, one on each side of her. "Wanna buy a side of beef?" She brushed them off, imagined Ormer in his cube, laughing at her, kept her eyes ahead on the crack of sunlight at the end of the block. From somewhere came shrieking, honking, gunfire. At the end of the tunnel of skyscrapers she stopped. The lake front winked with floating casinos, a torrent of shabby people pressing onto them. Someone grabbed the hem of her jacket and she jerked away, pressed in and out of crowds of loud trim executives going to lunch, tidy frightened unemployed people going to interviews, bums. Gunfire broke out nearby.

She turned another corner and was back at Sunco Tower, looking up its long green length to the pinprick of sky, down again to the row of noiseless revolving doors. On days when people were fired, extra guards were posted at the entrance. Ormer was safe. She ached. The dark beige walls of her cube that had seemed like a prison were like home now. She stood and people bumped her, pulled on her clothes, opened cases of merchandise in her face. She ran across the street to Sunco Tower's twin—the Holoco Tower—and flattened herself against its cold stone side. At the end of the block was the Paterco Tower, straddling the street with two giant plate glass legs, forming an arch above the traffic creeping below. She slid into the entrance of a ground-floor tavern, into the familiar shadowy feel of dark wood and brass.

She got a beer and sat with the plastic plants in the window, watched the checkerboard of screens on the far wall. She sat all afternoon, let television fill up her head, its light displacing her images of Ormer. She sat through a movie about a toothless bumpkin who tries to sue Holoco after a loose rack of discount automatic weapons falls on him in a megastore. The movie was followed by mid-day newsmag with a special feature, "Litigious Losers: Whose Money Are They Really Getting?"

Arel switched from beer to vodka. In three hours Ormer would be off for the day. The newsmag continued with more stories about arms and legs found in elevator shafts, people mowed down in casino lines, tubs of nerve gas released in a downtown tavern. At the airport, famous trilogy-writer Dr. Aslow and his son arrived to attend some swank event on the Gold Coast.

She started doing shots of tequila. Watched the row of revolving doors across the street. In an hour Ormer would emerge, his jacket billowing, his eyes scanning the sidewalk. She tried to watch the screen again, looked back at the doors. Did another shot. Curled her fingers around the trigger of her Flame-Off. He'd be going through the tunnel to the parking lot. He'd walk alone through the dark lot. The plastic trigger was cool in her palm. She ordered two more shots.

By eight o'clock she was drunk and hopeless, her face dropping into airless sobs that made her shoulders leap forward. She only had enough credit to cover her living expenses for three more months. It could take years to find another job. Tears flooded her face and couples at surrounding tables chatted.

She left the bar, dizzy, went down into the tunnel, crouched at the bottom of the stairs and waited. The cold air made her think she was sober. She sat, fingered the trigger, imagined Ormer emerging from the revolving doors. Imagined him pausing, looking right, left, nervous, sauntering toward the tunnel, trying not to look nervous. She smiled. Then heard voices at the far end of the tunnel—Ormer, Kadence, and Koo—chattering about the VP's gorgeous young daughter, whom Ormer simply didn't have the time for. They strolled past. Had Ormer thought of her at all? Fuck him. She followed, the extra set of footsteps lost in vague echoes. At the end of the tunnel she watched Kadence and Koo get into their cars and leave. Ormer headed toward the far end of the lot. She followed, ducked between cars, patches of gravel suddenly loud under her feet. He stopped, turned, saw nothing. Cleared his throat. Rattled his keys. Then walked faster to his car and jammed the key in the lock.

"Ormer," she called out, surprised at how she sounded—not vengeful or menacing after all, but small, his name a pebble sinking in the murky night air.

He turned and smirked. "Yes?" Crisp and detached.

She jumped out of the shadow at him and he flinched. She must have looked wild, furious and drunk. She opened her palm to show him the Flame-Off trigger, wrapped her fingers around it again.

"Why it's Arel. What a surprise. And now you're going to torch me? Oh help I'm so scared." He leaned against his car, crossed one foot in front of the other.

She extended her arm, aimed at his groin. "Why did you get me fired?"

He smiled, took a noisy breath, "Oh, why not? You're insufferable. You used to be okay—lazy and not much to look at. But now you're apparently out to reform society. Bombarding us with little facts at lunch. Thinking you're smarter than everyone else. You pretend that you like being different but the truth is you just can't fit in. You're only trying to change the system because you can't succeed in it. True?"

"No." She raised her hand, aimed at his face. She could do this. Nothing would happen to her. A son disappears, a brother, a lover—the middle class couldn't afford to hire the police. She squeezed the plastic trigger until it almost fired. Ormer crossed his arms.

"You're scared. Admit it," she yelled.

He raised his eyebrows. "Wrong again."

Almost crying: "Why don't I have an effect on you?"

"Because you're nothing, Arel. An annoying buzzing mosquito. Shoo. Go. Shoo."

With each word she was less able to fire, bound to him by his cruelty: now she needed him alive, to prove he was wrong. If he'd groveled, she might have fired. Her arm dropped. Three more months of credit, seven more years of car payments, eleven more years for electronics. Nineteen dollars and ninety-six cents in her purse.

Ormer eased into his car. She stepped sideways into the shadows as he started the engine, backed up, and drove away.

*   *   *

In her car, she cried. The highway was packed but moving fast and her head was fuzzy, replaying the list: Rent—$2550 a month; gas, electric, water—$750 a month; TV—$345 a month; sellfone—$600 - $800 a month; minimum interest payments on consolidated electronics, clothing, personal debts—$175 each, on and on. . . Through her tears the other cars were long red streaks of taillight.

She almost ran into someone, slowed down to eighty miles an hour, and a Buick Marauder rode up behind her, honked, tapped her bumper, honked. "Goddam motherfucker!" she shouted at no one who could hear.

She plowed into the center lane, let him pass, then whipped back into the lane behind him and punched her accelerator. She was so close she couldn't see his taillights, only the wide smoked rear window like a wide-open laughing mouth. She honked—long and mean. He flew into the center lane to lose her but she flew after him, rode up, honked. She knew what he was like—a skinny smug Ormer Bell, older and richer maybe—an Ormer Bell of the future. What would her future be?

Fuck him. She chased him down the highway, her car pinned to the rear of his. Neon signs soared by like an orange wall. She jerked into the center lane again, sped up beside him, lowered her window, and fired her Flame-Off at the side of his car. The flame streaked off his fender, a wild comet. He whipped in front of her again, across a few more lanes, and screeched off the highway at a Gold Coast exit.

"Motherfucker!" she yelled. He stopped at the toll booth ahead, inserted his toll card, dangled his arm from his window, oblivious to her presence. She crept up behind him and fired.

He screeched onto a side street and she laughed, screamed. Round a corner they went, round another. It was hard to drive and aim at the same time. Fireballs blazed into alleys, against stone walls. The Buick bounced onto a sidewalk, barely missing a group of ladies in fur coats, who shrieked and teetered away in a waving herd. Arel bounced her car onto the sidewalk too, momentarily chasing them, laughing out her open window. Laughed and fired at the awnings of a row of posh restaurants, watched the dancing flames devour green striped fabric.

Then her Flame-Off ran dry. She watched the Buick make another wild turn and she went straight, her foot rising off the accelerator, and listened to his tires squeal on in terror block after block.

She sighed, settled. The night was calm and she drifted down a narrow street of ornate buildings, every curly crevice scrubbed white. This was where the rich people lived. Through their windows she saw twenty-foot ceilings. Rich people squandered space. The furniture was velvet and seemed sparse in such big rooms. Through one enormous room was another, another. She turned onto Michigan Avenue, into a crowd of glamorous people draped with furs and jewels, and got stuck in traffic.

She hugged her steering wheel and watched them, imagined being them: TV stars and CEOs, talk show hosts, sports stars and rock stars. She watched and suddenly saw, in the center of them all, Dr. Aslow—*the* Dr. Aslow—his face big and glowing like a moonboard, smiling all his teeth.

Blonde buxom girls in stiff silver evening wear swarmed around him. At the edge of his circle of women was a gaunt tall man, about Arel's age, pale like Dr. Aslow but emaciated and unhappy, his face a piece of hard carved wood, very still, his hands raised, his palms out against the crowd. It must have been Dr. Aslow's son, grown up from the days of Aslow's "Getting a Happy Family" trilogy, when they appeared together on a never-ending lawn with fountains, statues, some sisters in the background. Aslow tossing up a baseball and catching it himself, the son moody-faced and dark, sometimes running around, weirdly slow. Arel examined him. He'd grown up strange.

She sighed, laid her head on the steering wheel. Traffic inched forward, stopped. Her eyes were still swollen and closing them stung, so she kept them closed, made herself used to the sting, adscreen images pricking the inside of her lids, carrying her away in some flashy dream. She was almost asleep when gunfire broke out.

She flipped the gear into neutral and ducked down, then rose up enough to peer through the passenger window. A man in old clothes was on the roof of a parked limousine shooting off two Sunday morning specials. On the sidewalk men in silk suits and ladies in strapless gowns swept to the right, then to the left, each time leaving a few bodies in their wake.

The hotel doorman took up his position behind a bush and with two shots picked off the gunman. The entire incident had lasted only three minutes. She'd be stuck in traffic for hours.

A crew of hotel janitors with push brooms appeared and swept the bodies into a pile. A hotel maid came out with a bottle of Blood Scrub and started on the sidewalk. Arel watched, grew sleepy again, realized she was hungry. She let her car roll ahead a few inches, even though the car in front had not moved. Her butt hurt from being in the seat so long.

But then a janitor became upset, gesticulated, ran into the hotel. A line of dark-suited managers dribbled out through the revolving door and collected on the sidewalk. She buzzed down the passenger window and stuck her head out. Someone was shouting that Dr. Aslow had been hit.

The managers began to pick bodies off the pile. One of Dr. Aslow's blondes was there—arms and legs and head flopping down from the torso. Someone pulled a man's arm out of the pile, but it wasn't Dr. Aslow's. A few unknowns rolled down. The crowd around the pile grew dense and she couldn't see, strained toward it. Then she heard sirens, the small wailing growing louder, louder. Lights came into view. She leaned out the window to get a better look.

Racing up the sidewalk was, first a motorcycle, a cameraman sitting backwards behind the driver, and behind them, in a single beam of light, was Dolla Dare, riding on the roof of the WRNL News van like a Roman chariot driver, one hand holding on to a gold shield mounted on the top of the van, the other hand whipping a microphone round and round over her head. Her voice boomed in the night, "Get out of the way you anorexic depressives! News team coming through!" Somehow Arel had missed this latest career move: Dolla had become a serious journalist.

Pedestrians were driven off the sidewalk and into the street, filling in the cracks between cars, and the news van rolled up. Far in the distance were the ambulance sirens.

The cameraman filmed Dolla's leap off the van and followed her saunter around the pile of corpses. "Who's in charge here?" she barked, and all the managers raised their hands. She picked out the best-looking one and said in a loud, no-nonsense voice, "Is it true that Dr. Aslow has been hit?"

The manager stepped close to the microphone, urgent, important. This would be the most meaningful moment of his life. "Dr. Aslow *has been hit!*" Shrieks from the crowd. "He is presently unconscious and awaiting medical attention. He *is not dead.*"

"Dr. Aslow *is not dead.* But *has been hit,*" Dolla summed up for the camera.

The manager tugged the microphone back. "However, Dr. Aslow's son is dead. And a couple of women. All these other people too." He tilted toward the pile.

"But Dr. Aslow *is not dead.*" Dolla repeated, perhaps disappointed, then brushed the manager aside and lunged toward the bystanders. "Sir! Tell us what happened here in your own words."

The camera lights landed on the long chapped face of a young guy who turned out to be shy, "Well, I was just walking down the street—" He took too long and Dolla cut him off. A mob closed in on her. "Get away you cancer brains!" she yelled into the microphone. Then pulled a guy out of his car—just three cars ahead of Arel's.

"Do you think there's too much violence on the street?" she barked at him. Together they stood in the beacon of light, the surrounding faces partial in the darkness—a pair of white eyes, a set of smiling teeth.

"Yes, Dolla, I think there is too much violence on the street," said the driver carefully into the microphone. Happy with this, Dolla pulled another driver out of his car—two cars ahead of Arel's—and asked the same question.

One more car, and she would open Arel's door. *Dolla Dare.* Dolla Dare would lean into *her* car. *Touch her.* She checked her face in the mirror: swollen and awful.

But what did she care about being on TV with Dolla Dare? She didn't, didn't, grew certain of it. Grew fierce and hard just as Dolla finished with the driver two cars ahead and yanked out the driver from the car right in front. "Dolla symbolizes all that's wrong with society," Arel cried out to her windshield, and decided to spit at the woman when she opened Arel's door. Better yet, Arel would go on TV and tell the world that journalism had become nothing but mere sensationalism and that, by constantly showing grotesque acts of violence, it was in fact advertising them, ensuring their repetition by people longing to be important, to be newsworthy.

But when Dolla finished with the other driver, she turned away, the camera lights went off, and Arel sat in the dark again.

Goddam! Goddam! *Almost* on TV. It wasn't *fair!* She wanted to run after Dolla, grab at her black satin jacket. Dolla Dolla! Me me! Arel flung open her car door and jumped out onto the soft blacktop, felt the cold through the soles of her shoes, then stood frozen: Ormer Bell was right. What Arel really wanted was to be seen, to feel important, just like everyone else in the world. Everyone desperate for visibility, existence. If Dolla Dare had pulled her from her car and stood with her in a dazzling glow, Arel would have babbled, "Yes, Dolla, we should do something about all this awful violence on the street," with an eager bobbing nod and adoring eyes, trying to soak in Dolla, wanting to be Dolla, gladly mowing down pedestrians for a chance to strike a pose in a beam of light.

three

Three months later she ran out of credit, was evicted, and had to go into Self
Storage. Spaces were scarce. Though no one could say what the actual storage bin rejection rate was, the local news was always showing flashes of
people evicted and rejected, alone on the sidewalk with their stuff blowing
away. Arel had to fill out a 10-page application and go to an interview,
which couldn't be scheduled until the day of her eviction.

The interviewer was a beautiful young blond man with a carefully
scrubbed face and pressed suit, which did not glimmer in the dark cata-
combs of SunStorage. The interview room was an empty storage bin, brown
and loosely crated. The young man rocked forward, deskless, his mini-com-
puter resting on his crossed knee. He punched in numbers to call her up.
Beyond the top of his bright head, in the next bin, fragments of someone's
belongings were snagged into the cracks of splintering unfinished boards.

"Arel Ashe," he finally read. Pause. "No job interviews for three
months?"

"Well," she cleared her throat. "I have one tomorrow morning, to
become a temporary person."

"Tempee," he murmured, typed, punched in a number. Then read silently.

"It's a phone interview," she chatted, unused to having someone to talk to.

He nodded, reading, then exclaimed, "You got *fired?*"

She grinned, shrugged though he wasn't looking at her, kept grinning.

"You left this space blank," he commented. "Family."

"I don't have any."

"No one to help you pay the monthly fee?"

"No."

"Mmmm." He punched in another number." She tried to read the tiny screen upside-down. "Now, here's another blank—phone number?"

"Oh." Embarrassed. "They cut my sellfone service."

"And here—what's your new address?"

"I don't know yet."

She saw that he was entering points for each answer. The last one scored a "10."

"Any medical conditions?" he asked, a fingertip poised over the mini-keyboard.

"Well. I've been depressed."

"Ah." Another "10." Then he looked at her for the first time. "You understand that if you miss one monthly payment we'll seize and auction off all your possessions."

She nodded. He handed her a docu-screen with these exact words on it and she signed it. He smiled.

"Does this mean you've accepted me?"

"You bet!" He beamed. "It's the best score I've had all week!" Then he rocked forward. "Cot option?'

"Oh no," she said, attempting to sound privileged. She did have a place to sleep: the back room in the library. She would be okay, as long as she had the library.

"All right then." He stuffed his computer into his pocket and stood, cupped one hand under her elbow, raised her out of her chair, and steered her through the narrow lightless tunnels toward the heavy locked door to the parking lot. He clanked open the door and edged her out into the blinding heat, into scorched-dead air, and clanked the door shut.

She walked alongside the row of bright yellow SunStorage trucks, one of which would come to carry off her stuff: her sofa sleeper, her roll-away dinette set, boxes of electronics and clothes and shoes, the twenty-gallon stock pot. She would close the door to her apartment for the last time. Empty, it would seem suddenly large, so fashionably taupe. Her body ached, but her eyes were too dry to tear.

Still, she had her car, she told herself, and the luggage that fit into it. She had fourteen dollars and ninety-two cents. She had the clothes on her back, her skin.

She pushed through the heat to her car, swept the adflyers off the windshield, climbed in. "I'll be okay," she said to her dark dashboard. Her

library salary would cover her car payment and the minimum interest payments on her consolidated electronic debt, clothing debt, furniture debt, personal debt, and the library employee fee. With a temp job, she'd be able to
afford the monthly Self Storage fee, and food.

She drove toward the library, past the glaring mega-malls and mini-
malls and burning cars abandoned at the curb, with less than fifteen dollars
in her pocket, with a pounding head, with no credit. She felt every muscle
contract, but this was her fault: she'd done this to herself. She'd been blam-
ing the world for her problems, when the problem was her. She couldn't fit
in, wasn't good enough, just wasn't good enough. Her thoughts like a sack
of rocks dragged her to the bottom of the lake. She'd blamed everyone else
for her lack of energy, lack of ambition, careless appearance, and now here
she was, a person with no place to live, no job, no money, no credit. A person with no value.

She remembered her mother saying, to someone walking out their
door, "What is the value of one human life?"—one of those questions with
no answers—her stupid mother. Stupid mother, *promising* she'd always be
there, promising, and Arel sitting on the old brown stool in the small cold
kitchen peeling carrots, putting pots on the stove like her mother liked—the
way she used to do with Arel's father. A cold day. All the food cooked and
her mother still not home. Carrots and beans and potatoes soft in pots on
the stove and still her mother not home. Arel dragging the stool into the living room, sitting at the window, watching down the dark street, a statue in
the window watching for her mother to suddenly appear, suddenly, imagining it, any moment, suddenly appearing, rushing up the gray sidewalk in
quick cat steps, her hair full of wind and bright against the dark sky and leaf-
less trees, against the graying-yellow brick of the tenements heavy and
splashed with black paint. Imagining her, into the night, into the morning.
Sitting as the next day kept going on and on unthinking, vegetables soft and
soggy on the stove, watching down the street into the twilight. No phone
call. How could she have promised? Just gone. No word. Nothing.

In the library storage room she opened her suitcases and laid them flat,
shoved boxes together to make a bed, layered shirts and skirts and towels
on the tops to make a mattress, found a sheet to tuck under the corners of
the boxes, wadded up her bathrobe for a pillow. Then lay down on her side
and curled her knees to her chest and started to drift off to sleep, though it
was still mid afternoon.

*　　*　　*

Arel did not wake until noon the next day—past the time of her SunnyTemps interview. Her eyelids slid down, down. Then she heard herself sigh, sat herself up, tossed her legs off the side of the boxes. She could reschedule the SunnyTemps interview—she'd slept through it twice before. Once, when she called to apologize, the woman on the phone said they didn't usually hire people who'd been out of work for less than three months anyway, because people out of work longer were more cooperative employees.

She stood, walked in a circle around the tiny room, pulled on a skirt and top and went out through the videobook racks, walked behind the counter, walked in a circle. Looked out the window across the parking lot to the megamall across the road. The Fourth of July decorations were already up on the mall roof: a gigantic popped piece of Dr. Popp's popcorn, several stories high, next to a huge dancing cigarette butt with a line of red smoke twisting eternally off the top, through an invisible tube that spelled out *Be Elite, Smoke a Neat,* next to an enormous Bud can, upside-down and crumpled, driplessly delicious, next to the new Dr. Drink tamper-proof straw wrapper, designed to protect your straw from being secretly dipped in cyanide by psychos. All in red, white, and blue. At the end of the row of decorations was a fat flag pole on a big ball, making an exclamation point, waving a little American flag at the top.

Birds milled around on the beer can. She watched them. Yawned. Watched birds. Dropped her forehead against the glass. God. Unemployment was as boring as employment. And now she would have to call SunnyTemps with some excuse. What would she say? Even a real excuse sounded like an excuse. Was this the third or fourth time she'd missed?

She dialed the library phone and a young woman with a voice like Koo's answered. "So, here's what happened," Arel said fast, in her falsest happiest voice. "Just as I was about to call you this morning 'The New Shopping Spree' came on and I just couldn't turn it off! I bought the cutest outfits!" She detested acting happy.

"Oh that happens to me all the time," the young woman laughed.

"So you understand?"

"Oh sure, sure, doesn't matter though." Then, in a different tone: "Our policy is three strikes and you're out. Temp jobs are in very high demand and very hard to get." She must have been reading this.

Arel tried to think of a reply that would be effective, blurted out, "Please—" accidentally sounding miserable. "I'll do anything." Pause. She thought she heard a few clicks on a keyboard, then a beep.

"You'll do anything?" the agent echoed. "Well, there is one thing we might do. We'd be making an exception—just for you." The intonations were in the wrong place. Another pause: Arel's turn to talk.

"Oh, great."

"We could place you on our TempeeTemp list. You'd be filling in temporarily for temporary people who fail to report to work on a given day."

"Does that happen?"

"Oh, sure!" The voice was natural again. "People get sick, take shopping days, even go on vacation—some people are at their temp jobs for years you know." The bright voice stopped, perhaps sensing its mistake.

"I didn't know." Arel replied and envisioned the rest of her life: striving to be a permanent temporary.

"Of course TempeeTemps cannot expect the same generous wage as our real Temps."

"Well, that's understandable."

"Then congratulations!" the buoyant voice said. "You are now an official TempeeTemp!"

"Great."

Then no one spoke. Was it the end of the script?

"Soooooo—" Arel said. "Anything available, like, now?"

"Oh," said the agent. "Let me check."

Silence, humming, distant clicking. Arel hung on the line, imagined her stuff in the storage bin, imagined food. Stuff, food, stuff, food.

Finally the chirpy voice returned, "Why, yes"—surprised—"there is something! Wow it's a good thing you asked!"

Arel's heart jumped: she'd actually succeeded at something. The job was phone soliciting for Sunco's Good Health Outreach program—headquartered in the Sunco Tower downtown—the same building that Adstories was in. She was to start the next morning.

She danced on the stool, leaped onto the counter. "I can do it! I can do it!" Then settled onto the stool, relaxed, turned on the TV. She speed-flipped through the channels, found her twelve o'clock favorite: the new Dolla Dare talk show— "Dare To Talk." It had already started but the theme was stamped across the screen on a waving gilt-edged scroll: "Supermodels Who Date Famous Men With Missing Body Parts." One couple had already chatted with Dolla and was sitting quietly to the side. Whatever body part the man was missing was not apparent, and Arel felt sorry for the supermodel, though she'd heard the prosthetics were usually bigger than the originals.

Dolla's audience cheered as the next couple bounded down the center aisle—the woman in front, raven-haired, big-breasted, and braless—and the man behind—much older, reedy, gray. It looked like Dr. Aslow. Arel leaned forward: It was Dr. Aslow, greatly aged since the Gold Coast Massacre—the skin looser over a thinner face. But he was smiling, arms raised high overhead, waving at the crowd with artificial hands.

The crowd cheered louder and Dolla stood at the bottom of the stairs whooping along, twirling her microphone over her glitzy yellow hair. Since getting her own talk show, Dolla had a softer, more compassionate look—her hair was teased a bit closer to her head, and her black pants, though still skin-tight, were nylon instead of leather. Her shirt was pale pink with a giant ruffle flouncing from the tip of one shoulder diagonally to her waist, the wide neck designed to shift often across the black lace straps of her bra.

"And here he is guys!" she shouted, careful not to call the audience names like "schizoids" or "hemorrhoid heads."

Dr. Aslow did a little jig down the steps and up onto the stage, and the supermodel rushed up to hang on his shoulder. He moved a hand into her hair, demonstrating how the life-like thing could move its fingers in hair without accidentally yanking it out.

Arel watched the hands, imagined she heard a mechanical whir, though that wasn't possible. Their movement was like a film with its frames running a fraction of a second too slow. If you weren't looking very closely, you'd never know they weren't real. They were even creased to look as aged as Aslow—or a few years younger. They had little, too-wide fingernails, little beige hairs.

"A-maz-ing!" Dolla bellowed. Dolla talked too loud to be a talk show host, but no one expected her to stick with it.

Aslow and his friend took seats next to the first couple, who were not as famous. Dolla shimmied over to Dr. Aslow and sat on his lap. The supermodel looked upset. Then Dolla sprang up and growled into the microphone and Dr. Aslow comfortingly patted the supermodel's thigh.

"Dr. Aslow," said Dolla, and the studio audience fell silent. "This is your first public appearance since the Gold Coast Massacre."

"Yes it is, Dolla," he replied amicably.

"Tell us. What has your life been like," dramatic pause, "since that terrible tragedy?"

"Well, Dolla. . . " He leaned forward. "I like to say I've been in R and R—recovery and revelation."

The camera cut to Dolla's nodding head, her face carefully knotted into an expression of interest. Dr. Aslow leaned farther forward, cocked his head, took on the genial, questioning expression that was his trademark. "I've been thinking, Dolla." Pause. "Why, Dolla?" Another pause. "Why, why are we all so unhappy?" Dolla's head nodded, nodded, Aslow went on: "That's the question I take up in my latest trilogy."

"Fascinating," said Dolla, nodding too much, not fascinated. Behind Dolla, audience members were pointing at themselves on camera behind Dolla.

"You see, Dolla," Aslow went on in his melodic voice. "I have suffered a great personal tragedy. I lost my only son. But through this personal tragedy, I have heard a message. Dolla, my only son died for you, so that you could hear my message."

Dolla appeared on screen again, nod-nod, eyelids heavy.

"*Why* are we so *unhappy?*" cooed Dr. Aslow. The audience behind Dolla was nodding too, sleepy-eyed, nodding off. No one expected him to really answer. Then, suddenly, he did: "Because Satan walks among us!"

At first no one seemed to hear. Then Dolla looked up, and in a moment of not posing, glanced in confusion at someone back stage. "Pardon?" she asked Dr. Aslow, and the audience's attention was caught by her natural-sounding voice. Dr. Aslow rose from his chair, smiling pleasantly, then pressed his feet together and spread his arms straight out, turning himself into a cross. His head tipped back dramatically, but his voice was still friendly and calming: "Because Satan walks among us."

Arel burst out in three loud laughs: religious fanatics were a classic scorch. The studio was dead silent, and the camera remained unthinkingly on Aslow. Moments passed and he let his arms swing down, hands behind his back, one foot taking a short step to the right: a soldier at ease. When Dolla finally reappeared on the screen, her mouth was slowly closing—a look of shock hardening into killer-sarcasm that pushed her eyebrows up and her head forward. "Excuse me, Dr. A," she said so politely. "Did you say, Satan walks among us?"

Cheerfully: "Yes Dolla I did."

Dolla began to whip around in mock fear, like she thought Satan might be sneaking up behind her. Then began to yank people out of their seats. "Are *you* Satan? Are *you* Satan?" she kept saying, her nose in their faces and her eyes bugged out. The audience roared.

Finally she sauntered down toward the stage, her head bent sideways to mimic concern. "Uh, Dr. A?" she asked innocently, surrounded by delighted audience faces. "Just one more question before we bring on the next couple." A dramatic pause. Audience members leaned forward in their seats. Dr. Aslow tried a pleasant smile. Dolla made them all wait, swaying by the stage, pretending she couldn't keep from grinning, then bellowed, "Did they amputate part of your *brain too?*"

More laughter. The camera lingered on Aslow, who kept the smile pressed on his face, his eyes staring down, his head bobbing and foolish. Arel was kind of sorry for him. No one deserved that.

Then the next couple came on stage—the supermodel pushing an armless, legless man in a wheelbarrow.

Arel turned off the screen and remained on the stool. God. Dr. Aslow had clearly lost his mind, she thought—poor guy. Then thought, *Satan walks among us?* and couldn't help but laugh. Being on the side that was laughing felt so good, felt safe and unalone.

✳   ✳   ✳

She parked in the old lot, walked through the old tunnel, went through the same revolving doors. Everything seemed smaller and oranger. She got on the elevator and was startled by her reflection in the mirrored walls: so extra-poofed and professional in her skintight crimson minisuit. She had to remember to push 6 instead of 15. She recognized people on the elevator but didn't say hello: to them this was an ordinary day. On the sixth floor she stepped off into a different yet oddly familiar maze of cubicles.

The coordinator of the Outreach Program was a man with gleaming black hair and big handsome features: eyes, lips, nose. Arel stood to the side as he strolled through the maze with his hands behind his back, pausing to overhear the quality of the various solicitors' phone performances. Eventually he noticed her at the end of a row of cubes.

"You're the new temp!" he boomed in a big Southern accent.

"Temp temp," she chirped and he gazed, confused. She tried adding, "A temp for a temp—a TempeeTemp," but this was not clarifying. This was her awkward old self. She spent too much time alone. She sighed.

"I'm Raz Shae." He said and gave her hand one hard shake.

"Arel Ashe."

He looked her up on his miniscreen. "You used to work upstairs! In Adstories!" he exclaimed. "For a long time! Then you got fired!"

"Yeah, well."

"That happened to me too!"

"Really?"

"Yeah—I was in Adstories too and I got fired too! Years ago. I was too smart for them—that was the problem. I had a real knack—The Sound-Master, that was me—I knew when things just didn't sound right. They did-n't appreciate me."

"Me either." She replied, not quite convincing. Then leaned toward him, trying to be flirty. He was dark but good-looking, and maybe he was smart, like Ben, maybe different, like Ben. She chattered: "Where *are* you from?"

Still reading his miniscreen, he replied, "Nwallins."

Silence. "Oh—New Orleans."

"Right."

Still trying to flirt, she leaned closer, about to ask what he'd been doing since Adstories. But that was obvious: he'd worked his way up to become boss of phone solicitors, probably at half his former salary. Still she leaned, and was about to invite him out for a drink when he yelled, "Vena! Vena baby!"

A very young, tall, very black woman darted out of a cube and ran to his side. He slid one hand around her waist, squeezed, then opened the hand and let it slide down her butt. "This one's new," he said about Arel. "Break her in, will ya?"

"Sure baby!" Vena said and he released her and continued his over-seer's stroll through the maze.

Vena was an instant friend. She had a wide raspberry smile and long thin hands that floated around, fluttered onto Arel's arm. Her skin-tight dress was crinkly metallic, like a space suit, and her spike-heeled shoes had silver laces up the ankles and calves and over the knees and up her thighs. She seemed a foot taller than Arel, her light black hair in a high fat pillar. She led Arel to the List Station and explained: "Now every morning as soon as you get in you *run* over here to get yourself a list—and when I say *run*, baby, I mean *run*—and you get yourself a NS not a SS, got it?"

Arel nodded.

"Now see—" Vena held up the only list left, marked SS. "Now 'cause you're starting later in the morning you're stuck with a SS and baby you'll be lucky to get one appointment let me tell you." Vena talked too fast. "But here's what you do baby—you wait till lunch. We have to turn in our lists at lunch. That way the first people back from lunch get another shot at the NS lists. That's fair, don't you think?"

"Oh yes."

"So what you do is you only go for a five, ten minute lunch and you

run back and you get yourself a NS. Of course you take mine and I'll kill
you!" she laughed. "Just kidding baby. It's all based on who gets back first,
see—who can run the fastest. That's fair don't you think?"

"Oh, definitely, definitely."

"Now here's your script. You gotta match up your script to your subcategories. For example this week you could get a SS-GSWK or a NS-HCI or
a NS-DSI. You look right here and make sure it matches up, got it?"

"Uh-huh."

"Good. You're quick. Hey, Raz! Arel's quick! Raz likes quick. Now
here's the key to success: happy cheerful. Got it? Think how happy you are
talking to these dirt-brains. Happy happy cheerful."

"Uh-huh, uh-huh."

"So once you got your list and your script you come over here to the
cube next to mine. That's so you can ask questions. But you'll be fine I can
tell—you're quick and a happy cheerful person."

"Yes, yes, uh-huh, uh Vena?"

"Now sometimes these phones get stuck in your ear—" she was lead-
ing Arel to their adjoining cubes. "You gotta be careful pulling them out,
okay baby? If you get it stuck in there you pound on the wall and I'll come
rescue you."

They passed Vena's cube. Inside was an 8 by 10 glamour shot of Vena
in a sapphire swimsuit. In the photo she was stunning; in person she was
not. They went into Arel's blank cube and Vena sat her down, began to plant
the phone in Arel's ear.

"Uh, Vena?"

"Hold on baby I need to concentrate so I don't stick you in the ear."

Arel waited. Vena's careful half-circle eyebrows drew together in a
wrinkle-less frown on her smooth young forehead.

"There. Got it. Now you just pound like this"—she demonstrated—"if
you have any questions and remember—friendly happy—that's the key—
and remember—there's no such thing as a stupid question."

"Vena?"

"Yeah baby?"

"What does it all mean?"

Vena's half-circles flew up. "What?"

"All these. These codes."

"Oh!" she laughed. "Baby, at first I didn't know what you were asking
me!" She pointed to Arel's list with a long robin's-egg fingernail. "SS means
South Side—short for South Side Medical Group. GSWK is Gun Shot

Wounds-Kids. That's the only injury that really hooks these people, but it's still tough to sell 'em. We're trying to get Raz to drop it. He's already dropped several SS subcategories, but he's stubborn about this one, he says it'll sell if you do it right. He says it's all psychology—that parents will bring in their kids for extra CT scans even after they recover because it makes the parents feel better to know what's *inside*. He makes a good argument but I personally have never sold any and baby, if I can't sell it, no one can. Now NS is North Shore—they're a cinch. HCI is health club injury, and DSI is depression-suicidal ideation. Now those people are very suggestible. Remember—happy friendly!"

Vena vanished and Arel sat. It was already mid morning: soon people would go to lunch, and she could run for an NS. Happy friendly! Across the back wall was a banner that read: "Friendship Is The Ship That Sales." Probably Raz had thought that up. It sounded so good.

Arel made the first call. A tired woman answered the phone. "Hi!" Arel read. "This is——" Blank. "Arel!" She inhaled. "How *are* you, ——" Another Blank. She searched the SS list for the name. "Farla."

"Fine," said Farla. "Do I know you?"

"It's Arel from the doctor's office!"

"Oh?"

"How's——" Search, search. "Zeza?"

"She seems fine. Doesn't think much of school." Pause. "Are you Dr. Blare's nurse?"

A question. The script didn't allow for questions.

"Uhhh. . . " Arel flipped pages. Who was she supposed to be? "Oh, no I'm the imaging technology assistant." But now she was ahead in the script and didn't know what to say next. "You know, I assist with imaging technology."

"Uh huh. . . "

"Yeah, you know, I was assisting with Zezee's technology."

"Zeza."

"Yeah, yeah—we all started calling her Zezee, you know, 'cause she's such a pleasant, friendly child!"

Long pause. "Zeza?"

"Yeah, so. . . " she began reading from the end of the script. "I can schedule her for another CT scan."

"Why would you do that?"

Why? The answer was probably somewhere in the middle of the script. She improvised: "Why not? Can't hurt, right?"

"Those scans are so costly."

"But what's cost, really," Arel tried to sound wise, "when Zezee's health is at stake?"

"Is Zeza's health at stake?" Farla sounded suspicious.

"Well. . . isn't it always?"

"What did you say your name was?"

"Uh, gee, Farla I gotta go—the doctor's paging me. I'll give you a call back later. Bye!" Arel hung up and looked around. Raz had been across the room the whole time, and she heard Vena's voice chattering happily on the other side of the wall. She dialed another number, this time sticking closely to the script and talking too fast for the callee to ask questions.

"Now I don't want you to feel alarmed," the script told her to say. "But I've been looking over past CT results and it wouldn't hurt to bring —- in for another scan. Now I know this is costly"—clever script—"It's completely up to you. This is *your* choice."

Everyone said they would do it, but they all needed time to find the money; they all intended to call the doctor themselves when they had it. No appointments, no commission. Her fellow solicitors were beginning to go to lunch.

Raz let Vena go first, which didn't seem fair—she got to have a long lunch and get a good list too. But Vena was a real temp who'd apparently worked there a long time. Arel waited. Raz began to let others go. Another hour of dialing, reciting. She tried to remain upright in her seat, to hear peptalks in her head, but after another hour she didn't care about sounding happy or making a sale, she just wanted her butt out of that chair.

"Arel," Raz breezed by and commanded, "Lunch."

She ran. Into the elevator and down to the lobby, where she headed for the glass wall beside the revolving doors. Her forehead pressed against the glass, she gazed out: sunshine, outdoors, the freedom to walk around. She watched people hurry along in and out of highrise shadows, back to their cubes or to interviews for jobs in cubes. She was a lucky one: she had a job. She took a moment to feel appreciative, then checked the time: fifteen minutes had already gone by. Time outside of cubes passed so much faster than time inside cubes.

She flew back up to the sixth floor and ran for a list, got an NS-HCI— the only good one left. "Fortuitous," she said out loud, not knowing how she knew that word or what, exactly, it meant.

In her cube she flapped through the pages of the Health Club Injuries script. The approach was different. Rather than pretending to be a concerned technologist, she was to pretend to be a flirtatious nurse who'd noticed the patient in the waiting room and taken a "special interest." All the names on the Health Club Injuries list were men's— since men tended to be wealthier than women, they were the main Outreach Program targets.

Script pages flipped. She was to ask the callee if he had any slight twinges in any body part and make him think these were abnormal. She dialed and tried to sound happy cheerful and sexy, but her chair seat was immediately unbearable, sucked dry of all its padding, pressing her butt into a painful bone. She accidentally deviated from the script, lost sales. Eight more hours of this. She wasn't allowed to go to the bathroom until 4:30. She twisted in the chair, which screeched in torment. She was hungry, having skipped lunch, and slurped the last drops of diet Coke off the ice cubes in the super-double-jumbo cup. Her mind wandered, and suddenly she was thinking of how the whole phone soliciting operation was designed to prey on people's fear and paranoia to sell them health care they didn't need.

Of course, if people were going to be that stupid, they deserved to get taken. People needed to be more suspicious of each other.

After her bathroom break, Raz dropped by. "Been losing some?" His face in a cheerful contortion.

"She'll get the hang of it!" Vena called out. Her head appeared, her hair freshly frizzed. "I'll coach her! She'll catch on! She's quick!" Vena winked and he grunted and shuffled away and she whispered to Arel, "Come out with us tonight, baby, we'll get you on his good side."

Arel whispered back, "How are we going to do that?"

"You leave it all to me." Vena grinned.

Still whispering, "But my evening job—I'm not off till midnight."

"You come out then—you can't miss the Fourth!"

She'd forgotten: today was the Fourth.

"And the launching!"

She'd forgotten the launching.

"But Vena," she blurted. "I'm already so tired and I don't think I can make it."

"Oh, come on Arel!" she whimpered. "It'll be more fun with more people! Please please please. We're going to the Park Forest River Oak mall."

That was where Ben lived. "Oh," she replied, "okay," and Vena heaved a huge dramatic sigh, whispered, "We'll take care of things with Raz," and her head slowly descended into her cube.

Arel sat, facing blank nubby plastic walls and the rest of the day.

*　　*　　*

At midnight Arel drove to the mall, tired, looking less poofed and not quite professional, but jumpy with the thought that she might see Ben. Inside the mall, bright as a sun-scorched day, her excitement faded: Ben would never subject himself to this mob, in the mall, on the Fourth of July, to stand in front of a megascreen and watch a moonboard launching.

Arel pushed through the shoulders of drunk shoppers, garish in their American flag clothes: minidresses and skintight shirts decorated with red, white, and blue sequins, rhinestones, feathers, ribbons, logos. The center pillar adscreens flashed their red, white, and blue images. Giant flags flapped, *Get Real! Shop Real!* which annoyed her: What did Holoco care if people bought their stuff online or from the mall? The sign robots maneuvered in and out of the crowd, their tin-can bodies flashing human body parts and products. Bored maintenance men followed the robots through the mob, ready to make adjustments and prevent them from tumbling down the steps into the mall park between adscreen pillars.

Arel was to meet Vena and Raz at the Good-Buys Pub. She pushed through the crowd. The megastores were linked together by glitzy specialty shops and restaurants: Disney Electronics, Kentucky Fried Tacos, Buns & Guns. She paused at the window of a store that sold real vacations: Arctic Adventures, Ghana Get-Away, Chinese Shopping Sprees. Then she spotted the Good-Buys Pub, across the mall park, between the Post 'n Pets and a novelty shoelace store.

Vena loomed tall and bored in red spiked six-inch heels and a blue and white striped strapless glitter minidress. On her soft black cheeks were painted red stars. Raz stood beside her, also bored, holding two Biggie Beers.

"Vena!" Arel shouted as she approached and somehow Vena heard her over the crowd, became animated, waved a long lovely hand.

"Hey baby!" Then, to Raz, "Go get Arel a beer." He gazed at her, annoyed, and she walked her knife-point fingernails up his arm and across his shoulder and tweaked his chin. Then she whispered something close to his ear, which made his face crinkle into a wicked grin. He went in to get Arel's beer. Vena smiled, began swaying to the music blaring from the pub, and Arel wondered just what she'd have to do to get on Raz's good side.

Then Vena said to Arel, "Is that what you're wearing?"

Raz re-emerged with a cardboard tray full of Biggie Beers. Vena lifted up two of them, handed them both to Arel.

"All this?"

"It's a special!" Vena exclaimed. "You save a buck and a half if you buy two at the same time!" She lifted her own two off the tray, and everyone began to drink. No one could get their hands all the way around the cups.

"Okay babies!" Vena whooped over the noise of the milling mob. "Let's shop!"

Vena, Raz, and Arel and their huge beers were sucked into the crowd and swept along. Raz kept his eyes on the ceiling screens: baseball, football, basketball, bikini soccer.

Vena called out, "What are you going to buy Arel?"

Arel had seven dollars and six cents. "Mmmm. . . " They passed the Post 'n Pets. "Stamps!"

Vena maneuvered them into the store. This Post 'n Pets had a rain forest theme and a sale on exotic fish. Along the tops of the caged pacing dogs and cats were screens explaining how owning a pet relieves stress. The stamp counter was in the back of the store. Vena and Raz stayed up front, looking at the fish, and Arel walked back for stamps. The salesman was a beautiful young blond man, not much taller than she.

"Have you ever thought of exotic fish?" he said, holding the bag of stamps just out of reach.

"No. Thank you. I just want the stamps."

"Let me explain our sale and our unprecedented money-back exotic fish guarantee."

"No, really, just the stamps."

"Our exotic fish are most exotic."

She yanked the bag out of his hand.

"You could at least take a look!" he scolded and she bolted out.

They stopped outside the store to take slurps of beer. Arel was exhausted, increasingly irritated, increasingly drunk. Blurted out: "Do you guys ever get tired of people always trying to sell you things? I mean, is that our only purpose in the world, to buy stuff?" They gazed at her. Vena said, "Whad'ya get?"

Arel shook the stamps out of the bag, popped open the stamp case, and there, smiling up at her from ten little white squares, were ten little Hampton Dranes.

Then Raz shouted, "It's starting it's starting!"

The crowd compressed in front of the megascreens, each screen displaying a piece of the moonboard launching. People shoved into Arel and she began to shove back. Her first beer was gone, and she started the second one, which was now warm. She stood, in the mob, everything too bright and too loud, with a gigantic warm beer and a fucking bag of stamps. All faces were fixed to the screens, to the ads on the screen, not wanting to miss the moment when something apparently important would happen. Arel scanned the crowd for Ben's face, tried to imagine it was there. But she couldn't even imagine it. Foggy-headed, she saw instead how bizarre everything was: faces painted with stars and stripes, hair sculpted into the Statue of Liberty, hats in the shape of the Liberty Bell. On the edge of the crowd were a bunch of teenaged boys with muskets and red T-shirts with "S.W.A.U.T." printed in big black letters across their backs.

Arel looked at these boys, poked Vena. "Hey Vena." Vena was swaying to the admusic—Blackie White's "Oooh Oooh Baby"—her head tossed back in an expression of dreamy ecstasy. "Hey, Vena!" Arel called louder. "What is that? S-W-A-U-T?"

Vena snaked a long soft arm around Arel's shoulder. "Oooh oooh baby," she sang, then abruptly, in Arel's ear: "Now's a good time—before the launch starts, while he's still kinda sober. Go over there and *sell* yourself—show him what a go-getter you are!"

God, this again. She'd much rather have group sex with them.

"What do I say?"

"Say anything baby!"

Pause. "Could you be more specific?"

A commercial came on, for diet wine, and Vena began to bounce in time with Killer Cum's version of "Heard It Through the Grapevine."

"I like this song!" Vena said. "Did you know you can get the sound track for this commercial?"

Arel squeezed behind Vena, around the other side of Raz, and she yelled into his ear, "I'm so excited!" She took big gulps of warm beer, grew thirstier.

"Yeah!" Raz replied to the screen.

"No, I mean because of my great new job!"

"You got a new job?"

"No—" It took all her breath. "I mean the phone soliciting."

"Oh." He kept his eyes on the screens. Topless women were chasing Paul Revere on his horse: an ad for McSpress Mail.

"You know what I really love about phone soliciting?" she went on, not sure what would follow this.

Raz jumped, pulled out his sellfone, bleating out a newzip: *It's Almost On!* Raz yelled out, "It's almost on!"

"Raz?"

"Whad'you say Arel?" Eyes still on the screen.

"I said, what I really hate about phone soliciting is preying on people's fears to sell them expensive medical testing they don't need, which is perhaps the worst example of how people are exploited for profit in an unregulated capitalist society that I have ever encountered!"

Raz's face registered nothing.

She continued: "And by working as phone solicitors we are in fact serving as co-conspirators in an inherently unethical system!"

Raz's dark eyes began slipping to the corners, catching glimpses of Arel. "Inherently unethical?" he blurted out. "God, Arel, you sound like a nerd!" Then he burst out laughing.

She finished her beer and the launch began. Suddenly blaring trumpets quieted the crowd, and the screen faded to black. Then sprang alive with spinning stars and wiggling stripes. These images swept to the side, like a curtain, revealing the launch pad. Standing in the windy night were the celebrities with champagne bottles to christen the boards: Dillie Dare, Dolla's voluptuous, ruby-haired, seventeen-year-old cousin, and Hampton Drane's young rippling sand-colored nephew, Hootie Grate.

"Wow," Arel said. They were both so stunningly gorgeous. She couldn't help but think of Dr. Aslow's son, conspicuous by his absence, and in her haze felt sad, though she hoped they wouldn't start that whole America's Lost Son thing again.

Vena was trying to cover Raz's eyes, apparently jealous of the bouncing Dillie Dare. "Seventeen," Raz drooled.

"Hey," Arel said. "Wasn't she seventeen five years ago in that old Dolla Dare video?" No one heard. Who cared. The crowd compressed and held its breath at the countdown, "Five, four, three, two. . . "

Off they went, two more moonboards—one for Coke and one for Bud, identical to the first two—up into the hot orange night sky. These moonboards were made of slightly different materials, and everyone hoped they'd show better through the pollution. Arel's eyes drifted from the screens to the crowd, to another bunch of young men in S.W.A.U.T. shirts standing just in front of her, downing their beers.

When it was over, Arel, Vena, and Raz shoved out the exit with the rest of the crowd, dissipating in the dark parking lot. They walked to Raz's Jeep Mangler, stood around. Arel's head felt elongated. She kept standing, thinking how, if sleeping with Raz would save her job, then she'd get to have a job *and* sex. But Raz and Vena were climbing into the jeep, waving good-bye, leaving her behind. "Bye baby! Bye baby!" Vena kept yelling and waving out the window and blowing kisses. "We love you! We love you!" Arel waved back.

In her car she turned on her entire dashboard. The noise kept her awake on the drive back to the library. She cranked her window down, and the loud wind helped sober her up. In the library lot, window rolled up and dashboard off, the silence startled her. Silence was frightening. She opened her car door, pulled herself up and out, staggered once, sighed.

Then walked toward the library door, across the dark long lot. Car alarms began to wail, familiar and comforting. She listened to the wailing, the shuffling of her feet, then stopped, and heard more shuffling feet, stopping. "Oh God."

She began to walk again, faster, heard the steps behind her, walking faster. Car alarms, footsteps, footsteps coming closer. She was almost to the library door. She felt for her Flame-Off, shivered, walked faster. Heard the steps growing louder, then felt someone's presence right behind her.

She whipped around, aimed her Flame-Off, and shrieked: there stood a handsome young man, clean and neat, in expensive silk clothes.

"Oh God!" she cried out. "You scared me half to death! I thought you were a homeless person."

He looked at her with sharp, pale eyes. "They're everywhere. Those people." He lowered his hand—his Flame-Off, stared at her, then looked up at the library. "You work here?"

"Yeah, at night."

He straightened up, put away his Flame-Off. "I'm sorry I frightened you," said his voice. "You be careful. Homeless scum are everywhere." He took a few steps back. Her blurred head began to worry, told her something was not right here. He turned and she watched him vanish into a shadow, watched his silky clothes cease to catch light, saw the big black letters on the back of his shirt disappear before she realized what they said.

*   *   *

She tried to get up early the next morning, to get a good list, but barely made it in time. She sat all morning exhausted and hung over, with a bad list, making no sales.

Vena kept peering over her cube wall to smile at her. Arel cried, "How are you not hung over?"

"I'll get Raz to let you go to lunch early with me, then we'll come back and get you a DSI—you can sell them anything."

"Depression and suicidal ideation," Arel recited.

"Right!"

"God Vena," she said abruptly. "It's like I'm stuck in a box and I try to get out and just when I think I'm out I realize I'm in just another box. Do you ever feel that way?"

Vena dropped her face and raised her eyebrows. "Ooh baby, you got some hormones today!"

Raz let them go at noon. In the elevator they straightened their skirts and examined their faces. Vena's eyes landed on Arel's hair in the mirror, and she whipped out her comb and plunged it in. By the time they reached the lobby, the top half of Arel's hair was teased.

"I was just going to get a bag of fries in the sandwich shop," Arel said, expecting Vena to object, but instead Vena trotted along beside her. She asked Arel's advice on which salad to get and which brand of water was best. At the register, Arel couldn't decide whether to spend the extra 25 cents on a packet of salt, and Vena sang out, "Go for it baby! You're worth it!"

They stood together in the crowd of orange and yellow tables and shoving employees. Arel glanced toward the old booth, thinking of the old days, expecting to see strangers in it, and instead seeing Ormer, Kadence and Koo.

"Oh my God."

"Do you know those people?"

She wanted to run away. But Vena had begun to stroll over, with her big swishy walk, catching everyone's eye. Ormer, Kadence, and Koo watched her, then Koo noticed Arel.

"Arel!" shrieked her little voice. "Hey look everyone it's Arel!" Arel approached the table. "Hi Arel!" Koo hadn't changed. Ormer and Kadence looked older, too suntanned. They looked up without speaking.

"And. . . Vena!" Vena sang out, sounding spontaneous and fun. She eyed Ormer, slid into the booth next to him, slid closer to make room for Arel. "How do you do?" She held out a loose hand, shook Ormer's limply.

"That's Ormer Bell!" Koo was introducing everyone. "And I'm Koo and this is Kadence. Are you a friend of Arel's?"

"Yes I am," Vena's voice seemed to take over the table. "Arel and I are colleagues and close personal friends."

In the mirror between Koo and Kandence's heads, Arel saw herself look confused.

"Oh wow! Arel what are you doing now? You never called me!"

"Oh. Sorry." Had Koo been serious about that?

"So you got another job already?"

Vena replied, "Yes, we're both in sales."

Kadence looked suspicious.

"Sales? Sales?" said Ormer, annoyed.

"Yes, yes," replied Arel.

"But only temporarily," Vena put in. "I intend to go into show business. I'm going to be the next Dolla Dare."

Kadence snorted. Arel considered it: "It could happen." Minority women were in.

"I have an interview Sunday with a man who says I could be in commercials," Vena went on. "Do you think I can pass for seventeen?"

"How old are you?"

"Eighteen."

Silence. Koo's face worked into a miniature frown: "Ormer, maybe you could get her a part in the new Hampton Drane movie. There are *so* many young girls in that one. Isn't that a good idea? Ormer?"

"I hear you, Koo."

"Just as an extra, you know—anything, don't you think? You could get her in. Couldn't you? So she doesn't have to go meet that man on Sunday? Ormer? Ormer?"

"What is your problem?"

"You're working on Hampton Drane," Arel said, too sadly, revealing too much. Koo looked embarrassed. Kadence smirked.

Vena leaned forward and craned her neck to look at Ormer, the bare top half of her breasts squeezing together. "You know Hampton Drane?"

Ormer chewed, chewed.

"He certainly does," Kadence replied. "He's Jonquil Adams' new right-hand man."

"Yeah!" Koo said. "He could get you in the movie easy."

Kadence chewed loudly.

"Ormer," said Vena in her sexiest phone voice, "What exactly do you do as Jonquil Adams' right-hand man?"

Kadence replied: "He drives her to parties at the CEO's. And he works with Austin Carl too, and he calls Hampton Drane on the telephone. *And,* he manages to do it all in addition to his regular duties!" She flashed a grin at him, her eyes closed, which he didn't see.

"He's a doer!" Arel commented.

"Yes he is," Kadence barked. Kadence was still carefully stylish, sitting cramped in the corner, her hair done in the new windy style—cut and straightened and sprayed into a solid on just one side—like a sculpture of a wind-blown head. Arel looked closer: the hair was lacquered with sand-colored glitter.

Then Arel's eyes dropped to Kadence's lapel. Pinned to it was a red and black campaign button: S.W.A.U.T.

"What is that?" Arel asked. No one replied. Everyone was chewing, silent, except for Vena, who was pulling her personal card from her purse and passing it to Ormer: "Just in case you need any extra young girls."

Ormer croaked: "Purge the Earth of those with no worth."

"What?" Arel said.

Vena giggled.

Koo asked, "Do you like your new job Arel?"

Kadence continued munching a diet Frito, and Ormer stuffed the last bit of a hamburger pita in his mouth. They'd expect her to brag, puff it up, so Arel calmly replied, "No, Koo, I detest it." Everyone looked at her, startled to hear something real. Arel went on, in a happy cheerful voice, "I'm not even a temp—I only fill in for temps. I barely earn enough money to eat. I got evicted from my apartment and will probably lose all my worldly possessions." Everyone was speechless. "That's why I'm unhappy." Then, to Kadence and Ormer: "So, why are you unhappy?"

Kadence snorted, popped another Frito in her mouth.

Vena piped up: "Come on, Arel, we gotta go get our lists." She took Arel's hand, rose, and trotted her out of the Sandwiche Shoppe. At the elevator, she leaned down, close to Arel's forehead, and bubbled, "Do you think he'll call me?"

"What?"

"Do you think Ormer will call me and get me into the Hampton Drane movie?"

"No."

"Oh you're such a—what's that word?"

"Pessimist."

"Yeah!"

Going up in the elevator, Vena looked in the mirror, tried out different poses for Raz for when the doors opened. Arel watched her and the short, unhappy-looking man beside her, with a S.W.A.U.T. button on his lapel, the letters black against a blue background, to match his lapel.

"Vena, what *is* that?"

Then the elevator doors whipped open, and they had to run for their lists.

∗   ∗   ∗

Arel settled into her cube with a long list of depressed and suicidal people and tried to feel cheerful. Nine more hours. She dialed the first number, but the callee's "Hullo?" was so depressing she hung up.

But this was her big chance—this was it.

She dialed another number and hung up again, felt herself slip, sinking with the sack of rocks. Ormer Bell writing screenplays with Jonquil Adams and Austin Carl, chatting with Hampton Drane on the phone, a regular rising star, and it could have been her, but she wasn't savvy enough, she wasn't something enough. It could have been her, but instead this was her: this person desperate to keep a temporary job as a phone solicitor. With only herself to blame.

Raz strode by, glanced in. "You got a good list," he remarked. "You ought to get a lot of sales." Then worked his eyebrows into some significant expression.

Vena's voice called out, "She'll do great now baby! You wait and see."

"Yes," he said ominously and strode away.

God.

She dialed another number. "Hello?" said the sad young man's voice.

"Hi. Hi. How are you?"

"Who is this?"

"Who?"

"Do I know you?"

"No," she replied, accidentally telling the truth.

"Who are you and why are you calling me?"

"My name is Arel. I used to have a real job but I got fired and now I have to be a phone solicitor, and I have to call up strangers and pretend like I'm their friend."

"Wow. That's brutal."

"I'm sorry I bothered you."

"That's okay. Do you want to talk? I don't have anyone else to talk to."

"Me either, really."

"Mm, that's brutal. So." Pause. "What are you selling?"

"Prozap. No—Prozap Plus. Ever tried it?"

"Mm—I think I tried Prozap Extra, one, two, three years ago, but I got depressed again."

"I got depressed when I lost my job. Is that what happened to you?"

"Mm, basically I lost my job when I got depressed, you know—that whole getting out of bed in the morning, that's brutal. I still can't do it. But I'm back living with my dad. Basically my dad's loaded. He makes how-to-get-rich videobooks. Basically you get rich by making how-to-get-rich video-books. Did you know that?" Low, solemn laughter. "But I don't have anyone to talk to. What are you selling again?"

"Prozap Plus."

"Yeah, that stuff, yeah, I tried that four, five years ago."

"God. How long have you been depressed?"

"Mm, how long?" He laughed again—a laugh always just starting. "I don't know. Long time. How long? Mm." Silence.

"Why are you so unhappy?"

"You ask some wild questions. Why am I unhappy? You know—it's those brain chemicals, those chemicals like you used to mess with in high school, that stuff in test tubes that eats the paint off the counter and fizzles up and smokes. You know that stuff. That stuff's in my head. That stuff makes you think all kinds of wild shit, you know? Like I used to think my dad hates me. Once I thought he was trying to kill me. I really thought that, you know? That's because he really was. But you can't just blame your parents. You gotta take responsibility for yourself, you can't blame other people, you know, it's just yourself that's all fucked up. Like my dad—he only beat me up because he loved me and he was doing his best. Mm. I'm all fucked up. It's like, I know that's true, but I can't remember it, you know? Mm. I get confused. Those brain chemicals, they're brutal. What are you selling again?"

"Prozap Plus."

"Yeah, I oughtta try that. I'm on something else now. It's called, uh— Prozap. No. That's what you just said. You think that'd help? Can you get me an appointment? I just can't remember stuff, you know? It's like every day I think, I'm not gonna last another day, you know? You know how that feels? Like your skin's on fire and you want to jump in the lake and stay down there on the bottom of the lake, all peaceful and quiet, till the burning stops and you're so full of water you're not thirsty any more. And then your skin just peels off and all your insides float around free and peaceful till the end of time. Nothing burns anymore. Ever feel that way?"

"No. Yes. I don't know."

"Mmm. Can you get me some of that stuff? I just need someone to talk to. I need to remember things, you know?"

"Hang on." She had to leave him on hold for ten minutes while the psychiatrist's appointment administrator coordinated her screens and found a time when the doctor would be in. All the fifteen-minute slots were full; she had to take a five-minute prescription appointment. When she came back on the line, he was still there, hopeful, obedient. "Next week's the soonest I could get you in," Arel said.

"Yeah? Well I feel better just talking to you. Next week huh? Well I'll still be on this earth probably. Basically I'm too much of a coward to kill myself, you know? It's like—cutting yourself, shooting yourself in the face. God, that shit would hurt, you know? I'm not into that, that hurting yourself shit. Shit, I'm all fucked up. It's like, nothing seems real. Why isn't anything real?"

When they hung up she leaned her face into her hands, breathed, then realized the room was too quiet. She turned to find Vena and Raz gazing at her over the top of Vena's cube.

"Interesting approach," Raz said. "Real honesty."

"It suits her," Vena commented.

"You strike me as a creative individual," Raz continued. "I'm sorry to see you go."

Go?

"Go?" Vena barked. "Where's she going?"

"The regular temp's coming back tomorrow. They just called me."

"Raz," Vena pouted, punched his arm. "You always spoil my fun." She looked at Arel with big brown sad eyes. "That's too bad baby, but you call me up, anytime. We'll go dancing!"

Vena descended into her cube, Raz shuffled away, and Arel panicked. Eight and a half more hours. She dialed nonstop, and with the DSI list and the real honesty approach she made twelve more sales—$130 for the day plus the base wage—not enough to pay the storage bin fee, but enough for some decent food.

When the day shift left and the night shift trickled in, she hung around in the bathroom, drank water from the tap and tried to untease her hair. Then she waited for the elevator, braced herself for the devastation of joblessness again. An elevator arrived, she got on, braced. Then realized that she did not feel devastated: she felt relieved. In the empty elevator she cried out, "Thank God! I'm free!" She jumped up and down, laughed out loud, pushed all the elevator buttons going up: Free from phone soliciting, from the cubicle, from the cushionless chair and Raz and free from lying for money.

She rode all the way up to the top of the Tower, peered out at Chez Tres Chic when the doors slid open, then pushed the button for the fifteenth floor and rode down to Adstories. Would it look the same? Sometimes they reassembled the cube maze into a new and different pattern. Sometimes they replaced the beige cubes with gray ones. When the elevator doors opened, she saw that everything was the same.

Nearly everyone had gone. The only sound came from the Xerox room, the copier grunting and wheezing out copies of piles of paper left in the overnight trays. She walked by her old cube, looked in. A picture of a strange bottle-green sports car was taped to the wall. She walked on, toward the chunking sound, then looked into the Xerox room. It was a new machine—huge and broad, with two silver robot arms attached to each side, like a squashed headless human. One arm scooped copies out of the exit trays, the other shoveled originals into the entrance trays. She moved closer, read random words off the pages of the original before they were sucked into the machine: "very young". . . "vicious attack". . . "man with a". . . "Oh, doctor!" Tidy rainbow-colored copies slid out the other side: "Hampton Drane: Man With a Mission," the title page read. "An original screenplay by Jonquil Adams, Austin Carl, and Ormer Bell."

She pulled a lilac copy out of the stack. She would be late opening the library, but she settled onto the floor where the security camera couldn't see her and started to read.

Ormer had used some of her ideas. Except in this script, the homeless torch victim that Hampton Drane rescued was a poor but not homeless beautiful young Latino girl, brutally raped by a gang of twenty-nine Latino boys who throw her onto various car hoods and break her legs with a tire iron and stab her with sharpened popsicle sticks, then use her own Flame-Off against her. In the dramatic torching scene, the young girl's sleeve catches gracefully on fire, and her lovely raven hair is singed. She sits crying in the snow, and Hampton Drane appears, mysterious and divine, to scoop her up and carry her off to his special clinic devoted to the Higher Ideal of Restoring Beauty.

In the meantime, the girl's beautiful older sister wins the Sunco Lottery and hires a sexy blonde police detective—a possible Dolla Dare part—to find the girl. The girl is found, and the sister lavishes gifts and money on Dr. Drane. The girl, the sister, and the sexy detective all fall in love with Dr. Drane and his practice is overrun with sexy young Latino, black, and Asian girls and sexy blonde detectives who offer to do various jobs for him in exchange for plastic surgery. In the end, all the sexy young girls at the special clinic attract hordes of new male clients with plenty of money for little adjustments to their noses, chins, dicks.

"He'll *hate* this," Arel said to the machine, which had finished with the Drane script and was now spewing out sherbety sales charts. She looked around the room. There were disc mailers on the top shelf, above the reams of paper. By the door was the huge canvas mail cart, half full. The disc with her version of Hampton Drane Part 2 was still in her purse. But the disc mailers were directly in front of the security camera, and Sunco could sue her for office supply theft—if the security guards in the basement were still awake in front of their wall of security screens. Still it was risky.

She stood up, climbed onto the counter and grabbed a mailer. She would not spend her life dreaming of peace at the bottom of the lake, of her skin burned away, her organs drifting without awareness or purpose like sightless bloodied fish. She turned and smiled and waved at the camera, grabbed a mailer. She wrote on the envelope: "Dr. Hampton Drane, c/o Sunco Adstory Department, Sunco Tower—PERSONAL." She folded a piece of lily-white paper around her disc, wrote "from the woman with the flying hair," put the disc in the envelope and the envelope in the mailbag. Then she grabbed an entire ream of paper—plain white. She had another plan.

She waved at the camera again and walked out with her package of paper. Tomorrow she would earn no money: she would work with a real purpose.

∗　　∗　　∗

The next morning she rose early, sat weightless at the counter, and wrote in big bold letters in black marker on a white sheet of paper: "Why are you so unhappy? Come to the mall park tomorrow at 7 PM." She loaded the stolen ream into the library copier—an old disposable model that trembled and wheezed as it sucked pages in and spat them out.

Then she took her armload of pages—dramatically black and white— to the parking lot of the Park Forest River Oak mall—Ben's mall. He'd like this. Her mother would like this: A grass-roots movement to raise consciousness and challenge the oppressive capitalist system in which we live. That's how her mother would have said it, the sound clear in Arel's head.

In the parking lot, the sun scalded her air conditioned skin. She squinted, walked fast to the far end of the lot, and began sweeping the other adflyers off windshields. She spent time positioning each of her flyers straight and directly in front of where the driver's face would be. "Why are you so unhappy?" All alone on the windshield. A lone flyer would be an eye catcher. She moved down one row of cars and up another. The other advertisements—red, yellow, orange and green—piled up like hot bright snow between cars. Her skin burned but didn't sweat; she was thirsty. She looked up. The sky was cloudless, as flashy blue as an adscreen. Across the parking lot was a Mexican-looking man also putting ads on windshields, but not sweeping off the other flyers first, and she wondered why no one had thought of this before—adflyer stealing. Or maybe they had. Maybe Paterco flyermen pulled off the Sunco ads and the Sunco flyermen pulled off the Holoco ads. How can you know what's been taken away before you arrive?

She drove back to the library, thinking of her mother, growing bolder. Thinking of Ben, of seeing his face in the crowd, smiling at her. She felt like her old self again, and he'd like that. At a stoplight she whipped out her miniwriter and zipped an anonymous message to him: *Why are you so unhappy? Come to the mall park tomorrow at 7 PM.* Then she zipped one to Kyler too.

That night she fell asleep easily, with the language of books and her mother's voice in her head, rehearsing what she'd say: The highly specialized and segmented nature of the work process in a capitalist society not only alienates workers from the *product* of their labor—dramatic pause—but also from *themselves*—another pause—because we experience work as something unpleasant to be gotten through quickly, viewing it as the opposite of pleasure—pause, pause—which deprives us of one of the most important sources of meaning in our lives.

Over and over again her speech replayed, sometimes in her voice, sometimes in her mother's, and she closed her eyes, let her thoughts wander and discover pictures from her past: tall dark bookcases and the old-fashioned computer screen that hummed, her mother's back at the screen, Arel falling asleep in her mother's lumpy bed, in the room that was the living room and the dining room and her mother's bedroom and her mother's office. Seeing her mother's face in early morning light, long and creamy next to hers on the pillow and dead asleep, her mother's fingers wiggled into the curl of her own, holding her hand. Pale damp light, holding hands.

*   *   *

The next evening the mall was so crowded she had to park in the remote lot and take the shuttle. Inside the crowd was denser than usual, shoppers packed in and only milling, not running as usual, not sprinting up and down moving escalators, into stores, racing other shoppers to the check-out counters to get back to work sooner. She pushed into the mob and rolled with it toward the center of the mall, toward the mall park, where the crowd was even thicker and not even milling. Then she realized that all these people had come to hear her.

"Oh God."

She'd had no idea there'd be so many. She'd imagined herself poised on the planter, calm and picturesque above a small collection of sullen, polite shoppers. Suddenly she was nervous, pushing through the crowd, her speech replaying faster and faster in her head and suddenly making no sense. Did people used to *like* being at work? Didn't an office always feel like a jail? What made work meaningful? *Meaningful work?* In a smaller group, she would have posed these questions. But a mob of miserable shouting people suggested the need for a different approach. She thought of sneaking away, or running away, but then tomorrow would come with nothing to think about but finding another tempeetemp job.

So she climbed up onto the planter above the sea of blond and dark heads and bright padded shoulders. In the atrium over her head were giant white bird cages swaying, containing giant bright parrots squawking. She surveyed the crowd: faces pale and tanned, old and young, frowning, framed by the metallic oranges and limes of this summer's hottest fashions. She didn't see Ben or Kyler, but who could see anyone in a mob like this?

The crowd was clumping into bitterly talking groups. Arel cleared her throat and yelled as loudly as she could: "We're here to discuss what is wrong with our lives and our world!" Her voice carried, echoed in the atrium, startled her. The crowd quieted and looked at her. Actually looked. She was amazed. She was visible. She paused and felt its force: visibility, voice. Felt twenty feet tall. Then yelled out passionately: "Why are we so unhappy? What is wrong with our lives?"

A short man with bleached hair and narrow shoulders yelled out, "I got one! I got one!"

"Tell us about it, brother!" Arel shouted back and everyone was excited, straining to hear him. He said: "Every day I'm five minutes late to my night job and I get docked an hour's pay!"

The crowd grumbled in sympathy and Arel chimed in enthusiastically, "Why does that happen, brother? Why?"

He shouted back, "Because people take too goddam long ordering at the McDonald's drive-throughs! I sit in line forever and it makes me late!"

"Yeah!" cried out a middle-aged woman. "People at the drive-through should decide in advance what they want, pay up, and hit the road!"

"People are idiots!" someone shouted. An angry yelp of agreement went up. An old heavy freckled man complained, "You know what else makes me late? Women with children. They're so goddam slow, putting their kids in their cars—"

The first man cut in,"—strapping them in, walking around the car, getting in themselves—"

"God!" shouted the second man, "I'm growing old waiting for these stupid broads to pull out of their parking places!" Arel felt her mouth smiling weirdly, had no idea what to say.

The mob was reminded of other time-wasters: people who made left-hand turns, people with too many items sneaking into the 40-item or less check-out lanes, people who didn't have the bullet-proof glass option on their cars and caused traffic jams when someone blew out their windshields and scattered glass all over the highway. It was especially inconvenient when the driver got killed, because then the car just sat there till the body sweepers came, which caused an undue burden on SunMaint, which would soon have to hire more bodybag men and be forced to raise the price of the road tolls.

"All because *some* people can't afford bullet-proof glass!" a woman yelled.

"Well," said Arel thoughtfully, with no thoughts in her head. This wasn't going well. Her prepared speech would be ridiculous here, and she realized: to truly be heard, she had to speak their language, not the language of old Marxist books. Moments passed and she grew self-conscious, picturing herself standing around on a planter. Then she saw the image of her mother at the head of a class, irreverent in loose-fitting clothes and loose hair, while Arel, six years old, sat in a corner desk, coloring in Cinderellas with gold crayons. "Well," Arel said, recalling what her mother would say. "Perhaps there's a larger issue here."

Faces were blank, but willing to listen.

Arel continued, "Clearly we all need more time."

"Yeah!" voices called out.

"That's right!"

An angry man shouted above the crowd: "And more space! I've been cramped up in the same goddam dinky studio apartment for over ten years and you know why?"

"Why?" people demanded.

"Because last year when I applied for a bigger place, two gay guys came in with better credit and I lost it! Of course they have better credit— they have two big incomes because they're both men."

"Yeah! They're like fashion designers and interior decorators and stuff like that pays a lot of money!"

"That's right!" another angry voice realized. "Homos bug the shit out of me!"

"At least they have jobs!" another voice called out. "Last year some unemployed scumball shot me in the back and I was in the hospital so long I lost my job!"

Someone else shouted: "The worst is when some black homeless scumball mugs you, because you can never understand what they're saying!"

Another voice said, "See? It's these people without money costing us money!"

The crowd formed clusters again, their angry talk growing angrier. Eventually the mall police arrived—four guys with massive upper bodies in cheerful orange and yellow uniforms. One of them looked at Arel. "What's going on here?"

She replied, with authority, "We're having a rally! Did you know that Americans have the right to assemble to discuss issues that are important to them?"

"What?"

"It's in the First Amendment—the Bill of Rights."

The officer called over to the other three: "Hey, guys—does anyone remember the Bill of Rights?"

"Yeah!" one of them said. "I remember that!"

"This lady says these people are allowed to have a rally here, because of the Bill of Rights."

"The right to peaceably assemble," Arel corrected, growing nervous. She'd looked this up on an old mini-pedia and had found only a mini-version of it, written in convenient, easy-to-read words.

"Oh yeah," the other officer answered. "But not on private property."

The first officer turned toward Arel and shrugged. "Don't know what to tell ya." He cupped his hands around his mouth and shouted, "People in the crowd. Return to shopping. Return to shopping."

"No don't!" Arel screamed. "Don't go shopping!" Which caused a stunned silence. "Listen!" commanded her voice, and everyone did—even the puzzled mall police. "Something's wrong here. Can't you feel it? It's the crummy jobs we have and the time we don't have, and, and the stuff. God, who needs all this stuff? Imagine: less stuff—more space. Less stuff, less expense—less work. Less work, more time. See?" People kept listening. "More time. What would you do with it? Try to imagine." She tried to imagine, but what would she do? Watch more TV? No one else could imagine either, but in the remarkable silence, she could tell that they were trying.

Then suddenly there was movement in the crowd. Someone was shoving excitedly toward the planter—a guy in a green Video-Infinity shirt—waving one of Arel's white flyers. He jumped onto the planter, jumped up and down, and pointed to the Video-Infinity store window. He kept jumping until everyone looked toward his store. The grid of screens in the 30-foot store window flashed and there was kindly old Dr. Aslow, frozen-faced, a different piece of face on each screen—Dr. Aslow as a giant jigsaw puzzle, Dr. Aslow in a huge hamster cage.

The bright light naturally captured all attention. Arel looked out at the mass of people, stretching from the mall park to the escalator, from the Good-Buys Pub to the novelty bottle cap store, everyone expressing their individuality in wild clashing advertising colors, all strangely alike. They'd come, wanting something, unable to say what. What would she do now? She had no plan B and her heart sank. Things couldn't possibly get worse.

Then Alsow's face came alive and the speakers boomed: "Greetings, my children." He smiled, lips closed over the teeth, benign, serene. He looked different in this video—less confident, simpler, tenuous, older, bruised. He began:

"I have been praying—for me, for you, for our happiness in this world of Satanic influences. I have put this question to God: 'Why are we so unhappy?' And now I put the question to you." The face got even larger, too huge for the frame, his ears, hairline and chin shaved off. "Why *are you so unhappy?*" He was looking directly at Arel—directly at everyone. Elbows and shoulders and feet stopped twitching. His voice was empathetic, full of sorrow. "You work so hard to be happy. No one works harder than Americans. You buy things to cheer yourself up, you buy your self-help videos, your exercise equipment, your entertaining shows. But nothing seems to help. Nothing makes a difference. You are unhappy, day after day, struggling along as best you can but losing hope that things will *ever change.*" The crowd was mute, motionless, expanding as shoppers passing by stopped to see. "You tell yourself—just get over it! Just be happy! Be positive! Don't think so much. Just get better! But it doesn't help, does it? Nothing helps!" His face was too close to turn away from, too revealed—its creases and bumps raw without makeup, too real. Arel tried to look down but the voice brought her back: "Why?" he cried out. "Why?" His eyes grew watery and red; he blinked and caught his breath. Then continued:

"Because you have suffered tremendous personal losses. You've been robbed, assaulted, disabled. Perhaps, like me, you've lost a loved one—a family member dead, gone. My son, my only son, my son gone. Gone. Your loved one—gone. And—there's *nothing we can do about it!*" He seemed surprised by this. "Our lives, forever darkened. Our hearts, forever torn to shreds." He paused, tried to compose himself, but when he spoke again his voice was even wilder: "We *try* to get over the loss. But we *just can't*." Now tears ran from his eyes, his grief unleashed. It was embarrassing, intriguing; no one could look away. He sobbed, kept sobbing, stayed on screen sobbing, and Arel's chest began to knot up. He was making her remember. She didn't want to remember, couldn't help it: the wait at the window, the night sky dark as tar, Great Aunt Ashley finally phoning to say they ought to go look at that week's unidentified bodies. Aunt Tiffany in the car patting Arel's hand but not comforting, not her mother, reminding Arel of something her mother had once said: "You know why I love you so much? Because I know you so well."

Dr. Aslow wiped his tears with his satin hanky and talked on bravely: "God has advised me what to do to ease our common suffering." Calmer now, with a purpose: "My son's murderer is dead, but I ask you, is that enough? One agent of Satan is gone—but there are tens of thousands, hundreds of thousands of people just like him, waiting to take his place—to murder your son. Satan still walks among us today! We must purge the earth of these worthless creatures and *never* suffer again!"

"Yeah!" said someone in the crowd.

Dr. Aslow continued, his voice still shaky but happier now, repeating his familiar words: "I have a simple, three-step plan." He paused, grinned hopefully—sweetly—at the audience, pleased with his plan, with faith in the crowd.

"One, identify *who* in our great society is an agent of Satan, sent to make hard-working Americans like us suffer. This is easy. Obviously, homeless people make us suffer. These creatures steal from us—our money, our time, our loved ones. These people are of *no value* to our society. They are unemployed and impoverished, contributing *nothing* to our economy. They exist merely to prey on us.

"Now, most homeless people are easy to spot." Dr. Aslow's face began to shrink, encircled by its gold oval, and floated over pictures of Chicago city streets. "We trip over them when we're hurrying to our jobs—" Lumps lay bundled in old brown clothes in doorways, alleys, next to dumpsters. "They follow us to our cars at night and demand our wallets." The scene cut to a simulation of a sinister, faceless form in a worn coat following a glamorous young woman to her car. "They are smelly and unclean. Their clothes are unclean." Back to the Chicago streets: to the dazed stubbled unwashed face of a black man crouched in a doorway, then a lone rat, big and black or brown and sniffing on a pile of garbage.

"But be warned!" Dr. Aslow barked. "Satan has many guises. The visible homeless are only the tip of the iceberg! There is also the problem of the *hidden* homeless—people with no steady employment and no permanent address, who roam from place to place, freeloading off friends." The screen now showed pictures of people in last year's fashions loitering in a mall. Arel began to shift, conspicuous in her outdated clothes, but no one was looking at her, no one pointing and whispering to the person next to him. Aslow went on: "Though these people are not as worthless as the visible homeless, they are people of low value to our society and are undoubtedly tomorrow's street creatures.

"And who is at risk for becoming a person of low value? Just look around you, take note of who doesn't get along with their co-workers, who is uncooperative at work." On screen now were still shots of sloppily dressed people at Xerox machines, people sleeping in their cubes. "Such people merit close scrutiny.

"Now," Dr. Aslow's face grew again, breaking out of its oval, and scrunched into its renowned look of puzzlement before the revelation of a great truth. "We must think—*how* do we solve this problem? Americans are great problem-solvers. There's nothing we can't do when we put our minds to it! We are the nation that built spaceships and created interactive video games! So how are we to solve this latest problem? Just how are we to purge the earth of those with no worth?

"This is Step Two of the Aslow plan. I have been working round the clock to solve this problem and I have discovered a shocking truth about the current American criminal justice system." A dramatic pause, then, incredulously: "I have discovered that our justice system is old and *outdated*—it is, in fact, the *same* system of justice we had under Big Brother Government fifty years ago!"

The crowd gasped.

"In that old and outdated system, criminals are sometimes *set free* on some tiny technicality and allowed to roam the streets again, menacing innocent hard-working individuals like us! My plan—the Aslow Action Plan—is designed to streamline justice production in this country, to ensure that no agent of Satan will ever again go free to plague our society. You see—" and here his face grew even bigger, about to explain a difficult concept— "since all these homeless scums are either criminals or about to be criminals, we can simply *assume* that they're criminals. This is a new improved strategy in the business of justice. Clearly, such people should be locked up." The camera panned back and Aslow was back in his armchair, relaxing into the richness of it, a satisfied man: "I have proposed to the Paterco board of directors that Paterco offer hard-working citizens like us some amount of money—say $30—for bringing homeless people to PrisonCo, where they will be put to work doing something of service to our economy."

Small noises of approval went up.

"Currently, the board of directors is doing a cost analysis of my proposal. Letters of support from the public, of course, could influence their decision—that's how a democracy works!" He beamed. "Now, the final step," he explained in a concerned tone, "is to safely and successfully round up these presumed criminals and bringing them to PrisonCo. You may wonder, how can we accomplish this great plan? I suggest forming small citizen action groups for this task. We must all work together to cleanse our society of its evils. Only by standing together can we free ourselves from the claws of Satan and be happy at last. Yes, my children, this is how we can be happy at last! Happy at last—because we *deserve* it! We are a great nation of doers—so let's just get out there and do it! Satan Walks Among Us Today—join the SWAUT team!"

Dr. Aslow smiled one last time, nodded genially, then blipped off the screens. Voices rose, quietly, then louder, then people began to roam away. Some filed into the video store; others drifted into whatever store was closest to them. Arel watched their faces and tried to tell their thoughts. Eyes shifted, drawn to the things designed to draw them—the pillar adscreens, the sign robots, the lifelike movements of the metallic mannequins in metallic clothes in store windows. The faces in the crowd did not look around suspiciously; they looked tired and slightly swollen from sleeplessness, from the pollution and the boredom, in search of something that seemed interesting and important—unaware that there might be something to see in the spaces between the flashing images. No one glanced back at Arel—no one noticed her at all—and she was relieved.

Then a hand pushed into the back of her hair, tightened around her neck, and a voice said, "Got ya!"

She screamed and jumped forward, but when she turned, it was Kyler. She threw her arms around his hard broad shoulders, hung on.

"I am so happy to see you!" she screeched and a look of thrill lit up his face—not especially because of her, she knew, but at the thought that someone liked him so much.

"How've you been, Arel? Where've you been? I tried calling you, but your phone was shut off."

"Oh, yeah."

"So I tried calling Sunco Adstories, and they said you got fired!"

"Oh, yeah."

"Hey, I oughtta get you on at the high school—it's part-time work, nothing fancy, your basic shit job, but it's something. Hey, do you still work at the library?"

"Yes —"

"Great!" he boomed, relieved. "I liked your pep rally! We didn't know it was you. Ben got some message and wanted to come."

Her chest contracted. "Ben's here?"

"Yeah!" Kyler squinted at the crowd. "Where'd he go?"

Arel squinted too, scanned the mob. Would he look the same? But he wouldn't be in the crowd, he'd be on the periphery, trying to stand apart, and suddenly she saw him, leaning against the wall. She knew him from his black-and-whiteness, his expression of expecting something surprising. Old lovers are familiar and strange at the same time, and always better looking.

"Wow!" she said. "Look how long his hair got."

He was staring at her, but her eyes would not glance away. Kyler waved him over with big flapping arms, and as he walked toward them, slipping through the crowd, she realized he was graceful.

"Hi Ben!" croaked her voice. His eyebrows raised.

"Hey!" Kyler bellowed happily. "It's like old times! The Three Musketeers, together again!"

Ben began to look miserable. Kyler put an arm around each of them and said, "Let's get some ice cream!"

∗ ∗ ∗

At the Cones 'n Phones, at the other end of the mall, they sat at a table near the mock window, painted black with pinpoints of white to look like the view from a spaceship. In the middle was the solar system, with scoops of ice cream where the planets would be—mocha for Venus, blueberry for Earth, raspberry for Mars. Saturn was a ball of lemon-ice with rainbow sherbet round it in sparkling rings, which seemed inaccurate. Underneath was written: "Our Business is the Universe."

Arel could think of nothing to say and Ben was silent as Kyler decided what everyone should get. For Arel, a triple-dark-fudgy-chocolate-chip-Oreo cookie-M&M cone with chunks of green mint and jimmies—because she needed more extravagance in her life. For Ben, a pineapple-orange piñata, because he needed to act more festive. Kyler punched in their order, boomed, "God, you two! Cheer up!" and began his tabletop drumroll.

"So much for my grass-roots movement to raise consciousness and challenge the oppressive capitalist system in which we live," Arel said and laughed at herself. Then, seriously, "You have to be a celebrity to have an effect," expecting to draw a response from Ben, who remained closed up.

Kyler laughed: "You and that stuff. You're funny. But you really had them there at the end—with that stuff about time and space and money and things. They were really listening before Dr. Aslow came on." He laughed again, wiggled his fingers at her like a hypnotist, "Ooooooooooooh, spooky creepy weirdo Satan stuff."

Then he got distracted by the display of phones through the glass tabletop: a starburst of slender curves of plastic in all colors—from French vanilla to midnight navy. She looked down too. Sunco had the technology to implant a phone in your ear, yet people still preferred the old-fashioned kind you held in your hand. Some had miniscreens, some minispeakers, and all had the stalker option to screen out harassing calls from ex-lovers, estranged spouses, deranged dial-a-dates and clever psychopaths who followed you on the street and somehow got your number.

"So many choices!" Kyler bellowed. "What a great country!"

Gloomy silence.

"God, cheer up guys! You two can be a couple of statues." He winked at Arel. "I know what you're doing—you're sitting there *thinking*. You think too much! Both of you. Two of a kind. Hey there's our ice cream!" Kyler jumped up and ran to the counter, and Arel and Ben were alone, sitting across the table from each other, glancing at parts of each other—chin, hair, hands—but not eyes.

"Kyler said you got fired," Ben said finally.

"Yeah."

"What are you doing now?"

"Making speeches in malls."

"I mean for a living?"

Silence. Then, "Oh, various uninteresting things. Temp stuff, you know."

"Mm, sorry to hear that," he said, as though he really were. Her throat closed up. He said, "You'll get something soon." Then, awkwardly, darkly:

"You have enough, right, to cover your rent and everything?"

Her throat made a sound, and Kyler returned with their cones. He already had a mouthful of ice cream, his teeth clenched in an ecstatic grin. He held his hands down so Arel and Ben could tug their cones out of his fingers, and he bounced in beside Ben.

"Oh, now what are you two talking about? Lighten up gang!" He bit off a chunk of ice cream and picked a topic to lighten them up: "What's up with that Aslow! It's like he's some kind of religious fanatic. Wha'd they do, amputate part of his brain too!" He laughed, chewed ice cream. "That plan of his—that's just plain a bad idea! Think about it. Say the three of us go out to nab a few homeless scums and cart 'em down to PrisonCo, which is way the hell on the South Side, right? So we get what—sixty bucks on a good day? Split three ways? Twenty bucks a piece for what—three, four hours of work? Plus the cost of gas? Naw. I mean, you couldn't pick up more than one or two at a time, or you'd need a bunch of guys and a minivan, and there goes your overhead, right Ben?"

Ben replied: "People would have to do it for more than just the money."

"Exactly," Kyler said. "Makes no sense! Ooh ooh!" He pulled his sellfone out and read his newzip: "It's Dolla and Dillie!" he belted out. "Oh no! They got in a mud fight at the Oscars!" He gasped. "Dillie got the part in 'Acquaintances' instead of Dolla! Oh my God!"

Arel blurted out, "Do you even realize that you pay money to know that garbage?" Kyler looked wounded, but Ben glanced down, suppressing a grin.

"Gee, Arel." Kyler squeaked. "That was just mean."

"I'm sorry." Arel looked at her cone, tried a small lick. It was too rich. Thick chocolate oozed like molasses over her tongue, clogged her throat. She tried to swallow. So thirsty.

Ben reached over, took her cone and gave her his more sensible one. She looked at him. The side of his mouth gave a twitch she couldn't interpret. But the taste of fruit on her lips was sweet and wet.

"Wow!" Kyler said. "She must really be stuck on you boy, to let you get away with that!"

*   *   *

Alone and lonely all evening at the library she sat on her stool and imagined the worst possible future. Somehow the Aslow Action Plan would catch on. The Paterco Board of Directors would adopt the scheme, and people would begin rounding up the homeless—they'd become adept at it, use their American ingenuity to make it pay, make it their second job. In a few months all the visible street people would be gone, and then these citizen squadrons—the SWAUT teams—the Aslow Actioneers—would start looking for the hidden homeless, and one night she'd be sitting in the library, on this very stool, and the door would burst open and a brigade of hard-working citizens with firearms would drag her off to prison.

But this was ridiculous. Kyler was right: Aslow's scheme wouldn't pay enough, especially since it would be dangerous—homeless people had firearms too. Plus Aslow came off like a lunatic religious nut and people didn't like that. Anyway it wouldn't be cost-effective for Paterco. How many chain-gangs did they need on toxic waste dumps? And no one would turn her in. Who knew she'd been evicted but Ormer, Kadence and Koo, Vena, and the guy at the Sunco Self Storage?

A ball of panic burned up her throat. She tried to remain calm, breathed deeply, closed her eyes and pictured the requisite deserted beach and tranquil lapping sea. But her thoughts flew: there'd be a newzip—Aslow's scheme implemented—then a pounding at the door—everyone she knew trying to nab her.

She breathed in, out, relaxed, and thought of Ben. He'd stared at her when she wasn't looking, asked how she was, smiled at something she'd said, given her his ice cream cone—he'd known what she'd needed, given it to her. The idea of him grew in her mind. Hour after hour, sitting on her stool, TV sounds murmuring in the distance. They were "two of a kind." He was different, like her; he could care about her, he could keep her safe.

She called him and on his machine invited him to lunch the next day. She said she'd wait for him in the school cafeteria. She tried to sound provocative. She pointed out that he had to eat anyway.

Then she went into the back room and tried to go to sleep. Restless and stiff on her boxes, she developed a strategy. She prepared, figured out how to sell him on the idea. There had to be something in it for him. When she had the pitch scripted out in her brain, she was able to relax, feeling pleased with herself: she'd learned this much—you need a certain savvy to get what you want in this world.

*　　*　　*

The next day, in the airless heat, she walked to her car, peeled off her imitation-silk jacket, felt the sun dry on her bare dry shoulders. She wore the strapless buttercup bodice she'd bought two years earlier and the black skirt that was not skin-tight but had a slit—clothes that were sexy but not too trendy. Ben would like that, she thought. It was too early for their lunch date but she went anyway, drove to Holoco Central High to wait for him in the cafeteria.

She parked in the underground visitors' lot and took the glass bulb elevator to the fourteenth floor. Holoco Central High was cylindrical, and the cafeteria was at the top, slowly rotating. She stepped off the elevator into the cool hum of a lush gold and silver room, watched the red and blue rooftops of the malls through the window glisten gradually out of sight. Another half-turn and she was facing southeast, seeing the Chicago skyline far in the distance, evaporating in foggy heat.

She crossed the gold carpet to the long semi-circular bar, made of old metal with blinking lights to look like a crashed space ship. She climbed up on a stool and posed, rested an elbow on an instrument panel. No need to be nervous, she told herself. She was well prepared. With six of her fourteen dollars she bought an enormous purple rum drink. *Well* prepared, she reminded, and watched the elevator doors. She was twenty minutes early. Students began arriving for lunch—high school juniors and seniors—young faces attached to tall adult bodies with suit jackets swinging open as they headed toward the other side of the room, where the decor was more silver than gold. They collected at tables with little polished ruby-colored trays of food, talked in controlled polite tones with smiles on their faces. One boy was making some elaborate point with big hand gestures, and another boy threw a french fry at him.

She finished her purple drink and couldn't afford to buy another. Could just barely afford another. Shouldn't buy another. Raised a finger, ordered another. Then drank it too fast, in loud extravagant gulps. And now she would only be able to order crackers for lunch. She was licking the purple foam from the sides of the glass when Ben stepped off the elevator.

When had he become so handsome? She stared at him. His thick dark hair was down to his shoulders, blew back as he walked toward her, not looking at her.

"Hi," she said with a dry throat. She followed him to a table and kept looking at the back of his hair, the flashes of face when he turned his head.

Their table was not next to the window, but they could see around the chunky forms of the school CEO and VPs to the steamy streaks of sunshine on the rooftops and streets. She tried to think of something clever to say about the view, but Ben's eyes were drifting around the inside of the room, not on the view or on her, which made her think of how he'd looked at her the first night they were together. That look gone now.

Suddenly she said, "I was so happy to see you yesterday." He looked startled. "Were you happy to see me?" she tried. His eyes remained on her face and her hands trembled.

"Sure." He opened his menu and his eyes shifted from the taco side to the stir-fry side.

Sure? She looked down and tears pushed into her eyes, nearly enough for one to almost creep down her cheek. A waitress arrived and Ben ordered a jumbo eggroll. Arel ordered the crackers.

"So," said Ben. All business.

"So, yeah. I got fired."

"Yeah, you said."

"I got evicted from my apartment. I've been living in the library."

Silence.

She went on: "Do you suppose that's a problem with all this Aslow stuff?"

"Mmm," he replied. "Mmm." No reply.

The waitress returned with their food and he seized his knife and fork, concentrated all his attention on sawing off a small crusty corner of eggroll.

"Maybe I'm just being paranoid," she said. "Do you think so?"

He kept his eyes on the eggroll, nodded, frowned, shook his head, took too long chewing. Finally finished chewing, frowned. Then pried off another wormy bite.

She took a cracker out of the basket and crinkled the end of the wrapper between two fingers. Counted to thirty. He was still silent.

"Anyway," she said, making her voice cheerful and composed. "I had the greatest idea!"

He looked up.

"How much does your cleaning service cost?" she asked.

"A hundred ten, twenty? Something like that."

"Do you ever get behind on your junk mail returns?"

He replied, finally animated. "Constantly. Last month I didn't return one of those HoloSport cards on time and yesterday I got a fuckin' slalom ski in the mail. A fuckin' $528 on my card."

"Sounds like I could save you a lot of money."

He looked at her, blank.

"In exchange for a place to stay," she spelled out.

He looked down again, dug a fork tine into the open mouth of the eggroll. "Why aren't you asking Kyler?"

"I don't want to ask Kyler."

"Why not? You've got something going with Kyler."

"I never had anything going with Kyler."

His eyes flashed up, black with rage, and she was frightened.

"Not like with you," she said.

"Whatever."

The puddles in her eyes deepened and a tear spilled out, snaked slowly down her cheek.

"God, Arel. Don't cry." Annoyed, passing her his napkin. "My place is too small."

"But I'm so short."

He grinned for an instant. "I work there in the evenings. I have stuff I do. I'm up till three in the morning some nights."

"I wouldn't make a sound."

Another tear leaked out, the piece of scrap metal in her chest jabbing harder. The dry skin of her face and hands drank in the tears, wanted more. "Ben, please, help me out." But this was pathetic. Everyone knew that being pathetic was a turn-off. She caught her breath, closed her eyes, felt the slow motion of the cafeteria rotating like the earth—this glassed-in cylinder the whole world.

When she opened her eyes, he was looking at her, looking tired. He didn't want her in his space, she knew and understood: in your own quiet square you grow comfortable alone, not safe with a lover but safe from them—the people you know for a month or two and remember in catch phrases—the intense brunette, the congenial blonde, the sullen redhead.

"My expenses would go up if you stayed there. I barely make ends meet."

"I wouldn't cost you a cent, I swear, if I do, I'm out."

He shook his head.

"And I could give you some money," she went on. "I have these temp jobs you know."

"You have one now?"

"Oh yes," she lied. "I'm cleaning cages at the pet cloners in the mall."

More silence.

"I know you're mad at me about Kyler," she dribbled on. This was not part of the script, and she felt she ought to stop talking, but couldn't. "That was an awful thing I did, God, I'm really sorry about that. I guess, I don't know, I just wasn't thinking about you, you know? Or, I didn't care, I don't know."

He stared at his plate, his face reddening.

"I know this is a huge favor," she went on, wishing she would stop, "but I don't know, Ben, I mean, this Aslow thing has got me freaked out, you know? I mean, the whole thing sounds insane but there's something about it, something about it, something's nagging at me—am I just being paranoid?"

He shrugged, gazed out the window.

"Please, Ben. Can I stay with you?"

He turned his face toward her, slowly, burned his eyes into hers. Then relaxed his shoulders, his back, sank into his chair. "All right."

"Oh, yes! Thank you! It's just till I get a full-time job and then I'll be gone, I promise."

His eyebrows eased out of their perpetual frown, and his eggroll seemed to dissect more easily. "When would you have to move in?" He didn't seem unhappy.

"Well, today's convenient."

"*Today?*"

"Tonight?"

"Do you have a lot of stuff?" he asked hopelessly.

"Oh no, not at all. It's amazing how little you really need. Some clothes. Shampoo. Toothbrush," she smiled. Added: "Toothpaste," so he wouldn't think she planned to use his.

He ate the last bit of eggroll slowly, glanced up at her, almost shy, and grinned. He wasn't unhappy. She smiled back, sat straighter and ate another cracker. But looking out the window, the same view passing by, passing by, she began to sink again, her mind forming an image of herself, living with Ben, taking up space, cluttering up his bathroom. Stepping out of his shower and dripping on his rug. Whipping a towel around her hair like an efficient old wife as he gazed out the window at some beautiful stranger dashing by.

*   *   *

He had no place for her clothes or her suitcases, so she left the clothes in the suitcases and pushed the suitcases into a tidy line along the walls of the main room, shrinking its perimeter. She waited until he was in the bathroom before spreading a case open across the floor and rifling through for her toothbrush. Then snapped it shut quickly and rolled it back into place before he returned, to spare him the sight of less space. She was hungry, having had only the noon crackers, but she wouldn't ask him for food.

In the evening she went to work at the library dressed in an efficient eggplant suit, looking not at all like a depressed unemployed freeloader, and when she returned after midnight she sat considerately on his sofa until he finished working at his computer, trying not to wonder what on earth he was doing, definitely not asking. She sat, picked at the tiny black checks on his sofa-sleeper, tried to see the screen, too small and far away. The skeleton with the kilt was still there, and beside it were the chunks of another computer, an ancient model, which he appeared to be assembling. On the wall was the row of pictures he'd ripped down, rehung: Mars hand-drawn by someone named Sarah and the cryptic fuzzy wormy structures below. She stared at them, knowing she'd seen them long ago in grade school. At last it came to her: "Chromosomes!" His back jumped, and he squealed around in his chair, "God. Arel. I forgot you were there."

Not flattering but she was smiling anyway, so lonely she was grateful to be talked at. She said, "And I forgot you were into molecular biology"— a conversation starter. "The basic building blocks of human beings!"

"All animals," he corrected.

"Oh"—not a conversation-extender. His chair began to reel back toward his screen and she called out, "Heredity!" startling him again. He turned just his face toward her and she heard herself ramble on, "What we inherit from our parents, and our grandparents, and our great-grandparents, great-great-grandparents, great-great-great-grandparents." Stopped finally. "I never knew my father. He and my mother got divorced when I was a baby. How about you?" Silence. "Who on earth is Sarah?"

"My sister," he replied.

"Cool! You have a sister?"

"Not anymore."

She shut up.

He went back to work and she began to fall asleep, sitting up, bobbing-headed. At two o'clock he switched off the screen and she jumped up: "Want to go to bed?"

He pulled the sofa out and together they looked down at the wrinkled sheets. He clicked off his one lamp, undressed in the dark. She slid nude between the sheets and watched his form cross the room to yank open a window, letting a musty summer smell waft in. His form grew more distinct as he walked back toward the bed: he was still in his boxer shorts.

"You opened the window," she commented.

"I like to save on air conditioning."

"In July?" Sarcastic. She was mad because he was still in his boxer shorts. He climbed into bed.

"I have to be up at five tomorrow morning," he said and was silent. Apparently going to sleep. How could he go to sleep? He must have had sex more recently than she had. Her mind raced to all the pretty little dark-haired teachers floating round the cafeteria. She was wide awake. Surely he wasn't really going to sleep. She tousled his hair, pretending to be nonsexual. "Night night," she chirped. Silence. Minutes crept by.

"What time are you getting up?" he asked.

"Oh early!" she tossed around, messed with the sheet. "To get to that . . . pet cloning job! I get there early to show initiative. You know? I just know I'll get a promotion there!" Optimism was a turn-on, everyone knew, but he said nothing. He was really going to sleep.

"Good night!" she said cheerfully.

"Good night," he replied and turned his face toward her. So close. His jaw steeply cut, the crease from his nose to his mouth deep. His lips would sink into it if he smiled. She grinned. He closed his eyes and went to sleep.

*　　*　　*

The next morning she jumped out of bed before he did, put on a suit and headed for the door, pretending to rush off to work. She'd only gotten two hours of sleep but it didn't matter: after he left she would sneak back and take a nap.

She spent the morning in the mall park, unable to stop watching the thirty-foot pillar screens. There was a new channel that broadcast Flash-News twenty-four hours a day. She bounced a knee in time to The Hangmen's version of "You Keep Me Hanging On" and watched: burning cars on the Eisenhower, an old hooker and a young hooker crawling up the embankment, an old photo of a mother and infant, the two hookers dead, an empty cheerleader uniform doing cheers by itself, an old aluminum house with neighbors milling in the yard looking through the windows, "Murder?" writing itself across the screen. Then Streetbarf's "Hit the Road Bitch" began and a plane landed, a pile of luggage appeared and disappeared one suitcase at a time, smiling faces flashed on the screen—TV stars, CEOs, a basketball player dyed blue.

Dr. Aslow kept appearing on screen, in various locations around the country, preaching against Satan and the lingering evils of Big Brother Government. It was hard to make out what he was saying in the Flash-News format. His face alternated with other millisecond images of small groups of followers, cornfields, more followers, city logos, more followers, the huge rocky West, a statue of Jesus, then the big blustering face of the Wizard of Oz.

Sitting so long on the planter gazing at the screen made her look like a mall loiterer, of course, but she told herself not to worry. Aslow was a nut. Everyone knew. No one liked a religious fanatic. She was safe. Everything was fine. Safe, fine, fine, she kept hearing in her brain and got up, strode from one end of the mall to the other, practiced looking like a person with a job and a place to live, then went back to Ben's place to take a nap.

His lumpy mattress was a feather pillow compared with the boxes in the back room at the library, and she slept till mid afternoon. When she woke she remembered the junk mail. She trotted down three flights of stairs, pulled the day's mail out of the tall metal wall box. It was heavy and slippery, pieces cascading over her arms as she carried it back up three flights of stairs. She had to drop it all on the floor outside his door to get the key back in the lock. Then kicked the piles into the apartment. She sat on the carpet, back against the couch, picked up the first fat envelope.

Inside was a tiny magazine titled, "I've Always Wanted To Be A Blond." The man on the front cover was lean and dark-haired—like Ben—thinking hard about becoming a blond. She flipped through the pages to find the card declining the monthly supply of hair color, and with a thick black marker ex'd the box next to, "No thanks, but keep me on your list!"

Then wondered if perhaps Ben would like to become a blond. Like Kyler, she thought, thinking of his amazing hair, all shades of yellow and gold. Thinking of his bare back, shoulder muscles rounding forward, his perfect butt as he pulled up his pants. She shifted to sit cross-legged with her heel shoved into her crotch, but she didn't have time. She grabbed another envelope: a pamphlet full of lean, dark-haired men smiling because they finally learned how to make time. Half an hour went by: Envelope after envelope of lean, dark-haired men discovering ways to look better, work better, acquire more stuff. She made slick piles on the floor, went to search for his Pater-Recycle basket. Then sat on the floor again with the bin and the piles, trying to shove the piles into the bin. God. After this she'd have to sort through the junk mail on the Holonet.

She stood up with the bin and noticed a piece of mail that had escaped under the couch. She knelt, pulled it out: It was a red and black disc mailer. With the return address: Aslow Actioneers, Chicago Team. Across the back: SWAUT.

She stood up and looked at it. Ben's name and address were printed clearly on the front. Slowly she became aware of some feeling, something trying to creep to the surface. "No," she said out loud. "I'm sure they send these things to everyone. This doesn't mean anything." She began to feel strange in the hot bright silence of Ben's small place. She ripped open the top of the disc mailer, pulled out the disc, snapped it in half. Then buried it in the recycle bin and carried it downstairs.

They send those things to everyone, she told herself. She was safe. Everything was fine. All evening she sat in the library, watching all the regular shows: "Deadly Affairs," "Liar, Liar," "Fifty Ways to Get Rid of Your Girlfriend." By the end of the evening she was trembling, calling Kyler from the library phone, "Hi Kyler!" she said to his machine, trying to sound cheerful and calm. "So, how's it going? So, what about that job at the school? Call me, call me soon, okay? But, call me at the library—don't call me at Ben's! Don't call Ben's and ask for me, okay? Okay, okay." She hung up and sat until the end of her shift, stayed late, not wanting to leave, thinking of crossing the deserted lot in the dark airless night.

*　　*　　*

Kyler knew the Vice President of Quality Control for HoloLearn—the Holoco school company. He told Arel to put on her flashiest suit and meet them for lunch at Holoco Tower, across the street from Sunco Tower.

She arrived early, tried to stand for a moment in the shoving crowd between the two highrises, looked up, felt dropped into the bottom of a glowing green glass pit, then pushed across the street to Sunco Tower, where Ormer, Kadence, and Koo were in their usual booth in the sandwich shop. Vena was there too, cuddled up beside a stiff Ormer.

"Hey everyone!" Arel said.

"Oh look," Ormer droned, "It's the chewing gum on the bottom of my shoe," and Vena said, coldly, "Hello Arel." Kadence peeled the plastic wrapper off a plastic fork, crumpled and tossed it, watched it uncrumple. Her SWAUT button today was a shade of celadon that did not quite match her suit.

"I can't stay," Arel said. "I have an important business meeting across the street. I have this great new job, and a great new apartment!"

No one seemed to took note.

"It's such a fabulous apartment! You can all come over and see it! Vena you can bring Raz!"

Vena kept her eggplant lids cast down. "Well I don't know Arel, we're mad at you."

"You and Raz? Why?"

"No, me and Ormer." Vena wiggled a hand inside Ormer's elbow, and Ormer crunched a bread stick to show his contempt.

"I *said,* leave him *alone,*" Kadence hurled a tiny tomato at Vena's column of hair.

"Why are you mad at me?" Arel asked.

Koo chimed: "I'm not mad at you! I think it's really neat!"

"What's neat? What?"

Vena tossed her head back, turned her face toward Arel but still did not look at her. Tiny eggplant veins fluttered. She enunciated: "Somehow Hampton Drane got hold of that old screenplay of yours and now he wants to do yours instead of Ormer's."

"Oh my God really? You're kidding!" Arel leaned over the table and slapped at Ormer's sleeve. "I told you he'd like my script! He *liked* it." He liked it. She smiled so completely, her whole self rose into it. "God!" She began to laugh, a long rolling, uncharacteristic laugh.

"We aren't producing it," Kadence informed.

"You're not? Why not?" Disappointed, but still happy.

"Because it's incompetent," Ormer said. "It doesn't sell plastic surgery and it makes no sense."

Vena patted Ormer's forearm. "Ormer had to write a big long memo to Hampton Drane explaining why your screenplay was so incompetent, didn't you baby?" Ormer chomped more bread stick. "Why was it you said, baby? Her script didn't even—what was it?"

"Meet the minimum criteria," Kadence sneered and tried to catch Ormer's eye. "Sex by page 25, violence by page 35, car chase by page 90. Right?"

Ormer snapped, "I don't have it memorized."

Vena laughed at Kadence, and Kadence threw a broccoli head at Vena's nose.

"But Hampton Drane is insisting on that screenplay you wrote!" Koo said excitedly. "He thinks it's wonderful! He said he liked—what was it?—the ideas!"

"Yeah? Yeah?" Arel laughed again.

Kadence continued, "Sunco is selling him to Paterco."

"And I won't get to be in Ormer's screenplay," Vena whined.

"You were never going to be in Ormer's screenplay," Kadence barked and dug around in her salad for something else to throw.

"God you guys," Arel sang out. "Make some progress!"

"Aren't you late for your meeting?" Ormer said, which she was. She darted out, feeling like the star of something. In the elevator lobby, glancing back through the sandwich shop window, she stopped to look at them, in their usual poses: Kadence tall and pissed; Koo alert and puzzled; Vena arrogant and oblivious. Ormer ignored them all, peeled the cellophane off his diet spaghetti salad. Arel swung through the revolving door and flew across the street, feeling separate and privileged—like an individual in the crowd.

The Holoco Tower sandwich shop was strangely like the Sunco Tower sandwich shop, she realized, though the decorative plastic border along the top of the wall was red-orange instead of blue-green and the glittering company logos on the melon wallpaper were in gold circles instead of silver ones. The booths ran across the south wall instead of the north, but they were the same—brass-trimmed with thin plastic seats big enough for one and a half people on each side.

She looked for awhile before seeing the top of the back of Kyler's glistening yellow head. The woman across from him was older—fifty or fifty-five—with meticulous plum stripes in her white hair, which was pulled back and poofed out, spilling out the top of a crimson head bow in millions of tiny lacquered curls. She leaned across the table with elbows and hands unable to keep still, smiling the way all women smile at Kyler. Kyler was smiling back, devouring a double-jumbo salad burger.

Arel walked toward them, catching glimpses of herself in the mirror wall—small but striking in her short tight marigold suit, striding and buoyant—a writer of screenplays with good ideas, a person with an effect. She strode, felt taller.

"Here she is!" Kyler yelled out, trying to rise in the booth. "Arel Ashe," said his clear loud voice, "this is Ramy Vine."

"Hello," Arel said, low and professional, giving Ramy's hand an overly hard shake. Then bounced in beside Kyler, full of confidence.

"Gee Arel," he said. "You look great."

"I'm ready to roll," she said and drummed the tabletop.

"Aren't you getting lunch?" he asked.

"I've put on a few, so I'm fasting today," she said, slapping her thighs. She couldn't afford lunch today.

"Now that's willpower!" Kyler gushed and Arel smiled at Ramy, who looked worried. Then he explained: "Arel's my best friend's girlfriend," and Ramy looked happy again.

"Ramy's my pipeline to power," Kyler clicked and Ramy giggled and Arel hoped this wouldn't take too long.

"There's a job opening, right?" Arel said.

Ramy lowered her voice by crouching over the table, "It's very confidential." She paused to frown seriously, and Arel realized she had no eyebrows. "As you know," Ramy continued, "Holoco takes education very seriously. We're committed to developing young minds and making the future a better place."

Arel glanced at Kyler, who nodded occasionally and stared past Ramy—he was bored, Arel knew, but trying to look interested, not knowing what genuine interest might look like.

Ramy went on: "We're dedicated to doing what works."

"What's that?" Arel asked.

"What's what?"

"What works? I mean, what is it that works?"

"Oh, I mean, whatever it is—whatever works, that's what we do."

"Oh."

"Part of what works, of course, is excellence in teaching."

"Well, it would."

"Would what?"

"Work. I mean, I would think that excellence would work."

"Yes, *yes.*"

Kyler put in, "And very well."

Arel summed up: "Excellence works very well."

"Yes, *yes.*"

Kyler smiled. "Didn't I tell you? Arel's a real smartie. Arel's different." To Arel: "Ramy's *different* too."

Suddenly Arel was annoyed. "What a lot of different people you know."

"Ramy's very caring," Kyler went on.

"Oh?" Arel waited for someone to elaborate. Ramy was acting more flattered than she should have been.

"Tell her, Ramy!"

"I'm very concerned about the *children,*" she said. "Not just with meeting the Holoco quotas for future workers. I really want these kids to acquire the skills they need to get the really high-paying jobs so they'll be happy."

"That's nice," Arel replied.

"I think children need to be well-rounded individuals," Ramy continued. "For example, I think they should all have courses in new product development as well as the principles of packaging."

"Ramy's radical," Kyler smiled. "So's Arel. She knows all kinds of stuff out of old books. Tell her something, Arel!"

Arel began in a loud voice: "Well, at the turn of the century, many scholars objected to the privatization of public schools—"

"Ha ha!" Kyler bellowed. "*Privatization.* You and your words! What does that even mean?"

Arel ignored him, "And one scholar, elaborating on a quote by Thomas Jefferson about democracy and literacy, wrote that American democracy is only as good as its public education." Ramy's forehead wrinkled where her eyebrows should have been, and Arel went on: "The concern was that education would be redefined solely as vocational training. See, before the capitalist forces in American society—"

Kyler cut in, "Wasn't your mother a teacher?"

Arel looked at him, his expression carefully blank, practiced, designed to make people doubt their guesses about what he was thinking. Arel replied loudly: "She lost her job when Sunco bought out the University of Illinois and downsized."

"Ahhh," Ramy said. "She remembers what things were like when the state ran the schools. Terrible, just terrible. They used to close the schools in June and let the kids just loaf around all summer! And of course the buildings were so unattractive. See," she became very serious: "there was no *motivation* for Big Brother Government to care about the children. At Holoco, children are our business."

Kyler grew impatient: "Tell her about the job."

"It's part of our Program of What Works, to guarantee excellence in teaching. See, in the past we used to do periodic teacher inspections—"

Kyler cut in: "Some of the mirrors in the classrooms are two-way, and there's a secret passageway running all through the building between the rooms," he grew excited, it was so like a spy movie. "And the inspectors used to come in sometimes with checklists."

"Unannounced, of course," Ramy added. "The teachers weren't supposed to know when the inspectors were coming. But somehow the teachers always found out. And of course they were always on their best behavior the day the inspectors came. We began to suspect that, between inspections, some teachers were deviating from their scripts."

"So they have this new plan," Kyler lowered his voice. "Very hush-hush."

"Really, Kyler shouldn't know about it. He caught me in a weak moment," Ramy giggled.

"I swear I won't tell a soul," he winked and clicked.

"So what's the job?" Arel asked.

"You set up the minicameras. That way we can see what the teachers are doing all the time, without their knowledge. Then, on a trial basis of course, you and a team of other teacher inspectors watch random segments of the videos, to ensure the teachers are following the script." Pause. "As far as I'm concerned, the job's yours!"

Arel didn't speak, not quite happy. She ought to be happy. She sat, not smiling. Being a teacher spy made her not smile. "Great," she said without enthusiasm—with no choice. She dug a resume out of her purse. "There's my *permanent* address," she pointed out, "and phone number."

Kyler was bouncing, elbowing her: "I knew you could do it!"

Ramy said, "You'll start in three or four weeks."

"Weeks?" Arel cried out. Too late to save her stuff in Self Storage. "I mean, great!" Why was it that, to upper management, only unimportant things were urgent?

Kyler jumped, pulled out his sellfone, read the newzip. "Huh, huh, huh. . . "

"What is it?" Ramy asked, too interested.

"Dolla's signed on for another six weeks of Dare to Talk!" He frowned, shook his head, clucked. "That can't be a good sign for Dolla's career."

"Oh, dear." Ramy sympathized, patted his hand. "Oh dear." Paused to look sad.

"Let's go," Arel said, and she and Ramy both walked Kyler out and stood together in the street corner mob until Ramy admitted she had to go back inside—her office was in the Holoco Tower. She kissed her fingertip and pressed it against Kyler's lower lip, and he winked.

Arel and Kyler crossed the street, Kyler talking fast: "I figure that lady's gonna get me into Administration—that's where the big bucks are. Company car, expense account—I'd be launched. I'd be launched. I'd be safe."

＊　　＊　　＊

At the library that evening she thought about Hampton Drane instead of the Holoco High job. He liked her script, but Sunco wouldn't produce it,

Sunco was selling him to Paterco. But Hampton Drane was a millionaire, he could produce it himself, that was possible. "Anything is possible!" she sang out in a voice trying to believe it. Pause. "Right?"

Then the door alarm wailed, and Ben walked in. Walked up to the counter, stood across from her, in an old canary cotton shirt full of sweat. He didn't like air conditioning in his car, he'd once told her, but he didn't like the windows down either, so he drove around sweating and suffocating.

She wasn't sure what to say. "This is a surprise."

"I heard you had lunch with Kyler."

Arel tensed. "Oh."

"You got a job at the high school." His voice neutral.

"Yeah."

"Congratulations!"

She stared at him. He wasn't angry. He seemed perfectly fine.

"Oh, thank you."

"You'll be good for that job."

"I will be?"

"Yeah. It's that PR assistant job, writing adflyers, right?"

"Oh." Was there a job like that open? "Yeah," she replied—it sounded so much better than "teacher spy." He smiled at her.

"Is that why you came in? Just to say congratulations?"

He shrugged. "I was tired of working."

"You were?"

Silence. The pale brown of his eyes was flecked, scattered, the color of faded oak. She let her gaze drop, down to his neck and chest, pale inside the canary shirt, and she remembered the feel of his chest bare and bony against hers, the way he breathed—audible, catching. Sex with Ben had been too intense, their bodies touching naked in too many places, their faces too close.

In the silence her body shifted, tried to get comfortable again. Her eyes rested on his fingers and hands, knuckly, on his wrists, unexpectedly small. She stared, leaned the top of her head toward him. Had he come in to restart their romance? But he wasn't resting his elbows on the counter so that his body would tip toward hers.

"Yes," came the belated reply to her question. "Sometimes I walk to clear my head, get new ideas. So I walked over here."

"Oh."

"The new job—when do you start? It's full-time, isn't it? Are you looking for an apartment?"

"Oh." So that's what he'd come to say. *That*—leaving no room for mis-interpretation or possibility. Her insides folded up into tiny squares. "Actually, no, it's only a part-time job. But it's better than the tempee job— it pays better. It's permanent."

"Oh."

She slipped her hand away, hid it behind the counter, listened to the hum of silence, imagined the adscreens popping on, fragments of products and people flashing around, taking up her mind and pouring desire like molasses into her empty chest. All she was to anyone was a potential con-sumer. Her eyes started blinking too fast and wouldn't stop. Stupid. Old lovers never returned. Lust passes, and all that's left are personalities—awk-ward, needy, unable to stay interesting. But this time was hurting more than usual. She looked at his face and thought how stupid he looked with no tan and a skinny neck and how he wasn't as smart as he thought he was; then realized he was about to leave. She blurted out, "When I first met you I thought you were different."

He turned, startled, ready to be angry: "I thought you were."

"I am."

"No. You want to be. You want to think you are. You want other peo-ple to think you are—"

"You don't know me."

His voice rising: "You're just like every other female, Arel. You think you're different? You'll do me for awhile until you can get into Kyler's pants, you and—"

Her voice shrill: "God. I said I was sorry!"

"When did you say that?" He turned red. "Anyway you aren't and you'd do it again if he wanted it."

"That's not true."

"Bullshit."

"It's—"

"Fuck it." He stepped back, into the videobook racks, locked his arms to his sides, wouldn't look at her. She leaned on the counter, let time pass, softened her voice, and tried again: "Really, I am sorry. I didn't think you'd get *that* mad. I don't think about him anymore. I think about you."

Then his arms flew up and knocked over a rack. Hard plastic boxes clattered to the floor, started to slide. "I don't care!" he shouted. "I'm done with all of you. You. You all start thinking I'm not good enough for you— that you deserve better than me. Me." He bent over, as though he meant to pick up the rack, then suddenly straightened up again and kicked over another rack, so hard that the four behind it fell too. Videobooks flew. "Fuck," he said and sighed, looked at her, inhaled noisily. Then waded into the videos and nudged them around with his toe, muttered, picked up a rack and kicked the videos around some more.

She climbed over the counter, walked around him, kneeled in the sliding piles. "Come on." She began handing boxes to him, and he began clicking them into their slots.

"Don't they have to be in some order?"

"Who'll know?" She kept passing him videobooks and they fell into a rhythm: pass, pick up, pass, their hands brushing.

She waited awhile, until he seemed calm, absorbed in the mechanics of his task, and said, "I know what you mean, you know. I'm hardly anyone's dream chick. The guys I meet are always looking for some fantasy too. And people constantly lecture me on how to improve myself. Usually its change my hair. People are really bothered by my hair."

"Your hair's not bad."

"Yeah, well. I wish, I want. . . " What? Just to not be rejected again. He did not look at her expectantly. He took boxes from her hand, put them on the rack, his face closed, thinking of someone else, maybe, some woman from the past who'd left him for a good-looking go-getter like Kyler. Maybe for Kyler himself. Who knew? No one ever talked about their past; it was bad form, everyone knew.

Arel picked up videobooks, passed, brushed his hand. The bones of his knees showed their shape through his gauzy slate pants. Kyler's body had no edges; it was perfect hard padding—effortless, plastic, prefabricated, with no variation or history. Ben's body looked hand-made, nicked in places by some old sculptor who had grown fatigued and worried, susceptible to his own humanity.

"The thing is," she said, "you and I are different from other people, because we know we have to change to do better in the world but we just don't. We kind of try, but we don't really try. Because deep down, we think we're just fine, you know? There's some voice in our heads telling us, 'It's not you. You're fine.'"

"Yeah, and so fucking what," he said. "That's what the other voice says, 'So fucking what.' This world is dog shit. Everyone in it is dog shit."

"But you're not alone—"

"Yes, I am, Arel," he spat out. "Totally alone, the last one. I used to have a family—two parents and a little sister. We were actually happy. Our parents liked us. They were teachers and they liked children and I actually had a happy childhood. Believe it?"

"What happened to them?"

"They're dead, what else? Twelve and a half years ago." Then he was silent, not explaining how, and she squirmed, wanting to know how. People's deaths made interesting stories. Finally he continued: "They were murdered in the Ravenswood Massacre, all three of them. My little sister was ten years old. I was in college, trying to learn the fuckin' basics of human life."

She was silent, running through her mental list of massacres. The *Ravenswood*. Was that when the disgruntled former HCTA worker jumped on the Ravenswood train and opened fire? Or when the disgruntled former busboy ran into the Ravenswood Cafe and opened fire? Or there was another one, too, she thought—on the street Ravenswood—an evicted tenant or something trying to mow down his former landlord.

"Well I sure fuckin' learned the fuckin' basics of human life," Ben went on, loud, oblivious to her presence. "People are dog shit."

Kind of annoying, this implication that she too was dog shit, but she let it pass; he didn't seem to be thinking of her at all.

"I'm sorry," she said in a sympathetic tone that sounded practiced, though she did feel sorry. She thought of taking his hand, just as a sympathetic friend, just to hold it. Taking his hand, squeezing it once or twice, then pulling him down onto the cascading videobooks and yanking down his pants. Tacky. She was so damn horny. She exhaled, passed videobooks, listened to them click into their slots.

He said, "I've never told anyone about it. Not even Kyler."

"Mm." So, just as well she hadn't tried to yank down his pants.

"It's kind of a relief to say it out loud," he said, his voice altered, but she missed it, her mind straying, trying to get used to the idea that he was only a friend, envisioning getting into bed with him every night forever like a sister, with quick good-nights and closed-lipped smiles and dry pats on the shoulder.

God, she thought. He wants me to be his lost sister. She glanced up to find him looking at her. Meaning nothing, no matter how much she wanted it to mean something. She sighed noisily, felt thirsty, wanted her double-jumbo diet Coke behind the counter. She started to stand and slipped on a videobook; he caught her by the hand, then didn't let go. She could feel him looking at her. *Means nothing.* Then he took her other hand and slowly spread her arms wide apart, bent down to gaze at her face. A burst of air exploded from her mouth. Then he lowered her into the pile of plastic boxes. Her skirt twisted up around her thighs and he pushed it up farther, peeled off her stockings, put his weight on her, kissed her.

It had been too long; she'd never make it through the foreplay. It didn't matter: he skipped it. His thrusting was slow, full of pauses. But it lasted long enough for the harsh light in the window to fade, for the adscreens to scream on and race around them and dissipate, for silence and softness to settle over them. Videobooks stuck to her back in sweaty patches but she felt untouched by anything else. Only him. She thought maybe this was making love: this urge to put your arms around your partner's neck and say his name.

* * *

Ben was back. This time she was determined to keep him. She sat in the library in the evenings playing and replaying Dolla Dare's, "How to Keep Your Guy," reciting Dolla's wisdoms: Don't burden him with your little worries. Don't sound weird on the phone, or, if you can't help it, explain immediately that it was just your hormones so your guy wouldn't think you were secretly a psycho-bitch or that you thought *he'd* done something wrong.

Then there was the scene with Dolla's sexy little cousin Dillie, standing in a cinnabar teddy in front of an anatomy chart, while Dolla explained that men and women have different chemistries and that's why men get bored with just one woman. In the video, Dolla recruited Dillie as a surprise treat for her guy, which, as Dolla explained, was a good way to keep him. "Take control!" cheered Dolla. "Be empowered! Don't let him get bored with your relationship! Show him you're full of sexy little surprises—that you understand his nature." Dillie Dare had long lush mounds of kinky curly red-orange hair, which Arel had always thought clashed with that red teddy.

Arel didn't especially like that part and thought of asking Ben if he minded being with just her, but that would sound too much like relationship talk. Guys didn't like that.

But she was careful to follow the rest of Dolla's advice—careful not to be a bother, not babbling on and on about her little problems—like she didn't have enough money to buy food. She learned how to sneak food—one cracker out of each box, the smallest carrot out of the bag, paper-thin slices of cheese. She learned how to press the toothpaste tube evenly, with the palms of her hands, so it wouldn't look used. Ben didn't notice. He was preoccupied with something on his computer—something "conceptual." She was careful not to bother him while he worked.

Every day she cleaned his apartment and sorted his junk mail: the new virtual adventures from Holoco, the new anti-spill cup lids from Holoco, the new junk mail sorter service from Holoco. She found no more disc mailers from the Aslow Actioneers and couldn't believe she'd ever been suspicious of him, of *Ben*. *Her* Ben. He was different, he was good.

Every night they made love, touching every part of each other, their bodies pressed tight and his face against hers. Then they would fall asleep, Arel holding him, her breasts against his back, her legs curled up under his.

*   *   *

Every day she waited for the Holoco High job to start. Ramy could call at any moment, Kyler warned her, so she stayed by Ben's apartment phone, watching daytime TV and sneaking food. She sprawled on the lumpy mattress, watched reruns of "Movers and Shakers" at 10:30, "Real People Videos" at 11:00, "The New Murder Court" at 11:30. At noon, "Dare To Talk" came on.

During the commercials she trotted into the kitchen. In the refrigerator door was a bottle of creamy broccoli and onion salad dressing, half empty, the level sinking behind the label, which was perfect—he'd never notice that some was missing. She poured the dressing into a tablespoon and licked it off. Then found her double-jumbo diet Coke on the top shelf, old and watery and almost gone. She pried off the plastic lid, gazed down at the dark gleaming surface, iceless, but still with a bubble floating by. She gulped down the whole thing, then went to the faucet, filled the cup with water, and drank that too. Turned the faucet back on and let the water run over her hands. Felt it run, so wet. It would raise his water bill by several dollars but he might not notice. He might not mind.

Back in the living room "Dare To Talk" came on. Arel sprawled and watched Dolla's face glide across the screen in different geometric shapes, looking surprised, sarcastic, serious, sentimental. Then Dolla appeared behind the studio audience, did the Dolla dance down the steps, jumped into place with her feet planted apart, Catwoman-style, in her black pants and frosted melon pirate shirt, and introduced her first guest: Dr. Aslow. Some people cheered—Aslow fans in the audience.

On stage a lone harsh beam clicked on and there he was, seated in a too-low metal chair, his knees ridiculously high. Yet his face was powdered and composed, more controlled than in his video. His artificial hands were in two loose curls on the arms of the chair. He smiled and looked restful as Dolla paced in front of the stage and shot mean little smirks around the studio.

"That's right guys!" she bellowed. "He's back! And he's *still* talking about *God!*" A burst of polite laughter erupted. She kept pacing—it was distracting—and her eyes kept springing wide open, hyperalert to the audience response. "Now, Dr. A," she said in an oh-so-innocent tone. "I was wondering. . . " She pressed her lips into a thin tight grin, rolled her eyes to one side: "I mean I, I, I understand. . . that Satan walks among us today. . . " Rolled her eyes to the other side. "I was just wondering, though. . . " Pausing, pausing, really too long, rather amateurish. "Are you sure he didn't walk away with your *brain?*" The audience laughed slightly. Her timing was off. "Come on, Dr. A—what *is* the story?" She smirked with one side of her face. "You're going all over the country with your little bag of videos telling people that God is talking to you. What's the story?"

Dr. Aslow leaned smilingly forward. "Not everyone is able to hear the voice of the Lord, Dolla."

"And some people hear all kinds of voices!" The audience laughed louder at this and she bounced an outstretched arm upward to turn up the volume.

"You're a very funny lady, Dolla, but I know that deep inside you're unhappy. I can see that. I can look into every face in this studio and see the unhappiness. And I can tell people *why* they're unhappy."

"Look out!" Dolla threw up her hands. "It's Satan!" She spun around, whipped her head back and forth. God this joke was old. Dolla was too old, thirty-eight or forty, looking tired—tired of herself. By contrast, Dr. Aslow looked cheerful and purposeful, though he was surely past sixty.

He began: "It's like this, Dolla. Life in America has become unbearable. We try to be happy but we get nowhere, trapped in this meaningless dark pit we call life. And do you know why?"

Dolla replied in a vicious bouncing tone: "Because Satan walks among us today?"

He replied genially, "No no, Dolla. It's because we work too much."

Suddenly everyone was dead silent, including Dolla. The smiling Aslow remained on screen, the camera man too stunned to pan. No one had ever said this out loud before, and on TV. Eventually Dolla's voice was heard: "What?"

"You see," continued Aslow, "most Americans have to work two jobs just to make ends meet. We don't have enough time to shop, vacation, or just watch TV. We don't have enough time to spend with our families and friends—many of us don't even *have* families and friends, because we don't have time. Tell us, Dolla, are *you* in a meaningful relationship with a man?"

The camera remained unflatteringly long on Dolla, who couldn't answer, the significance of it sinking in: even the author of "How to Keep Your Guy" couldn't keep a guy. Finally Dolla blurted: "What are you talking about? What happened to Satan?"

"Oh, Satan is with us." He tipped forward. "Why do you suppose we have to work so much? Why do we never have enough money?"

Dolla looked suspicious, but everyone else wanted to know, strained forward. Including Arel. Aslow smiled kindly, then, calmly: "Because we are constantly being robbed. The homeless steal from us, and I don't just mean mugging us and breaking into our homes. Think about it. They shoplift—forcing stores to raise prices to cover the loss. They cause our insurance premiums to skyrocket—just by being in our neighborhoods! They push people off bridges onto the highway and we get stuck in traffic and get docked an hour's pay! We get caught in crossfire and end up with huge medical bills! Our co-workers get killed on the street, resulting in lost productivity for the company, which means lower profits and less money for us! How much of your income do you suppose you lose every day as a result of these homeless criminals in our country?"

"I don't know."

"Thirty-three percent of our money lost—every day!" The volume of his voice had risen to a boom. "What would *you* do with thirty-three percent more money!"

In the long stunned silence Aslow regained his calm tone, spoke again in the hypnotic tone of past videos: "Dolla, let me explain this to you." The back of Dolla's head nodded. "Our nation is a great nation, because our people are good people. Are you following me?" Nod. "Now, good people are people who do good things. They get to work on time, hold down their jobs, pay their bills. Are you following me?" Nod. "Unfortunately, we also have in our great nation a growing number of bad people—people who don't pay their bills, who get evicted, who steal our money, our possessions, and sometimes our loved ones." His tone intensified: "These bad people are a threat to the good people like us—to our great nation—to our very economy! And the threat grows with every passing minute! This is what God tells me, Dolla: Satan is at work in our great nation. God says to me, tell the people! Tell the people of the threat!" He began to rock, the powder on his face dissolving into a weird sheen. "You see Dolla, my son's death did have meaning. He died so that I could hear the word of the Lord. He died so that *you* could be saved." He lurched forward, boomed: "Satan walks among us, Dolla Dare! But the Lord reigns! Let both shores rejoice! Thick darkness surrounds us, but righteousness and justice are ours! Fire goes before Him and consumes His foes on every side and the mountains melt like wax before Him because he loves the righteous and hates the wicked with His very soul and on the wicked he will rain fiery coals and burning sulfur and they will be pulverized, pulverized, pulverized by His scorching wind!"

Then there was no sound, and Arel began to ache. Dolla let out a short shrill laugh, but no one laughed with her. Things didn't seem funny anymore. Things just seemed strange. No one had ever talked like this before—the way God might really talk.

Aslow rocked forward, hugged himself, straightened up, stared off, the shadows of his face supernatural in Dolla's joke lighting. The silence and confusion grew awkward, and Dolla cleared her throat.

"Well Dr. Aslow I must confess—*confess*—" she laughed, alone, "that I have someone waiting backstage who thinks you're full of donkey dung!" Into the camera she said: "Stay with us you pea-heads at home for that incredible sexy hunk of adorable doctor—Dr. Hampton Drane!" She whooped up applause as the cue music played.

"Hampton Drane!" Arel called out, as though he might hear, and bounced. Waited through commercials for disposable vacuum cleaners, ziplock garbage bags, genetically engineered rubberbands that would never break, the Dolla Dare show. When Dolla returned the audience was in midroar, Hampton Drane gliding across the stage with a big smile, radiant, unaffected, with the promise of normalizing everything. His smile brightened and the cheers grew louder. He was almost as old as Aslow but more handsome, with a full head of hair that was silver, not gray, and an effortless walk, and real hands. He was given a chair that was taller and more padded than Aslow's. When Dolla's joke stage lighting diffused, Aslow's clothes and face looked less creased, more human. Hampton Drane sat beside him, and Arel saw that they were wearing almost the same suit—burgundy with twinkling highlights, in almost the same style.

"Hello you hunky Hampton!" Dolla bellowed and he looked uncomfortable. "How are you?" she gurgled, crawled up on stage in front of him, wiggled her butt like a cat about to pounce. The audience laughed and clapped. Hampton Drane smiled and pretended to recoil—or pretended to pretend to.

"I'm fine," he said, then waited for her to climb down off the stage.

"But I do want to clarify that I never said Dr. Aslow was full of donkey dung." The audience laughed and clapped again—his way of talking seemed so unrehearsed. "I said I *took issue*—specifically with his scheme and his claim that it was divinely inspired."

"Oh, say it again," Dolla crooned. "*Divinely*. Don't you love it, guys!" Applause.

"Well thank you Dolla but I think this is a pretty serious matter," he replied and everyone stopped clapping to politely pay attention. "The Paterco board has appointed a committee to do a cost-analysis of Aslow's Action plan—which is in essence a plan to imprison a large segment of our population—which is both un-Constitutional and antithetical to the teaching of Christ, as I understand it."

Dolla's expression hardened into boredom and suspicion.

"Oh no!" Arel said to him. "You're sounding too smart!"

Dolla glanced at someone in the booth at the back of the studio. Then turned and raised an arm overhead, flapped her hand. "Oh, perfessor, perfessor, I have a question!"

Warily: "Yes?"

"Uh, uh, could I, like, go to the bathroom, like, for the rest of the show?" Laughter. She continued in a friendly tone: "Hampton, what *are* you talking about?"

"Social responsibility!" he bellowed. "Our obligation to one another as members of a democratic society. Long ago our grandparents accepted that responsibility. We took care of those less fortunate than ourselves and found meaning in those acts—"

"Oh, oh, I see, so what you're saying is—what the *hell* are you saying?" More laughter.

Aslow cut in. "I'll tell you what he's saying! He's saying bring back Big Brother Government!"

The audience gasped. Dolla was suddenly worried. "What do you mean? How can anyone do that?"

"Oh, it can happen Dolla," Aslow continued. "If we aren't careful, *history* can repeat itself."

"What are you talking about? What history?" Dolla said, upset.

Aslow went on: "Did you know that long ago Big Brother Government used to give money to people who were too lazy to work—*our* money! *Tax* dollars!"

"What do you mean? Why would they do that?"

Hampton Drane intervened, "I think I can clarify the issues by—"

"Because Big Brother is evil, Dolla!" Aslow roared. "We all know that! What we don't know is that Big Brother continues to interfere in our lives—restricting us from taking action to protect our money and our property! Forcing us to go through all the bureaucratic rigmarole of proving that criminals are criminals! Does that make sense to you Dolla?"

Dolla's surprised face appeared. "No!"

Hampton Drane began, "I think we're not appreciating the—"

But Aslow was in a private conversation with Dolla: "We've made tremendous progress over the past fifty years. We are almost completely free of government. Almost—not completely. We need to take the final steps to become the great liberated nation that God intended us to be—free of all government restriction—free to make money and create a true Paradise on earth!" The audience applauded and Aslow kept talking: "Dolla, sometimes I think they ought to teach history in school, so our young people won't forget how truly difficult life was for our grandparents." Hampton Drane's mouth opened but Aslow continued: "Our ancestors scraped and sacrificed to make this country God's country—America—Paradise on earth! But the work is not yet finished! We must weed our garden. Every single homeless scum must go! Believe in God! Do God's work! And all the riches of heaven and earth are yours!"

A brief silence, then a loud sigh: "May I talk now?" Hampton Drane said.

"Of course," said Aslow, reasonably.

"Recently I received in the mail a remarkable screenplay for my next movie—'The Hampton Drane Story, Part Two.' It was a story of compassion for the homeless—an amazing story."

"My story!" Arel yelled at the screen.

"In this amazing story, the hero actually invites deformed homeless people to live in his home. This story reminded me of the religious parables my grandmother told me when I was a young boy, and so I started reading the Bible, and I found a very different God from the one Aslow talks about. I found the teachings of Christ to be about mercy and compassion, especially toward society's outcasts, for instance—"

"Wait a minute—" Dolla said. "You've been *reading* the *Bible?*" Some people laughed. "The *book?*" More people laughed. To Aslow: "Is that what you've been doing too?"

"I don't have to, Dolla. God speaks directly to me. Entire Bible passages appear in my mind—"

Hampton Drane almost snorted, "I'm sure you're just recalling them from your father's sermons when you were a child."

Dolla shrieked, "His father was a *priest?*"

"A minister," Hampton Drane was growing impatient.

"Say no more!" Dolla looked happy again. "Please!"

Now he was annoyed. "Look, this is serious." To Aslow: "Rounding people up and putting them in jail isn't going to bring back your son." Then to Dolla and the audience: "Listen. Listen. I have my own plan. Let's call it the Drane plan. Let's do get the homeless off the streets. But instead of putting them in prison, I say we give them a home with us. Each one of us can take in one homeless person—feed him, clothe him, help him find a job—shelter him until he is able to get a place of his own." He looked so earnest, pitched forward and squinting passionately into the camera lens. Dolla's face appeared on screen, twisted into it's funny-frown. "I know it sounds a little impossible," he persisted, "but if you think about it awhile, it starts to sound less strange. It will all be in the Hampton Drane Story, Part Two, which I am currently producing myself—"

"Yes!" Arel screamed.

"Ah," Dolla said, "so *that's* the deal." Relieved. "You're here plugging your new movie."

"No, no—" But he was drowned out by the cue music.

Dolla said to the TV viewers: "Don't go anywhere you fart-heads out there in fart-head land. Audience reactions when we come back."

Arel waited through more commercials, became entranced by a giant talking sock, which complained to a shoe that its owner didn't use enough Static-Offs in the dryer, and it ended up squashed in a big wad of shirts and towels. The shoe and the sock began to march around a pair of woman's ankles with signs: "Stop Sock Abuse!"

When the show returned, Dolla was strutting down the center aisle in a nun dress, tight and short, and a nun hat with wings flopping on either side. A snare drum beat in time with her walk. Aslow and Hampton Drane flashed on screen, bewildered, then off again. Dolla got half way down the aisle, grabbed an audience member by the necktie and shoved her microphone in his face. "What do you think of all this stuff?" she asked, but the guy was too awe-struck to answer, standing so close to Dolla Dare. So she pushed him back down and pulled up a short fat woman by the sleeve. "What do you think?"

The woman was sweating but managed to speak: "Well, I think I know what Dr. Drane is trying to say. I think he's trying to say that, well, people should be nicer to one another."

"Oh, was that it?"

"Yes, yes, and I agree. I mean, I think people should be nicer to each other, don't you? I get so mad when other drivers shoot at me."

"Hey yeah—that pisses me off too," Dolla agreed and shouted: "You hear that, world? Be nice to me you butt-brains! I *deserve* it!" She continued down the aisle, shouting at various audience members to be nice to her. Then she grabbed an older man by the lapel and barked. "Well? Let's have your opinion."

"I don't know about all this religion stuff but I think Dr. Aslow is right about those homeless people stealing from us! And I think we should all stop and think about that history repeating itself thing—I mean, why can't we put these losers in jail? Who says we can't? Some bureaucrat somewhere with some list of *rules!*"

"Here here," she said and grabbed a good-looking man with piles of creamy hair. "How about you baby?" She began her sexy cat gurgle, ran a hand down the front of his shirt. He said: "All I know is, I can't get ahead! I try everything! I work my ass off, and I still can't get ahead!"

"Oh poor *baby*. Come on over to my place and I'll see you get some head!"

The audience roared. Dolla reached over several people toward another good-looking man, but a woman jumped up and got in the way.

"You know what I think!" the woman shrieked. "I think we should lock up all these homeless scums and make the streets safe again!" The women in the audience cheered. "I'm frightened to death to walk to my car after work! I could be robbed and whacked up with a machete and scattered all over the side of the Eisenhower! I want these scum dicks off the street!"

Dolla repeated, "Here here," a bit apathetic, and moved on to a young man who wasn't as good looking up close as he seemed from the end of the aisle.

He started to talk, in a voice that seemed familiar to Arel: "Well, basically I think the whole country is really a fucked up place, you know? The place is brutal. I used to get really depressed. Every morning it was like, basically, I can't even get out of bed. It was brutal. But then I saw Dr. Aslow's new video and I learned about God and it's like, now I can get out of bed every morning, because I don't care anymore that no one else gives a shit about me, because God does. Because, basically, God is my father, you know? Not that prick who just fucked my mother and that makes him my father. That shithead tried to kill me once, 'cause I was so fucked up. That whole thing. Brutal. But then I learned about God—God is my *real* father, he's *real*, and everywhere you go, he's *there,* and he *loves* me. And if you're good enough you get to go to heaven and be with God your real father. But you gotta be holy and do God's work, like Dr. Aslow says. You gotta make the grade."

"Thank you *so* much for *that*," said Dolla, mashing him back down into his seat.

"And one more thing I want to say, Dolla," he called out from his seat. "I think that dress you're wearing is basically an affront to God." People cheered at this. The camera caught Aslow's face, cheering along, the artificial hands applauding. Dolla smirked, wiggled back to the center aisle, posed, said, "I think *some* men would disagree with that!" and then the men applauded, and some women too—applauded everything, anything—and the end song came on. "Good-bye you bowel brains in TV land!" Dolla yelled and ran up and down the aisle, snagging men out of their seats and showing off her dress, tipping them backwards and kissing them with her tongue, one leg shoved in between theirs.

Arel turned off the TV and called Ben's machine: "Hey guess what! I'm famous! Well not really but I could have been. Hampton Drane was on TV and he didn't actually say my name but it was me he was talking about so he could have said my name! Right there on TV!" She stopped talking, wished he had the erasable type of machine. "Well I'll explain later."

She hung up and walked in tight circles around the living room, full of plans. She'd call Hampton Drane. She'd begin work immediately on Part Three. It would be brilliant, even more brilliant than Part Two. She pulled out her miniwriter, kept walking in circles. "Part Three, Three, Three. . . " Three parts would make it a trilogy, and people liked that. "Three, Three. . . " All she needed was to figure out what it would be about. She walked, walked.

Nothing came to mind. She sat down. "Okay. Think." *Think*. She sat, waited for something to pop into her head. Was that how she had thought of ideas before? "Okay," she said again, as though this word might dislodge a torrent of other brilliant ones. What was *likely* to happen next? What was *plausible? Think, brain*. The brain was silent, not blank so much as black— in some very dark shadow. Maybe she was thinking too much. "Be a doer!" she yelled at herself, poised her hands over the miniwriter. Nothing.

She got up again, wandered into the kitchen, around the kitchen. Something was making her restless. She strayed into the bathroom and looked into the mirror wall. Her face in mirrors was always disappointing: always the same, shiny and lined, never smoothed or painted, exfoliated, airbrushed or iced. She tried turning slightly, tried to think she was okay, but couldn't help thinking she just wasn't right: couldn't help thinking everyone else's thoughts.

She was silent for awhile, then said out loud to her reflection: "What's likely to happen in Part Three is Hampton Drane gets murdered in his bed by all those wretched deranged homeless people he takes in."

She stared at her reflection, which did not disagree. "The truth is," she went on slowly, "Hampton Drane's idea is the stupidest thing I've ever heard in my entire life!" She took a breath. "The truth is, Dr. Aslow's plan makes *much* more sense." There *was* too much crime on the street. It *was* committed by homeless people. People who don't earn money steal it. That was common sense. If there were no homeless people, the streets would be much safer. Her mother would still be alive. Hampton Drane was nuts. "Take in filthy deranged thieving homeless scums to live with us? They'd murder us! We'd be *lucky* if they just robbed us. And even if there were some honest homeless people to take in, who had enough space? Who could afford it?" How many mouths could you feed with one bottle of diet creamy broccoli and onion salad dressing?

Her thoughts raced on: Hampton Drane had gotten the idea from her screenplay but had evidently missed the fact that he was the only one taking in homeless people—him with his plenty of rooms and food and security guards. And so in the end he doesn't get robbed and murdered but that was easy—that was fiction—what does fiction have to do with reality?

The face in the mirror glared at her, an incredulous bystander, an accusing conscience. "What!" she yelled at it. She could make it turn slightly one way, then the other, could make it forget Hampton Drane and think about its features too close together, its nose too long, its creases deepening, its hair drooping. She could trick it into thinking different thoughts: with a few hair puffers and a tube of red or raven or buttercup blond, she could look more like she was supposed to. With a few tucks and nips—less nose and more mouth, sleeker cheekbones, a tighter chin, she could look in the mirror and look just right. All she needed was a good plastic surgeon.

"Shit!" She sneered at the sneering reflection. "Why did I ever write that stupid story?"

She covered both eyes with her hands and saw darkness instead of herself, saw white dots against the darkness, like snow on a night sky. Saw a face, raw, and translucent hands. Saw a man do a bright dance round and round, herself in a lazy pose by her car. The distance between them in that last instant, when the burning wrestling finally stopped, took effort to main-

tain. Driving away, it took energy to stick her thoughts here, there, anywhere but on the sight of her own hands in a white grip on the wheel,
reminding her of his. Six and a half months ago.

But if she encountered him now, surely she'd do the same thing. Kill
or be killed. According to Hampton Drane she was supposed to walk up
with a pleasant smile and invite him home to live with her. How could
Hampton Drane think this was anything but insane?

How could he? She thought about his face on the screen, searching,
open, intelligent—the sanest face she'd ever seen. What did he know that
she didn't know? What had he learned from the old books? Why did his plan
seem so crazy to her and everyone else, but not to him?

She opened her eyes and watched herself begin to smile. "Yeah," said
her reflected self, smiling, to the self standing small and alone in the outside
world. "Yeah," the face encouraged, and she stood straighter, watched herself grow taller, stronger, determined again. Her task now clear: Find
Hampton Drane.

four

For three weeks she tried to reach Hampton Drane. His private numbers were inaccessible, of course; she had to zip a message to his public site. Then she had to wait for a reply, which took a week, which thanked her for being a fan and regretted that Dr. Drane couldn't respond personally to all his wonderful fans. Apparently no human had even read her message. She tried again, marking the next note "PERSONAL," and in another week came the same standard reply.

"Shit!"

In the meantime, she tried to have ideas for Hampton Drane, Part Three. She'd dug through the boxes of books to find something about religion, but all she could find was a Bible—a huge heavy thing with minuscule print and narrow margins and a strange extra space down the middle of all the pages that turned out to be another margin. Her eyes ran down the first page, transmitted no meaning to her brain. She tried reading aloud: "Let there be an expense—*expanse*—between the waters to separate water from water so God made the expanse and separated the water under the expanse from the water above it." This not only confused her, it made her thirsty.

"Expanse," she said out loud, thinking perhaps she didn't know the definition of this word. She accessed Mini-Meanings for the convenient, easy-to-read definition—"A lot of"—put her head down. Why did nothing fit together? She sat up, cleared her throat, trudged on: "and so God called the dry ground land and the gathered waters he called seas." Nine hundred and forty-four more pages to go.

Every evening she forced herself through pages, the sounds of the words streaming through her brain and evaporating, cutting no deep ravines, not connecting to the existing landscape. Until Dr. Aslow no one had talked much about God. She recalled her mother saying something about organized religion but not about God in particular. Eight hundred eighty-four pages to go. She would not lose heart.

She flipped ahead to the middle, then passed the middle, to trick her brain into thinking she was almost done. She began to read again—short sections with little titles that started like stories but were instead about seeds and weeds and vines and sheep. Her attention was caught by a mention of tax collectors, after which Jesus Christ says, "It is not the healthy who need a doctor, but the sick," which didn't seem terribly profound, but then he says, "Go and learn what this means," as though it meant something different, and she was lost again, adrift on this expanse of syllables—sins, yeast, seeds, weeds vines and sheep.

Then she came to a passage she liked:

> the Father will give you another Counselor to be with you forever—the Spirit of truth. The world cannot accept him, because it neither sees him nor knows him. But you know him, for he lives with you and will be in you. I will not leave you as orphans. I will come to you. Before long, the world will not see me anymore, but you will see me. Because I live, you also will live.

She concentrated on it, memorized it: *I will not leave you as orphans.* She understood how Aslow could go around sounding so much like God talking—the language of books gets into your head, just like the sound of TV shows and adscreens and self-help videobooks, and talks in you until it's no longer a foreign presence, but you. *Another Counselor to be with you forever. . . the world cannot accept him. . . but you know him.* Like Hampton Drane, she thought, and made a note on her miniwriter: "HD could be this Counselor guy."

She put the Bible down, stared out the window. Black asphalt swam in late August haze and she was sweating, the air conditioner humming but emitting no cool streams. She picked up the book again, came to a section about unsalty salt, put it down for the evening and turned on the new Aslow channel.

"The Saviors" was about to start. She sat through the teasers for upcoming interviews with happy Aslow converts, old westerns, another remake of *1984,* and the infomercials for antidepressants, get-rich-quick videobooks,

Flame-Offs and other defense weapons. When the Aslow channel first aired, there were no commercials. Aslow funded it entirely with his own personal money. But as the ratings went up companies got interested and began to buy time. Now Dr. Aslow was a multitrillionaire.

"The Saviors" began and Arel sat ready to take notes on her miniwriter. She intended to "analyze" it—to notice things and write them down—something her mother would have done. The show began and Arel typed, "The Saviors all look exactly alike."

The point, she knew, was not to search for the subtleties, but to note what was most obvious and recognize it as odd.

She gazed at the screen as the Saviors soared down from the sky and formed an orderly line, all with huge shoulders and narrow hips and yellow semi-circles for hair. They were sexy, she realized. Their faces were always very serious. Only their mouths ever moved. She thought they resembled a young Dr. Aslow or maybe his son, though his son had been dark.

She typed, "They're all young, strong, blond men."

There was a nerd—a skinny guy who helped them sometimes by mixing up chemicals for explosives, but he was too cowardly to join the Savior team. Sometimes there were girlfriends—different ones in each episode—who were always easily confused. Of course there were plenty of dead women in the crowd scenes, and of course there was Devilla Dare, the garish aging woman in black and too much makeup who was not really a Scum but at times seemed worse, going around with her camera crew, talking too loud, getting in the way and thwarting the Saviors' attempts to rescue the hard-working citizens of Asville from the Scums. At the end of each episode, as the sun set over the now-safer city, Devilla got hungry and chopped off an arm or a leg from a guy on her camera crew, and sat munching on it as the end credits rolled. "Devilla eats body parts," Arel typed, not quite knowing what to make of it.

The episode began with the standard happy family out for a family day of shopping, swinging their purchases cheerfully down the street. "Character types—" she noted on her miniwriter, "Chatty dad, smiling mom, bright young boy, preverbal girl." Their chirpy chatter blended in with the tinkly music so that the writers didn't have to try to figure out specifically what a happy family might be saying to one another. Then the camera panned back to reveal the dark evil outlines of the Scums forming their pack, preparing to dart out, knock the family down, steal their wallets and their merchandise and shoot them all in the head. Sometimes they actually did this, and sometimes the Saviors stopped them just in time, which made you want to watch and see which was going to happen. Tonight the ominous music hummed up the scale and diffused into a heavenly tune as the camera raced up the side of a building to the Saviors, perched in open windows, ready to sail down on their white cape wings and pulverize the Scums with concealed eternal torches. But at any moment Devilla could appear and give away the Saviors' position and the family could get blown away after all.

The library phone rang and she jumped. "Hello?" she said, eyes still on the screen.

Ben's voice said, "Turn on Flashnews."

"Hi Ben!"

"Turn on Flashnews."

"Why? I'm watching—"

"I know you are. But turn to Flashnews."

She changed the channel. Men in football uniforms were skydiving from hot-air balloons. "What is it?"

"Damn, you missed it. Keep watching. It'll come around again."

"What? What?" Three headless corpses appeared, danced, disappeared. Then Aslow came on the screen, his face tossed back in a huge smile, then a row of grinning executives, then a blinking red neon number, a red white and blue coupon waving at the top of a flag pole, rats scampering down an alley. A golden horn dancing with a silver spoon. Then cheerleaders kissing football players climbing into hot-air balloons. "Is it over? What was it?"

"It was the Paterco board of directors adopting the Aslow Action Plan. They're paying $29.99 for every homeless person you bring in plus with every fifth person you get a ten dollar gift certificate to any Paterco store." She didn't reply. He added, "Very win-win."

"How did you figure all that out from that one bite?"

"I didn't, really, I got the newzip."

Silence. "You subscribe to the Aslow newzip line?"

More silence.

"Ben?"

"What did you say?"

"I said—" Stopped. Her stomach twisted: sometimes he was so odd. "Nothing." Remembering to trust people was hard. She wrote a note to herself on her miniwriter, "Just trust Ben!"

"You okay?" he asked.

"Of course."

"Can you come home early?"

"I don't know." She heard her voice sound odd.

"Close up early, come home, we'll talk."

"About what?"

"You're worried. Don't worry. Like Kyler said, no one's gonna spend their time trying to catch homeless people. Not cost-effective, too danger-ous, and anyway, it really doesn't apply to you."

"I didn't think it did. Did you think I thought it did? Why would I think it did?"

"I was just thinking of you."

"Oh," she said. Did he mean, in a considerate way? "Thank you." Who knew how he'd meant it?

He replied, "Okay, well, I better go." Sounding weird.

"What are you doing?"

"Working."

On what? she wanted to ask. But he never answered.

"Bye," he said and hung up, without waiting for her "bye."

She sat restless through the last half of "The Saviors," making no notes, hardly watching at all. Then waited through another show, waited long enough, and closed the library early.

* * *

She crept in soundless and found him tilted over his keyboard, his forehead propped up in one hand. When the door closed behind her, he whipped around, closed his document.

"Did I startle you?"

"No, no. You're early," he replied. His face too white in the grainy pud-dle of light cast by the only lamp that was on. Slowly, he reached up, clicked off the lamp, and she stood and he sat in complete darkness.

"What are you doing?" she asked and he replied, "What are you doing?"

Suddenly frightened: "Ben?"

The orange glare through the window began to lighten large objects. She kept her eyes on the spot where his shape would appear, kept them there, not wanting to blink and miss the moment when he would come clear. Then she heard his chair squeal and his few soft footsteps to the win-dow. His outline was strong against the tangerine sky.

"Look," he whispered. "Come here. Look!"

She took a few steps toward him, stopped. Through the window the two newest moonboards hovered, surprised uneven eyes at the glass. The first was a red and yellow ad for Mrs. Mom's banana butter-cream fudgy cookies, a Sunco subsidiary, the other a yellow and red ad for the See-Me Exercise Club, another Sunco subsidiary. The exercise ad flashed pictures of people running on treadmills and riding stationary bicycles. She said, "That is ironic."

"What? No. Look *between* them. See it? That's not an airplane."

"It isn't?" She walked closer to the glass.

"It's a star." He sounded serious.

"You've never seen a star before?"

"You're not seeing it."

"I can see it." She looked harder. "It's right there."

"Mmmm." Disappointed but throaty, sexy. Mmm—a sound he only made in the dark. He was different in the dark. But she supposed she was too. Invisibility made you freer, reckless enough to speak your thoughts out loud. "Ben."

"Mmmm?"

"What on earth are you working on?"

"Oh, different projects."

"Well, for example, what in particular?"

He sighed. "It's private, Arel. I don't think you'd like it."

"How do you know? Maybe I would. Give me a chance. Like, this extra computer here, that you're building. Why are you doing that?"

Reluctantly: "With that I can keep my own site running—I can't afford a site from Paterco, Sunco, or Holoco."

"Okay—" It was an answer, at least. "A site for what?" Silence. "Like, maybe, one of Kyler's schemes?"

Silence. Then, "Yeah. Yeah."

"Okay," she said, trying to sound positive. "Okay." More positive. The more you say okay, the more okay things are. "Want to know what I'm doing?"

"I know what you're doing." The shadows of his face shifted into a smile. "You're reading old books again. I can tell."

She smiled, relaxed: Ben knew her. Everything was fine. "You'll never guess what though."

"What?"

"The Bible."

His face was surprised but still smiling.

"It's even harder than those other books," she went on. "And it seems to be written by a bunch of guys who don't remember stuff very well, so you start thinking maybe they don't know what they're talking about, and then you have to wonder, if there is a God, why didn't he just write his own damn book? Did you ever believe in God?"

Ben's form shrugged.

"But then you start thinking, all these people all through history believed this stuff. There almost has to be something to it. It's, well, kind of convincing. But then you think, well, these guys could have made it all up. But then you have to think, why would they do that? There's nothing else like the Bible—how did they know it would sell? But if there is a God, why all the mystery? Why doesn't he just come out and say hey look, here I am! so people wouldn't have a bunch of doubts and we wouldn't have to be trusting all these various *guys*."

She stopped, considered it. Maybe that was the point. Maybe that's what Hampton Drane knew that she couldn't get hold of—trust. She looked at Ben's form, still and serene. She went on: "And I know you're going to think I'm nuts, but I was reading this stuff about a Holy Spirit, who goes around comforting people—doesn't that sound nice? And God says this Holy Spirit person walks among us but we don't know it, and so I started thinking, maybe Hampton Drane could be this Holy Spirit, in Hampton Drane Part Three, and then I started thinking, well, what if Hampton Drane really is the Holy Spirit, for real!"

Long pause. His face turned and tilted back, his eyebrows crept up.

She said: "Not that I'm becoming some weirdo religious fanatic. I sound like a weirdo religious fanatic, don't I? Those two words always go together—religious, fanatic. Religious fanatic. Religiousfanatic. Say it real fast three times—*religiousfanaticreligiousfanatic*—it's easy!"

He laughed his sane-sounding laugh, loud and unscrolling. She began to laugh too—small hard gulps of air knocked out of her lungs. Laughing in the dark with Ben made her feel larger, more permanent; it felt like hope for the future. He slid the back of his hand down her arm, around her elbow, to her hand. Held her hand.

He whispered, "Let's go to bed." They walked over to the couch, threw off the pillows and unfolded the bed. Then she knocked him backwards onto the bad, straddled him. The room was dim, cool, quiet, remote from the eyes of cameras and bulbs and people on screens. She leaned forward, kissed him, kissed him, as he squirmed out of his clothes and peeled off hers. She ran her hands along the tops of his small hard shoulders, and there was nothing in her head but the feel of his skin, muscle under the skin, bone under the muscle. She began to slide herself along his dick, up the shaft and down, until he took it in one hand and pointed it up and slid it in. Nothing in her head but the feel of him: no pictures of frat party orgies or visiting plumbers with enormous dicks or Dolla and Dillie Dare. Sex with Ben was personal. She kept the rhythm slow, leaned forward, slid her arms around underneath him, and he rolled her over on her back, pressed her knees to her shoulders and started to pound. Paused to put a pillow behind her head. Then he came, sprawled on her, breathed slowly, limbs sinking, though not too heavy, falling asleep. She rolled him off her.

"Mmm, sorry," he said. Falling asleep. He twitched when he fell asleep. His arms and legs jerked, like the legs of a dog dreaming of chasing something, or of being chased. She put an arm across his chest to keep him still, smiled.

Then lay awake. Next week she would start the Holoco High job, after the three-day weekend summer break, and she wanted to tell Ben about it. She didn't like deceiving him, didn't want him not knowing she was going to be there, just on the other side of his two-way mirror. But she didn't want to admit she'd lied before. How would he be able to trust her? He'd lie awake in the night wondering if he could trust her, or she'd worry that he would, and all the unsaid stuff in their heads would make them fall silent, look at each other with tense lonely glances.

She rolled onto her stomach and felt her body sink into the lumps of the old mattress. Anyway, said her thoughts, in "How to Keep Your Guy," Dolla said having secrets was okay. Getting too close was unhealthy: people need to keep a distance.

*   *   *

The halls of Holoco Pre-Exec High were a bright smooth peacock blue with surreptitious curves that turned you in hidden directions. The empty corridor knew she was there—the wall sensors tracking her path so that the ceiling-high wall ads could flash as she passed by: ads for teen shows and teen show stars in ads for blue jeans, acne medicine, mini-Flame-Offs. No real people were visible anywhere, but when she got to the main office she heard a gasp, then a click. Then an arm reached out from a supply closet door and grabbed her wrist and yanked her inside.

"What are you doing out in the open?" Ramy scolded.

"Sorry."

Surrounding them were shelves piled with promotional materials in blinding primary colors. Arel picked up a flyer for prospective customers explaining the advantages of sending their special teen to Holoco Pre-Exec

High. Inside was a chart of the annual salaries of Holoco Pre-Exec Alumni, printed over an artistically blurred photo of a young man handing his old dad the keys to a new Ford Meltdown with a giant bow on the hood. Underneath the script read: "Your kid. Your best investment for the future."

Ramy pried an unmarked box off a bottom shelf, then maneuvered it around the floor with the pointy point of her shoe. Behind a false box front was a secret lever that opened a secret door behind a false box front.

"This is exciting," Arel said.

"Shh."

The passageway was dim and sterile, lined with stark metal chairs spaced every several feet in front of the two-way classroom mirrors, left over from the days of live teacher inspectors.

"Now," Ramy pulled out her tiny note-screen. "What's your sellfone number?"

"Oh, you know, you wouldn't believe what happened to my sellfone. . . "

Ramy stared at her.

"I was crossing the street, and it fell out of my pocket, and a bus ran over it. Like, just now."

Ramy snorted and handed Arel one of her extra ones. "Now that's school property. It's not to leave the school grounds. I expect you to take proper care of it."

"Yes ma'am!" Arel cried out. A telephone! She began accessing Hotnews, Celebrity Line, Horoscopes. Ramy reached over with a jagged fingernail and turned it off, then nudged Arel into the passageway and began to leave.

"Hey wait," Arel said, "Aren't you coming along to show me what to do?"

"I have a breakfast meeting." Adding suspiciously, "Aren't you a self-motivated worker?"

The secret door closed and Arel was alone in the long gray soundless hall. She wished she could find Ben's classroom immediately, just to look at him through the window. Instead, she slid the phone into her suit pocket, next to her miniwriter, and crept down the corridor, plopped onto the first chair she came to, yanked open the flaps of a box. Inside were neat rows of minicameras, each encased in huge tough plastic cubes. On top was a direction sheet with lots of diagrams and easy-to-read text: "Step One. Take a camera out." She took one out and wrenched it out of its plastic armor. The camera itself was soft, strokable, nestling in the palm of her hand. She popped off the lens cap and looked into its eye. Under the lens was a "90."

"Shit." She'd have to replace these things every ninety minutes, when the film ran out.

Step Two: "Get the small red box out." The small red box was full of supergluey velcro strips for attaching the camera to the glass. "Will stick to concrete, plaster, beaverboard, formica, glass, cloth, leather, skin, and all other surfaces," said the box. She removed a strip with the very tip of her finger, pressed it onto the camera front, and whacked the camera onto the first window. Then looked through the lens into the empty room beyond and saw only the top of the wall and part of the ceiling. She tried to reposition the camera—pulled, twisted, wrenched, pounded, but the supergluey velcro strip was unbudgeable, the camera permanent. She kicked the wall and nudged the box down the corridor to the next window.

This classroom was lit and full of students. Arel gazed in. It had been sixteen years since she'd been in high school, but the classroom was basically the same: around the long perimeter was the line of yellow cubicles, each one angled so that the students couldn't see one another to cheat, each with a built-in desk and mini-screen. At the front of the room, between the dusty portraits of Charles Darwin and Horatio Alger, was the mega-screen listing all fifty-five students' names in rank order of the day's mounting incomes. The students were taking a test on their screens, and with each correct answer their daily incomes increased by a dollar. With each incorrect answer, the amount dropped by two dollars. Arel watched the names on the mega-screen jockey for position at an amazing pace. "Dormer K" was at the top of the list, fluttered down, then up, in close competition with another Dormer and kids named Chute and Sill. The list was reproduced on the mini-mini-screens inlaid in each desk screen so the students wouldn't waste time leaning out of their cubes to check their status. These students were highly motivated.

She stood and watched. One by one the students finished their tests and switched their screens to something else: Ad Trivia, Intergalactic Holocaust, or Holoco's ever-popular teen romance, "Area Code 362436." When everyone was finished, they stood and stretched for ten seconds, then began the next test. The test schedule was posted on the wall: 7 AM to 2 PM—two hours a day longer than when she was in school. She popped a camera onto the glass and moved on. She was taking too long.

The next class was also testing, and Arel tried to be more efficient, doing her work without noticing anything, but this classroom had a wall display of slogans by students, impressively professional in bizarre colors. The slogans were for the new McDonald Mall opening downtown, where vendors with state-of-the-art hot carts were going to stroll through the various clothing, furniture, jewelry, and novelty stores, so the customers could choose to eat while standing in line to make other purchases. "Power to the Purchasers!" one slogan read. "Vote for Value!" said another. "Life, Liberty, and Convenience!" Arel had forgotten it was an election year.

The phone tweeped.

"Hello?"

"Shhhh," Ramy's voice said. "You're very loud."

"I am?"

"Meet me in the closet." Click.

In the closet Ramy was smiling genially, her mouth freshly ochred. "I had a spare moment to pop in and perform an assessment of your work." Then, caringly, "How is it going?"

Arel had to say, "There's a problem. I can't get the cameras off once I stick them on, and I have to change them every ninety minutes."

"What do you mean every ninety minutes? They're supposed to be one-eighties! What idiot placed this order? You have to watch these people twenty-four hours a day!" Arel trailed after Ramy down the passageway.

"And what's this?" Ramy barked.

"That's one of the cameras."

"Where's the label!"

"Uhhhh. . . "

"Didn't you even read the instructions?"

Arel was silent, revealing her guilt. Ramy made her pull out the instruction sheet and Ramy read, nodded and hummed. "You write the room number, teacher name, date and time. Let's do one together so you can *visualize* it."

"That would be so great."

Ramy had very neat printing. Then, suddenly, "What is this?"

"What?"

"Is this as far as you've gotten? In all this time? You have two more wings to cover!"

"I do?"

Silence. Ramy whipped out a mini-evaluator. "Your objectives at this time are to work at a faster rate," she typed in, "And to apply labels with care." She punched a side button and a long strip of tape curled out with these objectives printed on it. Then Ramy began to rush off.

"What about the velcro problem?" Arel shouted after her, sounding truly concerned. God.

"What!" Ramy shouted back. "No one ordered the velcro remover? I have to watch these idiots twenty-four hours a day! I have to do everything myself!" and vanished.

Down the corridor Arel went, sticking new cameras alongside old ones, cameras accumulating on the glass like a crowd of mindless eyes, storing up pictures for some later use.

*　　*　　*

The day wouldn't end. Eight more hours at Holoco High, then four at the library. With five hours of sleep between this day and the next. She tried to motivate herself by looking for Ben's classroom, but she couldn't find it: the rooms along two corridors were empty, the students gone to their lunch half-hour and Health Club period.

Arel sat, lost and lonely in the small intestines of Holoco Pre-Exec High. She closed her eyes and the insides of her lids were bright with rows of rectangles receding down a long dark hall. She was thirsty and hungry and wanted to run out into the sunshine or throw herself through one of these windows. Ramy's phone began to vibrate with a newzip. *Fashion Alert! Fashion Alert!* ran the purple words across the flashing silver screen. *The sky's the limit for the new shorty skirt! pater.fashion.com.* She examined the phone, front and back, trying to find a way to turn off the newzips, but couldn't. She accessed Celebrity Line: *Aslow Action Plan's a Real Hit! pater.aslow.com. Is Hampton Drane Insane? sun.drane.com.* She clicked on Hotnews: *Aslow Action Plan's a Real Hit! pater.aslow.com. Is Hampton Drane Insane? sun.drane.com.* Her Horoscope said it was a good day to work hard.

She got up, shoved boxes, planted cameras, shoved boxes. She came to the school library, which looked just like the Sunco Public Library. Behind the counter was an old frowning wire-haired woman, made mean no doubt by years of working with teenagers who imagined great lives for themselves and laughed at her for having such a stupid one. At the back of the library was a short girl, not pretty—too beige and flat—turning a videorack without looking at it. Arel watched her. The girl looked guilty, glancing at the librarian then back at a closed door behind the rack. Under her thin periwinkle shirt she was hiding something flat and rectangular, but too large and thick to be a videobook. Then the bell sounded and the girl hurried out the library door.

Arel followed her path. The girl entered a classroom, ran to her cubicle, settled in as the other sixty kids settled into their cubicles. They began to take a test and Arel sat, pulled out her miniwriter, typed "Hampton Drane Part Three. Surprisingly, Hampton Drane does not get murdered in his bed." She could never get past this line. It seemed to have no possible story to follow it. She deleted it and wrote: "Hampton Drane is taken hostage by all the homeless criminals in his house and brutally tortured for days—" delete "—weeks." That sounded more like the beginning of the story. "But still he vows to rescue homeless people." Stared at this: "What's his motivation?" she asked herself, no self answering. She mashed down the delete key until the entire tiny screen was blank and looked up.

Through the two-way mirror, test time was up, and the students scrambled to finish. Too late—their little screens went as blank as Arel's. On the teacher's mega-screen, words appeared:

"Family—A group of 2 or more people living together who are related by blood, marriage, or adoption."

The teacher was diminutive but bright in chartreuse beside the screen. The students—ninth or tenth graders—had turned their chairs in a neat U around the room.

"What do we know about families?" the teacher said. "Dormer?"

A boy replied, "They're more likely to comparison shop on big-ticket items!"

"Correct!" The teacher hit a button on her mini-control. There was a ding, like an old-fashioned cash register, and the big screen flashed the class list. "Dormer R" leap-frogged over a few other names.

"And families with small children?" asked the teacher. Fists punched up. "Valance?"

A girl replied, "They're more likely to pay more for brand name products even when they believe no-name brands are just as good!"

"Correct." Another ding, and "Valance S" jumped up a line. "Families with babies?" Fists. "Mortar?"

"They'll pay more to get pink products for girls and blue for boys!"

"Right!" Ding. "Upper-upper class families?"

Fists. Boy: "They spend with good taste!"

Ding. "Lower-lower?"

Fists. Girl: "They're impulsive shoppers, they overpay, and they buy on credit more than other people!"

Ding. "Lower-upper!"

Fists. Boy: "They, uh, they, uh, huh?"

"Focus up!" the teacher shouted and there was a click instead of a ding and the boy's name dropped.

More fists. Another boy: "They feel insecure! They have. . . they have. . . conspicuous consumption!"

"Correct!" Ding. Silence. Then: "You're slow today. You better review your section on families for the test tomorrow if you think you're gonna beat Miss Kord's class." More silence, then slowly, slowly, the teacher squinted at the students. The students squirmed. The silence stretched on and on and on, then snapped: the teacher pounced forward, hit another key and sent the final student ranking to the screen. Mostly Dormers were at the top, with a few Valances toward the middle. Some students cheered and some moaned and the list vanished.

"Section Four," the teacher barked. "Understanding Basic Human Motives." A list appeared on the big screen:

Hunger reduction

Safety

Sex

Feeling Important

Underneath the list was an addition line, and beneath it: " = MONEY." A sample ad flashed on screen to exemplify how you might appeal to all four basic human motives at once: A wealthy smiling man was driving an expensive armored car crowded with women offering him round pretzels. The clothes and lips and eyes and car seats and hood were all bright blue or red and below the photo was a giant white command: "Save $3500 Now!" The teacher was about to say something when a fist went up.

"Yes?" she was surprised. "Dormer?"

"Last night on Flashnews they had this story about all these people who actually like Hampton Drane, they're like, his followers or something, and they think we should all be nice to each other." The way he said it made his classmates laugh.

"Yes?" The teacher laughed too.

"Well, so, what's their motivation? To be nice?" More laughter.

The teacher explained: "Sometimes being nice to other people makes you feel good. Now," she probed, glancing back at the screen. "Why is that?" It was an opportunity to check comprehension.

A Valance raised her hand: "Once I actually stopped on the street and gave a homeless person my left-over snack-a-long, and that made me feel good because it was like, wow, I have all this power over these people, I can say, 'You eat or you starve.'"

"Okay!" the teacher sang out. "It made you *feel important*." She tapped the screen.

Another girl said: "And my mom bought this new sign for her car window that flashes out a real friendly 'Hello' so that other drivers maybe won't shoot at her."

"Safety." The teacher tapped the screen. "See how this works?"

An excited Dormer called out, "Let's think up new products to sell these people! These Dranee freaks! For real! Can we?"

The teacher twittered. "Oh Dormer. Always the *intra*preneur."

"I got a slogan!" yelled another, envious Dormer. "Doing good for others is good for you!"

Everyone liked it. The Dormers got extra dings. Then there was a lull and a flattened hand rose steadily into the air. The teacher tried to ignore it but it didn't go away.

"Mrs. Breen," a girl called out: it was the short girl from the school library. The teacher sighed, "What is it Rela?"

"Well," the girl shifted, took too long to speak. "Well," perhaps no longer wanting to speak.

"Rela, you're wasting time."

"Well, why don't we just put 'Being Nice' up there too? As a basic human motivation?"

"Why would we do that?"

"Well, if we did that, then we could look up there and say, oh, those people are motivated by that motivation." Pause. A few giggles. She went on: "And then we'd think oh that's their motivation instead of one of those other things."

"I have no clue what you're talking about."

The girl seemed to nod.

"What are you talking about?" the teacher pursued, and more students laughed.

"I guess I just thought there should be more words up there."

"Does that make any sense at all?"

"It's just an impression I had," the girl kept on, a bit quieter, but kept on: "That we've left something out."

"And you think I ought to just climb up on my chair and scribble in something else?" The students laughed openly and the girl began to slide down in her seat, with a look on her face that Arel remembered the feel of— that Arel had learned to avoid when she was a girl, sitting in a classroom with some thought pricking at her head, something she didn't have the vocabulary for. Trying to express it anyway and never succeeding so just stopping, her unnamed thoughts eventually rearranging into images of fair-haired boys and mansions and herself as a rich and brilliant adstory writer someday.

But suddenly this girl stopped her downward slide, sat up tall, looked directly into the teacher's eyes and replied, "Yes. Yes."

The teacher smirked and moved on to the next topic but the girl still sat erect, her face a mask of defiance, and Arel was amazed, recalling her own self-doubt at that age, her search for validation in the blank busy faces of Great Aunts Ashley and Tiffany. But this girl—Rela—had found courage somewhere. It was kind of inspiring. Arel sat straighter too and went back to writing: "Hampton Drane is taken hostage and tortured until his homeless captors are brutally mowed down by his security guards." She smiled, scrolled back, added "good-looking and daring" to "security guards," and laughed: She would trick people into starting to watch it. "But," she continued, "in the hospital HD declares to his brilliant personal script writer that he still has faith in his plan for rescuing the homeless. The script writer asks "Why?"—and sets out to understand." Arel stopped, took a breath. What would the writer discover?

The phone chirped: "And where are *you?*"

"In the psychology hall."

"Well I'm in the main passage and I'm looking down the hall and I'm seeing only one camera on each window even though the tapes ran out hours ago."

Arel jumped, spent the rest of the day sliding the box, getting a camera, cracking the plastic, sticking the velcro, planting the camera, sliding the box, sliding the box. Hour after hour. Sliding, cracking, thumping. By the end of the day she was exhausted, slipping out of the building, sitting in traffic, sitting in the McDonald's drive-through, sitting in the library, falling asleep with her head on the counter while hour after hour "The Saviors" blared from the wall screen. When she woke up, it was past closing time, and the Aslow Channel Update was on: Dr. Aslow was climbing into his jet, which had angel wings painted on its real wings, with the CEOs of Sunco and Holoco, who had just joined forces with Paterco in Aslow's great and holy mission to rid society of its Satanic evils. The deal was the same, though: $29.99 was as much as you could get.

Numb, still exhausted, she crept out the library door, locked it. Turned. Her car was always so far away.

For a moment she stood surveying the dark lot. So hard to see around the trucks and minitrucks, minivans and megavans. She listened, heard nothing but the wail of car alarms. She set off across the parking lot, fast, faster.

Half-way to her car she saw shadows shift ahead of her, heard a sound. She walked faster. Heard feet shuffling. Suddenly a form leapt out from behind a jeep—a chunky young man with lumpy hair and a face scarred from acne. She screamed.

"Oh, I didn't mean to startle you," said the young mean sweetly, extending his hand and holding out, not a weapon, but a daisy. "Jesus loves you. Peace be with you." Pinned to his shirt was a giant yellow button: Be Nice!

She took the daisy, still shaking, surprised that its real stem felt so rubbery. "Thank you." Then expected him to go away. But he stepped toward her and kept talking: "Jesus loves the lost and abandoned."

"I'm glad."

"*Do not worry. Look at the birds. They do not sow or reap or store away in barns, and yet your heavenly Father feeds them. Are you not much more valuable than they?*"

"I don't know, I never thought about it. Or is that one of those questions without an answer?" Then: "Oh, God, you think I'm homeless! Do I look homeless? I look homeless! I'm not, I'm not—" She tossed the daisy at him and started to run, ran to her car, jumped inside, and sped back to Ben's.

✳   ✳   ✳

At the school the next day she was calmer. She had a home: she had Ben. And at any moment Hampton Drane would reply to her zips and send her a big check for her brilliant screenplay and then hire her to write another screenplay. She was certain, certain. She paused to zip him again: *Qualified Personal Script Writer! Available Now! Call. . .* She shoved boxes, planted cameras.

She passed the school library and saw the flat-haired girl again, who was pretending to look at the videobooks and instead eyeing the librarian. Arel stopped to watch. The librarian sighed, glanced at the wall clock, scurried across the library to the bathroom, and the girl ducked through the door at the back of the room. She re-emerged in an instant, long-necked and bug-eyed, stuffing a book up under her shirt, and ran out of the library. Arel paralleled her path and watched as the girl filed into a room in a line of other students returning from lunch.

The teacher was in the center of the room unfolding a portable disposable mini-conference table, and a small group of students were gathering. The rest were steadfast at their screens in their cubes. The teacher, slick and shiny, blonde and tall in a cranberry suit, snapped the table in place and seated herself majestically at the head. Students dragged chairs over. Rela was the last to the table.

The teacher barked, "Who's pitching adstories?" Half the hands went up. "Who's pitching news stories?" The other half went up. Arel whipped out her miniwriter. One by one the students pitched their ideas: a group of schoolboys bludgeon another boy for being nerdy and having acne, a girl and her friends decapitate her boyfriend for buying a cheap birthday present, two teen lovers shoot each other in a spat over the last slice of pizza. Arel typed, "You can't tell the news stories from the adstories." The teacher sat with a mini-checklist, which beeped pleasantly or not. A boy named Brace got an extra beep for thinking up a teaser for his news story: "Stepping outside your front door can kill you instantly! Story at 10." Arel typed, "Fear sells as well as violence and sex. Lots of marketing opportunities in a brutal society."

Then the teacher called on another boy—the same jet-haired, strong-jawed Dormer who was at the top of the list in the other classes, who rocked back on the slim shaky hind legs of his chair with no fear of falling backward. He didn't immediately reply when the teacher said his name, and the teacher leaned forward, her fingers wiggling together, her lips twitching in an out-of-control grin. His pause made her say: "What's the Devven Lee Jeans girl up to now?" Her shaky grin broke into an excited smile. "Denvver Dee," she recited, *"She's smart, she's sassy, she's a survivor."*

Across the table a different, envious Dormer said: "She still gunning down homeless muggers while she's out night-clubbing?"

"Nope," said the brilliant Dormer, and everyone around the table leaned forward in anticipation, except for Rela, who leaned back, hiding her miniwriter under the table and not paying attention. Dormer revealed his stunner: sexy teen beauty Denvver Dee gets hit on the head by a homeless mugger, gets amnesia, and becomes homeless herself. Some students gasped, and the teacher leaned even closer to Dormer. Arel typed, "The teacher wants to suck this kid's dick."

"Then what?" demanded the excited teacher.

Though homeless and amnesic, Denvver Dee is still sassy and really sexy in her jeans, and she rises above her circumstances, lands a modeling job, and even gets engaged to the boss. The Devven Lee Girl has simply *got it.*

The teacher was thrilled and seized the opportunity to lecture the rest of the students about why this idea was so brilliant: "This character is first-rate because she's who we all want to be—a strong person who knows what she wants and has the guts to just go out and get it. A real doer. Not one of these whiny people who think all her problems would go away if people would be nice to her. She doesn't blame other people for her problems. She *owns* her own happiness. Excellent, excellent. Dormer you really ought to send a memo to the CEO of Devven Lee and pitch this idea. All right who's next. Rela."

The girl raised herself and spoke in a voice approximating fearlessness: "Well lately I've been thinking about all this God stuff, and I wanted to understand it better, but I couldn't find God on the Holonet, so I tried to find some old books to read, so I did, I found this one book, and it's really different, it was written at the turn of the century, and I don't understand all of it, but it has some stuff about organized religion and the democratic process, compared with the democratic process in the absence of the wide-spread practice of religion—" Faces around the table began to contort— "and I guess it's a little hard to describe but it seems like people used to be different, well, no not really but something was different, I can't quite put my finger on it. . . " A long pause. She coughed, added, "Did you know that p*oliticians* used to be elected President?"

The teacher exploded: "You're supposed to be pitching an adstory!"

"Oh, yeah, I'm getting to that. I was thinking, wouldn't it be cool to have an adstory set in the past? Like, an *adhistory*."

"How is that going to sell Devven Lee Jeans?"

"Well, I haven't worked out the particulars yet."

Someone laughed. The teacher said, "Are you saying you haven't done your homework?" Then no one laughed. A heavy, horrified silence descended. The big screen at the front of the room lit up, and Rela's name dropped from the middle to the very bottom. The teacher allowed a long embarrassed silence, and Rela's eyes began to redden. Then the brilliant Dormer spoke up, "Not a bad concept, though. Once you work out the particulars."

The teacher smiled her small boysenberry mouth at him. "Yes, someone with a knack could make it work. Someone with an *instinct*. Not some Ivory-Tower-head who just sits around reading books and doesn't know the *real world*."

An ambitious Valance called out, "I know! Denvver Dee could time-travel back to the twentieth century and shoot homeless people there too!"

"Okay, okay," the teacher nodded in conditional approval.

Rela added sharply, "Yes, that's right, to keep them from reproducing. She's very civic minded. She really cares about the people of the future. She wants to make the world a better place. She wants to be nice."

The teacher's head continued to nod, responseless. She couldn't have missed the sarcasm, Arel thought; probably she was so unused to it, she didn't know how to respond. "Blatant sarcasm," typed Arel, just for fun.

The students at the table went back to their cubes to make room for the next batch, and Rela walked directly toward the mirror, toward Arel. The girl jerked her chair back into her cube and plopped herself into it, not turning on her screen, instead pulling out her book, small and pale orange. She ran her hands over it, slightly bent it. Arel looked closer to see the book: "Twenty-First-Century Obviousnesses," she read out, slowly. "Obvious-ness-es." She spent so long on this word that she almost missed the name of the author, in thin black letters below the title, before the girl opened the book. "Meghan Ashworth." Meghan Ashworth—a series of syllables that slid easily through Arel's brain, unheard, unthought for such a long time: her mother's name.

✳   ✳   ✳

She told Ben about it that night: "A girl at your school had it, I saw the name on the cover—Meghan Ashworth."

Ben sat on the floor, assembling the old computer. "Wow—is that your mother?"

Another odd response.

"So. You're putting that together finally, to run your own site. Right?"

"Hm?"

"For what. Sign Shine?"

"Hm?"

"Or is Kyler onto some new scheme? Ben?"

"Yeah?"

"What on earth you do need that site for?"

Ben stopped, looked at her, did not respond.

"Oh that's right, it's private." She tried joking: "Porn."

He laid his screw driver down and pulled out his sellfone, which was buzzing out a newzip. He read it in silence, then put it away.

"What was that?"

After a long moment he replied, not looking at her, "You know what Arel? You're getting paranoid."

More silence. "Hey. I got my paycheck yesterday, for the week. Want some money? For electricity and stuff?"

He concentrated on fitting two parts together. "Well, thanks. It's not really necessary."

"Oh?"

He said, "It's too bad I never get to see you at the school. Do you ever see me?"

"What's that supposed to mean?"

He stopped to stare at her. "I thought you might see me sometimes—in the halls or something."

"No, no, they never let me out of that little office. Ha. More like a storage room." Then, trying to make it convincing: "Actually it is a storage room."

He went back to fitting pieces of plastic together, then, out of the blue, he said, "Arel, have faith."

What was that supposed to mean?

Later that night, in bed with Ben, she lay awake while he slept. The ceiling and the walls were light and dark with shadows that appeared to be moving but weren't. She watched them, not moving, and realized the room was seamless—the front door and the closet door side by side and frameless, blended into the wall with invisible hinges and concealed knobs. Everything so smooth, so hidden. In her mother's old place, the doors were visible, lumpy with ridges and hinges splashed with imperfect coats of paint. There was a separate bedroom in her mother's place—Arel's—and she remembered her mother standing in her bedroom door every night, mouthing goodnight, clicking the bedroom door shut behind her, closing Arel into a cool scary darkness. But every morning when she woke the door was wide open, through it gleaming the cream and oak tones of the hall and kitchen and pantry through a series of door frames at odd, quirky angles that made the small place infinite.

Modern places had no angles. They were perfect cubes. Arel rolled onto her side, tried to watch Ben sleep. She thought of climbing on top of him, knowing that when he was this asleep he couldn't be roused. Then thought about knowing this and all the other things she knew about him: his voice in the dark, his coffee maker, the long rich black of his hair, his bathrobe hanging on the bathroom door, his shoulders folding up when he sat and crossed his legs. A lot to know. But what did these things add up to? The more she knew about him, the less able she was to place him. He was atypical, unidentifiable—unpredictable. In contrast to Kyler, who she'd known just as long but was never a mystery. The thought of Kyler relaxed her. She supposed that he had secrets too, but they were easy to guess—some business scheme, some woman. She pictured him as a little boy, beautiful, clear-faced and blond, crosslegged in front of the screen, his eyes fixed on some blond handsome hero: *I want to be like him, I'm like him, I'm him.* Then she pictured Ben—a dark little boy with a too-long head and matted hair, distracted by something in the three-dimensional world—the sound of distant slowly dripping water, the feel of unwaxed wood—missing the options of who to be.

She got up and went to the kitchen for her left-over double jumbo diet Coke. The burst of refrigerator light like a scream in the night. She felt agitated, by something, by everything, but there was her Coke, so comforting. She left the door open, sucked up the last of the soda, ran the straw around the bottom of the cup still sucking, then popped up the lid of the disposable trashcan to throw away the cup. The cup dropped in, shifting the trash, and something bright caught her eye. Something flat and crimson, stuffed into a crack in the trash—an empty mailer. She looked closer. An empty video mailer—from the "Aslow Actioneers, Chicago Team."

She pulled it out, stared. An empty video mailer. She held it, couldn't budge. He must have sneaked it out of the mail before she got home—deliberately. He must have slid it into the garbage, deliberately—pushed it down, not just dropped it in.

Slowly she shoved the mailer back into the trash, along the side where it had been, then stared into the refrigerator at all the bright boxes and cans plastic wrapped, all with pictures of perfect food, bright with deception. Making you hungry for something that wasn't really there. Nothing was ever what it seemed. She stared at the pictures of food. Thirsty. Stared and tried to tell herself, It means nothing.

She closed the refrigerator door and stood in a blue glow cast by a sign outside the window. "It means nothing," she told herself firmly. Ben wouldn't join the Actioneers. Ben was good and kind and wouldn't assault people, even homeless people. She stared into the refrigerator again, stood in the cold bright blast. Ben was angry and unpredictable and secretive and strange and his entire family had been wiped out by a homeless person.

She stood and her stomach clawed its way up her chest. But no—what did it mean really? Really? Maybe he was just thinking about joining the Actioneers. Maybe for just a little extra cash, understandable, intending to nab an occasional drugged-out guy in a doorway. Understandable. Certainly she was in a whole different category, surely. And for $29.99? Surely she was of more value than that. "Money isn't the only thing that motivates a person," he had said.

She closed the refrigerator and crept back into the living room, into bed, careful on the thin mattress to avoid waking him. She was under the sheet when she realized he wasn't there.

"Arel," said his voice from no where and she screamed. "*Arel.*" He was by the window.

"What are you doing?"

"Watching the night. It's my favorite time of day. Even in the city. Though there's nothing like the country night. In the country you can find a spot in the middle of a field and look up, and the blackness is like a bottomless sea of stars— you can look up and revel in the past—a universe of pasts."

What a bizarre thing to say. "When did you ever do that?" asked her skin-tight voice.

"Hm? Mmm. After my family was murdered. I would drive to Indiana and stand in the middle of a field. For days, sometimes. Come sit with me."

"No thank you," she squeaked. "I'm exhausted. I feel sick. I have to sleep. I have to get up early."

He didn't reply. She closed her eyes and pretended to go to sleep, kept pretending as he climbed back into bed and did not put his hand on her shoulder. She listened to him stretch out, roll, roll, relax his breathing.

She had to find Hampton Drane. She'd tell him she was working on Hampton Drane Part Three. He'd not only hire her, he'd take her in. She'd be safe. She'd find him, he'd take her in, she'd be safe.

∗   ∗   ∗

She sneaked out at lunch the next day. She was short enough to conceal herself in the current of students flowing down the hall and slip out a side door to her car. She crept along the Kennedy, toward downtown. Koo could access the executive directory and get Hampton Drane's private number and everything would be all right. Even if Sunco had sold him to Paterco, Sunco wouldn't delete that kind of information. Everything would be all right.

She parked in the old lot and braced for a long hot nervous walk across the lot, through the crumbling tunnel and through the street vendors to Sunco Tower. But when she got out of her car, the lot was silent and clean. She felt almost safe, walking between rows of cars, their alarms unruptured, their headlights blank and serene, gazing passed the spot where she had torched the homeless mugger, seven and a half months earlier.

She approached the opening of the tunnel, nervous again, her eye on its dark mouth. But once inside she saw no vague forms slumped on the ground and heard no moans. Nothing but daylight appeared at the other end. She went up the stairs and stepped out onto the sidewalk and stopped, stared, amazed. The sidewalk was tidy and quiet, stretching into the distance alongside the shimmering green glass highrises to the cemented edge of the bottle-green Chicago river, shimmering. The vendors were gone—the short horrible brown-coated people who stood against the sides of buildings and darted out with their clumsy boxes of cheap jewelry, spiked dog collars, monogrammed spark plugs. Arel took a few steps into this pristine place. Even the wafting trash seemed gone. And the sky, she noticed, was weirdly blue, implausibly blue, melodramatic with its few fluffy clouds. She took a few more steps, stopped. People passed by her in a pleasant gentle stream, in clothes as immaculate as the street, bright and new and wrinkle-free, fitted perfectly to their trim bodies. There had always been such people, but now there was enough space to see them, each one in a frame of blue sky. Arel was entranced: it was not just that they looked attractive; they looked happy. Then she turned.

On either side of the tunnel entrance stood two lines of forms unmoving, unspeaking, in long thin white garbs like choir robes or angel costumes, with sleeves like wings. They wore flesh-colored helmets with face masks painted alike: large round blue circles for eyes, large round red lips serenely smiling, no nose, a yellow semicircle for hair. They'd been soundless behind her, watching her stand. She couldn't stop staring. She'd never seen them in person.

"Excuse me," she said to one of them. No reply. She gazed at its mask, believing that if she looked long enough, she'd see the real face behind it. The heat of the sun increased. Was the face staring back? In the centers of the big round blue circles were eye holes like dilated pupils. A single larger hole was punched in the center of the lippy grin, so that the mouth looked like a painted clown smile over a true mouth, hung open in surprise.

She stepped back. Their robes were buttoned to their throats but ended at their knees, allowing them to run, she imagined, and she could at least see which were men and which were women. Their shoes in a line were bright red, yellow, or blue, coincidentally matching the paint on their masks.

"Well," she said finally and turned, walked through the Sunco Tower revolving door, feeling the prick of their eyes on her back.

Inside everything was normal in the elevator lobby and she was relieved, comfortably dwarfed. Through the sandwich shop window were the same old faces in the same booth. She strode toward them, worked to sound happy, "Hi everyone!" Bounced in beside Koo, then realized: "Hey. Where's Vena?"

Kadence and Ormer glanced tiredly at Koo, who blurted unhappily: "We don't know! We haven't seen her for days! I went to find her on the phone soliciting floor and everything was gone! Even the cubes!"

"God." Arel replied. "The cubes?"

Ormer let out a noisy sigh and Kadence barked, "Of course phone soliciting is gone. It's far more cost-effective to use prisoners. Face reality, Koo: Vena got the ax."

"It can't be true!" wailed Koo. "What will Vena do?"

"Oh I bet she's already got another job," Arel said. "She's such a positive person."

"Yeah. Yeah. You're right." Koo sighed, relieved, and began to eat again, tilted forward to sip from her straw. Arel watched her face, simple and round, pointing here and there, eager to be happy. On her lapel was a big yellow campaign button, "BE NICE!" the letters arranged in a smilie face, the B and the E making eyes, the N in the nose position.

"And for your info," Kadence continued, energized by Vena's disappearance, "Hampton Drane is also gone."

"Gone where?"

"No where," Kadence smirked.

"He went off to produce my screenplay himself," Arel said.

"It's a free country," whined Ormer, his fork twisting fettucine, and Kadence burst out, "The man's a total case. Telling people to take in criminals."

"He's a nice man," Koo insisted, and Ormer droned, "It's all so. . . *co-dependent.*"

There was a silence, while forks twisted noodles, then Kadence burst out, "It's insane!" and everyone jumped, even Ormer. "Be nice to homeless scum. We ought to round them up and shove them against a wall and pulverize them. That's what I'd do. Get up a torch squad and line them up and blast away till they're nothing but a pile of black bones. And then I'd keep blasting until they were *nothing.*" Her fury stunned them all—a fury with no particular audience, no awareness of its appearance. They all sat silent until Arel slid an elbow across the tabletop, slowly, leaned forward. "Why would you do that, Kadence?" she asked.

Kadence didn't look at her: "Why the hell not?"

"Oh, God," Koo whimpered. "All this conflict. I feel like throwing up my entire stomach."

"You know what you should do?" Arel said to Koo, sounding helpful. "What?"

Arel bellowed, "Go shopping!" and grabbed a napkin, pulled out a pen. "Here's my new address." Quickly she wrote on the napkin: "Urgent! Find Hampton Drane's private number (access old exec dir). Call me at library!" and wrote the number.

"What a long address," Ormer said, his eyes not even on the napkin.

She gave the napkin to Koo, who stuffed it in her purse without looking at it and burbled, "Great!"

"Let's go tomorrow!" Arel persisted. But Koo was eating again, her eyes roaming off, and Ormer had begun to smirk.

∗   ∗   ∗

Back at Holoco High she was safe in the network of corridors, her thoughts spinning but hopeful now. Koo would get Hampton Drane's number and she'd call the number and he'd be there, in person, on the other end of the line.

She pictured her escape from Ben: dramatic in the night while he fitfully slept, suspensefully sneaking one suitcase after another into the hall, with a sudden final dash down the staircase. Then she pictured herself safe at last in an airy silent sun-striped bedroom in Hampton Drane's divine mansion, resting on a soft cream bed with hands folded across her chest, gazing at a far-away ceiling. Thinking of Ben. Missing Ben. Never touching him again or talking to him again, which was not possible to imagine.

Arel headed off down a corridor, not sure where she was going, trying to find Ben. But it was only mid-day and many of the rooms were still vacant. She passed the teacher's lounge, peered in and saw Kyler, lolling on the couch with an attractive yellow-haired teacher. Something must have been wrong with the sound system in this room—Arel couldn't hear him. She banged on the window, but the glass was unshakable. She pressed her nose against it, yelled, "Kyler!" Of course he couldn't hear.

So she pulled out Ramy's phone and dialed his number. She saw him sit forward, mouth "Excuse me" to the attractive teacher, pull out his phone and say, "Hello?"

"Hey Kyler! Kyler! Hi! It's Arel!"

"Well hello Arel." It was odd to see his mouth move through the glass and hear the words through the phone. "How are you?"

"I'm fine, fine."

"Hey how's the job going?"

"Oh fine, fine, hey Kyler?"

"Yeah?"

"What do we really know about Ben?"

"What?"

"You know, I mean, how well do we really know Ben? Don't you think he acts awfully strange sometimes?"

"I think he acts strange all the time." Pause. "What's goin' on Arel?"

"I don't know, that's the problem."

Then Kyler's face broke into a smile. "You think Ben's two-timin' you? He's not. He doesn't do that. He's a good guy. Don't go all psycho on him. You're fine. Just relax!"

Brief silence. "Okay."

"Hey, where are you? Aren't you here somewhere?"

"I'm right through the glass."

"What glass?"

"Outside the teachers' lounge—I can see you. There you are."

"*The teachers' lounge?* Oh, man! They've got those two-way mirrors up on the teacher's lounge too?" He squinted right at her. "You mean you're there?"

"Yup!" And though he couldn't see her, she waved.

"God, there's no privacy anywhere! Hey, Arel," he lowered his voice. "Don't tell Ramy you saw me in here with Miss Loob, okay?"

"Okay, Kyler."

"Thanks, you're a pal."

"Okay."

Still whispering, "I'll talk to you later."

"Okay," she whispered back, hung up, and spent the rest of the day planting cameras, trying to just relax.

* * *

In bed that night she lay beside him, her arm across his chest to still his twitching. She kept her eyes closed and tried to fall asleep, but it was night and she was exhausted—the time when her head would not shut up.

She got up, went into the kitchen, and by the light of the refrigerator rooted through the trash: McDonald's wrapper, diet frozen dinner plates, a banana peel. He'd eaten a real banana? A few broken appliances—a clock, his hair dryer, the microwave oven. She reached down to the very bottom of the trash. Still nothing, still nothing. If she did this every night, she told herself, and never found anything again, then things were okay and she could stay. She pushed down deeper—still nothing, nothing. Then something—stiff and rectangular. Like a video mailer. She pulled it out: it was a video mailer, from the Aslow Actioneers-Chicago. The disks were gone, but there was stuff left inside—adflyers for Actioneer T-shirts and baseball caps, toy Aslow action figures, vacations in Aslow's Holy Holiday Hotels, and a blue card with a scrawl that may have really been hand-written, thanking Ben for the good work he was doing for Dr. Aslow and God.

She let everything drop back down, onto the top of the trash. Tears pooled but wouldn't run. Her mind a blank.

Then she slipped back into the livingroom, paused to check that he was asleep, and crept to his desk screen. She lowered the volume but the light from the screen was still bright; she turned, checked Ben's black-and-white face, unmoving. She would stay up all night if she had to find the file, then found it immediately—ProjAA—"Aslow Actioneers," she whispered and grunted at his incompetence at concealing it, then turned again to check him. Still asleep. She accessed the file and examined the screen—a sea of strange codes, almost like chemical names. "Explosives," she mumbled. "Or nerve gas." Or a virus to drop into the water supply. She scrolled down, passed a series of tiny letters and various shapes clustering around one another—some kind of chemical formulas—CHs and NHs and HOOCs. She didn't know enough science to figure it out, though it looked familiar—the HOOCs looked familiar. Under each picture was "AA" with a number designation. "AA," she whispered to the screen and the pictures began to look more and more familiar. HOOC, AA, AA—then it came to her: "Amino acids," she said out loud, and Ben's voice replied, "What the hell are you doing?"

She turned. He was sitting up in bed, and had been.

"Uhhhhhhh—"

He got up, marched around her, turned off the screen, turned on the light.

"I was just uhhhhhhh. . . curious!" She was actually smiling innocently.

"Yeah well I said it was none of your fuckin' business." He put both hands on the back of the desk chair and shoved it hard, with her in it, against the wall. She flew forward and hit the wall. "Damn you! Fuck you!" He hunched over the screen, tapped keys, apparently checking to see if she'd changed anything. She stood up, arched her back against the wall, "Well what the fuck is it that's its so fucking private?" He was silent, clicking. She yelled, "I know why you won't tell me. I found out, Ben. You're working for Aslow!"

Not looking up: "What the hell are you talking about?"

"I found the disk mailers in the trash. I know what you're doing."

"You're going through my trash?" He straightened, too tall, reddening. "What the hell is wrong with you?"

"I was looking for evidence and I found it."

"Evidence? What the— Evidence of what? You are totally paranoid!"

"You're denying that you're working for Aslow?"

"Why the hell would I be working for Aslow?"

"What about the disks?"

"Jesus fucking Christ. You mean those free disks? I copy over those disks. See?" He pulled one out. He'd covered Aslow's orange picture with a plain white label.

"Then what the hell is that?" She yelled at the computer screen.

He was rigid, severe in shadows and planes of light. Then relaxed slightly, into a kind of fatigue: "Arel, I don't like to tell people because they'd think it was stupid for me to spend my time this way."

"Well, I won't think it's stupid, Ben, this is me you're talking to, remember?"

He sighed. "All right, all right, I'm theorizing how basic life might be able to exist on other planets. I want to see if it's possible."

She was silent, trying to consider this, feeling her entire face squint at him, then burst out: "Theorizing about life on other planets? *Theorizing* about life on other planets? *That's* what you're doing? Christ Ben! That's the stupidest thing I ever heard in my life! What the hell is the use of *that?*"

His eyes grew fierce and remained on her face. "No *use,* Arel. I just wanted to know what's possible. I wanted to think that somewhere else life could be different." Then a silence, confused and hostile, his eyes still pasted to her, her face still feeling its frown, her eyes finally darting away. She was tired and her shoulder hurt from hitting the wall and she couldn't help thinking the whole thing was stupid. Then he walked to the closet, grabbed some clothes, forced his feet into a pair of shoes.

"Where are you going?"

No reply. In the dark he buttoned his shirt.

"Ben?"

His arms rustled into his jacket sleeves—the sound of a lover leaving.

"Don't go. You don't have to go. Ben, I'm sorry."

"You're always sorry. Why don't you quit doing things you have to be sorry for?"

"You're right. What a good point. I'll do that. From now on, okay?"

He was still leaving. She kept talking: "Really. I'll be totally better. You'll give me a chance, right? Right? Come on. You have to."

"I don't have to do anything." He yanked open the door and she followed him out into the stairwell.

"You're right, that's true, but—" She began to follow him down the stairs. "Wait, just—" The door slammed below and didn't open again, no matter how long she stood and waited.

Alone in his bed, she watched the lime green lines of his clock shift from 2 to 3 to 4. What had she done? But he'd come back, eventually, he'd have to. He'd want to. He'd have to. What had she done? But he'd be back and they'd make up and they'd stay together. Wouldn't they? "What have I done?"

She rolled onto her side, pulled her knees up to her chest. Pieces of herself slid down a serrated blade, from her throat to her stomach, and piled up bloodied and dying.

*　　*　　*

He wasn't back by morning and she was angry, exhausted, ripping her clothes off their hangers to dress for another unbearable day in the bowels of Holoco High. She arrived late but would be there much too long; she stood at the beginning of the first endless passage about to perform the first task of the day and felt the old familiar squeezing in her upper chest: these were her days, day after day. This was her life. Thirteen more hours. And now, apparently, there would be no Ben at the end of it. No Ben and whose fault was that—hers. She kicked the box of cameras, kicked the wall, whacked cameras onto glass, went down the hall like a fireball.

But by mid-morning she was angry at him again. What the hell did he expect? What was wrong with *him,* she should have said. He calls *her* crazy. What did he imagine he was? Amino acids on other planets? What the hell was that? "Highly fucking weird," she said, loud, and grew suspicious again. Too weird, really. Highly fucking unlikely was more like it. And what about the computer he was building for his own site? What was that for—The Amino Acid News? For amino acids to get in touch? It didn't make sense— it was all a cover. Who knew what all that chemical stuff meant? Probably he was making chemical weapons for Aslow, which would explain why he'd overreacted and gone stomping off. At the first possible opportunity he could, she couldn't help but note, men and their personal freedom, men and their attitudes, men and their everything. She kicked the box again.

By late morning it was all her fault again and she was tearful, limping along with the box, barely able to pull out the cameras. She'd have to move out now, but who cared? She'd rather get torched on the street than have to live without Ben. She loved him. "Oh my God!" she screamed out. She did love him. Maybe he'd come back. Maybe it wasn't really over. She shouldn't get her hopes up. She plummeted onto the box, told herself that he might not come back and that she would just have to get over it. She could do that, she'd done it before.

And maybe, really, it *was* for the best. No—it was for the best. He was so moody and even kind of violent, and plus he was untidy, and awfully damn weird. Amino acids on Mars. She got suspicious again, remembering the note on the card from the Actioneers thanking him for his hard work, which looked like it really had been handwritten. A thought seized her: maybe, in the evenings, he was looking for amino acids in space; he was weird enough to do that. But what was he doing during the day? Showing Aslow videos to his students? Preaching Aslowism? Turning the next generation into Actioneers?

She left the box and ran down the passage, looked through every window, full of students taking tests. At last she found the science corridor and turned down it, began to run. It branched into two narrower passages and she went up one and back down and headed up the other and finally found him. She stopped, panting, gazed in.

There he was, he was there, tired and crumpled, sitting on the edge of his desk. He was smiling. He so rarely smiled. At first she saw only him, his amazing face, the hard angles and soft creases that drew her in, drew her in, the smile—the teeth a bit too small but somehow perfect anyway. The imperfections perfect, making his face stunningly unique. She couldn't take her eyes off him. She pressed against the glass like a ridiculous teenager, just to get closer to him.

Gradually she became aware of the rest of the room. Slowly she realized that things were wrong. The big screen over his desk was turned off. The portrait of Charles Darwin was up, but Horatio Alger had been pried off, a lighter shade of paint in a rectangle marking his absence. And the students: they were not taking their tests. How was that possible? Some of them were sitting on the floor talking, and some were in their cubes reading their screens, not necessarily science, and some were reading books. The trendier students—the Dormers and the Valances—were playing videogames. What the hell? Arel kept staring. A girl walked up to his desk, hopped up beside him, brushed the hair back from her face—it was Rela. She had Arel's mother's book and was showing it to Ben.

"Okay I don't understand this either," she said and read: "The belief that we all get what we deserve, be it good or bad, is one such notion, serving to buttress—buttress—"

"Support."

"Okay—the existing. . . sociopolitical. . . structure that permits excessive wealth to coexist peaceably with extreme poverty, indeed redefining luxury as a right."

"Do you like this book?"

"Yeah—it's neat that the author is your friend's mom. It's an *analysis,* like you told me, and see, it's not too long!"

He smiled.

"But if I don't start doing my homework instead of reading these old books I'm going to end up owing Mrs. Fran money, and besides what is all this reading going to get me?"

"I can't answer that. What I do know is that your time and your life aren't worth anything to anyone but you, so you have to be able to figure out for yourself what's important."

The girl sighed and went back to her cube and Arel kept staring. "God," she whispered. This was where Rela had found courage. Arel kept staring. She really could trust him. And probably, probably, he really did love her. She hardly believed it, so hard to believe. She let her forehead rest against the glass. Why hadn't he ever told her? He was sitting with another student now, explaining some chemical formula, smiling, the student laughing and joking. "Pretty radical Ben," she said to him, then jumped back and screamed at the glass, which was full with cameras.

But all the cameras were still there—all the film still unseen. No one knew but her, and suddenly it seemed preordained: she was to be the teacher spy, so she could protect him. So she could save him.

She tried to pry the cameras off, yanked and wrenched as hard as she could, "Damn velcro!" she screamed and began to punch the cameras. Their smooth indifferent sides bruised her hands. She jumped onto the chair and tried to kick them off the glass. Even the glass didn't rattle, the structure so solid. She pried a metal arm off the chair and started to bludgeon the cameras—began to make progress. She concentrated on just one, beat it again and again, until the seamless black case began to crack. The tiny crack spread into a bigger one, and finally the entire side chipped off. She could see the film cassette inside. "Ha!" she yelled and took aim again, but this time her metal bat didn't swing. She turned. Behind her stood Ramy, holding the end of the chair arm. Melodiously she said, "And what are we doing here?"

Ramy escorted her back through the tunnels, toward the exit. Arel looked up at the dark ceiling: Of course they would have quality control cameras to keep an eye on the person installing quality control cameras. At the front door Ramy released her to the security guards, who walked her across the lot in a suffocating heat that resisted the changing season.

five

Three days later Ben was fired. He only had enough credit to cover one month's rent: it was Arel who figured this out and called Kyler, but Ben agreed to go with her to talk to him at the Good-Buys Pub. They sat waiting against the far wall, beneath a gold-plated wagon wheel: this Good-Buys had a Wild West Gold Rush theme. Shrunken Indian heads hung over the bar, over the gold-rimmed upside-down wine glasses. Ben said only one thing: "Nobody shrunk American Indian heads," contemptuously, "That was scalping. Fuckin' inaccuracy."

When Kyler finally came he sat and leaned forward over the table to appear concerned, but did not look either one of them in the eye. He gazed at a nick in the tabletop, in front of Ben's tensed hands, began to fidget, wished aloud too loudly for the waiter to hurry up with his jumbo Apache tequila. He pulled out his sellfone and checked Celebrity Line: no news of Dolla Dare. He let out a painful breath, looked up at Arel and Ben, blurted, "God guys! You look like death!"

"Oh it's not so bad." Arel said, chirpy and fast. "I'll get another temp job soon"—not true—"and Ben can temp too!" After three months. "And hey," she raced on. "It's all just temporary! Things always look up. And in the meantime maybe we could stay with you!"

A long, shocked silence, then hysteria: "With me? Me? Both of you? Oh my god! I can barely fit myself in that dinky place! Shit! God! Both of you? Where would we all sleep? Shit! You two would get the bed and I'd have to sleep on the floor and I'd be a wreck every morning and then I'd lose my job too and then what would happen?"

Arel was prepared for this, said kindly, "Now, Kyler. Don't catastrophize."

"Christ, guys. How did this happen? God everything just gets worse and worse! What happened to you Ben? You loved teaching. How'd you get yourself fired?"

More silence from Ben. Arel said, "You could fit one of us, couldn't you. You keep the bed, and Ben sleeps on the floor."

Kyler doubled over till his forehead nearly touched the tabletop. "Yeah," he croaked at the blue-painted wood. "That would work."

"No," said Ben's underwater voice.

Arel replied, "I can go back to the library, to that back room. I'll move some videoracks over to hide the door. I can avoid the cameras. It's really not bad. Kind of like home. The most important thing is to stay off the streets."

"Oh, God," Kyler moaned. "Ben staying with me—won't everyone find out?"

"Shut up," Arel said. "You'll be all right."

"Oh, shit. Do you think so?" He finished his drink and wanted to leave. He scraped back in his chair but Ben got up first and shot out ahead of Arel and Kyler, into the mall crowd.

"He's mad at me," Arel said.

"For what? Getting him fired?"

She was silent. Out in the mall, pressing through the crowd, she stuck close to Kyler's tangerine sleeve. "Kyler, I need a favor."

"Oh God!"

"Shh. Not a big one. There's a girl at your school named Rela—a short girl with flat hair."

"Oh yeah. She's in my third period."

"Tell her Meghan Ashworth's daughter wants to borrow the book. That's all."

He recited the message, tired. "Okay. Will you be at the library?" She nodded, put out a hand to stop him, then put her arms around his neck. He felt unfamiliar, his body bent at an awkward angle. She didn't stand to watch him disappear into the crowd. She left first, headed to Ben's place to pack.

*　　*　　*

The leaving was not theatrical. Most of her stuff had never been unpacked: she did not have to search for socks under the sofa or hairbows in the bathroom drawers. She had always been careful of his space. She rolled her suitcases toward the front door one at a time, glancing and glancing into the kitchen, where he stood at the counter with his back toward her, his back bare. She heard him tear a wrapper and crunch something. She was leaving and he was snacking. She stood at the door and tried to think again that his shoulders were too narrow, his vertebrae too steeply cut. But his sides slid gracefully into the waistband of his jeans, worn thin, showing his contours down to his heels—bare. She ran her eyes back up his body, intending to be critical of his flaws. Then realized she wasn't looking for flaws—she was attempting to memorize him.

She thought she would leave without speaking, roll her suitcases out one by one and then just click the door shut so he would have to wonder if she was really gone and turn to find that she was. But after she rolled her suitcases out and stepped back in she said, "I'm going now." The sound of his eating stopped, but he did not reply. She said, "I can call you. Do you want me to call you?"

No reply.

"If you don't want me to call, say 'Don't call.'"

"Don't call."

She couldn't move, couldn't catch her breath. Filled up with acid. Her eyes burned with tears, and razor edges sliced long slow lines down her cheeks. Then she began to sob, sobbed, salvaging no pride. He must have heard her. He kept standing with his back to her. Began eating again.

She caught her breath and managed to control the sound of her weeping and said, shaky but clear: "You can call me." Pathetic, she knew, but it allowed her to leave. She hurled herself out the door before he could say no again and steal all her hope. She stumbled down the stairs with her suitcases and her shred of hope and no pride, had to stop at the second-floor landing to finish her crying. This stolen bit of hope made it easier now but would make it harder later, she knew, when he didn't call and didn't call, the hope dying by painful degrees, fighting to renew itself, dying again. But maybe that was the point of the pain—to make you finally understand that real disconnection had too high a price.

*　*　*

Outside, she began to feel better, her eyes in a squint in the sun, her body absorbed in rolling suitcases and hoisting them into the trunk of her car. She would feel okay, she knew, as long as she had things to do: walk, roll, arrange her space in the storage room. Her suitcases became a puzzle to solve, not quite fitting into her car, giving her mind a problem to work on. She set them all out on the pavement again, visualized them as the pieces of a Chinese puzzle.

Across the lot was the Mexican flyerman, who was there every day with his adflyers, lining windshields with canary, fuchsia, jade, plum, fireball. Pages lifeless against scorched glass, no wind to flutter them. He was so fast—his arms working in different directions—taking a flyer out of his bag, smacking it on a windshield, reaching into the bag again. Arel watched him, somehow comforted.

Then, a few rows behind him, she saw a cobalt convertible weaving toward him, packed with young broad handsome men waving cowboy hats and a few wild girlfriends—a group of rugged individuals. They rolled up next to him and said something she couldn't hear, then began to yell, and the flyerman began to run away. Homeless people knew when to run now, which had become a problem—catching them was more difficult. But more exciting too, which made rounding them up especially popular among young people. The trick, she'd heard, was to torch the ground around them to make them stop running without actually setting them on fire. A dead homeless person was not worth $29.99.

One of the guys in the convertible stood up, whooping and firing, gripping the top of the windshield as the car sped after the Mexican. But the guy in the convertible was a bad shot: he hit the Mexican squarely in the back. A long moment transpired between the hit and the combustion, then up went the flames.

Arel watched. Thought of yelling, Roll on the ground! The flyerman tripped and fell, yanked himself around the ground for awhile, for awhile, awhile, until he stopped. Arel felt the heat of the flames, though she couldn't have, felt a numb rush in her head, something lifting out of her, something like slow steam going up and dissipating in the dead air. She turned away.

She thought, perhaps a parking lot is not the worst place to die, full of sunny cars like gleaming neon and asphalt softly melted.

She turned away, thought, Perhaps a parking lot is not the worst place to die. People like cars.

Turned away. She leaned into her open trunk and tried to inhale the carpet smell but couldn't escape the odor of burning flesh. Vapors like hands slipped around her neck, covered her face, made her gag and cough and press her hands to her chest. She looked down at her hands, thin corpse hands with ridges casting shadows.

Then, "Hey," said a voice behind her. She looked up. Now the convertible was behind her. Seven stylish faces pointed at her, smeared in shades of red, each head of hair a different shade of blond, from raspberry to glitter. "Did you know that flyer scum?" One of the faces said.

"No," replied Arel. "I didn't know him."

"You ever see him before?"

"No, never."

"You ever talk to him?"

"No. No."

The faces remained on her, the car idling like churning, exhaust going up and dissipating in the dead air. She tried not to tremble.

"What's with the suitcases?"

"I'm going on vacation."

"You?"

"Oh, I usually look much better than this. I'm having a bad face day."

"You've been crying."

"You're not going on vacation."

"You're right," Arel answered. "I just dumped my boyfriend."

More silence—a figuring-out silence. "Then why are you crying?"

Arel stalled, lifted a heavy suitcase, wobbled it into the trunk. "Because I'm not eighteen anymore," she replied. "It's not easy to get another guy at my age."

The faces smirked, satisfied.

"Where are you going now?"

"Home," Arel barked, and one of the faces squeezed up in suspicion. Arel said, "Feel free to follow me," and loaded the rest of her suitcases, slowly. Smacked the trunk shut, climbed into her car, not quickly. But the convertible was still there. It backed up so she could pull out of her space, then began to follow her. Down one row, back up another, out onto the street. She drove slowly, straight, turned a few corners, went straight again. She couldn't think. Her body hardened. "Go *somewhere*." To Kyler's, she thought, and crept around another corner, watching the convertible in her rearview mirror, knowing that Kyler wouldn't be home and that she'd end up standing around outside his door, unable to get in. The convertible stayed with her, not growing impatient and going away. She turned toward the highway. They'd never follow her onto the highway. They wouldn't want to get stuck in traffic. But what if they did. Then what? They'd get frustrated, stuck in traffic, and shoot her for the hell of it. She drove on slowly, on and on, and they followed, followed.

Then she passed another mall parking lot. At the opposite end was a short black woman, elderly and tidy, moving down rows of cars, putting flyers on windshields. Abruptly the convertible made a turn into the lot and headed for the woman. Arel drove away fast, catching her breath, safe, not relieved, crying again, not feeling fortunate.

*　　*　　*

In the library on her stool she wrapped herself up in her arms and rested, soaked in the familiarity. She jumped when the adscreens came on, but then they went blank and she settled, every bit of herself, like a cloud of dust coming to rest on an empty surface. Then she turned on the screen, passed the Aslow channel, searched for something mindless and distracting on one of the Sunco channels.

"Guess the Prices of the Rich and Famous"—perfect. She laid her head on the counter. The contestants were in mid-bounce behind their podiums, one gold and one red, the merchandise wheel in mid-spin. Round and round, slowing, slowing, clicking to a stop at a picture of a pewter fireplace poker.

"Okay, Contestant Red!" said the fun-loving bronze-suited host. "Can you match prices with. . . " a dramatic pause, and the Celebrity Cube appeared on screen—a 30-foot structure divided into nine squares, one celebrity per square. The audience waited to see which square would light up randomly—a dramatic moment, but, Arel thought, not so dramatic to merit this long of a pause. She pulled out her miniwriter and made a note, then looked back at the screen, still waiting along with the audience, and gasped when the top middle square flashed on: it was Dolla Dare. Dolla Dare in the Celebrity Cube. Arel sat up, made another note, "It's only been a few weeks since Dolla lost the talk show." Poor Dolla.

Dolla cackled and Contestant Red quivered, and the audience actually booed. Dolla roared, "Come on tuna brain! Take a guess! What do think I'll write this time?" Dolla had a huge card across her knee, held the fat marker over it like a dagger about to strike.

"Okay Dolla," said the host, with squirming eyebrows. "Now remember we're looking for your *best guess*. What do you *really* think this would cost?"

Dolla bit the top off the marker and wrote. Wrote and wrote. How could she be writing so much? When she finished she pressed the card against her chest and grinned the evil Dolla grin, like the cartoon Devilla, and Arel tried to think which one had the grin first and which was the copy.

"Contestant Red?" said the host sympathetically. "What do you think Dolla wrote?"

"Uh, uh, uh. . . " Tears sprang to the contestant's eyes. He had to guess the celebrity's price within fifty dollars to get his fifth Big Chance card, which he needed to enter the Final Spin to get into the Final Round, where he might win a Jeep. "Uhhhhhh. . . Fifty cents!"

"Ah ha ha ha!" shrieked Dolla and whipped her card around, which said "79 Trillion dollars and you're not only Stupid you're Ugly TOO!" The audience was furious, booing and screaming. It was no fun if no one could ever win.

The show ended, everyone unhappy. Arel wondered if Kyler knew. Flashnews came on: Actioneers marching in angry flapping robes, Dranees meandering in the airport with daisies.

She went into the storage room, opened her suitcases and laid them flat, shoved boxes together to make the bed, layered the shirts and skirts and towels on the tops, tucked the sheet under the corners of the boxes, found her blanket, wadded up her bathrobe for a pillow. Lay down. "I can survive," she told herself, then thought about death. Everyone was so afraid of death—of having even less existence than they had now. What did the Bible say about dying? She closed her eyes and tried to imagine being dead but could imagine only sleeping, with its inevitable dreaming, its mindfulness, its eventual waking. Death was something you could not imagine from the inside; it could be only an appearance of others. She kept her eyes closed, tried harder to see it. Pictured corpses with chalky faces, charred limbs. Pictured them bloated or blackened and twisted into the shape of tree branches, row after row arranged on asphalt like cars in a lot. She pictured eyes sprung open, noses chewed off, lips baring teeth or expressions serene. She saw every kind of dead face imaginable, but hers was not among them.

*　　*　　*

In the silent morning she lay on her bed of boxes, calculating and recalculating. All her minimum interest payments were automatically deducted from her library check. She had only one option: to quit the car payments and let Sunco-Toyota repossess her car. She had to choose between her car and food. She thought this shouldn't be difficult, but it was: could she live without the car? With no possibility of jumping into it one day and taking off down the highway, escaping from this place—could she live with no hope of a better life down the road? Her eyes drifted dry across the beaverboard ceiling of her small clean cinderblock cell. She had no place to drive to—no place different from here. But she couldn't give up the car. To survive here, she needed to believe that she could leave.

On her miniwriter she typed a list of where to find food: "free samples at grocery stores, free samples in people's mail, free pretzels at Happy Hours"—though the salt would make her thirsty. Then, after an airless moment: "At night, garbage. But only as a last resort."

Do not worry, hummed the Bible voice in her head, but didn't continue, and suddenly it pissed her off—stupid metaphor, useless faith. She didn't need faith, she needed God to ring the doorbell with a pepperoni pizza. A large stuffed pepperoni and mushroom pizza with extra cheese, and maybe some onions and green peppers too. In the distance she heard a ringing, like a doorbell: "And there he is," she said to the beaverboard, "God with my pizza," then realized it was the library phone.

"Hello?"

"Arel Ashe?" said a cheerful female voice.

"Koo! Thank God you called!"

"Oh, no," replied an embarrassed stranger's voice, "Sorry—this is your Sunny Temps agent, with a special request for you!"

No Koo: no Hampton Drane. "A what?"

"A request! A special request! Raz Shae in the Sunco Prison Division asked specifically for you—called you that 'smart gal.' Wants to know if you can come right away, right now!"

"Yes, yes! Right now? Yes!" Money. Food. A pepperoni pizza. "Where do I go?"

✳　　✳　　✳

She had to go through the city, down the long vein of highway from the North to the South Side, past open fields of broken concrete and glass and the skeletons of trees and buildings, past the exit for the Paterco University of Chicago and Comiskey Park, where the HoloSox played ball, then off on the ramp and through neighborhoods once full of people.

The Sunco Prison Complex was a collection of old institutional buildings in scarred gray concrete with flat roofs. Uncheerful. Arel waited at the front gate for the guard tower to verify her, then drove in. Huge guards hung around the prison yard, former football players and basketball players, draped with mega-torchers, bored, joking around. She grinned as she rolled by and they smiled and waved large hands.

Raz Shae had an office in the headquarters building, which was under construction. Crowds of workmen were narrowing the halls to make the rooms on either side bigger to fit more cubicles. Raz didn't have a cube, though, he had a real office—a converted closet, which would have impressed Arel a year ago, but which seemed now like just another small enclosed space. It was lined with shelves that were empty, powdered deep with dust. The ceiling was low and the floor bare concrete. The only light was one nude bulb dangling overhead, burning out or not bright to begin with.

"Hello, Raz," she said. He was sitting on the floor, balder than she'd remembered, surrounded by old office equipment, various-sized screens, and stacks of actual old paper files.

"Thank God you're here!" he shouted and leaped up, which made her lurch back. He grabbed her hand and yanked it wildly up and down. He was either friendlier than he used to be or very desperate. She pulled her hand away, rubbed it, and realized she didn't know if he worked here or was incarcerated here. "How are you!" He smiled right into her face as though they'd been friends for years.

"Okay," she replied.

"Do I have the perfect job for you!" continued his bouncy voice, though he'd never been especially bouncy-voiced. "An ex-adstory writer, a person with a brain—you're perfect! And it's a full-time permanent position!"

"Oh my God you're kidding?" Her head was suddenly full of carbonation. Was it a dream? In her mind her future unfolded on a soundless set: food, an apartment, a place to go every day, people to talk to.

"Ha ha!" He threw out his arms. "Congratulations!" He threw his arms around her, spun her around, tossed his head back, released her, sprang back. Did a little jig. She leaned away. He whipped out his sellfone and pushed a button, "Hey Vena baby come on up do I have a surprise for you!"

"Vena's here too?"

"Oh yeah! Couldn't do without her! I got a promotion, you know. Health care phone sales is now only a small part of my operations. I'm in charge of the whole medical-administrative division for Sunco prisons! Isn't that great!" He threw his head back again and let out a crazed *ha ha ha*.

"Great, I guess. I mean, congratulations, I guess." She didn't know what she meant. She wanted to leave. Coughed. "I'm glad things are going your way."

"Oh yeah, oh yeah, you'd be surprised. These prisoners, well you'd be surprised. I was. I used to think homeless people were all deranged crazies, didn't you? Turns out they're former managers, salespeople, teachers, even script writers! Plus most of them actually had some kind of job when they got picked up—menial jobs that wouldn't cover rent anywhere. So they're capable of doing the work, you know—good talkers, fast thinkers, experienced in the work world. Problem is they're just plain lazy! I guess that makes sense—if you weren't lazy you wouldn't have lost your high-paying job and be homeless in the street and then you wouldn't be in prison in the first place. But productivity is too low Arel and my bosses are really on my ass. *Really* on my ass. So I came up with the greatest innovation!" He continued, increasingly frantic: "Prison motivation! A dynamic new concept! And you'd be the very first prison motivator!"

"Shouldn't that be, prison*er* motivator?"

"What? What? No that doesn't sound good—too many *er*'s. Prison motivator—Chief Prison Motivator, that's what you'd be, 'cause I want you to help me out with all this administrative stuff too." He looked down at the piles of old files, looked terrified.

"What does a prison motivator do?"

"Well, you pretend to be a prisoner, see? You sleep here and everything. But all your meals are at the employee discount! You do the phone soliciting thing, same as before, but, at night, before lights out, and at mealtimes too, you start telling stories."

"Stories."

"About prisoners you used to know who worked so hard they got promoted out of prison."

"You mean, set free?"

"Yes! Yes! That sounds much better! I knew you'd catch on! What you do is, you tell all these stories and the prisoners get motivated, without even realizing it!"

"Clever. Is it true?"

"What?"

"That working hard will make you free?"

"Well, it could be true, right? It could happen. All that really matters is that it'll work. We have to do what works."

"What works for whom?"

"For whom? For whom? God Arel, when did you start saying whom? Makes you sound like a nerd."

Arel was silent. Up the hall came the noise of buzz saws, planks snap-
ping in half and clattering onto the bare floor. Arel began, "Raz—" and Vena
burst in, glossy and chic in a skin-tight mini-dress made of red- and-yellow-
striped prison uniform material. She wrapped her long dark arms around
Raz's neck and wetly kissed his cheek. "Hey baby."

"Look who's here!" he said. Arel stepped forward.

"Baby! Look at you! You lost weight! Lookin' good, baby!" She wrapped
loose arms around Arel's neck and gave her a kiss too, less wet.

"She'll be working with you again," he said and shot a secret wink at
Arel. "So you show her around, okay baby?"

"No problem baby, you give her a cell next mine, okay?" Then she
turned with a flourish and raised her chin, spent a moment towering over
Arel. "I'll show you around Arel baby, but I won't be here long. I got people working night and day to get me out of this place and I'll be gone by
next week, next week at the latest. I got plans and I got connections and
I'm going places. Baby I'll be out of here by tomorrow. So you remember
what I tell you about how things work." Vena whipped around and tweaked
Raz's chin, pressed her nose against his, baby-talked something. He laughed
low and squeezed her butt, let his hands open wide and slide down and up
again. Then Vena turned on one spike heel, like a model, or a queen, and
began to strut out the door. "Come on Arel baby."

"Wait," Arel said and saw how it startled them, her tone much too
authoritative, more than anyone would expect from her. Vena stopped and
Arel said, "Raz—" He interrupted, "Vena baby go back downstairs and I'll
call you."

Vena blew him a kiss, then blew Arel a kiss too, all lipstick and lips,
and waved bye-bye. Raz closed his office door.

"Raz—"

"Remember, you pretend you're a prisoner to *everyone*, even Vena.
She's here for real."

"You mean, she's a prisoner."

"Ohhhh," he winced. "That *sounds so bad.*"

"Raz, I don't want this job."

He did not look as surprised as she'd expected. Mostly, he looked
fatigued.

"But thanks for the offer." She put out her hand, and he dissolved, "Oh
my god, you're leaving. Wait, okay, you don't want to do the story thing,
okay, but listen Arel, could you stay for awhile and help me out with all this
stuff? Just for the day? I'll pay you out of my own pocket. I just can't get it

done by myself, I can't do all this Arel! They downsized again and merged another two jobs with mine and I couldn't believe it, I even went out on a limb and told my boss there was no time to get all this work done, and he sent me to a time management seminar and now I'm three more days behind!"

"I'm—"

"Arel I can't lose this job. I'd be out on the street in a month and I'd get picked up, I know it."

She looked at him, gave him time to realize what he was saying, but he just stood scared and frazzled, his thin hair flying out, chick-like. She said, "So, you'd be picked up and brought here, and you'd be here night and day working your butt off—"

"I know, I know." He took a breath. "But I need to think I'm free, Arel. I need to think it in my *head*."

She agreed to stay for the day. They sat on the floor together, cross-legged, among the stacks of old paper files. Their task was to design a cost-effective system for allocating Sunco healthcare resources to incoming prisoners, most arriving shot or badly burned. The system was to be based on existing calculations of the relative value of different types of people, but with prisoner data factored in.

"It's so complex!" wailed Raz. He showed her the example provided on his assignment miniscreen: Middle-aged black female nonprisoners were good consumers but not as productive as young black female nonprisoners, and no minority groups over age sixty-five were worth much, because productivity declined so sharply after that age they typically lost their jobs, which tended not to be the type of work that transforms into consulting, and so they curtailed spending too. But then there were the prison factors: how productive were the various groups after incarceration, and how likely they were to buy big-ticket items in the prison shop? Raz and Arel had to refigure all the current tables to reflect the new prisoner data, some of which were in old paper files.

Raz burst out: "Some stupid anti-techie must have kept these old files!"

"Mm," Arel replied, "Some people like to touch things."

In a panic, Raz began to delegate: "You go through all the old paper files and add up all those numbers and figure the means and read them off and I'll enter them okay?"

Pause. He'd gotten it all out in one guilty breath. God. But Arel said cheerfully, "Fine!" and was cheerful all day, sometimes giggling, sometimes even laughing out loud, while Raz frowned and perspired and commented on how goddam cheerful she was. He had no idea. All day she gave him wrong numbers, inflated everyone's value, while he punched them in—erroneous figures that would probably never be recalculated. All day she was happy, imagining a long future of managers surprised by the unexpectedly high value of everyone.

At the end of the afternoon Raz gave her sixty-three dollars and a tearful hug and promised her a favor someday.

* * *

She took her sixty-three dollars to the mall and could once again buy shampoo, toothpaste, aspirin, and best of all the dinner she'd missed most: a two-pound cheeseburger at the Good-Buys, which came with all the french fries in the world. She took her time eating it, lounged in a back booth, feet up, her shimmering bag of purchases beside her, melted cheddar running down the sides of her hands.

When she finished she was still hungry, but she wanted to save as much money as she could. So she bought only another diet Coke, and asked for the free Happy Hour pretzels.

"We don't do free food anymore," said the efficient-talking, navy-suited, clipped-haired bartender, eyeing her. "Attracts the wrong kind of people."

She bought pretzels instead and returned to her booth, felt fine, let the back of her head sink into the soft Indian-design fabric. Then began to notice strange images on the screen.

She straightened up. There were pictures of children playing and elderly people and husbands hugging wives—whole people, not body parts—pastel, peaceful, drifting by. Then peaceful pictures of various Holoco discount stores and a serene voice-over: "You care about people. Holoco cares about people too. And now we intend to show you. With our bold new Campaign of Caring. Now, for every dollar you spend at a Holoco discount store, Holoco will donate one cent to the Holoco Foundation to Help the Homeless. Providing discount coupons for the homeless to use at our discount stores. What a convenient way to say, *I care*." After a few more pictures and tootling music the voice returned, low-pitched and faster: "If you do not wish your money to go to this cause, simply mark the red box on your monthly screen. Holoco respects your right to choose."

Arel pulled out her miniwriter but was distracted by the purple script writing itself across the TV screen, humble yet professional: "The Hampton Drane Story, Part Two. Produced by Hampton Drane Productions."

"He did it!" she screeched, and there it was—her screenplay. With some changes, she couldn't help but notice, but which did improve it, she had to admit. She drank melting ice and watched Hampton Drane giant on the screen, gliding divinely through dark streets, wrapping homeless torch victims in cloud-soft blankets and carrying them back to the Hampton Drane Home for the Homeless.

"It's even timelier now!" Arel called out in glee and the bartender pointed slitty eyes on her. She saw him, smiled, gave him a thumbs up.

Then saw Kyler stride in. "Kyler!"

"I've been looking everywhere for you. Why aren't you at the library? Why don't you get your sellfone turned back on?" He plopped down beside her.

"Look it's my screenplay!" She grabbed his knee and jiggled it.

"Really? No kidding? Wow. You're launched. What's he paying you?"

"Oh. I expect he'll hire me as his personal script writer."

"Wow." He got a tall thin flashy drink and another diet Coke for Arel, then pulled out a book and tossed it on the table. She spent a moment looking at it—her mother's book—then reached out to touch it. But it felt like a book, not her mother.

"That little girl was really impressed that I knew you, and that you were that lady's daughter—all that. She wants to meet you."

"I'll zip her a note. What's her last name?"

"Huh? I don't know."

"Well, can I send it to you and you forward it to her?"

"Huh? Sure, okay." He planted his mouth on the end of his straw, his eyes down and looking at nothing. He kept this position too long. No bouncing, no talking.

"You looked all over the place just to give me this book?"

"Huh? No. I've been carrying that around with me for days." Silence, then he said to the shimmering surface of his drink, "It's Ben. You have to talk to him."

"He won't talk to me."

"You gotta try. He just gets weirder and weirder every day." She waited for him to explain. He sighed: "See I thought he was working on my new product idea I thought of. It's total genius—major bucks. I mean, major." His voice livened up. "It's a special fragrance. You know how you'll be walking down the street and all of a sudden there's that annoying stench of burning flesh?" He waited for her to nod. "Well with my little mini-squirter scent you just do a little squirt in front of your nose and poof—no more stink. I call it, *Per-Fume,* get it? Ha! That's where the big bucks are, Arel, that whole torch and nab industry. That's what you gotta do Arel, think future, future, that's where the big bucks are."

"What about Ben?"

"Oh, yeah, well he said he was in on it! Pisses me off. He made all these lists of chemicals and plastic parts he was gonna need and I've been going out buying all this stuff, and day and night he works down in my basement storage bin but he never *finishes*. He keeps telling me he needs more supplies so I go out and get stuff and still no results. I'm a results kind of guy, you know? I go down in that damn basement to talk to him and he's got himself locked inside that damn storage bin and I knock on the door and, God."

Long silence. "You have a storage bin?"

"I mean, he was always kinda out on a ledge. But now he's just weird. Big-time weird. The hair—the guy never showers! He never speaks. He's like some insane homeless guy living in my apartment! God, Arel, what if the neighbors see him! And then, a few nights ago, that was the weirdest. I woke up and he was gone. Not asleep on the floor, not in the basement. I thought maybe he was with you."

"No."

"No, I know. 'Cause when I woke up in the morning he was back again sleeping on the floor pretending like he'd never left. Then he gave me another list of weirdo chemicals to buy. Will you call him?"

"He won't talk to me."

"You gotta try. He's got to straighten up if he's gonna stay with me."

"He's—"

"I know, I know, he's my friend and yeah I said he could stay and he doesn't have anyplace else to go, I know all that. Don't make me feel guilty, okay? If I'm out on the street too, that doesn't do him any good either."

"Kyler—"

"Oh—just a minute." Listless, he pulled out his sellfone, read the newzip. "Oh, man! Dolla lost her job on the Cubes! What's she gonna do now? Everything's awful." He rose. "I gotta go. Hey—congrats on the screenplay thing. You're launched! I always knew you would be." Then he left.

Arel stayed for the final scene of Hampton Drane Part Two: one last dramatic rescue, Hampton Drane's first faithful companion torched again and lying blackened in a crystalline snow, Hampton Drane appearing just in time, his silver-white heavenly hair and his smile sparkling in cool moonlight as he reached out and held the man's hand.

*   *   *

From the library she called Ben's phone and listened to his sullen, suffocated voice saying leave a message. She hung up without speaking, then called back, hung up again without speaking. The third time she said: "Ben, this is Arel. Kyler and I know what you're doing. Come to the library."

Probably he wouldn't come that night, but she thought about it anyway and let her heart hammer against her ribs. Waiting. She tried turning on the screen, then turned it off: even TV wouldn't take her mind off him tonight, wouldn't replace the image in her head of him walking in suddenly, his face on the other side of the counter.

So she took out her mother's book, said to the words on the cover, "I never knew you wrote a book. Why the hell didn't Great Aunt Tiffany ever tell me you wrote a book?" What the hell was wrong with those women? She peeled back the front. Inside the print was not too small and there was enough space between the lines to keep you from losing your place. Arel heard the words in the half-laughing tone she remembered: "Having a daughter when you're a woman, like having a son when you're a man, is unnerving: you are not as free to believe that your child is of some completely different 'nature' and thus you must continually accept responsibility for what the child is becoming." The sound of half laughing began to slip off the words, and Arel continued in a more somber tone: "Our fascination with 'inherent tendencies' allows us to avoid admitting that our children know only what we teach them."

These words should have been as strange as the language of the other old books, but they weren't. These words traveled easily down an old familiar highway, blocked off for years, toward an old home.

Arel kept reading: "We believe that human beings are inherently violent, lazy, deceptive, cruel, greedy, and above all, motivated only by self-interest. We believe these traits are inherent because we despise them so deeply we cannot bear the thought that we create and recreate them. We must believe they are natural, not cultural; that we have no power, no effect. How could we live with the realization that human nature is not violent and viciously competitive, that we have been, all along, perverting human nature, that all our violences toward others and ourselves are a byproduct of that perversion?"

Arel read on: "This is why we are obsessed with our fictions—our projections of who we are and who we might be—because we sense that we are not quite right, not who we were meant to be. Confusion begets stories.

Stories represent possibilities. But in America those possibilities are limited by the need to sell: in America, we create models of ourselves and each other, of life and the entire world, in relentless fantasies intended to sell cars, vacations, and laundry detergent. This is how we educate the next generation: generation upon generation, immersed in advertising fantasies, in deceptions, in nothing real."

On her miniwriter, Arel wrote a note to Rela: "It's funny how vividly we remember sounds—each other's voices. I remember my mother's voice so well. And I remember her peeling potatoes in the kitchen with one foot on the bottom rung of our old brown stool, singing some old song—*It's easier to learn than your ABC's. . .* " Then suddenly she remembered the whole kitchen: the puddly countertops, the same two plates standing side by side in the white plastic dish rack, the white door of the refrigerator covered with her little-kid drawings, held up by alphabet magnets. The feel of plastic sliding along her fingers as the magnets popped onto the refrigerator door. The feel of the old woven rug on her bare feet, the sound of the shower curtain whipping back, the squeaky folds swallowing up the green daffodils. "Is that what those are?" her mother had said. Her mother could never identify flowers. "They look like mutant tulips." Her mother in an old red robe at the bathroom mirror, brushing her hair in hard yanks, to make it look fluffier.

"My God," Arel said, remembering everything: the lines of light on the miniblinds in the morning, stacks of books and papers on every tabletop and radiator cover, the paint on the ceiling beginning to blister. Why had remembering always been so hard? The doors of closed-off rooms swung open in a different part of her head and light poured out: Suddenly she was a person with a frame, a history, an entirety.

Excitedly she typed: "Hampton Drane Part Three—a history! A history of Hampton Drane, and Dr. Aslow, and my mother—" who would have been the same age as Hampton Drane and Dr. Aslow.

She spent the rest of the evening looking at the old books with new eyes, trying to piece together what the world would have been like at the turn of the century. She found the words to use: "Republicans and Democrats"—the old political parties. "Political Correctness"—another term for liberal. "Libertarian"—which was everywhere for a while, then was no where, apparently substituted by words like "American" and "common sense."

She looked at the photographs and imagined herself on streets with houses in nude yellow brick; boxy cars with strange rectangular metal signs imprinted with numbers, apparently not advertising; tall glass booths housing chunky telephones with tails attached to matching boxes.

She fell asleep trying to dream these scenes, trying to feel herself hur-tled down a corridor to the past, dropped among scattered images new and old, and for a long moment she walked hand in hand through a parking lot with her mother.

∗   ∗   ∗

The next day Arel drove to Sunco Towers to find Koo. She had to reach Hampton Drane.

Crossing the sandwich shop, her reflection surrounded her, gave her away: her hair washed under the faucet in the sink and dried under the hand dryer, her clothes old and wrinkled. She was beginning to look homeless. Strangers in booths watched her with eyes glancing or eyes staring.

"Oh, Arel!" Koo's voice lamented loudly. "I wanted to call you but I never have the time anymore! Did you hear? They moved all the Adstory clerical functions to the Prison Division but there aren't enough prisoners to do the work yet so the assistant juniors have to do it all and they've got me answering the phones on the executive floor in addition to all this other stuff I have to do because I have a cheerful voice!"

Across the table Ormer smirked. Arel slid into the booth next to Koo, looked at Ormer, then back to Koo. "Where's Kadence?"

Koo replied, "Oh Kadence is too good for us now. She goes out with her other friends every day, out on patrol. So then once I did have time to call you and I went to get that phone number you gave me but I couldn't find it in my cube and that's just not like me! Losing things!"

Ormer smirked.

Arel grew uneasy. Then she saw Koo's barely eaten salad and could think of nothing but eating. A huge tomato wedge sat at the side of the plate, and Arel thought of eating it, not even caring who saw, biting through the skin and letting the soft seedy part linger on her tongue for several moments, forever. She'd never especially liked tomatoes.

"I looked and looked!" Koo was going on. "I dumped my whole purse. . . "

Tomatoes.

"Where is it?" Koo threw up her hands. "I tried your old number but you're sellfone's still shut off. Why don't you get it back on, Arel?"

"Yes," said Ormer. "Why not Arel?"

Arel's hand dive-bombed Koo's plate, snatched the tomato, popped it into her mouth. She chewed slowly, eyes fluttering, then looked up at the surprised faces of Ormer and Koo.

"Sorry," she said, her mouth full, lingering over the feeling of talking with her mouth full. "I'm starving. I'm on this god-awful diet. Don't you think I look thinner?"

"Yes," admired Koo.

Ormer fingered his straw. "How's your new job Arel?"

"Great!"

"Amazing how you always have time to show up here for lunch." He looked at her forehead instead of her eyes and tilted his head back to squint. A bit of tomato stuck in her throat. But he couldn't know anything. How could he know anything?

"I don't always have time. I came today to talk to Koo today. Boyfriend problems. Girl stuff."

"Why didn't you just call her?" He said and suddenly his eyes were on hers. He grinned.

"I do call her."

"You do?" Koo's voice jumped out of her. "I've never gotten any messages! Oh, Arel! Messages disappearing, notes disappearing! Entire Sunco departments disappearing! I don't like this!" She gasped, dropped her plastic fork. "And now I'm late back to work! How can a person eat lunch in ten minutes!"

"Eat at your desk like motivated people do," Ormer barked. Koo's lower lip began to quiver. Tearful, she began rummaging in her purse. Then handed a folded piece of paper to Arel. "Anyway, here's that number you wanted." Arel held it, felt it: Hampton Drane's private number. She unfolded it, watched it grow from a tiny square to a large one. The number was printed out in Koo's careful, childlike print. "Thank you," Arel said and immediately memorized it.

"Oh no problem. It was easy to find."

Arel was silent for a moment, then Ormer cleared his throat, pointed at his watch, and eyed Koo, who leapt up and ran back to work. Leaving half her salad.

Arel should have run away too, not risked staying with Ormer. But she stayed with the salad. Her eyes rested on it, unable to look away, until the sound of Ormer's snicker was all around her. She looked up at him: So he did know something—maybe everything. It was easy to find things out. Only rich celebrities could afford privacy.

She said, "Quit. Just quit. Why do you bother with me anyway? You say

I'm nothing but then you bother with me, and that makes you the pathetic one because you think I'm nothing but you need me, don't you? Ever think of that? I'm everything to you."

"As usual, I have no clue what you're babbling about."

"You need all of us. You sit here while Koo runs around doing everyone else's work and Kadence runs around torching people and you think you're on top, just sitting around on top. Superior. That's what you think. And that means you need me. Without me to persecute and feel superior to, you'd have to face the meaninglessness of your life."

He spat out a laugh.

"Laugh—I don't care. It doesn't make what I'm saying less true."

He worked his grin into a yawn, noisy.

"Fine. Don't listen. I don't care. I'll talk anyway. You've built your life on deceiving and hurting others and you've got all the power—you can find things out about people, get them fired, stick them in prison, hell you can even shoot them down on the street. You could shoot me too. But you know what Ormer?" She held his disgusted gaze. "You can never really get rid of me. I'm permanent. I'm here forever. Ha! You don't know what I'm talking about, do you?"

"You're a total case," he said and swept a hand around. Almost knocked over his cup. Then repeated himself, "A total case." He rose, took an awkward step out of the booth. He tried to mash his balled-up wrappers into his empty cup but they kept sprouting out again, up and up over the top. She laughed. He started to walk away.

"Bye bye!" she called out merrily. "See ya later!"

"Yes you will," he replied in a leaden voice, and when he was gone the place was too quiet, too empty, and she shuddered.

Then she began to eat Koo's salad. Leaves, big, green, rich, unfolding, drenched with creamy peppery dressing, big clean chunks of mushroom and carrot and cheese. Croutons, celery, onion. Tomato. She ate slowly, chewed each bite a dozen times, had never tasted anything so good.

∗　　∗　　∗

Back at the library, she punched in Hampton Drane's personal number. The recorded voice of his personal assistant answered, offering to take a personal message. She called every hour, day after day, and the recorded voice of the personal assistant answered, explaining that Hampton Drane was unavailable—on a case, on tour, on the air, everywhere but on the phone.

"Christ!" she finally barked after the beep. "Will *you* at least return my call? I'm—" she paused, not wanting to reveal too much to a stranger, "—just so eager to tell him about Hampton Drane Part Three. Everything's going so well!" But this message didn't sound urgent, just bitchy. She hung up. "Shit."

She pulled out her miniwriter: "The History of Hampton Drane," she typed. "A mere boy at the turn of the century, Hampton Drane. . . " What? Things would have to happen to him—sexual abuse, physical abuse, or maybe he had a nice family who all perished in some street massacre. Or maybe he had a sexually and physically abusive family that perished in a street massacre and he's relieved yet guilty. Which somehow motivates him to be nice to homeless people? She sat, sat. A failure to imagine, as her mother had said: the inability to dream beyond the walls of this small square room—a room lined with mirrors to reflect itself into an apparent infinity, a bogus universe of possibilities.

She thought that probably nothing bad had happened to Hampton Drane and that's why he grew up trusting and generous, but a story needs a conflict—everyone knew that. Only trouble is interesting. She typed: "The audience expects trouble, and if they don't get what they came for, they feel ripped off." She paused to think about this, and the door alarm wailed.

It was Ben. Her heart thumped up her throat. He walked up to the counter, rumpled and unshaven, and she felt her eyes move across every inch of his face, drinking him in. He did not say hello.

"Hello," she said. He stood like a suit of armor. She knew the posture. He started to speak in his locked-up voice: "You lied about Kyler knowing."

"Yes. To get you over here." She smiled stupidly, couldn't help it. "But you must have figured that out so why did you come?"

"I wanted to know if you knew."

Sarcastic: "Just curious?" It was so hard to talk from the innermost space, from that soft part underneath the old crusty deposits of pain and defensiveness. He didn't reply and to keep the talk going she said: "Well I could take a guess but I never seem to guess right about you. Maybe you're building a rocket ship." He smiled. "Are you?"

Regretful: "No."

"So why do you care if I figured it out? You think I'd tell someone? Interfere? Turn you in?"

"No of course not."

She nodded, a little grinny nod, and thought of nothing to say, searched for anything to say so he wouldn't leave. Thought of saying, *Don't leave, stay, stay, say you miss me, please miss me, please say you want me back.*

Then suddenly he said, "I miss you. I came to say I miss you and I want to see you again. I want you to join us."

She heard a rush in her head. Gritty toxic air burst from her lungs and she gulped in smooth air. Her body finally free of sharp debris. Her eyes, hot and dry, flooded. "You're kidding," was what she said. Then whispered, "God." Return. Constancy. She climbed up onto the counter and wrapped her arms around his shoulders and her legs around his waist. His face fit itself between her ear and collar bone. "Oh my God," she laughed. "You smell awful."

"Sorry." He held her and she held him and she thought she'd fall asleep, she felt so relaxed. She let her eyes close and her mind drift. Then the adscreens snapped on and she tensed up, clenched through the entire screeching cycle of pieces and bits of people and things. He held onto her, but it was too late: something had reminded her, had broken her calm. She remained still but unsmiling, her eyes wide and unblinking. She asked in a mechanical voice, "What do you mean, 'join us'?"

He let a moment pass. "You really haven't guessed?"

"I can't guess about you anymore, I said that. What are you doing?"

"I'm doing an Arel," he said, which seemed unlike him. Seemedi ngratiating.

"What?"

"I'm organizing." He lifted his face from her shoulder, tired and excited. "There are already so many of us—more and more every day."

"Who?"

"The 'hidden homeless,' as Aslow would say—people about to be evicted. We're almost an army!"

"An army," she echoed and thought: The computer set up to run his own site. The storage bin in Kyler's basement. Chemicals and plastics. "What have you done? What are you making in Kyler's basement?"

"It's so basic it's brilliant." He smiled and she recognized his old enthusiasm, his love of problem-solving, the thrill of creating. "Basically it's a gigantic water gun, filled with, well, essentially it's battery acid." He was so excited. "The gun shoots a stream wide enough to burn the entire face off a person in one hit! It's concealed inside various items—umbrellas, shopping bags—so when you raise your arm to take aim the other guy doesn't immediately know what's about to happen."

"You aim for the face?"

"It's a beautiful strategy—think about it. Something's burning your face, what do you do?" He demonstrated; he bent his face down and pressed the palms of his hands against it. "You want to touch it, don't you? You want to put your hands up to cover it. Like you're trying to hold your face on. Now look what's happening!" He extended both palms toward her. "Acid burning off your fingerprints! There goes your simple identification. Those rich pigs will have to spend a fortune on DNA analysis."

Arel didn't speak and he seemed disappointed, all alone in his excitement.

"Admit that's pretty fucking brilliant," he said, shaking his palms at her. "Do I know human beings or what?"

She imagined the universal gesture: the hands holding the downturned face in agony.

He grew irritated. "You look weird. What's wrong with you? It's the revolution, Arel! It's what you used to talk about."

"Is that what I used to talk about?"

"Organizing the masses against our capitalist oppressors, remember?"

"So you're just going to kill CEOs?" she asked, finding she didn't much like this idea either.

"Them too—anyone—everyone—whoever's a threat. What's wrong with you?"

"Don't do this, Ben."

"God, Arel. What else is there to do? Turn the other cheek? You think you're so smart but you're naive. You want to be Nice? You turning into a Dranee? Shoot first or die, Arel, that's the way it's always been and always will be. You're the predator or the prey."

"That's what they teach us to—"

"Excuse me, I have some pretty compelling evidence here."

"But—"

"Why are you arguing with me? You love me, I know you do. You want to be with me, and I want you to."

"In your army? Scorching people's faces off?"

"Fine, go be a Dranee. Go be a dead Dranee."

"So I'm either a mass murderer or a mindless sheep? Those are my only choices?"

"God you're stubborn." He backed away from her, flung out his arms.

"It's not right. Sometimes things *are* black or white, Ben. you can't do this."

"I can do whatever the fuck I want!" He backed toward the door.

She said his name once, heard it, kept hearing it. It sounded sad. When he got to the door he stopped and they looked at each other, his face wild, sorry. He wanted to stay, she could tell, she knew, no doubt: He wanted to stay, and he left.

*   *   *

This time, she knew, he was truly gone. For days she cried. Cried, cried, rested, then cried some more, with her face in the crook of her elbow on the counter, listening to her breathlessness, the screen on, crying amid images of moronic grinning Dranees with daisies and Aslow Actioneers with torchers as big as small cannons, patrolling the streets in choir robes and faceless masks, and bodies in alleys, bodies in trucks, bodies stuffed into the back seats of cars, dead, alive, and Dr. Aslow riding in a convertible, under a bullet-proof bubble, both arms raised and both hands twisted weirdly on their real wrists with the thumbs pointed up, pointed heavenward, patriotically, victoriously. She rested and sat up and cried some more, amid images of Aslow riding thumbs-up in his bubble bombarded by ticker tape, red white and blue, the convertible striped red and white with the blue on the rear—tiny blue Paterco logos instead of stars—driving past the side of a building that lit up in solid neon, then lit up to spell Aslow, a box after his name with a checkmark in it. Faceless faces, billowing choir robes, homeless people in alleys eating daisies.

She cried until one day she just stopped, aching, and slowly resumed her usual routines. She washed her hair in the sink, read, thought of lines from her mother's book: ". . . the wealthy are wealthy only because they are skilled at making money and value it above most everything else. . . not because they work harder or are smarter or somehow more deserving. . . If you don't have the knack for making money and don't value it above all else, do you really deserve a life of suffering?"

"American capitalism and American democracy have always been uneasy dance partners. . . "

She read, thought, began to write again. Ben was gone, and she had work to do.

*   *   *

"The History of Hampton Drane," she typed and thought of food. "Something will turn up," she said aloud. "Have faith." Concentrate:

"Hampton Drane," she typed and thought of chocolate, cake, cookies, milk, "Hampton Drane," and cheese oozing down the sides of a burger, "The History," and noodles swimming in cream sauce, marinara, broth. Bread and butter, thick-crust pizza thick with cheese, spinach, mushrooms, pesto, meat. Soft bread smeared with jelly, smooth, or lumps of marmalade or unmelting slabs of butter that crumble the bread and sit on your tongue undissolved, and too big a bite of bread sliding whole into your stomach and making you full, fat, filling you up and spreading you out and absorbing the acid that burns holes up and down your soft linings, turning the acid to cream. She had to find food.

It was late afternoon but already twilight, pale and almost cool. She slipped out of the library and around the back of the line of stores, through the back lot and into the neighborhood that lay between this mini-mall and the next one. The rows of brief lawns were packed with personalized mini-boards for area stores: "The Drumms say, Shop at Pants & Parts!"

The Halloween decorations were out, though it was barely October: Jointed paper skeletons bent into running positions and black witch silhouettes stuck onto the corners of the house signs and mini-boards. There were more corpses than usual strewn around—life-sized dummies made to look homemade—old clothes stuffed with rags with faceless burlap sacks for heads—tossed across the lawns and over the signs and even on the sidewalks to look like a massacre. Some had daggers stuck into their chests and some were chopped in half. But most popular this year was the scorch-corpse, the clothes and burlap bodies singed or blackened and twisted up tight to simulate the tree-branch look of a badly burned body. Arel walked on.

Her plan was vague. At the mini-mall on the next corner were several restaurants with mega-dumpsters in a row in the rear. She'd never picked through garbage for food before: Was there a strategy? Do you look for stray bites balled up in wrappers? Do you pick chunks of chewed-up meat directly off the gross garbage? A wind whipped up, cold and yanking at the tree-tops and her sleeves and she liked thinking it was God feeling bad for her. Of course it was only her feeling bad for her. Weather was just weather, the sky just air.

She came to the back lot and began to walk across, between rows of cars, in deepening darkness. A few distant alarms shrieked but mostly it was still, peaceful she supposed but still such an oddity, soundlessness and light-lessness compressing her. Pressing so hard on her ears she thought she heard ringing, footsteps. She stopped, turned, observed the cars vanishing in the night. Nothing else. She walked on, through scattering twilight. Suddenly a car alarm blared and she jumped, stopped, hugged herself hard and looked around. But the cars sat still in their tidy rows, innocent, and at the edge of the lot the streetlamps cast their flecks of light on nothing. She walked, heard footsteps—her own. Soft thuds. Then she stopped and the footsteps continued, heavy and crackling. Then stopped. She turned and called out, "I know you're there."

A face appeared over the roof of the car next to her and she gasped: raw-cheeked, red, wrapped in a balding scarf from the nose down: it could have been the face of the man she killed nine months earlier.

"Give me your money and I won't kill you," he said and she tensed in automatic fear, then laughed. Above the colorless scarf his eyes jumped open in surprise.

"I don't have any money," she said. "I came here to look for food in the trash."

The eyes grew intelligent and the arm lowered—he'd been pointing a gun at her. Did he believe her? Did she look like a person with no money for food? His voice was muffled by the thready scarf: "You can't rummage in the dumpster. They put cameras up, the employees do, with their own money, to catch people for a little extra cash. They catch you and lock you in the freezer until closing time and then they all ride down and take you in and then they go for a beer."

"Oh."

"Don't try to eat the frozen meat."

"No, I wouldn't, I don't think."

"I'll tell you what you need."

"What?"

The face above the scarf began to smile, slowly, eyes crinkling up, and he bellowed: "A shopping bag!"

She was silent. He reached into his jacket and pulled out a folded up bag from Estella's Bow-Teek, which sold hairbows and furniture from Scandinavia, and passed it to her along the roof of a car. She took it, because he had handed it to her. He dug his other hand in his pocket and said. "And you'll need two dollars and seventy-two cents." He passed her the money. "Now listen and don't blow it."

"Okay."

"Go inside the McDonald's. Buy a small Coke with the money. Carry that bag like there's something in it. Make a big deal out of needing a drink after all that shopping. Then you sit down and look around for other people with a shopping bag and a small Coke. Got it?"

"Yeah."

"Then do exactly what they do, and don't get caught."

"Okay."

"Your clothes are still pretty nice. You're new at this. Still have your car?"

"Yeah."

"Okay now listen. Don't sleep in the back seat. That's the first place they look. You gotta curl up in the front under a dark blanket, on the driver's side if you can stand the pedals, and leave the back of the seat tilted forward, it casts a good shadow. You're short. That's lucky."

"Thank you," she said and felt guilty, because she had the library to sleep in. She didn't need this shortness too. She had too much.

"But remember you have to keep thinking of new ways. They catch on to our tricks. Keep thinking of new ways."

"Okay."

He slipped away and she wanted to call out thank you again but was suddenly scared. She opened the shopping bag with a shaky hand, took a breath, then did something she hadn't done in years: went inside a McDonald's.

It was full of teenagers and mean-looking moms with unhappy kids and bright screaming surfaces and screens, posters and menu boards circled with bulbs blinking out a racing-around light. Behind the counter the workers in their garish colors stood shoulder to shoulder, moving robotically— one reaching for cups, one filling cups with ice, one filling cups with Coke, one passing Cokes to the one assembling the trays beside the cashier. Behind this line of workers was another line handling the food. Arel stepped up. The greeting girl in a jaunty hat smiled, noticed Arel's bag, chattered: "Doing your Halloween shopping early?"

Arel sighed too dramatically, "Yes."

"Seems like everyone is."

Then Arel was passed along the line for her diet Coke. She looked for a seat, wedged herself in between teenagers and moms. In the center of the McDonald's was a tall sprawling plastic play structure in the shape of McGulp's face. Little kids climbed over its teeth and into its grinning mouth, pushed each other across the tongue and down the esophagus slide. The blues and reds and yellows and greens were repeated in the plastic tables and chairs and planters and window posters advertising new kid movies, new kid stores, new kid TV shows. All Paterco. The posters filled every inch of the windows and Arel didn't know where to look, ended up looking at a poster for a new series starring Dillie Dare and Hootie Grate, "Saved by an Angel," about a sexy angel who works as a lifeguard and runs down the beach with several other bikini-clad angels to rescue handsome drowning men. *Entertainment for the whole family!*

Arel glanced around, spotted the other bag people among the noisy crowd. They sipped their Cokes slowly, quiet and nonchalant. An elegant silver-haired woman in a bronze suit sat silent beside a frazzled mom with three children, all with double-jumbo McValue-Happy meals—gigantic Cokes, burgers, fries, beans, fruit bowls, and pumpkin pies—more than three adults could eat, but a good deal because each item was cheaper in the McValue meal than it would have been by itself. The mom began to slap her children for playing with their McValue Meal Aslow Actioneer figures instead of eating, and the homeless woman let her hand drop casually near a french fry on one of the kid's trays. Then lifted her hand to her mouth to cough. Her chewing almost imperceptible. It was masterful. When the mom stopped slapping the kids and let them go play on McGulp, the homeless woman said, "Can I give you a hand with these trays, dear?" The mom looked up, startled, amazed, "Sure, thanks," and the homeless woman moved in a series of awkward poses, gathering wrappers, boxes and cups—"No, you sit there, let me do this for you—" then carried the trays to the nearest trash can. It was hard to see, but Arel knew what to look for: all the wrappers and boxes, which had been full of left-over food, were empty now, going into the trash. All the food had gone into the shopping bag. The homeless woman picked up her bag and her left-over Coke and strutted busily out the door.

＊　＊　＊

So Arel ate. Her library paycheck covered her car payments and two weeks of Cokes—she needed another thirty-eight dollars and eight cents for Cokes every day, but eating every other day was all right for the present, for a short time, until she found Hampton Drane. She still had not heard from him or the personal assistant, who was probably some Dranee upset by her message's lack of serenity. Arel came up with another plan. She called Kyler, whose voice did not sound happy to hear from her.

"I need to talk to you."

"Okay, okay," evasive, guilty, "Maybe next week."

She was diplomatic, offered to buy him a drink to make him think she'd gotten a job, and he agreed to meet her that afternoon.

When he walked into the Good-Buys, glowing, back-lit, his loose suit shifting, she made sure to call out, "You look so great!"

"You look tired," he replied. "Or old, or something. . . " the voice trailing. He sat looking like a bucket of water had been dumped on his head.

"What's wrong?" she asked.

"Arel," he whined and then bounced—huge out-of-control bounces—then stopped. "I'm an awful friend, I know, but I don't want you calling me anymore."

"Oh."

"I know, I'm awful, I'm awful. You two are my best friends but I don't have enough money or clout to take a risk. Ramy's getting all into that Aslow stuff and she constantly asks me about Ben—Did he get a job yet? Did he get his own place yet? I think she wants to nab him for 29.99! Anyway, I was lying to her about it, but she can check up on those things, you know? She could fire me Arel! I swear she's *this* close to it. She's still pissed about that whole Miss Loob disaster. Bosses—Christ. I ought to buy a franchise. That's the American dream, isn't it—own your own franchise. But who the hell can afford it! I told her last week I didn't know how he was because he left and he didn't tell me where he was going, and I want to keep it that way. I'm sorry. Do you forgive me? Tell Ben I'm sorry."

"Me?" Pause. "Isn't he with you?"

"I thought he was with you." Another pause. "I thought that's why you called. I thought he wanted to come back for his stuff."

"He left his stuff? What are you saying? He disappeared?" Making it a question, not a statement.

"I thought he was with you," said Kyler uselessly.

"He's not, he's not. Quit saying that."

"Christ. That's not good. You haven't heard from him at all?"

"Not for two and a half weeks."

"Christ. That's not good. That's when he disappeared. That's not good."

"Quit saying that!"

"Christ, Christ. Something must've happened to him. He got picked up. Maybe he's dead. Shit, Arel. Shit. If he got picked up, wouldn't he have called? People in prison make calls, don't they? Shit, Arel. He must be dead."

"He's not dead!" she barked. "You don't know that. Why do you have to think that? You don't have to think that. He's pissed off at us and that's why he hasn't called or maybe he took off somewhere. That's possible. He just took off down the highway, maybe. Anything's possible." Possible, possible, probable, true.

Kyler tried to sit up straight, which seemed to hurt him. "Yeah, okay. Yeah, maybe, I mean, he was pretty weirded out at the end there but I don't want the guy to be dead or anything."

"Kyler—"

"I mean I never would. You believe me don't you? You don't think I turned him in do you?"

Pause. "God, Kyler, no. That never crossed my mind. Did it cross your mind?"

"Christ! I can't stand this stress! I gotta go." He jumped up, his drink unfinished, then stood frozen, half-turned—a picture of himself. "I'm sorry," he said and let his hand drop onto her low shoulder. "Do you need some money?"

"Don't feel sorry for me. Don't stare down at me."

He took back his hand, looked offended, took a step back. She knew he was about to say, *hormones!* But he didn't. He turned but didn't go. She wanted to say, You know where to find me, but didn't, and he began to leave, slowly, maybe wanting her to call it out. He spent a long time walking across the bar, putting on his coat, going out the door. Then glanced back. "You're still working at the library aren't you?" he asked, and she nodded, and he nodded, and left.

She drank her drink, then drank the rest of his, pulled out her miniwriter and listed all the reasons why Ben wasn't dead. He was smart and wouldn't take foolish risks. He always surprised her—what seemed likely was never true. He was organizing; maybe he just got hurt and his friends were taking care of him somewhere. He could have left town. He couldn't be dead because he was a major character in her life and only minor characters get killed off. He couldn't be dead, even though he could be. She stared ahead, he could be. She tried not to picture it, Ben becoming a body, a thing tossed on the sidewalk, blackened or bloodied or both. People stepping over it.

But it wasn't true. Denial. No, she just didn't know. She had to wait. He'd call. That's what she'd do. She settled back into her seat and watched the screen for half a minute, then jumped up and ran out, through the mall, across the lot to her car, drove to the library and dialed Raz Shae.

"I need that favor," she cried out.

"What's wrong, Arel?"

"A friend of mine is missing."

"A friend?"

"So maybe he's there and just didn't call me or maybe he's in the prison hospital and can't, I don't know, can you check?"

She waited while he checked, an eternal moment, until his voice returned: "He's not here," not knowing whether to sound cheerful or sad—was this news good or bad?

"He could be at the Paterco or Holoco prison," Raz said. "Hold on while I check."

"You can check?"

"Oh sure we're all linked."

"You are?"

"Oh sure. More cost-effective."

Arel replied, "More cost-effective for whom?"

Silence. "You really gotta drop that whom stuff. Hold on."

She waited again, a longer eternity, and this time Raz knew the tone: "Sorry, kid. He's not at the others either."

Arel fit together the possibilities in her mind: He was in hiding. He was sneaking away from Chicago. "Will you keep checking, Raz? Every day? And call if he turns up?"

"Yeah, okay Arel."

She left the library and drove around, crept along neighborhood streets thinking that she'd suddenly see him, that she'd turn a corner and there he'd be, and she'd buzz down her window and call out to him. She kept picturing it, kept driving, drove until she ran low on gas, long after she was due to open the library.

✳   ✳   ✳

Day after day she cruised the streets, waited for Raz to call, began to feel small again, effectless. She took a week's Coke money and went to the Good-Buys to get drunk, bought a double-jumbo tequila in a glass with a cactus on it. The liquor made her feel sick, her stomach empty, but she kept drinking it anyway and ordered another when it was gone. She sat for one hour, two. The late afternoon bar crowd shuffled out, and the evening crowd milled in. She sat through "Murder Trivia," "The Secret Shocking Stories of Ex-Sports Sweeties," and a movie about a gigantic alien space ship that descends on America and pulverizes a bunch of cities and mountain ranges and minor characters. When this finally ended, a guy at the bar called out, "Hey it's seven o'clock! Change the channel!"

Everyone got excited. Arel straightened up to see. A football-field of horns announced a special presentation, then the screen was momentarily, dramatically blank, then a screen-shaped American flag appeared and a menacing voice-over said, as though resounding from the past, "If we don't remember history, we are doomed to repeat it!" It was Dr. Aslow's voice. The American flag faded into a still shot of Dr. Aslow looking martyrly yet determined, standing at the downtown intersection where you could see all three conglomerate headquarters in the same shot: Paterco, Sunco, and Holoco were all behind this spiritual giant. Arel pulled out her miniwriter and made a note.

A different voice-over said, "In an unprecedented event, Paterco, Sunco, and Holoco have joined forces to bring you the following special movie presentation."

That was odd, she thought. Why would they do that? Why would they say they were doing that? She made another note. The opening credits flashed the names of the actors: Hootie Grate, Dillie Dare—the new generation of rising stars. Then came the names of the writers: Jonquil Adams, Austin Carl, Ormer Bell. The title appeared in big black intentionally ugly block letters: "1994." It was an adhistory.

The movie began with the camera eye sweeping across rows of colorless marred tin-looking barracksy buildings, then stopped at large sign: Big Brother University. The place was full of blowing snow and howling winds, as if it were Moscow. It was, however, Chicago. Arel recognized the configuration of highways in the background, stripped of their colorful billboards and screens for the shooting of the movie, repainted to simulate urine-stained concrete. The camera eye moved fast across this desolate landscape and through the window of a barracks into a classroom.

A woman stood at the head, her hair, face, and suit all plain straight lines, brown, unshiny, burlappy. Written on the board was a laughably long word, "Histosociofeminology 101." The story began mid-scene. "What's your point Mr. Smith?" said the uptight pinched-face professor bitch.

"Well, just that—" Hootie replied, putting on a frightened face. He was such a bad actor. But so gorgeous, with his pile of yellow hair and lavender eyes. Similarly good-looking students surrounded him, with similar looks of terror on their faces. "Don't you think that, that," stuttered Hootie, "I mean, for hundreds of years blacks and Mexicans and all those other people like that have lived in slums and basically had no money to speak of and so, I mean, like, since this is a history class, don't you think that *history itself* proves that other races are genetically inferior to whites?"

The teacher barked, "Mr. Smith! Didn't you memorize the University

Rules for What You Can and Cannot Say? You have an 'F' for the course."

A clanging bell sounded and the students slunk out of the classroom in fear, down the hall, silent beneath the watchful eye of Big Brother University's cameras. Hootie and his friends scurried through whipping snow and piled into a minivan.

"What a bitch!" said the beautiful Dillie, pulling her parka over her big red hair to reveal giant thin-sweatered breasts.

"I knew what you were trying to say, man," said a buddy.

"Yeah," said another buddy. "If blacks are so equal to us, why didn't *they* sail over to America and grab *us* for slaves?"

Hootie replied, "And if I have a problem do I mope around for a hundred years?"

"You never would!" said a raven-haired friend of Dillie's.

Hootie went on: "I pay to come to this place—I'm the customer—and I have a right to say whatever I think! I'm fed up. I'm quitting school and starting my own company and when I make my first trillion I'm gonna go to the dean and say, Hey, man, I'm gonna build you a building, but first you gotta fire that femi-bitch!"

The story went on, with no commercials. Arel took frantic notes. Hootie quit school and made his trillion, because he was a doer, but the dean wouldn't fire the professor bitch, so Hootie seduced her instead. All she really wanted, it turned out, was to be loved by a powerful man. Then he set her up in a grand apartment and tormented her by never fucking her. Eventually she went insane and jumped out the window and then it was over.

The screen went blank and stayed blank too long, dark and quiet, making you think something was wrong with the TV, until slowly a grainy circle of light solidified into a spotlight, a too-bright column illuminating an old-fashioned stage with an old-fashioned burgundy curtain that hung in motionless folds. Suddenly the curtain whipped aside, and out stepped Jonquil Adams, Austin Carl, and Ormer Bell, their faces glazed to perfection. They were all dressed in white. Was that significant? Should she make a note? How could you tell what anything meant? A cheer track began, and Ormer, Austin, and Jonquil began to take bows. Ormer Bell in a spotlight on TV. On a phony stage, with a phony audience, but someone in the bar started to clap too, and others joined in, until the whole crowd was applauding.

When it ended, "Real People Videos" came on—about another marketing director—and the bar crowd dispersed. Arel sat. Sat, unable to write. Ormer Bell in a spotlight on TV. She sank into an old bad place, into old bad thoughts: Ormer Bell in a spotlight, while she sat invisible in a bar. Ormer Bell taking bows, while she sat paralyzed at her miniwriter. Ormer Bell writing screenplays, while she was wordless, worthless, hungry and thirsty, lonely and so scared of the next day. She looked at her dark mini-writer screen. What was the use of even trying? What did she have to say? She put her head down on the smooth hard tabletop and couldn't think: she was hungry. How could anyone think with all this hunger? Think or work or live in this place—*such a small space*—hungry for everything—hungry for clothes, cars, computers, TVs and stereos and all the gadgets in the world, power and status and a good fuck. A place where all your desires are dire needs, desires and needs that flash on and off and on and on in your head, running your thoughts off the road.

Arel's thoughts slid down one chute after another: She couldn't concentrate, it was no use. She was of no use. She had nothing to sell, only a few ideas that seemed wrong to people. Her life was hopeless. Ben was missing, gone, dead. Of course he was dead. Classic denial, stupid hope. Gone out, now gone. So easy to go out and be gone. Day after day, dead and still dead, and her left behind imprisoned in moments of thinking maybe it's not true, maybe he'll come back, maybe they'll come back, *if only I watch hard enough, sit still enough, keep my face against the glass, not blink my eyes, because if I blink my eyes they could slip away, slip away forever because I blinked my eyes.*

Her eyes stung. She thought of how his body fit hers, chest and stomach, arms and legs, cradling her. Soon she would start to forget his body, his hands, his face. Hunger rumbled through her, invaded every inch of her, tightened around her throat and made her cough, cry. Her tears were real, silent but sliding in hard straight lines down her cheeks. She tried to stop, thinking her body needed the hydration, and she choked, a harsh sound too loud in her head. She thought she heard a voice speaking to her but the noise in her head suffocated the words. The voice seemed familiar. Her body took in a breath, breathed out, turned. It was a woman speaking to her—a woman alone in the next booth. Arel tried to see the face in the dimness, couldn't tell if the untidy hair was gray or light brown, but the woman must have been homeless, her clothes so old and old-fashioned. "Go up to the bar," she whispered with such authority that Arel obeyed without hesitating. She walked to the bar, slid onto a stool.

A man who was not the usual bartender glanced up. He was young looking, not neat, with curly brown unruly hair and a beard and a lazy way of standing. He looked at Arel's face for a long moment before approaching her. Crying was suspicious. She planned a remark about a romance gone bad but the bartender never spoke, simply walked over, reached under the bar, and put a basket of crackers soundlessly in front of her.

"I didn't order these," she said.

He shrugged. "On the house." Then he pulled out a paper cup and filled it with real red wine.

"What's this?"

"This?"

"I didn't order that."

"I know." He drifted back to his spot against the back counter and crossed his arms and gazed off as though he'd never budged. She examined him for daisies but saw none—he seemed to be a regular person. She turned to look at the woman who had spoken to her, but she was gone. Arel picked up a cracker, let her fingers linger over the feel of cellophane peeling off, bit off a small piece. The crackers were not stale; the wine was not cheap and filmy. They were remarkable. They made her feel full and relaxed, calmed the storm in her brain. She turned again, but the bar was completely empty now. When she turned back the basket and her cup had been refilled. A stranger was feeding her, without her even asking, with no affectation, as though stinginess and suspicion did not exist.

She started to cry again, let go of real tears, no longer fighting to hold on to what she feared she might need later. Believing that water, salty and sliding down her face, was not a scarce resource after all. The bartender stepped up again to refill the basket and her cup and she cried, easily, not loudly, realizing that everything she'd been grabbing for—safety, love, and a meaning in life—could not be acquired, only received. When everyone tries to take them instead of give them, they no longer exist—they become intangibles in a world that despises intangibles, disregards what cannot be seized and secured for personal use.

She ate, drank, wrapped warm in this feeling of having enough and growing strong enough to think of Ben again. Great Aunt Ashley had said to someone, in front of Arel, "The important thing is to find the body. It's always worse when you don't find the body. Feels unfinished. You need that last good-bye." Someone else saying *hush*.

What you need, Arel thought, is to make the body safe, to stroke it gently, so that the last touch is not the rough handling of people who don't know you. She closed her eyes and pictured Ben laid out in his own bed, with the stillness of the dead, not burned or perforated with bullets or sliced open. Intact. Himself. She imagined her fingertips loose on his cheeks, slipping down, his skin registering the gentle touch. Him locked inside, inside his deep dead sleep, somehow knowing she was there.

A voice on the other side of her brain tried one last time: It's possible he's not dead, and she responded out loud, "He's probably dead." When people vanish, they are gone forever. She had to accept this. Sometimes you find the body and sometimes you don't, but you never find them alive.

*　　*　　*

The intake room was frigid and tall and narrow, metallic like a freezer, reflecting vague blocks of Arel and the beautiful young blond man sitting across from her, his computer resting on his crossed knee. His legs were short—he was short—but the room was so small their knees almost touched.

In a crisp friendly practiced voice he said, "And you're looking for. . . " the tone singing on, waiting for her to fill in the blank.

"White single male, thirty to thirty-five, tall, dark hair, dark eyes. A scientist."

"That's pretty specific," said the beautiful man, typing frantically.

"Is it?"

"Oh, sure. Most people don't really know who they're looking for. They think they know—an account executive, an adstory writer—that's what they say. But when I ask for the physicals, they don't seem to know."

"That's odd. Does that seem odd?"

"Depends, I guess."

Depends? she wanted to say, but he'd gone back to his frantic typing. "Income range?" he asked.

Silence. "Mine or his?"

"His, of course. I assume you can pay for our services." He laughed, and she laughed too.

"I don't really know. Forty to fifty thousand?"'

"Okay." More typing. "See, that's important."

"It is?"

His sky-flecked eyes flashed up at her. "You've never done this before?"

"Not for a very very long time."

"You ought to subscribe to our flyer, updated daily—pictures in the privacy of your own screen. Far more convenient. It's fine that you came in this first time, but who knows how long your search will take? Obviously you can't come in every day."

"Well—"

"Take it from me, you don't want to miss anyone. I can tell you're serious about finding your special guy."

"Yes."

He passed her a raspberry brochure with bold banana letters: "GET ON LINE!" went on and on about subscribing, "You'll save 2% on the subscription price if you sign up before you leave today. . . " She held the brochure, nodded, didn't listen, and finally his tone signaled the end of the spiel. "Ready to start?"

"Sure."

He led her from the frigid front room down a narrow passage, equally icy and gray, lined with thick metal doors. As they walked he murmured, "White male thirty-thirty-five," glancing at each door. Then he stopped and opened a door with a long arm, keeping himself out in the hall.

"You're not coming in?" she asked.

He shook his head with a look of horror. She went in and the door crashed shut behind her and she was frightened.

Long bright yellow bags lay on haphazard gurneys, shoved in too fast. The room was so crowded there was no place to stand except right beside one. She looked down at the first one. Tried to picture herself unzipping the bag. She reached, let her hand drop, reached again. Took a breath of icy air and reached again.

The zipper stuck. Her hand had to yank, yank. Hair was caught—rich thick blond hair—which spared her having to look at the face. She glanced around the disorderly room with its disorganized bodies. She'd need a system to avoid missing one, to avoid looking at the same one twice.

She breathed in, moved clockwise around the perimeter, breathed in, unzipped the sunshiny bags down to each chin. The faces looked pale and supple, like very realistic mannequins or rubber humans. All so still. Background music began to play—a light instrumental version of "Every Time I See Your Face." The zippers made the up-and-down sound of a long tormented moan. She tried to move quickly. But in the instant before her hand pulled down each zipper, fingertips cold on cold metal, something caught her and made her imagine the curling back of the plastic and a slice of face appearing—Ben's. Each time she expected to see it, and each time she saw someone else's, but only after a long instant of looking, the reality of the features separating slowly from the image of Ben's in her mind. Zippers ground back up with a resisting squeal.

She walked in an inward spiral. Some of the faces were badly burned, by flame or acid, and she had to unzip the bag down to the waist, but she could tell that these men weren't Ben by their unfamiliar shoulders, by the backs of their hands.

At the last bag she stopped, stared at the crinkly sparkly plastic, tried to see the outline of the head and torso without unzipping the bag. This one was Ben's size, and the hair caught in the zipper was dark. She thought of not looking, to leave herself some hope, but then she would always believe that it had been him. She reached for the zipper, pulled: not him. Not Ben. He wasn't there. She went back down the corridor.

"Ready to sign up for our flyer?" called out the chattery voice.

"Are you still talking about that?"

His eyebrows flew up.

She said, "It's cheaper to come in person," and handed him the rest of the month's Coke money.

"Cheaper? Well you have to figure in the cost of gas money—have you figured in the cost of gas money? And what about our suburban branches? MorgCo has twelve locations in Chicagoland alone. And what about northern Indiana? False economy! False economy!—"

She walked past him and through the door, through the parking lot to her car. It was mid-October, and leaves in brittle piles were collecting on the sidewalks and narrow lawns. The wind was always blowing now, slapping her face with winter-smelling air. She sat in her car and thought of the expense. The bartender at the Good-Buys continued to feed her, and not just crackers but slices of apple and carrots and sometimes bread and cheese and meat. She told herself to have faith, that it would last, and part of her believed: she could afford to find Ben. She would have to drive to every morgue in the city, every day, day after day, circle rooms of corpses zipped into bags like cheap garments, and see each charred, bloodied, chewed-off face. But she would find him, and she would take him into the country, dig him a grave under a brilliant night sky, make a pile of rocks, and write his name in indelible ink.

It was the best she could hope for. She thought of his shoulders, the way he would stand around and glance down. When she got back to the library she called Raz Shae.

"Still no trace of him," Raz said, sounding sad, "I promise I'll call if he turns up, Arel, I promise, I'll give ya a call right away. . . " he went on, as though he were saying good-bye but then not hanging up, "Arel," he said finally. "Something happened to Vena."

"What?"

"It was a terrible thing. One minute she was just sitting in her cell and the next minute poof, she set herself on fire. Who woulda seen it coming? She burned a long time. She wasn't screaming. Her roommates were asleep."

"God, Raz, I'm sorry—"

"Don't say sorry to me—wasn't me who caught fire." Long pause. "She gets the best care though. Turns out black female prisoners eighteen to twenty-two are real valuable! I was a little surprised, but with all she's got comin' we can afford the best—we could probably call up Hampton Drane himself!"

"You could? You could," she gasped. "That's it—Raz, get Hampton Drane! And tell him you know the woman who wrote his screenplay—tell him that, tell him I need his help."

*　　*　　*

The next day she tried to work again. She thought about Ormer's adhistory and realized that anyone could write anything and call it history, whether or not it was true. She typed: "Dear Rela, Your adhistory idea is harder to do than I thought it would be—it feels like a responsibility. Maybe all stories are. Figuring out the past—knowing which history is true—seems as impossible as predicting the future, I may as well do that!" She may as well. Why not? She thought about it, grew excited: She could write a story about the future—about a perfect place where nothing flashes in garish colors and people don't cage one another in miserable lives; where everyone has a purpose beyond consuming, a purpose instead of a use. Where work and love make you feel whole, not fragmented, not blown apart and packed into separate small boxes. Where you can walk down the street without being hit by a random bullet. The story of a utopia.

She was typing out her idea for Rela when the phone rang. "Arel?" It was Raz. "I just had a long chat with Hampton Drane. I never talked like that before in my entire life! We talked all about me. I talked about myself to this big-time celebrity—"

"You didn't mention me?"

"Oh yeah, sure I did! He knew all about you! He said he wondered why you hadn't tried to call him!" Silence. "Arel? Isn't that strange that he remembered you?"

"What did he say?"

"He said you ought to come right over, to his personal mansion! He gave me the directions and everything. He said if you wanted to, you could even move in and be his, how did he say it?"

"Personal script writer?"

"How'd you know that?"

"I don't know. I dreamed it."

He recited the directions, then said: "Arel, I can't keep checking on that friend of yours. I'm leaving town. I'm going back to New Orleans."

"Wow." Now she envied him, taking off down the highway. "Nice."

They hung up, and she floated into the back room to pack. Was this really happening? Was it possible? Suddenly it seemed not only possible but inevitable: She'd tried so hard, worked so hard, and she'd suffered: she'd earned her reward. Hampton Drane had called for her at last. Hampton Drane, God's Comforter, her savior. Now, finally, she would be happy.

six

Three hours later she was ready to go, in her best newest suit and her too-old coat. She stopped at the library door and looked back, looked hard at the silent crowds up and down the videobook racks, the crooked orange forest reflected to infinity. This had been her home. Any home was hard to leave, she guessed. Familiarity felt palpable, like something you could take hold of, hold onto. She paused, gazed, then left.

Hampton Drane's personal mansion was north of the city, even north of Wilmette, beside the lake. She crept up the highway, so far north the traffic thinned, and exited onto a wide walled street. The directions told her to turn, turn again, turn again, and she wound through neighborhoods of mansions and old twisted trees, past guard towers, where guards sat alone in high bright glassed-in rooms watching TV.

Finally she came to Hampton Drane's address: ONE. She pulled up to a gate, waited for the guard to verify her, then drove toward the residence: a sprawling place of yellow-painted stucco—a jumble of turrets, bay windows, balconies, gables, parapets, flying buttresses—anything that generations of wealthy people could think of to stick onto their mansion. On top of the roof, on its own little pillar, was a giant plastic fluorescent dove, its wings outspread and flapping on the wind.

Arel pulled into one of the many driveways, behind a parked parade of Mercedes, climbed out of her car slowly, lifted her old suitcases out of her trunk, and walked up several winding walkways. The front door was at least twenty feet tall. She rang the bell, which played a grand pipe organ tune that wouldn't stop, and the door opened a crack, revealed a sliver of a beautiful young blond man, though as short as Arel.

"Hello," she said and wondered if, technically speaking, you were still homeless if you lived in the Hampton Drane Home for the Homeless.

"Hello," replied the young man in the familiar voice of the personal assistant.

"I'm Arel Ashe. Hampton Drane is expecting me."

"Oh? Well I'm Eden Wall, Hampton Drane's personal assistant, and I have no knowledge of you." He squinted at her. She stood on the stoop, shivering.

"Perhaps you could check."

"That could take time.

"How much time?"

"Oh, days."

"Oh, I don't think so," she replied and wedged herself between the door and the frame. He stared at her, sniffed. Pulled out a yellow sellfone, murmured something. Sniffed again, and opened the door for her, "Well are you coming in?"

She stepped in. The front hall was as big as a ballroom, ornate with bronze statues, marble statues, metal statues, gilt-framed mirrors, carved wood door frames, gold antique tables with huge Oriental vases holding huge bouquets, a parquet floor with a gigantic oval rug woven in gold, silver, lilac, peach, aqua, rose, apricot, orange and kelly green. Hanging on the gold-papered walls, among paintings of graceful landscapes, were stone gargoyles.

She hesitated, then glanced up. On the sweeping double marble staircase stood Hampton Drane himself, the serene Hampton Drane, so silvery he sparkled, dressed in a fuzzy yellow bathrobe and yellow slippers.

"Here you are!" He exclaimed. "Arel Ashe! My personal script writer!" He rushed down the stairs, held out his hands, gave her a gentle hug and seized her bags. "Come in come in! How are you! Now your room is all ready for you, but first," he twinkled, setting her suitcases down gingerly at the foot of the stairs. "Let's have some cocoa!"

"Okay." They began walking through the front hall, toward a distant doorway, "Your house is so. . . so. . . "

"Thank you! It's been in my family for generations—for nearly 150 years!"

"Ah."

"Yes, yes," he said softly, steering her through the doorway and into another room, which looked just like the first room. "I grew up here."

Pause. "Hard to imagine."

When they got to the end of the second room, they entered a third room, as big as the first two but with a definite decor: it was full of mermaids—mermaid statues on pedestals in corners, mermaids mounted up and down sea-blue walls, mermaids suspended from the ceiling. He smiled. "I like this room."

"What's it for?"

"Pardon?"

"This room. What is it? What is it for?"

"For?" A puzzled silence.

At last they reached the kitchen, surprisingly normal-sized, with a regular-looking stove and refrigerator and a pink plastic table and chair set. She suspected this was not his only kitchen. He held a chair for her, and she wasn't sure how to move as he slid it in under the table beneath her.

"I like this room," he said. "I had it modeled after kitchens on old TV shows."

"Ah. Yes."

He padded to the stove and poured milk into an old-fashioned saucepan on a burner on the stove.

"My mother used to like to cook that way," Arel said. "It reminded her of when she and my father were together."

"Well well." He had a spoon, clicked it in circles round and round the pan. "Sadly, I myself never married or had children. I like to think of my guests as my family." He had an old-fashioned can of Hershey sauce. She feared he'd had it made specially for him. He pulled two plain white ceramic mugs from a cupboard, made two cocoas.

"Both of my parents are gone now," Arel said.

"Yes," he murmured. Seemed to know. "But now you're part of our family here. I'll think of you as my daughter, and you think of me as your father."

I will not leave you as orphans, whispered in her head, though suddenly she didn't want to think of Hampton Drane as her father. She'd seen a picture of her real father—a burly redheaded man in a Reggae-On Red Stripe T-shirt.

Hampton Drane carried the mugs carefully to the table, set one down in front of her, sat himself down beside her. "Well, here you are!" he twinkled again. "I bet you've already got lots of ideas for my next screenplay!"

"I do! I do!" she began. "It wasn't easy though. At first I couldn't understand—your plan—at first it sounded insane to me, no offense—"

He continued to twinkle.

"—but I kept reading and reading and trying to put it all together, to understand, and I think I do now! I think I do!" She leaned toward him. He lifted his mug, blew at it gently, took a sip. She went on: "It's not that I claim to know, really, what would make people happy. . . ." Then she stopped.

He tipped forward: "Oh, go on, dear. Please, go on. I want to hear all your ideas."

"Well, all anyone can do is speculate, and 'speculate' is one of those nerd-words, you know? What good is a process without a product? A salable product. That's how we think—how we've been taught to think. We grow up with all these sounds and voices in our heads—teachers and parents and soundbites and adscreens and TV cheer tracks—sounds that play over and over again and cut grooves in our brains, until all our thoughts slide into those grooves and we can't escape them. How do you think thoughts that wouldn't occur to you? How do you believe what you don't believe? Things like: maybe we don't need a mountain of stuff and to be on TV just to feel like we exist, maybe we're real enough without these things."

Hampton Drane nodded and frowned in fascination.

"But it's hard to feel real or worthwhile when all you see everyday is what you lack. We're bombarded by images designed to stir up desire— desire so intense it's like a prison cell. Like a gas chamber. And we think that the only way to get what we need is to take it from someone else. No wonder we can't trust each other. No wonder we end up completely disconnected. And then we congratulate ourselves for being so self-reliant, such rugged individuals, all the time growing more and more isolated, unhappy and so desperately lonely, with such a sense of meaninglessness that we seek out fads and trends, superficial likenesses, superficial belonging, and end up in groups waging war on other groups."

He nodded, nodded, sipped his cocoa.

"But that's just human nature, right? Kill or be killed. Everyone knows that—it's common sense. Then again, a long time ago everyone knew the world was flat—that was their common sense. What if we aren't born with some genetic impulse to maim and deceive others? What if that's another false story, told and retold because it justifies our economic system: survival of the fittest—if you survive, you must be fit, if you don't, you must not be. Excessive wealth and extreme poverty all nicely explained, all somehow deserved, and the corporate state goes whistling on, leaving us behind in a cloud of trivial choices—endless little product options, like particles in a smog that prevent us from seeing the choices we don't have—the freedom we don't have."

He leaned closer, nodded, waited for her to continue.

She went on: "Think about it. What if human nature is actually not dark and brutal? Or what if we've exaggerated that aspect of human nature because fear sells, because it's easy to profit from? What if we're actually all born with an equal or even greater impulse to take care of one another? If everyone were giving instead of taking, there would be no need to take. With everyone taking, we have nothing left to give. Everyone watching out for each other—maybe that's what it takes to be happy. Maybe human nature is divine."

Then he sat dead still.

"I know—this sounds corny. The *sound* seems wrong. What sounds right to our ears—what sounds natural—is combat. Someone wins and someone dies and we watch, spell-bound—we watch to learn how to act and what to think so we can be the one to win. So we can survive. You have to be tough. You can't be hesitant or sentimental or womanish. You can't be a nerdy weakling or a brainy bitch or a silly do-gooder. You can't be a scorch."

His eyes widened, intense on her face, unblinking. Then he looked down, concentrated, his face full of something he wanted to say. "Oh, Arel. Dear Arel," he said.

"What? What?"

He began to shake his head. "I'm afraid your cocoa's gotten cold." He jumped up to pour it back in the pan and reheat it. She sat, staring at his fuzzy yellow back: He had no idea what she was talking about. He was a sweet, warm, wealthy man with no personal knowledge of hardship—no experience of hunger, or of meaningless work, of fear, oppression, or loss. A sweet old man with a pile of old money, extraordinary luck, and no clue.

"Well," Arel said, straightening up. He worked hard at reheating her cocoa. Stirred frantically. "Well," she repeated. "My original idea for Hampton Drane Part Three was a history, but now I'm thinking, maybe not."

"No?" So polite, so interested.

"Now I'm thinking, a story set in the future! What do you think the world will be like fifty years from now?"

"I don't know!" he got excited, nearly spilled her cocoa. "I don't have your great imagination! I'm lucky to have you."

Her mother used to say that. She barely replied: "Thank you."

He went on: "Oh, you're welcome, you're welcome! But you must be tired! You have plenty of time—no need to rush yourself. You take it easy. I hope you'll enjoy the room I have for you." Excitedly: "I know! I'll carry your cocoa up to your room for you!"

"Okay."

They went back through all the rooms, up the grand staircase, up another grand staircase, down several hallways, then up another less grand staircase.

"Gee!" she teased. "I'm going to get lost in here!"

"Oh, don't worry—you'll find a map in your room."

"Oh." Pause. "Good."

Down several more halls they went, then down a half flight of stairs and through three more gigantic rooms, into a wide corridor lined with mahogany doors.

"Here we are!" He pressed open one of the doors, and there was her new room: enormous, everything in pale yellow satin: the king-sized canopy bed, sofa, chairs, rugs, wall carpeting.

"Wow."

He said, "Yellow's my favorite color," and sighed. "I like this room."

* * *

Morning after morning she awoke in the yellow satin room, gazed up at the yellow satin canopy and thought *I am safe, I am safe.* Then got up and roamed aimlessly through the mansion and the gardens. She was safe, safe. Excessively safe. Who needed all this safety? Who could stand it? The days passed, all alike, and she tried to work but couldn't concentrate. Couldn't help feeling that she was in just another box—a big spectacular extremely safe yellow satin box.

She roamed around, not bothering to get dressed. Sat outside in the minigardens in a fluffy yellow robe. It was early November, but Hampton Drane had outdoor mega-heaters, disguised as gigantic granite bunnies, to keep the minigardens warm enough to sit in year-round. She sat among quivering sunflowers, tall trimmed bushes, enormous white snoozing cats. Sometimes other homeless people were there too: gaunt listless people, some with healing burns, all of them dazed, all wrapped tight in fuzzy yellow robes. No one was plotting to murder Hampton Drane in his bed.

Sitting on the minigarden bench, in a row of mute Dranees, she would pull out her miniwriter and type, "Hampton Drane Part Three." Then stop: somehow Hampton Drane didn't belong in her future utopia. No celebrity did. Her utopia was full of ordinary people, equal in voice and visibility. She began to write about homeless people. She wrote about herself. She zipped paragraphs to Rela. Hampton Drane would see her working and twinkle at her, thinking she was writing his script. She figured he ought to write his own damn script. Figure out for himself what words to say.

"Do you need anything, dear?" he often asked. "Would you like some cocoa?"

She told him about Ben, and he hired some policemen to find out what had happened to him, but they never had anything to report. She curled up on the sofa in the mermaid room, her bare feet tucked into the folds of the yellow robe, and wrote paragraphs about Ben—his body, his face. The sofa in the mermaid room was shaped like a mermaid, upholstered with velvet aqua scales, its big tail flapping up to form a little roof over half the couch. To make it feel safe.

She wanted to find Ben. Hampton Drane said his chauffeur could take her around in the limousine to the MorgCo franchises, if she liked. She'd never been in a limousine. She pictured herself in the long sleek car, gliding up to the Sunco Tower, stepping out onto the sidewalk in glittering heels, strutting toward the revolving door, Ormer Bell standing stricken on the street. Ha. "Hello Ormer," she would say, extending a limp hand, "Did you hear? I'm Hampton Drane's personal script writer." Ha. Ormer in a spotlight on TV, Ormer looking stricken on the sidewalk. Couldn't she show *him*. "Well you think about it," said Hampton Drane, meaning the limousine.

One night she sat with Hampton Drane on the oversized leather yellow sofa in the TV room and watched TV. The personal assistant, Eden Wall, sat on Hampton Drane's other side. Arel and Eden swung their feet, which didn't quite reach the ground, and Hampton Drane put an arm around each of them, called them the daughter and son he never had, got them cocoa. They tried to avoid Flashnews, with its images of Actioneers chasing Mexicans and blacks and Asians, Actioneers pulling the petals off daisies. It upset Hampton Drane, made him cluck and gasp. Eden, who always had to have the remote control, found adhistories to watch.

They sat, sipping their cocoa, swinging their feet, and watched Holoco's latest adhistory: "The Last Coke Machine," about a secret Pepsi-Cola plot to buy up exclusive contracts with various institutions and replace all the Coke machines with Pepsi machines. Which meant that Americans couldn't have a Coke. But a team of daring handsome Coca-Cola executives, including Hootie Grate, and a sexy young journalist—Dillie Dare—worked day and night to uncover the plot and reveal the truth to the American public. In the dramatic last scene, in front of a cheering crowd, and after Dillie had confessed her passion for him, Hootie made a speech about Americans' inalienable right to always get what they want. "We must always fight!" yelled the tearful Hootie. "For our God-given right to choose!" Then he held up his hands, each holding a soda can: "Pepsi. . . or Coke!" The crowd cheered.

When it was over, Flashnews came on. Eden Wall pointed the remote at the screen, but Arel stopped him—"Wait." Images of the Graycoats appeared: Ben's army—young, angry, homeless-looking men and women, all in shabby gray jackets, shooting torrents of battery acid from homemade weapons. The Graycoats ran down alleys, vanished in parking lots.

Hampton Drane shook his head. "It's a vicious cruel world, Arel." Patted her hand. "You write down all those ideas of yours, for my next screenplay, and maybe it will help." Twinkled. "How's that screenplay going?"

"Oh fine, fine."

"Good! Now don't you feel like you have to rush—you take your time. Don't hurry yourself."

"Okay, I won't." She kept her eyes on the screen: another flash of the Graycoats, creeping down an alley. She thought she saw something:"What was that!" she yelled. Eden jumped, and cocoa sloshed. In fifteen seconds, the picture came around again. She watched this time knowing where to look: the last man in the line, face turned. The hair, the jacket, the way he raised his arm. "That's him!" she screeched. She grabbed Hampton Drane's sleeve: "It's Ben! He's alive!" She jumped off the couch, ran up to the screen. "Watch, watch! Do you recognize that street corner?"

They leaned toward the screen and squinted, waited till the picture came around again. Hampton Drane didn't recognize the corner, but Eden did: "It's Lake and Wacker"—near the Sunco Tower.

It was late afternoon, already dark, and Hampton Drane didn't want her to go out. "It's dangerous!" he cried and stood in front of the door to keep her inside. But she squirmed past him, out the door and down the walkway. She had to find him. She jumped into her car and sped toward the city.

*　　*　　*

On the highway, traffic was miraculously light—all barriers suddenly gone. She accelerated past the few other cars into the far left lane. She would get there in time. She would find him. She would bring him back to the mansion and he'd be safe and she'd have everything—everything she'd ever wanted, everything she deserved.

She soared and began to imagine life at the mansion with Ben. Imagined it unscrolling on a massive screen: Arel Ashe, humble yet elegant, strolling through the thick rich gardens of the Hampton Drane mansion, pausing now and then to make important notes on her miniwriter, and across the lawn—Ben—intense, dark, exhausted but softened, grateful, gazing at her in admiration. "The History of Arel Ashe," her thoughts announced to an invisible audience, and a cheer track went wild. "Arel Ashe, Part One." Then traffic closed in.

She sighed, slowed, slowed, stopped completely. A few miles ahead, news helicopters were swarming around a clump of cars. She turned on her miniscreen to find out what had happened, and there was a row of flags, billowing, whipping, running up poles. One unfurled on the roof of the Paterco headquarters building—a flag that must have been huge to be visible at all, but which was tiny and ridiculous compared to the massive structure. A scrap on a toothpick. Tiny flags flapped on all the headquarters buildings tonight, and Arel remembered that it was election day.

Dr. Aslow's face blinked on the screen, surrounded by more mini-flags, and Arel realized that he was running for President. He was the Paterco candidate. She tried to recall what exactly the President did and how a person could vote, annoyed at herself for not remembering—but she could ask Ben. Ben would know. Ben had the type of brain tha hung onto little facts that you really didn't need to know.

Traffic sat, stucker than usual, and snow began to fall. Giant silent flakes attached to her windshield, too tenacious for the wipers. Flakes silent and stubborn as her wipers wheezed across the glass. She sat, idled, squinted through grimy streaks, stuck in a pack of black and red cars turning ghostly white. In fifteen minutes she crept half a mile. This was taking too long: she would never get to him in time. She honked, then saw the problem—on Flashnews and in person at the same time—cars in a pile, the pile beginning to burn, the news vans blocking a lane, relaying close-up images to her screen: Sunco body sweepers shoving corpses around lazily with their body brooms. Arel groaned. SunMaint functions had been moved to the Sunco Prison Division, and prisoners were so unmotivated.

Then she began to panic: She was going to miss him. Right now he was alive, but what if she missed him? Would she get another chance? She honked again, useless honking. She crept up, crept up, sat, squirmed, cried out, then raced onto the shoulder of the highway, into the line of slightly faster-moving cars, and took the next exit.

Driving into downtown, she got stuck again. Ahead of her, another pile of cars was catching fire. She honked, screamed. Another ten minutes passed. So she turned into the nearest parking lot, got out of her car and started to run: still such a long way. She ran, grew breathless, kept running, stopped to lean against a building and breathe. This was hopeless. She leaned, panted—more than an hour had passed since the news flash.

But she had to try. She wouldn't give up. She caught her breath, prepared to go on, then realized where she was: across the street from Sunco Tower. And coming through the revolving door were Ormer, Kadence, and Koo. She yelled out, "Hey! Hey!"

This was fate. "Hey!" her voice lost in city noise. "Hey Ormer Bell!" she yelled louder. "Hey you prick!" She laughed. "Guess where I live now!" He paused and looked around, up and down, saw nothing. "Ha! Ormer Bell!" she screamed out again and watched his long face on his chicken neck search and search. She laughed, "I'm everywhere!" Then the three vanished into the mouth of the tunnel and she felt cheated. "Shit." That wasn't fair.

It wasn't fair. "Shit!" Her chance for revenge gone. Her chance to rub his face in it. Her voice replayed in her head: *Did you hear? I am Hampton Drane's personal script writer. At the mansion.* She had to tell him. She had to smirk at him as he'd always smirked at her. Stand cool and hateful with crossed arms and a sarcastic face and say, "I told you, I told you, I am better than you, I am bigger than you, you are *nothing.*" She had to catch him, she had to get him.

She was consumed.

She ran after them, into the tunnel, saw them at the far end about to walk out. She cupped her hands around her mouth and yelled "Ormer Bell!" in a spooky echoey voice, saw the back of his coat momentarily stop, then billow. Her laughter all around was enormous, ghoulish against the tunnel walls, the sound of her running footsteps sharp and clattering.

Through the tunnel and up the steps she ran, panting and thirsty, into the old lot. The car alarms were unsettled tonight, wailing, honking, shrieking in a digitized panic. She hesitated, spotted the trio on the other side of the lot. "Hey! Ormer Bell you prick!" The alarms drowned her out.

She slid fast along the cars, in and out of rows, bent her head against the sudden wind, her hands cold covering her raw cheeks. "Shit!" Ormer was getting away. No—she would not miss this moment of glory, her hard-won revenge. The three stood talking at Ormer's car, but soon they'd all leave, she knew, and she yelled out once more, rough and wild, "Hey!" and bolted toward them, her old coat flapping, her hair tangled in the wind.

Someone screamed—Koo. Then Ormer shoved Kadence in front of him, Kadence's arm rose, and a red-orange wave rippled forward.

It must have made a sound. A flame roaring at her. But Arel heard nothing for a long time except for a far-away crackle that slowly, slowly grew louder. Then there was the sensation of something—a gnawing at her arm, up and up toward her shoulder. Far away was the sound of her voice screaming. Something was chewing up her arm. She tried to shake it off, slap it off, the biting teeth, but they multiplied, clutching stabbing not teeth now but nails hot as the sun. Then there was a rush of heat along her chest and the stench of burning hair. Far away Koo's voice shrieked, "Roll on the ground!. . . Arel!"

She dropped into the snow but couldn't roll, could only writhe, the hard concrete like another flame fierce on her chest and arms. Then a sudden energy exploded inside her, a sharp shrill noise burst from her mouth, and her legs kicked with their own frantic force. She felt her body whip round and round, trying to escape the touch of the pavement. Then the energy was gone and her arms and legs and torso and face collapsed into shifting snow. Were her eyes open? She still felt the burning, but the sound was gone. Ormer's voice said, "There, it's out now."

Car engines started. Koo said something but Arel couldn't move, lay like hot scattered bricks, listened as three cars backed out of their spaces and drove away. Her skin smoldering but soundless. *It's out now. I'm safe now.* Now rest.

Pieces of her sank into snow. Now, rest, rest now, her voice said, not out loud. But it was late, and the library. She had to open the library. Her thoughts like stones sinking to the bottom of the lake. *Can't though* rest now. I'll be late. I'll lose that job. Ben said, Ben. Were her eyes still open? What was she seeing? Streaks of color and light moving fast in long streaks, in flashing patches. Part of her rose, sank, rose—she was still breathing. Bits of her sifted out through cracks in her skin, scorched skin, *hurts,* bone breaking apart and cracking into splinters and crumbling to powder, escaping through the breaks in her skin, escaping, the pain. Scorched skin cracking apart and cracking apart and all of her sifting out like heavy sand, into the snow, soaking there, in the snow, so cool and wet, snow-water running in through her skin and filling her up and drenching her, cool streams running through, her mouth, cool streams running in and out, the water rising, carrying her away. Not thirsty anymore.

Rest now, said her voice not out loud. Memories of days breaking up like sheets of ice drifting off, the water underneath deep and rushing, rushing her away, old thoughts rushing, voices and faces, highways and rooms, moments out of sequence, in a whirlpool, like dreams, dreams.

She dreamed that she was in her old cube, that she was waking up in the back room of the library, that she was at the counter when Ben walked in. She dreamed she saw Hampton Drane gliding in the snow, past rows of cars, through fluorescent circles and oblongs of shadow. Dreamed he kneeled down, so vivid—his voice and color, his fingertips on her cheek, his hand hovering, moving down, cupping lightly over hers in the snow. She felt his hand on hers. *I'm still here.*

She dreamed that Hampton Drane had found her. Dreamed he was lifting her up with a painless touch, lifting and walking her slowly across the watery soundless lot and holding her hand, squeezing it slightly, her face turning easily on its neck to smile at him. But it was not Hampton Drane, it was her mother, and it was not a dream, it was real.

seven

Just when you thought things couldn't get worse. God. Now Arel was dead and everyone was gone—everyone but him—and he should go home and get some sleep but he kept ordering triple-jumbo Apache tequilas instead. He didn't want to go home. He got too lonely at home; lately, he got too lonely everywhere.

The Good-Buys was packed with weirdo Dranee freaks in those fat yellow parkas, jumbo beers in one hand and megatorchers in the other. Used to be the worst thing the Dranees did was act too nice—that fakey nice he hated—and give you daisies. Now they had weapons and went around shooting at the Actioneers. God. What a mess. He tried to forget it all, watched the screen instead: cheerleaders chasing raccoons across a football field, President Aslow riding in his limousine, monkeys playing hockey, cars in a parking lot going up in flames, Hampton Drane in the mental ward, then that weasely little blond guy—some kind of personal assistant to Hampton Drane—standing on the cab of a truck tossing megatorcheres down to angry Dranees. Kyler grimaced. You could never trust short guys.

He sighed, looked around. The bar felt dark and cold, even with its crowd of sunshiny drunks. Funny how you could feel so alone in a crowd. He missed Ben and Arel. They were weird but they were his friends. He used to think how they'd help him make his billions—Ben, technical, Arel, creative—and how there'd be a movie about them, The Three Musketeers. Now they were gone and thinking up new products was no fun anymore. It just wasn't the same. He didn't want to be in a movie all by himself.

His head throbbed and he laid it on the table, then felt his sellfone vibrate. Happy for a moment, he yanked it out of his pocket, but it wasn't news of Dolla. It was never news of Dolla. It was a Presidential newzip: Aslow had appointed Ramy Minister of Public Education. God. Aslow was taking this whole President thing way too serious. And did people somewhere actually vote for him? Was someone in charge of all that?

Kyler drank, kicked his feet under the table, slouched, drank. On the screen, cheerleaders were putting raccoons into football helmets. Then a Dranee ran shouting into the pub—a group of Actioneers was coming out of the Post 'n Pets.

"God," Kyler moaned and started to slide down. The Dranees rampaged out into the mall, and the shooting began. He picked up his drink and slid all the way under the table, fit himself into the small space. The tabletop and booths formed a narrow box. He twisted up his long legs, sat on the floor with bits of popcorn, straw wrappers, cigarette butts, a crumpled beer can. Outside the pub were the sounds of shooting, screaming, stampeding. He peered out, saw no one.

How long would he be stuck there? He sighed, folded himself up tighter, and thought how the human race, which was so large, had certainly made itself very small. Then thought, What a weird thing to think. It was like a thought that wouldn't occur to him. Like something Arel would have said.

His arms and legs grew restless in the tight space and his thoughts kept going, like rocks rolling down a hill: That's why loneliness makes you feel small. You need other people to enlarge you, to make you more than you are. You need other people, not just to use—not just to fuck or boss around or mix chemicals for you—but to *know*. To really know. But how can you really know someone when you never have time to spend with them? Time traded for money, money traded for stuff, which you think is going to make you happy, and for a while you do feel happy, because you expect to, but then the happiness starts to fade—just like one of those old-time photos. That's all you really end up with: a snapshot of happiness.

Suddenly something exploded just outside the door of the pub; his hands squeezed his glass and his body tightened. Christ. Then there were several seconds of silence, and he relaxed, slowly. What had he been thinking? His brain was blank, then he remembered: weird thoughts—weird Arel thoughts. He shook his head to make them go away. Thinking too much never got you anywhere. Everyone knew that.

The chaos in the mall continued. He smelled burning. He drank tequila. Then settled against the wall, retwisted his arms and legs, took a long breath. Really, this spot wasn't so bad. He could see the big screen over the bar: scenes from the mall were already being broadcast—he recognized the Post 'n Pets sign behind a pile of bodies. "God," he said out loud. "Technology is amazing!"

But he got tired of watching the fight. Across the room on the bar was the remote control, and slowly he crawled out from under the table, wormed across the carpet, then sprang up, grabbed the remote, and scurried back to his place under the table. He got himself adjusted and started speed-flipping. There was a rerun of "Movers and Shakers," the one where Lil buys a new Dodge Detonator and finally gets the machine shop hunk into bed. The reruns were good. Lately, he thought, the show had been going downhill, ever since Lulu found the Lord and hauled the homely union organizer gal off to Prisonco. Since then, he thought, the show lacked a contrast.

He switched channels and found an old Dolla Dare movie—"Not Like Her Mondays." He had to admit she was better looking ten years ago. This was the one where she'd found her perfect guy and loved him madly—but not like her Mondays, when she insisted on staying home alone and watching the Monday night line-up, which included "Movers and Shakers." He remembered the megaboards ten years ago—*Not Like Her Mondays!* scrolling across the chests of Dolla, Lalla, Lulu and Lil. Four sets of perfect boobs. God. He switched to GrabBag and watched the spinning images of TV screens, Dodge Detonators, a preowned poster classic of Dolla, Lalla, Lulu, and Lil.

So many choices, he thought. Yet, it was all kind of alike. His legs unfurled, out to the edge of his spot, and he thought how, in the center of all the chaos, there was this sameness—this sameness that you could always rely on—and he sighed. It was like something to grab hold of, and that was truly a comfort. He relaxed against the wall and another rerun began. Like something to grab hold of, he thought again. Like bliss.

about the author

A.D. Nauman is an assistant professor of education and a prolific writer. She grew up in the '60s and '70s and considers herself classic "Generation W"—old enough to know what a social conscience is and young enough to still have one. She attended the Writers' Program at the University of Illinois-Chicago, where she also earned her Ph.D. in literacy education. Her short fiction has appeared in many literary journals. She has won the Illinois Arts Council Literary Award and has had a story produced by "Stories on Stage" at the Organic Theater in Chicago. Currently she lives in Chicago with her daughter, Maggie. *Scorch* is her debut novel.